Lavender Girl

Paula Hickford

Chapter 1

Liz watched through the gap in the curtains as the small Nissan pulled up in the road outside her house. She had guessed, as she was drawn to the window by the sound of the removal van arriving, that it contained the new occupants of the flat next door. As she watched she thought about her old neighbour.

The house next door had been empty for nearly two years, ever since Eve had gone to live with her daughter in a small village outside Exeter. She had been such a good friend. They had promised to keep in touch and visit often but it was difficult. Eve was not in the best of health and was therefore unable to travel by herself. Now she lived in her daughter's house, she felt awkward about inviting anyone to come and stay.

It was nine o'clock in the morning when the van arrived, banging the cab doors and rattling the shutter at the back. A short, fat, black woman struggled to manoeuvre herself out of the driver's seat of the Nissan. Her only passenger, a young girl that Liz guessed must be her daughter and looked to be around nine or ten, sat motionless in the passenger seat until the woman insisted angrily that she join her.

The girl flashed a look of defiance before sulkily slouching out of the car and slamming the door. The woman glared briefly at the child who pulled the bag she was carrying closer to her chest, but remained stony faced and rooted next to the car. She didn't look at all happy to be there.

The woman said a few words to one of the removal men before rummaging in her bag for keys. She found them quickly and went ahead to open the front door as the men started to unload the furniture. They placed a brown leather sofa on the pavement while they adjusted their grip and decided on the best way to get it into the flat. The woman stood by the side of the open front door and shouted at the girl.

'Tamika, don't just stand there, come inside.' The girl stayed silent as she moved slowly and deliberately behind the removal men, waiting while they squeezed through the door with the sofa before following them in.

The removal men were an odd looking pair. The one who appeared to be taking charge was very tall and very, very large. He had an enormous stomach which his jumper and jacket struggled to conceal. Bare flesh bulged between the hem of his jumper and the waist of his jogging bottoms as he bent and stretched to pick up bits of furniture.

'He must be freezing,' thought Liz, as he rubbed his hands together before cupping them in front of his mouth and blowing to warm them up. His small features were almost lost in the excess of flesh that made up his round face which was made to look even rounder by the woolly hat stretched across his head.

His companion, by contrast, was small and wiry with a face full of features, big, watery eyes and a bulbous nose underlined with a neat moustache. Both wore fingerless gloves and despite the difference in their heights Liz marvelled at how deftly they manoeuvred the furniture out of the van and in through the front door.

It had always been a quiet street, where people took pride in their houses. Liz had known all her neighbours. Eve had lived next door for forty odd years before she moved out. Their children played together outside as mums and dads chatted over garden fences. Of course it had all changed now. She hardly knew any of her neighbours. They all had foreign sounding names and the children very rarely played out in the street.

Her only son, Adam, had moved to Bury St Edmunds. He had lived nearby in Arkley when he first married Georgina. Liz saw him often when the children were small, although in hindsight it was probably because she was a convenient babysitter. He had done very well for himself as the Head of Corporate something or other at a German bank. He was now living in a very large detached house with five bedrooms and three reception rooms.

She would stress the size of the house when she was talking about him to anyone who would listen, like the man in the post office or the doctor's receptionist. She left out the fact that she only heard from him once in a while and from her grandchildren even less other than to acknowledge receipt of the money she sent them for birthdays and Christmas.

She sighed as she watched a while longer as beds and wardrobes emerged, followed by endless tea-chests, and a huge flat screen TV, finally all of the contents of the van had disappeared into the house and the street was silent again. She sank back from the window and went to the kitchen to put the kettle on. But wasn't there long when she heard the woman shouting the girl's name and the back door slam. She assumed the girl had gone to explore outside. Not that there was much to explore.

Eve's house had been bought by a builder who had converted it into two flats, making space for parking at the front and dividing the rear garden into two. Eve hated gardening and had most of the back paved over.

'Great for ball games, I expect,' Liz thought to herself, and it seemed that the girl agreed as seconds later she heard the thump, thump, thump of a ball against the fence.

Liz's garden was the opposite of Eve's, or at least it had been. Not that she was interested in gardening since Jim had died. Five years had passed since his death and yet the pain was still almost physical. He had loved the garden and it was now just a sad reminder of happier times. She couldn't even bear to cut the grass. Weeds had grown up in between the flowers and in some cases had swamped the plants altogether. Brambles and stinging nettles had gathered at the back of the garden and ivy, left unchecked, had grown up around the shed, almost covering it.

On her darkest days she wished the ivy would overwhelm and cover her too. She imagined herself laying down in the garden in the sunshine and falling asleep, with the ivy creeping silently over her until she was gone, subsumed by the garden and nearer to her beloved Jim.

On bright, sunny days she liked the ivy. Summer or winter it looked the same. It was resilient and even made the dilapidated garden shed look pretty.

She thought of the garden when Jim was alive. In the summer months it was a blaze of colour. Jim had been particularly fond of his lawn and could often be found leaning on his shovel and proudly surveying the grass which he regularly compared to a bowling green. She was surprised that he hadn't used a spirit level to make sure that it was absolutely flat.

In the summer they would sit in the garden together and have breakfast. After breakfast Liz would go back into the house to tidy up and Jim would either potter in the garden or go down to his shed. The shed was Jim's domain and the answer to every DIY problem was contained therein. Broken things went in and were occasionally even mended but more often than not Liz never, ever saw them again, the item having been dismantled and the composite bits and bobs added to his stock of useful parts.

Jim was equally meticulous about the garden. He knew the names of every plant including the Latin names. He even kept a journal of what was planted when and where. He had started it shortly after they moved into the house.

He had laid the lawn and organised the flowerbeds around the existing trees. A large Bramley apple tree had dominated one side of the garden and there were several pear trees in a line opposite.

Adam, in particular, loved the apple tree. Jim built a wooden platform across the larger of the branches and hung a rope swing from it which at various times had tyres or seats attached. Occasionally Jim would moan about the mud patch that developed beneath the swing because it ruined the look of the lawn and Adam would be banned from using it until the grass had recovered.

At the beginning of the journal Jim had drawn a grid with numbered sections. He carefully measured the garden to ensure the grid was accurate. Whenever he planted something new he would get out the journal and write the name, grid reference and date of planting. The last entry was made the week before he died, 29th March 2009, 9B and 9D Lavandula Augustifolia (Lavender).

Liz could barely look at the book now but equally couldn't bear to part with it so it stayed underneath the armchair in the living room. She didn't want to be reminded of how beautiful the garden had been.

She sat back on her kitchen chair and tried to picture Jim sitting in the garden writing his journal but the picture wouldn't form in her mind. Instead, tiny tears grew in the corners of her eyes as she drank her tea and chided herself for being a silly old woman.

She was startled by the phone ringing but glad of the

distraction. It was Adam, making his fortnightly call.

'How are you love, how's Georgina and the children?' Liz asked.

'We're all fine, mum.'

'Great.' She tried to keep her voice even. 'I do miss you. I haven't seen you in ages. When are you going to pop in?' It was hard not to sound desperate.

'Aaah… It's a bit tricky, mum, over the next few months,' was the usual reply. 'Can we make arrangements in a few weeks' time when I know where I'll be?'

'Of course' said Liz knowing full well she had been fobbed off again. It was always the same. Liz would make excuses to other people, usually that he worked too hard and his job was very important but in her heart she knew that she was quite irrelevant to his life. He probably considered her a nuisance. He certainly made her feel like a nuisance.

Liz set about doing the housework. She was very organised. She had one of those caddies that came from the Kleeneze catalogue where all the polish, sprays and cleaning cloths are held in a container with a central handle so you can take everything with you. The housework kept her sane, especially now she had nothing much else to do.

The bathroom and cloakroom were always first to get her attention. Then she would move on to the living room where she would polish the sideboard and side tables, dust the fireplace and vacuum the carpet. She did the same in the bedroom before changing the bed linen and then finally tackling the kitchen.

There was never much washing up, or washing for that matter. One person does not make very much mess and one house-proud person makes hardly any mess at all. She would save up the washing and ironing, just to give her a bit more to do at the weekends.

Weekends always dragged terribly and winter weekends were the worst of all. Short days and long nights full of sadness.

It was hard to find things to fill the time. She hated watching TV. Soaps and reality shows held no appeal. Life was depressing enough without seeing it played out over and over again in different locations. Instead she would read voraciously and occasionally she would paint, although she had hardly picked up a brush in the last few years.

Jim had cleared a space for her at one end of the garage. He had installed a window in the sloping roof and made her a bench with shelves above it.

He had not told her what it was for but on her birthday he had surprised her with a full sized easel and canvasses, unveiling what he called her 'Studio'.

She was absolutely thrilled. It wasn't ideal. It was too cold out there in the winter without a heater and the light wasn't perfect but it was fantastic to have a dedicated space to paint in. She had never been to an art class. Still, whatever she lacked in technique she made up for in talent. A half painted picture of a jug and bowl leant against the wall by the bench and remained a fixture.

The easel was back in its box. She would get round to it

someday.

Occasionally she would watch a DVD but only after she had scanned the blurb on the back to make sure it didn't include anything sad. Even watching something funny was not the pleasure it used to be. Laughing out loud by yourself seemed odd. She couldn't remember the last time she'd laughed.

She had tried a local club. Although she had retired she didn't feel anywhere near old enough to sit and play bingo in the day centre which was the only activity on offer on the day she popped in. The other 'service users' as they were called seemed to be a lot older and they sat about in winged armchairs. It reminded her of old people's homes and death. She didn't want to be reminded of death. She had almost run out of the place screaming.

It was a cold, dry day so she decided to clean the downstairs windows. When Jim was alive they had always done them together, with her doing the inside and Jim the outside. He would always joke with her by miming through the glass that she had missed a spot or two and point to different panes of glass. She would take him seriously for the first one or two marks but as he pointed more bits she thought were done he would start to laugh. He would play the same trick every time they cleaned the windows.

As she started on the front windows her attention was drawn to the house next door. Tamika was sitting on the front step with a sad expression on her face, clutching her shoulders for warmth. It was early January and very cold, too cold to be outside without a coat.

Liz watched for a while until eventually her mother opened the door and shouted at her to come back in. She had no idea if the girl was sulking or being punished. 'Either way, it's none of my business,' she thought to herself and carried on with the windows.

A few days passed before she saw the girl again. Liz noticed her sitting on the wall outside her house and assumed she was waiting for her mum to come home. She speculated on why the girl didn't have a key but didn't dwell on it for too long as the next time she looked out of the window she was gone.

A few days later, she was sitting on the wall again, eating a bag of crisps and drinking from a can. Most of the houses in the road had fences but Jim had built a wall around his castle, just high enough to sit on. Liz watched as the young girl ate the contents of the packet and then threw it into her front garden, closely followed by the empty can. Liz tapped on the window and gestured to the girl to pick them up. Tamika ignored the request and after giving Liz a filthy look calmly turned her back. Liz was incensed and went straight to the front door.

As soon as Tamika heard the door opening she jumped off the wall.

'Don't throw your rubbish in my garden,' Liz said firmly. 'Pick it up, please.'

'Get lost, you old witch,' was Tamika's defiant response. 'Pick it up yourself.'

Liz went to argue but instead turned on her heels and went inside. Tamika resumed her position on the wall assuming that she had seen the last of Liz. She was wrong. Liz was back within minutes.

Tamika again jumped up as the front door opened but this time Liz was ready with the garden hose. She had trailed it through the house and was now armed. Without saying a word she pulled the trigger and cold water shot out straight towards Tamika, who just about managed to duck behind the wall and avoid a soaking.

Liz shouted at her angrily, 'Put your rubbish in the bin, not in my garden, and don't be so bloody rude.'

She slammed the front door, leaving the child speechless. She half expected a knock on the door that night from the girl's mother but it didn't come.

Tamika was often outside after school, waiting for her mother to get home from work. Liz would sometimes see her there for half an hour or more. She didn't like seeing her cold and miserable despite her rudeness. It took a few days before she sat on Liz's wall again. There was nowhere else to sit. However, it didn't go unnoticed that she no longer threw her rubbish in the garden. Liz kept an eye on her anyway, concerned for her safety.

One particularly cold day she noticed that Tamika had been outside for over half an hour. There were dark clouds in the sky, making the early evening darker than usual, and before long icy rain was hitting the window. Liz went to the front door. As soon as Tamika heard the door she leapt off the wall.

'Don't worry,' said Liz, 'you can sit there if you want to. I just wondered if you would like to come inside to wait for your mother? We can put a note on your door to say where you are.'

Tamika eyed the old woman suspiciously, but shook her head to indicate that she didn't need help.

'Suit yourself,' said Liz, and shut the door.

More time passed with Tamika still outside and the rain beating down harder than ever. Liz looked out of the window every few minutes to make sure she was okay. Finally, she went to the door again.

'Tamika, please come inside. It's freezing out here. I don't bite'.

Tamika peered out from under the hood of her sopping wet coat with her huge brown eyes. She looked really cold and miserable and her stomach was rumbling, reminding her that she hadn't eaten since lunch time. She didn't want to go in but she was too cold, wet and hungry to sit outside any longer. Without saying a word she stood up and followed Liz.

Once inside Liz asked her to take off her wet coat, which she did readily. Liz placed it on the radiator in the hall before ushering her into the living room to sit by the fire.

'Warm yourself up,' she added, before popping to the kitchen.

Tamika looked around the room as she waited. Lots of photographs were on the wall. Family pictures of a mum, dad and two children. There was a younger version of the man with his mortar board and degree in his hand, wedding photographs and pictures of children, a young boy in his school uniform and a girl around the same age as Tamika, sitting on a pony.

However, it was the one on the wall next to the fireplace which caught her eye. It was a picture of the old lady, younger than she was now. She was holding hands with a man who had smiling eyes and a shock of white hair. They were in a garden, the sun was shining and they looked really happy.

Liz came back with a cup of tea and juice for Tamika plus a few biscuits on a china plate.

'Now then,' said Liz, 'I'll write a note for your mum to let her know where you are.'

She took some writing paper and a pen out of the top drawer of the sideboard and sat down to write.

'She's not my mum,' said Tamika. 'She's my aunt, my mother's sister.'

'Oh,' said Liz, 'well she will wonder where you are.' Liz wanted to ask questions but sensed that now would not be a good time.

She wrote on the paper, 'Tamika is with me at number seventy three.' She signed the note 'Elizabeth Bailey'. Tamika watched over her shoulder as she wrote.

'What's your name?' she asked, unable to read Liz's handwriting.

'Elizabeth,' was the reply, 'but everyone calls me Liz. You

can call me Liz if you like.'

'How do you know my name?' asked Tamika suspiciously.

'I heard your mum, I mean your aunt, call you on the day you moved in.' Liz replied.

'My mum called me Tammy. You can call me Tammy if you like.'

Liz smiled to herself. It was the first time that she had actually been up close to the girl. Tammy was tall but very slightly built with a round shiny face and big brown sad eyes. The rain had soaked through her coat to the shoulders of her pale grey school uniform cardigan and resembled epaulets. Her wet face was framed by a mass of frizzy curls as the scrunchie had given up its efforts to tame it into a pony tail and now clung on limply to an inch or so of hair at the bottom.

Liz left Tammy sitting by the fire as she popped to seventy one and pinned the note on the front door. When she came back Tammy was standing up looking at the photographs more closely. She asked Liz who they were.

'This is my son, Adam, and his wife Georgina,' said Liz, pointing to the wedding photograph, 'and these are my grandchildren.'

'Don't they ever come and visit?' Tammy asked directly. She had never seen them.

'They are very busy people,' Liz excused, 'and they live a long way away.'

'In another country?' Tammy asked.

'No,' said Liz, adding, 'Bury St Edmunds,' although it

may as well be, but she didn't say this out loud.

It was another half an hour before the aunt came to the door.

She introduced herself as Monica. She had a huge smile with dazzlingly white teeth and she was wearing a shoulder length auburn wig. She made a lot of excuses as to why she was late, something urgent at work and traffic was bad and she hadn't got round to having more keys cut. She didn't seem at all embarrassed about the fact that as far as she had known Tammy was waiting outside in the rain.

Liz replied that it was no trouble at all. It did occur to her that this may be a job for social services but Tammy was clean and well dressed and apart from having to wait for her aunt to get home there were no signs of neglect. She didn't want to cause any trouble, at least not until she knew that there was actually something to report.

The next day Tammy was again sitting on the wall looking cold and miserable. Liz was torn. She didn't want to make a habit of it but she hated seeing her on her own.

This time Tammy readily agreed when Liz asked if she would like to come in. She took her coat off, put if over the radiator and went straight to the living room, perching herself in Liz's fireside chair without waiting to be invited.

'Would you like a hot drink and a biscuit?' Liz enquired.

'Yes,' said Tammy.

'Yes please,' said Liz.

'Yes please,' repeated Tammy, eyeing Liz from underneath her fringe.

When Liz came back into the room with the tray Tammy was standing up looking at the photograph on the wall.

'Is that your husband?' she asked, pointing to the photograph of Jim.

'Yes,' Liz replied.

'Where is he?'

'He died a few years ago,' said Liz sadly.

'Did he have cancer?' asked Tammy.

'No,' said Liz, 'he had a heart attack.' She winced at the memory.

'My mother died of cancer,' Tammy said without emotion, and Liz was struck by the matter of fact delivery of the information.

'I'm sorry.' said Liz, and a look of understanding passed between them.

They were both silent for what seemed like ages but could only have been for a few seconds when the doorbell rang to indicate that Monica was home from work. Liz invited her in. Monica declined as she had to prepare dinner but thanked her profusely for her kindness. Liz watched as Tammy slowly put on her coat and followed her aunt outside into the rain.

Chapter 2

Liz woke early the next morning. She couldn't stop herself thinking about young Tammy.

She hated the thought of her sitting on the wall outside alone in the evenings. The recent revelation had made it all the more poignant.

Her own mother had died soon after Adam was born. It was completely without warning. Their doctor informed them afterwards that she had died as a result of a massive brain bleed, an aneurism. She could still remember how lost she had felt without her. She was sure that she would have gone mad had she not had a new baby to care for.

Her parents had been really happy together and Liz had quickly and painfully realised that she had, in fact, lost both her parents when her mother died. Her brother was a couple of years older and in the army so dad was alone in the house.

He died a couple of weeks after Adam's first birthday. He had lost a lot of weight and was both physically and mentally diminished without his wife, who was the love of his life, and he retreated into his memories. He was still breathing but he was dead inside and neither Liz nor her brother could reach him. He just gave up. She didn't feel nearly as sad when her dad died as she did when her mother passed and she took comfort in the hope that they would be together again.

She resolved to go next door and offer to look after Tammy until Monica got home from work. She dressed quickly and was trying to decide on whether to knock early or wait until the evening. The weather report on the radio decided her, more rain and a temperature of just three degrees Centigrade. It was only seven o'clock but she put her front door on the latch and, still in her slippers, walked down the path and through the gate to number seventy one.

When she got to the front door her resolve weakened. Maybe it was too early. She hesitated before ringing the bell to the ground floor flat.

'Maybe she'll think I'm poking my nose in where it's not wanted and tell me to bugger off.'

She raised her hand to the door, clenched it into a fist to knock and then pulled it back to her chest without touching the door at all.

'Oh, for God's sake!' she finally said to herself, 'if she tells you to bugger off at least you've tried.'

She turned her head towards the window and listened at the front door, still no sound. She was about to withdraw when she saw Tammy looking out through the glass with a puzzled expression on her face. Liz smiled and waved. Tammy did neither before moving away from the window.

Liz waited for a few seconds but couldn't hear anyone coming to the door so she retreated back down the path. Just as she got to the gate Monica called her. Liz turned back towards the house feeling a bit embarrassed. She saw that Tammy was now standing behind Monica on the doorstep.

'It's going to be very cold today and I wondered if you would like me to watch Tammy after school. If it's OK with Tammy,' she smiled at Tammy, 'until you get home from work.'

Monica looked at Tammy, who remained silent.

'I am not able to pay you,' she said defensively.

'Oh, I don't need to be paid,' Liz offered. 'It's too cold to be left outside.' That sounded a bit harsher than it was meant and Liz immediately regretted it and added, 'I would love the company,' by way of mitigation.

Monica's face softened as she looked at Tammy. 'Would you like to stay with Liz until I get home from work?'

Tammy shrugged but still said nothing. Monica interpreted that as agreement and it was settled. Monica told Liz how grateful she was for the offer adding that there was no after school club at Tammy's school and she was not able to afford childcare. She didn't know what she would do as work was unpredictable and it would be a relief to know that Tammy was safe.

Liz decided to go shopping and buy some child friendly food like squash and crisps, and perhaps some teacakes. She knew that Tammy could watch the TV until Monica got home but maybe she should get her a puzzle or something that she could do in case she got bored. It had been years since Liz had looked after a child and she had no experience at all with girls other than her granddaughter as a toddler.

She popped down to the supermarket in the afternoon to make sure that she would be home in time for the end of the school day but as she turned the corner she could see that Tammy was sitting on the wall outside her house.

It was only two o'clock and school didn't finish until three fifteen.

Tammy looked as though she'd been crying. As Liz approached she stood up and wiped her tear stained face with her sleeve.

'Hi,' said Liz.

Tammy didn't speak.

'Come on, let's go in. It's freezing out here.' She walked ahead and opened the front door. Tammy followed behind.

Once inside Liz helped Tammy off with her coat and hung it in the hall.

'Go and sit down and I'll make you a drink.'

Liz was back in a couple of minutes with tea and cakes on a tray. She poured Tammy a cup of tea, added the sugar and milk and placed it in front of her on the table. Tammy just stared at the cup as if she had never seen a cup before in her life.

Liz wanted to comfort her, to wrap her up in her arms and make the sadness go away, but something stopped her. She sensed that Tammy didn't want to be comforted and in a way Liz was grateful. She couldn't trust herself to hold it together. Some days she felt that she was just on the edge of breaking down and that would be no good for either of them.

'How come you're home early?' Liz tried to sound cheerful.

Tammy shrugged. 'I don't like tea.'

'Well, that's a strange reason,' said Liz smiling. Tammy looked up. 'How about some juice instead?' Tammy nodded.

When Liz came back with the glass Tammy was eating one of the teacakes.

'Do the school know that you were coming home?' Tammy shook her head to indicate no.

'I think that I should call them and let them know you're safe, don't you?'

Tammy nodded her assent. Liz knew the primary school that Tammy attended as it was one of the feeder schools for the secondary where she had been a teacher.

She managed to talk to the school secretary and found out that the cause of the upset had been a school outing. The children were given a letter to take home to be signed by their parents or guardians. A teacher had asked Tammy where her letter was in front of other children.

Tammy got very angry and upset. She ran out of the classroom, kicking a bookstand over before she left.

Liz was surprised that the class teacher hadn't been more sensitive. The school assured her that they would be apologising to Tammy and to Monica and there would be no further action against Tammy for running out of school. They had already called Monica and Liz asked them to give her another call to let her know she was safe.

'Would you like to talk about it?' she asked Tammy when she came off the telephone. Tammy shook her head.

'I can't say it out loud because that makes it real.'

Liz knew exactly what she meant. When Jim died she had been so paralysed by grief she could barely speak at all. She didn't know when Tammy's mother had died but guessed it must be fairly recent. It takes a long time to accept that someone you love is never coming back. It had been five years since Jim had died and yet she still had days when she half expected him to walk through the front door.

She looked around the room for a something to do. She asked Tammy if she liked to paint or draw. Tammy shrugged.

'Would you like to do some drawing?' Liz asked again, adding, 'One shrug for yes and two for no.' Tammy shrugged once so Liz took out the art box.

She had loads of art materials amassed over years of painting as a hobby. She took a couple of drawing pads and various pencils out of the box and put them on the kitchen table. She then sat down and picked up the nearest pad. Tammy came and stood next to her.

'Now what shall I draw? I think I'll draw you.' She turned to Tammy. She picked up a pencil and held it upright along the length of her thumb, her arm outstretched in front of her as if she was sizing up the subject before starting on her masterpiece.

She drew an oval shape on the paper before starting to add detail to the drawing.

'First the big brown eyes and now the ears,' she said out loud.

Tammy watched for a few minutes as Liz added pencil strokes to the paper, occasionally moving the pencil to and fro for shading. Tammy tipped her head forward to look over the top of the pad but as she did so Liz tilted it back towards her so Tammy was unable to see.

Liz continued for a few more minutes, adding strokes and tilting her head from side to side as if she was really concentrating.

Tammy was getting frustrated and could no longer hide her curiosity. She pulled down the top of the pad to reveal the drawing. It was more or less female, a large round head with sticking out ears and crossed eyes, extra-large hands, enormous feet and curly hair.

"Does this look like you?' Liz looked serious for a second. 'I think it does.' She started laughing.

Tammy looked surprised and then smiled before immediately picking up a pad to draw her version of Liz.

She drew an oval head with straight hair, slanted eyes and a half moon mouth with some of the teeth blacked out. She then added some wrinkles on the forehead and stickman legs ending in absurdly high heels to complete the picture. She turned the pad to face Liz in triumph and Liz laughed even harder, feigning outrage at the preposterous image before her.

Liz then resumed her drawing, adding freckles and a moustache to Tammy's face. Tammy added a witch's nose complete with hairy wart to Liz's. Liz drew an extra eye on Tammy's forehead. Not to be outdone, Tammy scribbled a beard onto Liz's chin. By now both of them were laughing hysterically as they scribbled furiously to make their portraits more and more outrageous.

It felt so good to laugh. It had been ages since either of them had really laughed.

'I knew there was a laugh in there somewhere,' said Liz. 'Will you sign it for me in case you ever get famous and I need to sell it?' She smiled again. Not really. I'd like to put it up in here.' She took some Blu Tack out of a drawer and pulled off a small piece ready to stick the drawing to the side of the fridge. Tammy scribbled her signature on the end just as the doorbell rang and Liz went to see who it was.

Monica was on the doorstep looking anxious.

'Don't worry,' said Liz softly as she invited her in, 'Tammy is fine.'

Monica felt a mixture of emotions. Happy she was safe, angry that she had run out of school and scared of what might have happened. She got the phone call at work and had to leave a training session.

'What happened?' she asked as she approached. 'Tamika, what were you thinking?'

'It was a misunderstanding,' Liz interjected.

Monica flashed her a 'mind your own business' look.

'I was worried sick,' she said to Tammy, who appeared unmoved. 'You can't keep doing this, do you understand?' Tammy just stared through her as if she was made of smoke. 'You have to talk to me, Tamika,' her voice softened.

Tammy remained stony faced. Monica turned to Liz.

'I need to go back to work, if that's OK.' She looked as if she was about to cry herself.

'No problem,' said Liz. 'It's nearly three now. She will be fine with me until you get home.'

'We will talk about this later, young lady,' she said to Tammy before leaving.

Monica gave Liz all her contact numbers, work, home and mobile. Liz did the same. Although she had a mobile phone it very rarely rang nowadays. She made a mental note to keep it handy, just in case. Monica began to walk up the path but turned to face Liz before getting half way.

'She hates me, doesn't she?' Liz felt for Monica. She had lost her sister and was now trying to look after her niece. 'I can't do this. I don't know how,' she said, shaking her head.

'I don't know much about either of you,' said Liz, 'but I think you need each other. Give it time.'

Monica smiled and promised to catch up at some point. 'Listen to your own advice,' Liz thought to herself as the words came out. 'How much time do you need?'

Tammy was quiet when Liz came back into the house. She was sitting in the living room looking at the journal. She had found it under the chair and was now studying a photograph that had been tucked into a pouch at the front.

It showed the garden in its full glory. Liz was taken aback but tried not to show it. After all, to Tammy it was just a book.

She left her looking at the journal and went back to the kitchen to make a sandwich. When she came back into the living room Tammy was studying the picture and comparing it to the one on the wall.

'This is your garden,' she said.

'Yes,' said Liz.

'Can I see it?' she asked.

'Not now,' said Liz. 'It's raining outside and it doesn't look its best at the moment.'

'When?' insisted Tammy.

'When the weather improves,' she replied forcing a smile, satisfied that she had fended off the inevitable for the time being. 'You know that your aunt was really worried about you, don't you?' Tammy shrugged. 'She cares about you very much.'

'Does she?' said Tammy angrily.

'Yes, she does,' replied Liz firmly. 'It's not easy looking after a budding artist.'

Tammy almost smiled but then changed her mind before adding, 'All she cares about is work.'

'I'm sure that's not true,' said Liz. 'I have an idea. How about the two of you coming here to dinner on Sunday? It's been ages since I've cooked for someone. What do you think? We can watch a DVD or draw some more. Shall I ask your Aunt if you're free?' Tammy nodded. 'Great,' said Liz.

'I'll speak to Monica this evening.'

Liz turned on the TV and left Tammy watching a cartoon while she went back into the kitchen. She pulled up the blind and looked out into the garden. It was a dull, grey day and the garden was almost devoid of colour apart from the evergreen ivy. The grey shed, at least the bits of it you could see, matched the grey sky.

'I'm sorry, Jim,' she said, looking at the neglected garden. 'I just don't know where to start.'

She pulled down the blind and filled the kettle with water. She found winter a bit easier than summer. In the winter she didn't have to see the garden. She could keep the blinds drawn and pretend it didn't exist. She had thought about moving but it didn't feel right. She just didn't have the energy to even contemplate it after Jim died and then nothing seemed to matter anyway, plus Eve had been such a good friend.

Eve had moved in a couple of years before Liz. At seventy she was ten years older than Liz but you'd never know it. She was very fit and active, at least she was until she fell and broke her hip. It didn't mend very well and getting about was becoming increasingly difficult.

Her daughters helped with the housework and shopping but she was finding it harder and harder to get up the stairs to bed. She could have made a bedroom from one of the rooms downstairs but would still have had to make room for a bathroom and that would have meant building work and money which Eve didn't have. She had been a widow for over twenty years but it was different. She didn't miss Alf the way Liz missed Jim.

Alf was an alcoholic. How he got to fifty had been a miracle according to Eve who had assumed it was because most of his organs were pickled. He was a functioning alcoholic in that he seemed to hold down a job but they never had any money. In the early days Eve was always knocking on the door needing to borrow something like milk for the baby, nappies or fifty pence for the gas meter. Liz felt sorry for her.

Eve would hide out in Liz's house when Alf was on the rampage, which thankfully was not that often. She would sometimes hear him shouting at the front door when he'd been out and was too drunk to put the key in the lock. She marvelled at Eve's patience and often wondered why she'd stayed but people did in those days. 'I've made my bed,' Eve would say, 'and now I'm lying in it.'

Liz looked at the calendar she kept pinned to a notice board in the kitchen, not that there had been any reason to keep a calendar for the last few years. Apart from the odd appointment and family birthdays she very rarely had anything to put on it. She pencilled in lunch with Monica and Tammy.

*****

Monica sat in her car outside Liz's house and thought of how different her life had been just eighteen months ago. After flat sharing for ages she had just about managed to save enough money for a deposit on a flat of her own. She had found the perfect place, a one bedroom flat in a brand new block with an ultra-modern kitchen and bathroom. The mortgage was manageable and it was convenient for work.

Her younger sister, Joanna, could not have been more different. She had no ambition in life bar marriage and children. She was thrilled when she knew she was pregnant. It was all she had ever wanted. Max was only her second boyfriend and a lot keener on the children than the marriage, at least the conception part anyway. He had left when Joanna rejected his proposal that she terminate the pregnancy. He wasn't ready for marriage or fatherhood.

Joanna was grateful that they were not married. She didn't really want Max having even a part time role in their daughter's life. Joanna never asked him for anything and let him slip out of her life as easily as he had slipped in. She didn't even let him know when Tammy was born. She was so in love with her perfect little girl that the everyday struggles of life were inconsequential. Tammy was a really good baby and Joanna loved every minute of being a mother.

She didn't keep her job after Tammy was born. There was no way her beautiful baby was going to be looked after by a child-minder, someone else hearing her first word or watching as she took her first step. She had worked as a hairdresser and still had a number of friends and clients who came to the house. This gave her an income and company and life was good. She was easy going and full of fun, tall and slim with smooth shiny skin and almond eyes. She was warm and friendly, she laughed often and the usual hairdresser banter was born out of genuine interest. She loved being surrounded by people.

Despite having a hairdresser for a sister Monica had had the same hairstyle for the last fourteen years, a mass of wavy hair that sat on her head like an old fashioned mop. She hardly ever left her hair loose. If she let Joanna work on it at all it was to have an inch or so lopped off the bottom and even then under protest. Most of the time she would pull it back into a doughnut shaped bun on top of her head, or when really desperate and late for work, conceal it under a wig.

'How can we be sisters?' Joanna would tease. 'We are nothing alike.'

This was true. Monica was short, which she always felt was unfair. At five foot two she didn't feel that short but she looked shorter because she was at least two, probably three, stone overweight. She wasn't entirely sure of her weight anymore as she had thrown out the weighing scales when they persisted in telling her that she was over twelve stone. She had the same smooth skin and dark almond eyes as Joanna but they didn't look nearly as elegant framed in her chubby face.

She hadn't always been chubby. The weight had just crept on over the last few years. She ate more when she was stressed and she was always stressed. That, coupled with working long hours and living alone, meant lots of nights in with takeaways and sad films for company while she saved hard to buy her flat.

She had been completely focused on her career and was doing really well. She loved her job as one of the senior accountants for a magazine group, even though she didn't really fit in with most of the skinny, image obsessed creatives that made up the editorial and advertising staff.

Added to which the amount of time she had taken off dealing with Tammy was now putting her job in jeopardy. It would be enough to send the most dedicated dieter into a spiral of cream cakes and chocolate.

When Tammy was due to be christened Joanna had asked her to be godmother. She reluctantly accepted, convinced that apart from looking pretty at the christening, with Joanna's help, her only involvement would be buying presents on birthdays and Christmas. Monica asked her if she was sure. Joanna was adamant that she was the perfect role model and was confident that she would be great mother material whenever she decided to settle down.

Monica was not convinced. She was entirely selfish and always had been. As if to confirm it on the very few occasions when she did hold Tammy as a baby she had screamed the place down. Hell, she could barely look after herself. How would she look after a little girl?

She was completely gobsmacked when Joanna asked her to be Tammy's guardian. To her shame she had said no at first. She didn't know how she would cope. She was terrified. She had no experience with children. Despite being thirty four she didn't feel grown up enough to be responsible for a child.

'There must be someone else,' she pleaded. 'You have lots of friends with children. They know what to do. I don't.'

'There is no one I trust more than you,' Joanna begged. 'I need to know that you will look after my daughter.' How could she say no?

Joanna had liver cancer. She had been going to the GP for months with various symptoms and pain but had been fobbed off with antibiotics, her doctor insisting that the pain was caused by an infection. When she was finally referred for tests it was more than six months after her initial visit to the GP. Monica had sat with her in the consultant's office as he delivered the devastating diagnosis. He was very sorry but the cancer was inoperable. She may have only three months to live. They both heard the words but neither of them could take them in. They asked him to repeat it two or three times. They were both numb.

Joanna only had seven weeks in the end. She died on the twenty third of August two thousand and eleven, just over a week after Tammy's ninth birthday. It was almost as if she was hanging on to make sure she didn't miss it. She had used up the last of her strength trying to organise everything. She left very clear instructions. She wrote page after page of what to do when. She gave Monica a list of all the foods that Tammy liked and, more importantly, the ones she disliked. She wrote down her favourite toys and games, clothes, colours, songs and the TV programmes she liked to watch.

She listed her friends and their contact details. She gathered all her school reports and other important information in a box file which included notes on vaccinations and illnesses. She gave Monica all of her photographs in a shoebox, a pictorial history of their lives to date. She reminded her to leave a nightlight on in Tammy's bedroom when she slept and to let her climb into bed with her if she was frightened or sad.

She made notes of the books that they had read together and the ones that they wanted to read. She listed the things they were planning to do in the school holidays. Visit the Zoo, go to the seaside, swimming, rowing, museums and a holiday abroad on an aeroplane. Joanna was most specific about this. They had to go by plane. Tammy had been on a boat and a train but not a plane.

The final item on the list was a birthday party. Monica was to organise a birthday party for Tammy's eleventh birthday. It would be her last year in primary school and Joanna had promised she would throw her a party and invite all their relatives, aunts, uncles and cousins, plus her whole class. Monica vowed to keep that promise.

When she came to collect Tammy at six thirty she was relieved to find that Liz had already fed her. She was equally grateful for the offer of Sunday lunch. Cooking was not her forte and just another thing she was failing at. She was not organised enough to sort dinner out every evening. She would have a run of a few nights when she thought she had cracked it but would forget to take something out of the freezer or run out of breakfast cereal or milk and feel like a complete failure.

Recently she had been really pleased with herself because she had remembered to buy Tammy's favourite pizza. Once in the oven Tammy had asked for sweetcorn to go with it. Monica felt quite smug as she was sure that she had bought some but after rummaging in the cupboard for five minutes or more she had to admit defeat.

'What have we got?' asked Tammy, daring her to come up with something. Monica sighed before rolling off the list. Tinned pears, condensed milk, plum tomatoes, spring vegetable soup or custard. She laughed. Tammy did not.

She was equally disorganised with washing and ironing and was grateful for the fact that Tammy had a school uniform, which meant she could stretch a school skirt or tunic for another day or so before washing it. The white shirts were not as forgiving and after washing were ironed on Sunday night in front of the TV.

This was followed by the ritual of hunting for the school tie to ensure Tammy wasn't late for school, which in turn made her late for work.

It wasn't made any easier by the fact that Tammy was so angry a lot of the time. If Monica tried to talk about Joanna, or even school, she would storm out of the room and slam the door behind her. If Monica asked her a question, or worse, asked her to do something she would remind her that she wasn't her mother and therefore couldn't make her do anything.

She had thought that the fact that they had both lost Joanna and had their grief in common would bind them somehow but instead it seemed to tear them further apart. She had initially resisted giving Tammy a key to their new flat because she didn't feel she could trust her in the house on her own. Tamika had broken quite a few things in the last flat. She would get very angry and throw the nearest thing to hand. The last TV had been the victim of the remote control through the screen.

Monica could not afford to keep replacing things. She had made arrangements with her employers to go in half an hour early and take a shorter lunch break so she could leave an hour or so earlier in the evenings, but still she didn't always get home in time. 'Must try harder,' she told herself as she drove back to work.

Chapter 3

Liz knew that half term was coming up and wondered if Monica would be able to take the time off work. She had thought about offering her services. After all she had nothing better to do, but finding something for a ten year old girl to do for a couple of hours in the evening was a lot easier than whole days.

Adam was busy at work when his secretary announced that his wife was on the phone. Georgina often called him at work and he was happy in the knowledge that it was likely to be for something trivial. During their sixteen years together Georgina had run their home like a well-oiled machine.

They had met at work. Georgina had been the personal assistant to the Head of Corporate Law while Adam was a rising star from the international division. There was an immediate attraction, although Georgina's was more calculated. Yes, she was attracted to his lean and handsome face, grey blue eyes and cheeky smile, but even more attractive was his six figure salary, not including bonus. He was a very good prospect indeed.

For Adam it had been altogether more romantic.

Georgina could play helpless damsel in distress with a performance that Dame Judi Dench would be proud of. She could also cry at the drop of a hat and Adam had been completely out of his depth the moment he asked her what was wrong sixteen years ago when he found her crying by the photocopier.

Georgina was pretty, with delicate features, tall and slim with hazel eyes, shoulder length blonde hair and a slightly wonky smile, a smile that Adam had found so endearing when she accepted the offer of his handkerchief. She had engineered the meeting and instigated their first date. Adam thought it was his idea but he stood no chance whatsoever. Georgina planned her life with military precision.

Within a year of meeting they were engaged and shortly after Liz and Jim were digging into their savings to contribute to their hugely expensive wedding. Adam didn't need the money but his parents were old fashioned and had wanted to contribute something. Georgina had helpfully suggested that they pay for the honeymoon.

After all, he was their only son and heir and they were so proud of him. They did their best to like Georgina but she was not easy to like. She would never put herself out to make conversation and although they were easy around Adam whenever Georgina was present there was a tension in the air.

Adam excused her rudeness as being caused by the fact that she was shy and sensitive. Georgina was neither. It was not that she disliked Adam's parents; it was merely that they were Adam's parents and she wanted to be his entire world. So under the guise of love and affection she had set about disaffecting her in-laws along with most of his friends.

Despite the fact that they lived locally they very rarely saw them. Adam and Georgina were always off somewhere sunning, skiing or sailing. Liz and Jim would keep an eye on their house and it seemed to Liz that they were most welcome at the house when they were away.

Things got a little bit easier for a short while after Sasha was born and then again when baby Leo came into the world. Jim could not have been prouder at the christening of Leo James Bailey and tried very hard to overlook Georgina's shortcomings. As for Georgina, she found it harder to find babysitters for two small children as her parents lived too far away, so Liz and Jim were finally called into service most weekends.

But it didn't go unnoticed that Georgina was only warm and friendly when she wanted something.

Adam was happily oblivious to the domestic discord in his life, he was so busy building his client base and getting to the top of the ladder. In addition to which he spent a great deal of time abroad during their early years together and was grateful for the fact that Georgina was so organised, which meant that he was never bothered by domestic trifles.

Georgina and Adam were equally ambitious. Adam wanted his CEO's job and Georgina didn't want to want for anything. In many ways they were perfectly suited. She was able to stay at home, employing a cleaner and a gardener.

The house was perfect and the children well behaved. He thought of himself as a very lucky man.

Georgina briefly considered getting a job after the children were born, or perhaps doing some sort of charity work. After all, she didn't really want to 'work' for anyone else. She had thought about starting a business of her own but hadn't been able to decide what to do, perhaps something in fashion or make up. She was fantastic at both, always beautifully turned out. Liz had never seen her without her face on, as she called it, both her faces, according to Jim.

Adam had not been keen on moving to Bury St Edmunds from Arkley when it was first suggested. It was a much more difficult commute but Georgina had persuaded him that their lives would be so much easier as her parents were local and could help with the children, who were by then one and three, when she resumed her career. Liz was still working full time and was therefore unable to commit to child-minding. It didn't take much to convince Adam and within three months they had moved away.

Georgina never did get back to work and seven years on she was still trying to 'find herself' with various schemes. Adam remained completely devoted. Jim was always of the opinion, at least early on in their marriage, that Adam was Georgina's career and they had both been fearful that should anything halt his march to the top Georgina would be looking for a new job.

Liz blamed herself for her son's selfish nature. She had spoilt him rotten. Adam had been born following two miscarriages and Liz had spent the final trimester in hospital, and there were other complications during his birth which meant that she was unable to have another child. She had thought about adopting but Jim wasn't keen and Adam was such a sickly child. He was in and out of hospital with asthma and various other childhood illnesses. By the time he started school at five he was fairly robust and she began to help out at his school as a classroom assistant.

Liz found that she loved it and fairly soon enrolled herself at university to study history, eventually qualifying as a teacher. She poured all the love she had into raising Adam and looking after the children in her care. Adam was a very bright child and, being a teacher, Liz was able to help him a lot in the early years of school.

He whizzed through the entrance exam for the best local secondary school, a 'Grade A' student, always at the top of his class. In fact he was so far ahead of his peers that he did a couple of the exams a year or two early . This was both a blessing and a curse. As he was speeding to the top of his form he was leaving many of his friends behind and his teenage years were fairly lonely.

Jim and Liz were incredibly indulgent parents and supported Adam while he studied economics and law, completing his degree and then his Masters. Things really improved at university for Adam where he managed to find an equally studious crowd to hang out with. He even found a girlfriend who made it home to meet his parents.

Liz loved Megan from the moment they met. Megan was

warm and friendly. She laughed, she joined in, she was funny and completely in love with Adam. She was petite with dark curly hair and serious brown eyes. She was passionate about the environment and in her final year studying bio-chemistry couldn't wait to be unleashed on the world. She really wanted to make a difference.

When Megan and Adam finished their studies they looked for work. Adam started his job search with the banking and finance sector but it was Megan who was the first to find her dream job. She was offered a research post with the World Health Organisation and the chance to go to Africa. She asked Adam to go with her but his devotion didn't stretch that far. His dream was to make loads of money.

It didn't take long for an employer to recognise Adam's talent. His first job at a bank in the city was going so well that within nine months he had usurped his former boss. A year later he had been headhunted by a rival bank in Canary Wharf. They tried to keep in touch, although Megan did most of the running, but she didn't fit with the banking crowd. She didn't look the part and had an inbuilt distrust of huge corporations. She also had a social conscience; Adam had no conscience, so they drifted apart.

It wasn't long after this that Georgina set her sights on Adam. The damsel in distress act had worked like a charm and he was happy playing Tarzan to Georgina's helpless Jane.

Georgina had called him at work to ask him to ask his mother a favour.

'Darling,' she began, 'Mummy and Daddy have decided to go on a cruise over Easter to celebrate their anniversary which means that you and I will have to cancel our holiday in St Bart's unless we can find someone to look after the children. Of course, I know it's still a few weeks away but I thought you might like to keep your mother in reserve in case we get stuck.'

'I'm sure Mum would love it,' Adam replied.

'She would have to stay at our house, of course,' Georgina continued, 'so the children could still see their friends and Sasha can ride her horse.'

'It would be like a holiday for mum, too,' Adam agreed. He actually believed that when he said it. 'I'll give her a call but I doubt there's any hurry. Mum never goes anywhere. I'm certain she'll be free. Leave it to me,' and with that he put down the phone.

*****

Liz still got postcards and invitations to visit from Megan now and again and mourned the daughter in law she might have had. Megan had since married and was now the mother of four children, blissfully happy and living in Cornwall where she owned a shop selling organic food. Liz would have loved to visit but Adam would not have approved and Liz was worried about appearing disloyal, so she contented herself with a letter now and again.

She looked over at the family photograph of Adam, Georgina and the children. They looked like the perfect nuclear family. Adam and Georgina were seated, holding hands in the foreground with Leo and Sasha standing behind them. They were all smiling. You could almost see the photographer in the background mouthing 'cheese' as they all grinned together. She picked up the phone to give him a call but glanced at the time and changed her mind. It was too early. He would still be at work and she couldn't face the rejection.

Besides, she had lunch to organise. The house had not seen many visitors since Jim died. On the very rare occasions when Adam and the children came to visit they were usually en route to somewhere else and never had time to stay for tea let alone dinner. So they had disposed of their dining table and instead converted the dining room into an office.

She liked the room very much and spent a great deal of time in there but it no longer lent itself to family dinners. She would have to think of something else. She wandered into the living room which overlooked the garden. Jim hated clutter and the room was functional rather than comfortable. There was a sideboard, two sofas, three side tables, a rug in front of the fireplace and the TV on the wall. It was certainly big enough for a table and chairs but did she really want to buy one? She had to do something; the small kitchen table was only big enough for two. Three would be a squeeze.

As she looked around the room she caught sight of the patio furniture through the window, she remembered the neat brown rattan set with a glass topped table and six chairs. It was sitting there, untouched, waiting to be of service. She opened the patio door and went outside. Only little bits of it were visible under the green protective cover, which was now stained.

A slimy green paddling pool had formed on top of the table where the excess plastic had been forced down by the rain. Liz went back inside to find her rubber gloves.

She returned with scissors to cut the ties which held the plastic in place, then lifting one side she managed to slosh some of the water away. She repeated this a few times until most of the water was displaced and she was able to lift the cover off completely. She placed it on the floor next to the door. She would get the yard broom and hose out to work on the residual dirt and slime that stuck to the cover later.

The furniture was still in remarkably good condition. Yes, no doubt it had been inhabited by spiders and various other insects. It was dirty and neglected but nothing a wash and brush up wouldn't cure. She could move the oblong table and three, no four of the chairs inside. Three would look unbalanced.

She pulled out the hose from the reel attached to the wall and, after clicking the nozzle into place, turned the selector to indicate a single stream of water which she directed at one of the chairs. She saw a spider run for cover as a stream of water rushed over the seat. She used kitchen towels to remove the excess water before drying the chairs with an old tea towel individually. She did the same to the table before polishing the glass and when she had finished it looked as good as new.

She lifted one of the chairs and was relieved to find it was fairly light. She tried the table and, to her surprise, it was not that heavy either but awkward to manoeuvre. She looked for a way to remove the glass and was happy to find that it just lifted off. This made it much easier to coax into the living room through the patio door. She put it in the centre on the rug and then brought the chairs in one by one, finally slotting the glass back into place.

The furniture looked odd in the living room so she moved the chairs into the office, followed by the table which she had to put on its side to get through the doors. It looked better in the office. It still looked out of place but less out of place than in the living room. She tucked the office chair in as close to the desk as it would go and stood back at the door to get the full effect. It looked great. She decided to leave it there until Sunday and went back outside to tackle the plastic cover.

This time when she went outside she paused to look around the garden before starting work. She hadn't had a really good look at the garden for a very long time but she took a deep breath and scanned the flower beds carefully. It had been ages since she had been this close. In some places it was almost impossible to tell where the grass ended and the flowerbeds began.

She tried to picture it in her head. She closed her eyes to imagine how the garden would have looked at this time of year. Crocuses and daffodils would line the front of the flowers beds and perhaps some hyacinths in the tubs. She inhaled deeply as if the act of drawing breath itself would recapture the smell of the fragrant flowers. There would be buds on the fruit trees and then blossom. She opened her eyes, almost expecting it to be as it was.

She turned her head to look at the pergola. In the spring it was magnificent, its dark wooden arches covered with stunning pink clematis with flowers almost the size of saucers. But now it was a mass of dead, brittle twigs twisted around the beams.

She recognised the leaves of a passion flower on a single, slender stem pushing its way through the ever present ivy. But she was most ashamed of the grass. She had no excuse. She could easily have handled the hover mower but she had not been able to touch it since Jim died and so the lawn now resembled a wild meadow with nameless plants a metre or more high in some places. Even the odd sapling was trying to stake a claim in the wilderness.

She stood in the garden and cried, hot tears falling down her cold face.

'Oh, for God's sake,' she said to herself, 'get a grip, you silly woman.' She turned and went inside.

Chapter 4

She spent Saturday morning doing her usual housework. Not that the house needed anything really. She had the ironing board up in the kitchen with Radio 4 in the background. She ironed everything these days, fitted sheets, towels, even knickers, not because she needed to but because it wasted a bit more time.

After lunch she made a shopping list. She had decided to cook roast lamb. It was Jim's favourite and according to him one of her specialities. Jim would not say he liked something too much when it came to Liz's cooking. He was scared that he would get it every other day so was sparing with his praise. He wouldn't have minded roast lamb every other day though, it was that good. Liz hadn't made a roast dinner since Jim died. It was not as though she had forgotten how, she just had no one to make it for.

Whenever they had roast lamb Jim requested apple pie. Crisp, melt in the mouth short-crust pastry filled with soft, sweet cooking apples. She didn't bother making custard nowadays. You could buy vanilla custard made with cream from most supermarkets.

She thought about wine. Should she buy wine? She didn't want Monica to think she was a regular drinker, especially now she was looking after Tammy, but it was nice to have a glass of wine with Sunday lunch. She hadn't had a glass of anything since the funeral. She was scared to have it in the house in case she was tempted to drink herself into oblivion. Bugger it. One red and one white were added to the list, Shiraz and Sauvignon Blanc plus lemonade or squash for Tammy.

Tammy had begun to come to Liz's every evening after school and they were getting used to each other. Liz learnt that Tammy liked toast with Marmite which Liz hated but bought anyway.

Tammy also liked salt and vinegar crisps and cheese spread. Liz obliged by making sure that she always had these in stock. She liked the company and Tammy was easy going and interested in everything.

She liked to read and had picked out Ann of Green Gables from the bookshelf in Liz's kitchen. Ann of Green Gables was Liz's favourite when she was growing up and she was really enjoying listening to Tammy reading aloud from the book, although Tammy voiced Marilla Cuthbert, who was Canadian, with an Irish accent and her brother Matthew could have been Welsh.

When she wasn't reading or watching TV she was asking questions. In fact Tammy reminded Liz of Ann Shirley from the book in that she was a very chatty companion, curious and opinionated. As she grew more comfortable in Liz's house she began to ask more and more questions, firing the 'why' word like machine gun bullets.

Why was Adam an only child, did she not want more

children? How old was she? Why didn't she do something with her hair? Did she ever have any pets? Why didn't Adam visit, had they had an argument? How long had she lived in her house? Did her grandchildren ever come to stay? Why was she on her own? A never ending stream of enquiries that often left Liz feeling like she was being interrogated by the junior branch of the FBI.

Liz was careful not to ask Tammy questions about her mother. She knew that Tammy would talk about her when she was ready. However, she didn't have a good word to say about her poor aunt Monica. Apparently nothing Monica did could compare to her mother, which was entirely natural but really hard on Monica who was doing her best. Liz always tried to get Tammy to see it from Monica's point of view but if the slamming of their back door was any indication of progress their relationship still required work.

Liz told Monica that dinner would be around two o'clock but she failed to put the joint in early enough as she was so out of practice and was just putting the roast potatoes in when the doorbell rang. Worse, it suddenly occurred to her that Monica might be a vegetarian. She began to panic. She hadn't even started on the apple pie.

Monica had brought flowers and wine. Liz felt obliged to own up to the fact that she had assumed that Sunday roast would be OK. Monica immediately put her at ease by telling her that it was her favourite meal, adding that she was completely hopeless when it came to cooking.

Liz felt her nerves evaporate and asked them both if

they would like to muck in and help with the pie. Tammy was really keen so Liz gave her an apron and put the flour and butter in a bowl. Tammy knew exactly what to do and didn't hesitate to tell Liz that she didn't need help. In no time at all she had formed a ball of dough in her hands and was separating it into two halves, ready to be rolled out.

She sifted flour over the pastry board and rolled out a pizza sized round to line the dish. Monica peeled and cut the apples. Liz greased the pie dish and marvelled at how well Tammy was able to fold the pastry over the rolling pin so it could be manoeuvred into the pie dish without help. She then arranged the sliced apples on top, added the sugar and topped it with the pastry lid which she pricked with a fork and dusted with sugar. Liz put it into the oven. Monica was very impressed.

The smells in the kitchen were wonderful. The roast lamb and roast potatoes were doing nicely and the vegetables were steaming on the hob. Liz made the gravy whilst Monica and Tammy helped to lay the table. Tammy, of course, already knew where everything was and got the plates and cutlery out of the cupboards and drawers. Liz apologised for the lack of mint sauce. It had been a long time since she'd had guests for dinner. But Tammy had never heard of it and Monica didn't like it anyway, so it wasn't missed.

Liz came in with the cold wine that Monica had brought along with a couple of wine glasses and a tumbler for the lemonade already in front of Tammy. She then went back to the kitchen to plate up the dinner. She looked at the finished meal and thought of Jim. She hadn't lost her touch. She took the apple pie out of the oven and left it on the kitchen counter to cool before taking the dinner plates into the office.

'Wow', said Monica, 'it looks delicious. I don't think I'll ever be able to make anything like that.'

'That's true,' Tammy interrupted.

'I'm sure you will,' said Liz, 'it just takes a bit of practice.' She gave Tammy a sideways glance and poured them both a glass of wine. 'I was a terrible cook when I first got married. I am grateful I didn't poison anyone, although I think I came close. I remember once buying a Vesta meal which was the closest thing to convenience food there was in those days. The tag line in the TV advertisement was 'Vesta knows how'. Vesta may have done, but I certainly didn't. They were Chinese meals with noodles and Jim was astounded that I managed to get the noodles perfect on one side, raw on the other and burnt in the middle. He was very skinny in those days. Luckily we had a fish and chip shop nearby.'

Monica laughed. 'Well, as you can see I am heavily supporting the local takeaways. They all know me by name.'

Tammy added that she was surprised Monica didn't look like a pizza. Monica bemoaned the fact that she couldn't lose weight and promised to learn to cook.

Dinner over, Liz picked up the empty plates and took them into the kitchen. She was soon back with a tray on which sat the gorgeous glistening apple pie, three bowls and the custard, which had now been decanted into a cut glass jug.

'Only a small piece for me,' said Monica, 'I should try to lose weight.' Liz cut the wedge in half and shared it between them.

'Custard?' she asked, holding up the jug.

'Better not. I only have to look at something sweet and I pile on the pounds. I do intend to start exercising but I don't get much time.'

Tammy had scoffed hers in five minutes. 'I used to make pies with mum.'

'Yes, you did,' added Monica, 'and they were fantastic. Joanna was a brilliant cook.'

'Maybe Tammy will teach you?' said Liz. 'She is obviously a dab hand in the kitchen. You could make dinner together.'

'That would be nice,' said Monica hopefully, looking at Tammy who said nothing.

'When I was your age,' said Liz addressing Tammy, 'we used to go blackberry picking in Parliament Hill fields. Parly we called it. We'd go all year round, summer and winter. In the summer we'd play hide and seek in the long grass and in the autumn we'd collect conkers and pick blackberries for blackberry and apple pie.

'Mum was from a huge family. She was the youngest of five sisters and three brothers. There was always a gang of us on the bus, with two or three of mum's sisters and loads of cousins. We would board the bus near to Chapel Market in Islington and stay on until it terminated just outside the entrance to Parly.

I was a terrible traveller as a child and my brother was no better, we were often sick on the bus. It would sometimes take half an hour or so sitting in the first field getting over being travel sick before venturing out to look for blackberries.

'Blackberry bushes are covered in thorns. The art of collecting the berries is to find a branch with a crook at the end and use it to hook the brambles and pull them towards you to pick the berries.

That's the theory anyway. In practice we would get covered in scratches and blotches of blackberry juice, risking life and limb and terrible splinters to retrieve a small box or bagful each. Not to mention the clusters of bumps on your legs from the stinging nettles which always seem to accompany blackberries.

'We didn't have much money either so mum always made egg sandwiches to take with us. We would sit in the top field in the sunshine eating sandwiches and drinking orange squash. I can't eat an egg sandwich now without being transported back to those fields. Then it was ice cream from the café at the entrance and back on the bus.

'Once we were home we all helped to make the pies which would seep inky black juice onto the plate and stain your tongue purple.'

'Can we do that?' piped up Tammy. 'Can we pick blackberries?'

'Yes,' said Monica, not really keen but happy to risk

personal injury for anything which might breach the gaping hole between them.

'You'll have to wait until autumn for blackberries,' Liz informed them, 'but strawberries are ready for picking in June. We could go there if you like, the farm is just up the road. I haven't been in ages. It would be fun.'

Monica was grateful for the prospect of doing something nice with Tammy. More wine was poured and Tammy retired to the living room where she settled in front of the TV.

Liz and Monica remained in the office at the table, chatting very quietly. Liz asked about Tammy's dad and Monica told her the story of Max. Tammy knew all about Max. Joanna had always been completely honest with her. Monica was surprised that Tammy had not asked to meet him, not that it would have been easy if she had. Joanna had no idea where he was although she had always told Tammy that if she ever wanted to meet him she would help her to find him. Tammy had never expressed an interest, not even after Joanna had died.

'How are you holding up?' said Liz presently.

'Oh, good days and bad days,' replied Monica.

'I know what that's like,' said Liz, 'you feel like you're under a cloud.'

'Most days she hates me but some days she merely despises me, so I think I'm growing on her. It's Mothering Sunday next week and I'm stealing myself for the tidal wave that's coming.

Tammy doesn't want to go to the cemetery with me and I don't know how to handle it. Some nights I wake up in a cold sweat with this feeling that a huge crushing weight is pressing on my chest.'

'Sounds like a panic attack,' Liz reassured.

'It's all I can do not to run out of the house,' Monica confided, almost whispering.

'I feel for you,' said Liz. 'I feel for both of you. It can't be easy. If it means anything at all I think you're doing really well, but it takes time. Tammy will come round and if I can do anything to help just let me know.'

'I am really grateful to you,' replied Monica. 'I was getting to the end of my tether with work and worry. I didn't have to think about things like holidays and homework before. I just went to work and came home and did whatever I wanted to do.

'Who would have thought that not that long ago I was footloose and fancy free with no responsibilities other than work and now I have a ten year old to look after. It's taken me months to get organised with the washing and ironing. Tammy used to have a packed lunch but I haven't got that sorted yet. I'm sure she resents the fact that she now has to have school meals. She won't let me help her with her homework and I am trying hard not to resent the fact that I had plans of my own which I have had to completely abandon. I didn't want to be a parent. I didn't choose...'

Her voice trailed off as Tammy called out from the other room. Monica panicked, terrified that Tammy had overheard, but she hadn't. Instead, when they went into the living room Tammy was standing at the patio door.

'What's happened to the garden?' she said, as Liz entered the room. Liz was momentarily taken aback but she recovered quickly.

'Oh, it's been a bit neglected of late,' surprising herself by the lack of emotion in her voice when she said it.

'More than a bit,' remarked Tammy, who had no discretion at all. 'It's like a bloody jungle out there.'

'Tammy, don't be rude,' reproached Monica.

'I've been meaning to do it, but I'm not much of a gardener. That was always Jim's job. I wouldn't know where to start.'

'But Liz,' said Tammy triumphantly, 'you've got the book.' She went straight to the spot under the chair where she had first found the book. She opened it at the grid.

'Look,' she said, pointing at the first page. 'I will help you. This is the time of year when you should start cutting the lawn, unless it's wet of course.'

'And how would you know?' said Monica.

'It's on page three,' said Tammy.

Liz couldn't help but smile. She felt a little tipsy.

Monica felt equally relaxed and thought about going home. Five school shirts had been left drying on the clothes horse and the ironing beckoned.

'We had better go soon, young lady. You have school tomorrow.'

Tammy watched the end of a film while Monica helped

Liz rinse the plates and fill the dishwasher. As they were doing so Monica turned to Liz.

'I hate to ask you this, and please don't worry if you can't, but I wondered if you would be able to look after Tammy over the Easter holidays. I wangled half term but I only get five weeks holiday and need to save some of them for the summer break. I can't afford to have any more time off work. I've been away so much.'

Liz didn't hesitate. It was great having Tammy around and she really liked Monica.

'I'd be happy to,' she said, adding, 'I was going to offer anyway but I didn't want you to think that I was interfering. Are you sure it's OK with Tammy?' Tammy was still sitting on the sofa with the garden journal on her lap. Monica shouted through the open door.

'Tammy, Liz has kindly offered to look after you during the daytime over the Easter break. If you would like that,' she added hopefully.

'Great,' shouted Tammy. 'We can start work on the garden.'

*****

On Friday the eighth of March Liz was surprised by a knock on the door, earlier than the postman usually arrived. On the doorstep was a very small man carrying a huge bunch of flowers which completely obscured most of his head and torso. Adam always sent beautiful flowers for her birthday and Mothers' Day. The bigger and more extravagant the flowers the less likely she was to be seeing

61

him any time soon.

There was a card, written in handwriting that Liz didn't recognise. 'Sorry, can't get to see you this weekend. Will pop in soon. Happy Mothers' Day, love Adam, Georgina, Sasha and Leo.' He didn't forget but the fact that he remembered was no comfort. It was automatic, as if it was a work commitment, a date in the diary but nothing personal. It was likely that his secretary had ordered the flowers and instructed the florist on what to write on the card. The flowers gave her no pleasure. She put them in a vase and hid them in a room upstairs. She didn't want Tammy to see them when she came home from school.

During the next week Tammy learnt that Liz taught history and had left her job a few years ago. She hadn't wanted to retire. She loved her job and loved being with the students, but Jim was a few years older than her and had been made redundant with a very good pay off. He was getting bored at home by himself so urged her to resign so she could be with him.

She found it really hard to adjust in the beginning but they spent some time decorating the house. They had lots of friends from Jim's lodge. He had been a Freemason for years so they were always out to dinner and often away for the weekends.

Jim never wanted to go anywhere for long because he hated leaving the garden. Liz would have liked to move abroad, maybe France or Spain. She loved the sun but it was partly the fact that she missed Adam so much that drove her to think it would be a good idea. She felt that if they lived somewhere more interesting Adam and Georgina might visit more often with the children. She certainly wouldn't see him any less.

Jim was not so keen. He preferred somewhere closer to home and had considered Bournemouth. They even got as far as going to see a bungalow but Liz absolutely hated it.

'I couldn't face living there,' she told Tammy. 'It felt like God's waiting room so we stayed here.'

Liz didn't mind most of Tammy's questions and even found herself laughing when recanting Jim stories. He would always read her the jokes or readers' letters from the paper, especially if they had made him laugh.

Tammy had begun to talk about her mother, too. She told Liz how she would braid her hair and when they were really busy she would get Tammy to wash the hair of the clients who came to the house for a hairdo.

Tammy could do a great imitation of her mother's well practiced hairdresser small-talk. She would move her hands as if she was cutting imaginary hair. 'Going on holiday this year?' she would ask, and 'How's the family? Phil out of prison yet?' Sometimes her mother would do the hair and the make-up too, if it was a special occasion. Tammy loved the before and after, seeing the people she knew transformed and dressed up to go out to parties.

The Easter holidays were fast approaching and Liz was looking forward to spending more time with Tammy and Monica and even to tackling the garden. This was usually her worst time of year. It was nearing the anniversary of Jim's death and she had to force herself to look at the garden.

Happy and sad memories were fighting for space in her head. The wonderful barbecues and parties they had in the garden with their friends, the bonfire nights and birthday celebrations for Adam and his mates growing up, and her grandchildren, the rare occasions that Sasha and Leo had toddled around the garden or splashed in the paddling pool.

But no matter how hard she tried to recall the happy memories the sight of Jim, his face ashen and his eyes rolling back in his head as he clutched his chest, haunted her. She caught her breath as, for a second; she was there again, re-living the moment when her world changed, paralyzed with fear for what seemed like forever before fumbling with the catch on the patio door in panic to get to Jim, who was already dead.

She shook her head and closed her eyes. She took a deep breath before opening them again slowly and forcing herself to look back at the garden. The sun was shining and the image was gone.

'I can do this,' she said to herself.

Friday the fifth of April was the anniversary of Jim's death. She was pleased that Tammy would be coming home a bit earlier from school as they were breaking up at two o'clock.

It was only Wednesday, so she had a few days to get some Easter presents to send. This year she would buy an

Easter egg for Tammy and perhaps something for Monica, conscious of the fact that she was trying to lose weight. She was still thinking about Easter eggs when the phone rang.

'Hi Adam, how lovely to hear from you.' She tried to sound as bright and breezy as possible. She hated the thought that he might think she was desperate and needy so she smiled as she spoke into the receiver, hoping that it might somehow be reflected in her voice.

'How are you, mum?' he began.

'Fine, fine,' she replied. She really was fine, for the first time in a long time.

'Mum, I've got some great news,' he continued. 'Georgina and I have booked a holiday for the Easter break, and we were hoping that you would...'

'Come with you?' Liz interrupted, knowing full well that it would be the last thing he'd say, but it threw him completely.

'Well, that would have been nice,' he continued, without a hint of embarrassment 'but Georgina and I have booked to go away for a romantic break on our own and we wondered if you would like to come and stay with the children. It would be like a holiday for you.' The man was deluded.

'Thank you, Adam, but no thank you,' was Liz's emphatic reply. 'I'm afraid I have plans for the Easter break and as much as I would love a holiday, I'll have to pass. Anyway, got to go luv, I'm in the middle of something. I'll have to call you later,' and with that she put the receiver down. It felt good.

Chapter 5

Adam was left holding the phone while his brain caught up with the conversation he had just had with his mother. Perhaps she misunderstood, he reasoned. He'd have to call Georgina and tell her. She would be devastated.

'What do you mean, she has plans,' was her plaintive cry on the other end of the phone.

'Well that's all she said,' Adam replied. 'She has plans.'

'Nonsense,' Georgina said. 'There must be a misunderstanding. She never goes anywhere. You'll have to go and see her.'

*****

Liz caught a glimpse of herself in the hall mirror and suddenly saw herself through Tammy's eyes. She had let herself go over the past few years. She was still fairly slim but her hair desperately needed cutting and was now almost completely white. She did look like a witch. She had taken very good care of herself in the past, always having her hair done and really looking after her skin. She looked young for her age but the grey hair now drained the colour from her face, adding five or ten years. It wasn't only the garden that had been neglected.

She rang the hairdressers.

When she got to the salon Yvonne, the colourist, recognised her.

'Hi, Mrs Bailey, haven't seen you in a while.' The last time she had been in the salon was the week before Jim died. They were going off to Prague for a long weekend and she had popped in to get her roots touched up.

Yvonne asked her what she would like done. Liz wasn't really sure except that her hair needed a complete overhaul. Yvonne suggested cutting in some soft layers and adding a colour. She then went off to mix the colour and a trainee stylist came over to help Liz on with her gown before going off to make her a cup of coffee.

Liz liked the coffee at the hairdressers. Filter coffee in a small cafetierre, a cup and saucer, small jug of milk and one of those crunchy coffee biscuits on the side, individually wrapped and brought in on a silver tray, which always made it seem special.

Yvonne came back presently with a trolley containing the bowl of colour and brushes and then proceeded to do exactly as Tammy had done when imitating her mother. She held up a strand of hair before painting on the colour and asking, 'What have you been doing with yourself?'

Liz was tempted to say that she'd just robbed a bank to fund her drug habit, she doubted that Yvonne was actually listening anyway. Anything was better that talking about Jim. She couldn't trust herself not to cry.

She managed to fend off most of the questions and

thankfully Yvonne didn't seem to remember anything concrete about her other than the fact that she was a teacher and used to come in regularly. Once her hair had been covered in the dye Yvonne placed a timer on the shelf in front of her.

'I'll leave you for thirty five minutes for the colour to develop. Want any magazines?' she asked. Liz indicated that she did not and instead got out her diary and proceeded to catch up on the last few days. Yvonne brought over a pile of magazines anyway.

'Must be something they pick up in hairdressing school,' thought Liz, along with totally ignoring requests to cut off a little bit, like cutting off four or five centimetres when you only asked for one. Liz's hair was in such bad condition that any style, any length would be an improvement.

She used to write everything in her diary but hadn't bothered over the last few years. There wasn't really much point in recording the same miserable day over and over again. She looked at this year's book, a brown, leather bound, A5 sized diary with a page a day. It was a Christmas present from Adam. She had started writing a diary when she first began studying, just names and dates initially, but as time went on it had become her inner voice. She would record important conversations, incidents in the class and things that went well or not so well during a lesson.

A page a day had been entirely unnecessary as she hadn't written more than a sentence or two in the last five years. She didn't exactly remember the dates of events but she decided to record her first encounter with Monica and Tammy. She wrote about Tammy's drawing of her and Sunday lunch. It felt good to have something to write about. She also skipped ahead to Monday the eighth of April and wrote 'Making a start on the garden with Tammy.'

She then flicked back the pages to today's date and wrote, 'Hairdressers' and then, 'Feeling different today, much more positive.'

When she closed the diary she thought about her conversation with Adam. She would have loved to see her grandchildren. She knew what they looked like. Georgina made sure of that with the annual family portrait but she didn't know them. She doubted that Leo or Sasha would actually like her to be there looking after them. They were not used to her, nor she them. She hadn't seen them since the Christmas before last and that was only a fleeting visit on their way to the airport. Besides, she had promised to look after Tammy and would not go back on her word.

The alarm on the timer went off and the trainee returned to wash off the colour before moving her to a different chair and the new stylist who would be cutting her hair. Sarah introduced herself and began chatting away. Liz was grateful that she could talk about anything she wanted to and she wanted to talk about the garden.

She told Sarah that she would be reviving a neglected garden. She didn't say why it was neglected or how long it had been that way, just that it required a bit of work.

'That's fantastic,' enthused Sarah. 'You have the

opportunity to change it completely. A revamp, like on the telly.'

'You're right,' said Liz, and she wondered why it hadn't occurred to her before.

When Tammy came home from school she did a double take as the front door opened.

'Who are you and what have you done with Liz?' she said eventually, taking in the new improved version. Liz's hair was now light brown with subtle blonde highlights and bouncy layers replaced the straight grey bob.

'I got sick of looking like a witch,' she said smiling. Tammy blushed at the memory. Gone were the shapeless tracksuit bottoms and in their place were jeans, flat boots and an olive green v neck jumper. A little eye make-up and blusher completed the transformation.

'What do you think?'

'You look nothing like a witch now,' Tammy replied smiling, which was as near to a compliment as she could manage.

'You'll have to redo my portrait,' said Liz, pointing at the picture on the fridge. Tammy grinned.

Liz had already prepared a snack, which was waiting on the kitchen table next to a notebook and pen. 'School ends this Friday for the Easter break and I thought we could make a start on the garden, if you'd still like to?' Liz asked cautiously.

'I would,' said Tammy, 'and I'd also like to do something to help bees.'

'Bees?' repeated Liz.

'We've been learning about bees at school and how important they are for pollinating and stuff. Did you know that they are being hurt by pesticides?' she asked earnestly. 'Too many gardens are paved over,' she continued. 'It's called habitat destruction, so bees can't find enough food.'

Liz could imagine the teacher standing in front of the class delivering the doom and gloom sermon and now Tammy was doing the same.

'Sounds serious,' she said.

'It is,' said Tammy. 'I want to do something to help them.'

'OK,' said Liz. 'Sounds like the garden and your project have a lot in common. We can work on it together. We can make the garden bee friendly. After tea we'll do a bit of research on the computer to find out which plants bees prefer. Maybe we could plant up some tubs to put in your garden next door too. What do you think?'

'Sounds like a plan,' said Tammy, who was pleased with the idea and both of them went into the office to work at the computer.

The next day Liz got up early. She had some shopping to do and decided to go to the garden centre first. She wanted to get a plant to take to the cemetery. In the months after Jim's death the only place she found any comfort was the cemetery. She would sit on a bench near to the black marble plaque which stated in gold letters, 'James Edward Bailey 12th March 1948 – 5th April 2009. Beloved Husband and Father. Always in our Hearts.'

She would sit on the bench and cry until she could barely breathe and her nose would get so bunged up she had to breathe through her mouth. Eventually there would be no more tears left and through soft, intermittent sobs she would talk to him quietly in her head. She was sorry she hadn't been able to save him, she was angry he had left her, she was lonely, so very, very lonely without him.

But today felt different. She was different. She would take the flowers to the cemetery but she wouldn't cry. She would tell him about Tammy and Monica and how she would be working on the garden.

The garden centre was huge. It was always a favourite of Jim's. They would often go in without collecting a trolley first. This was always a mistake as half way round Jim would spot some flowering shrub or bedding plants and would gather them up in his arms while Liz ran back to the front of the shop to collect a trolley. They would sometimes meet friends in the pub up the road and have lunch after shopping or sit and have a coffee, watching the world go by.

It always amazed her that couples could sit opposite each other with nothing to say. They always had plenty to say. Despite being married for thirty five years they would sit in restaurants and coffee shops, chatting and laughing like a courting couple. They would argue about politics, about religion, about what colour to paint the kitchen, but it was never dull. Liz could talk for England and Jim had never really grown up. He had a real sense of fun.

They used to have loads of friends but none of them were single and in the early months after Jim died the couples didn't know how to deal with a suicidal widow who could barely string two sentences together without wailing like a banshee. They just stopped coming to see her. She laughed to herself, 'What must they have thought of me? How do other people cope? How do Monica and Tammy cope?' She promised herself that she would get in touch with some of their old friends to let them know she was back in the world and hadn't gone completely mad.

She settled in front of a rack of potted azaleas in various colours and picked a plant with salmon pink flowers.

'Jim would love these,' she thought. She picked up two plants and then put them down again while she went back to get a trolley. Instead of going straight to the till she decided to sit down and have a coffee.

The coffee shop had changed since she was last there. It had been revamped and was now very modern. It still sold lattes and cappuccinos, tea and scones but it also sported a blackboard with 'Specials' like beetroot risotto with goats cheese and Brie and bacon quiche with pomegranate salad. Liz wasn't hungry. She ordered a skinny latte and sat down in a seat where she could sit and watch the world go by.

She thought about grief as she waited for the coffee to arrive. It not only robbed you or your loved ones, it robbed you of your confidence, your very self. She thought about Tammy and Monica. Just over eighteen months ago Monica had a sister and Tammy had a mother and now they were struggling to come to terms with their loss and coping a lot better than she had done.

She was completely lost in thought and hadn't noticed a man sitting nearby who was studying her closely.

'Liz,' he said presently. She didn't hear him the first time so he repeated it, louder this time. She turned to see a familiar face although the name escaped her.

'I'm sorry. I was miles away. I recognise your face but I'm afraid I can't place where from, and worse, I can't remember your name.'

'St Joseph's Secondary Modern,' came the reply. 'You taught history,' he continued, 'I taught design and tech but only stood in for a couple of terms.'

'Nick,' she said, 'yes, I do remember. We have both changed a bit I think.'

'You still look great,' said Nick kindly, 'and I still have my hair and all my own teeth.'

'A pony tail,' said Liz, 'you used to have a pony tail.'

'I am embarrassed to say that I did,' said Nick, now sporting a short back and sides with greying hair at the temples. 'Are you still teaching?' he asked.

'No, no,' said Liz, 'I left a few years ago. You?'

'I taught at another school for a while but soon got fed up with school politics and paperwork and decided to start my own business.'

'That's great,' said Liz.

'Well, it would have been had it worked,' said Nick, 'but it folded a few years ago and now I scratch a living as a painter. The pay is lousy but I work when I please and my office is fantastic. When I say my office I mean my spare room.'

Liz smiled. It was nice to have someone to talk to and a bit of light-hearted conversation was just what the doctor ordered. They chatted for a while longer, remembering old colleagues, until she finished her coffee.

'Well, I'd better be going,' she said presently. 'It was nice to see you. Good luck with your new venture.'

'Nice to see you too,' said Nick. He stood up to shake her hand as she left the table. 'Maybe we'll bump into each other again sometime.'

She grabbed the handle of the trolley and headed towards the tills and the exit. On her way she passed a large stand displaying garden tools and accessories. She scoured the shelves and was pleased to find a fork and trowel set with small flowers on the handles. 'Ideal for a little girl,' she thought to herself as she put them in her trolley. Finally she spotted the gardening gloves and picked up the smallest pair she could find and headed to the exit.

She toyed with the idea of going home first but decided instead to go straight to the cemetery. It was a beautiful sunny day and as she drove into the entrance she noticed more cars there than usual, which meant that a funeral was taking place. She thought back to the day of Jim's funeral. It was a bright sunny day, much like today.

Adam and Georgina brought the children who were quite young to be at a funeral but Georgina kept the children with her while Adam supported Liz, holding her arm as they entered the crematorium. Her legs had almost buckled under her as the mourners came in with the coffin and laid it on the stand at the front of the chapel, Jim's smiling face beaming out from a picture at the front.

The rest of the service was a complete blur. She had written something to read out but was unable to speak so the vicar had read it for her. Adam stood up and gave a very eloquent eulogy, accustomed as he definitely was to public speaking. Neither she nor Jim were religious and had discussed death but like most people they thought the day was a long way off and there was plenty of time.

Liz always said she would like a cardboard coffin and to be buried in the garden, after donating anything useful to medical science. She didn't feel sentimental about her earthly remains. They had asked her at the hospital if Jim was an organ donor but she couldn't get her mind round it at the time and had therefore not given her consent for the hospital to remove anything from his body. She regretted this now as it would have been something Jim had wanted.

How she got through the funeral and the months after were still a mystery. She was in automatic mode, walking through each day of the week like a zombie. Adam came to stay for a couple of weeks and Jim's sister, Doris, popped in from time to time. She lost weight, she lost weeks, she lost herself. Eventually Doris persuaded her to go to see the doctor who prescribed Prozac.

She remembered looking at the packet and considering

taking the whole lot in one go but the thought of Jim and Adam stopped her. As much as her heart ached Jim would not have approved so she flushed them down the toilet. Looking back she thought that she may have coped better if she had moved and not had to look at the garden at all.

Today she definitely felt stronger. She was now considering changing the garden and banishing the memories of that terrible day.

She parked her car and took the flowers from the boot before heading towards Jim's plot. She always took wipes in the car with her so she could clean the plaque. Luckily she had Tammy's new tools in the car so she would be able to plant them properly instead of placing them either side of the plaque as she had originally intended.

When she was happy with her handiwork she sat on the bench to talk to Jim. She told him how sorry she was that the garden had been so neglected, particularly the lawn. She mentioned the amazing flowers Adam had sent for Mothers' Day. She kept her real thoughts to herself on this matter. She didn't want Jim to think badly of their son. When she ran out of new things to say she told him she loved him and that she was going off to buy Easter eggs and something nice for Monica.

Chapter 6

On the way back from the cemetery she popped into the supermarket. All the supermarkets stocked up on Easter eggs immediately after Valentine's Day, and the shelves had been piled high. Unfortunately, with the Easter weekend fast approaching they were much less crowded now with obvious gaps where the most popular brands had been. Luckily they still had a few of the larger chocolate bunnies left.

She picked up three and thought she would post them to her grandchildren. She had not sent them Easter eggs for quite a while. She did buy them once when they were little and living locally but Georgina had informed her that she did not want them having too much chocolate and requested money instead. For the last few years she had done just that, no eggs, just money.

Sending money was easier but it had always jarred, especially when Leo had called to thank her for the money but let slip that he had an enormous egg from Grandma Betty and Grandpa Joe. This year she would send Easter eggs instead of money.

She left the supermarket and went straight to Boots,

spending what seemed like ages wandering around the aisles trying to find something suitable for Monica. Eventually she settled on a small basket of pampering products, a facemask, relaxing bubble bath, body wash and skin lotion. Poor Monica was always so stressed. She rushed home so that she would have time to wrap up the eggs for Sasha and Leo and pop to the post office before Tammy got home from school.

She also had to wash and repack the gardening fork and trowel and hide them along with the gloves and the chocolate egg. It was almost two thirty and she was starting to worry. Tammy's school broke up early for the Easter break and she was only ten minutes away so should have been home. Liz went to the front door to look up and down the street and was heartened to see that Tammy was having an animated conversation with a couple of girls in front of the house. They were all laughing.

Liz shut the door quietly and went into the office so she could keep watch until Tammy came down the path.

'Friends from school?' Liz enquired.

'Yes, Molly and Lauren are in my class. It's Molly's birthday in a few weeks' time and she is having a party.'

'That's great,' said Liz. 'Are you going?'

'If Monica lets me,' she added.

'Monica wouldn't want you to miss it. I think you know that too.' Tammy looked down. 'Where is the party?' said Liz.

'At the bowling alley on a Saturday afternoon,' replied

Tammy.

'Sounds like fun. I'm sure Monica will be happy for you to go and if she is busy I can drop you off and bring you back.'

'Thanks,' said Tammy, as she slipped off her backpack and put her coat on the hall stand. 'I've been working on my list,' she added as she came into the kitchen where Liz was inserting bread into the toaster.

'Toasted cheese sandwich OK?' she said as Tammy came in.

'Mmmm. I did some more research on bee friendly plants and I have some plant names. I thought we could look in Jim's book. He has a list of all the plants in your garden and you might already have some of the ones we need.'

'Good idea,' said Liz, as the toast popped up. 'We might have trouble finding them though. It's so overgrown.'

'Well, they can't walk,' said Tammy. 'Dead or alive they should still be where Jim put them.'

'True,' said Liz, 'and if they are dead we can always replace them. The garden centre is just up the road. Perhaps the three of us can go there next weekend?' Liz picked up the book confidently, no longer scared that it would spin her back into a well of sorrow. In fact she was actually looking forward to it.

Tammy ate her sandwich and Liz poured herself a coffee. Tammy rummaged in her backpack and retrieved a lined pad where she had scribbled a number of plant names.

'Wow, you have been a busy girl,' said Liz, scanning the

list.

They opened the book at the beginning. On the inside front cover there was a pouch containing a couple of photographs of the garden. Tammy took them out and laid them on the table.

'It was so beautiful,' she said.

'Yes, it was,' Liz replied, 'and it will be again.'

On the next page there was an A3 piece of paper, folded back on itself and sellotaped to the book. When unfolded it revealed a perfectly preserved scale drawing of the garden set into a numbered and lettered grid. On the next few pages Jim had listed every plant in the garden with the grid reference, its Latin and common name, the date it was planted, the date it would flower or fruit, even adding individual tips like prune in March or plant in dappled shade.

Later pages in the book were sectioned into months with each individual month devoted to what happens in the garden and when, plus the hints and tips Jim had picked up over forty years of gardening.

After the garden calendar section Jim had included a few pages on his beloved lawn. He had written down recommendations for certain products and what to do when. Liz scanned down the list of tools and was surprised to see there was no spirit level listed.

'We might not find all the plants in the garden yet,' said Liz. 'They flower at different times but we'll cross that bridge when we come to it.' They decided that if the plant was in the garden they would put a tick next to it on Tammy's list and the date that it flowered. Tammy read from the list and Liz scanned the book.

'Crocus,' said Tammy.

'It's here,' said Liz. 'It flowers March to April. Not sure if we'd still see that in the garden.'

'How about daffodils?' Tammy continued.

'They're here too,' Liz replied, 'but again, they're probably fading now.'

'Cowslip,' said Tammy.

'No, not here.' Tammy put a cross against cowslip.

'Honeysuckle.' Tammy had to sound this one out.

'Yes,' said Liz, 'L1 and M1, May to June.'

Tammy ticked and added the grid reference.

'Lilac.' called Tammy.

'Yes,' said Liz. 'J10.'

'Shall we swap?' said Tammy after a while, tired of writing and finding some of the plant names a bit difficult to read. 'You call out the name and I will look it up in the book.'

'Hawthorn,' said Liz, adding the spelling, 'H A W T H O R N.' Tammy ran her finger down the list of plants.

'That's funny,' she said. 'It's here, R9, flowers May to June, and it's Latin name is Doris.'

'Are you sure?' said Liz.

'D O R I S,' repeated Tammy. Liz leant over Tammy's shoulder to look at the book. Tammy was right. Jim had scribbled Doris next to the plant name and then it suddenly occurred to her why and she laughed out loud. Tammy, gave her a quizzical look.

'Why is that funny?' she said.

'It's Jim having a laugh,' Liz replied. 'Doris is Jim's older sister and they didn't really get on. Whenever she came to visit she would spend the first half an hour criticising him, the house or the garden. Hawthorns are prickly.'

'Oh,' said Tammy. 'Did he have a name for you?'

'I don't think so,' said Liz. 'I'll have a good look later.'

They continued to compare the list of plants that Tammy had made with Jim's garden history and by the time they finished they had discovered that there should also be Broom, Pieris, Ribes, Rosemary, Lavender, Wisteria, Thyme, Sage, Dog Rose, Chives, Lillies, Fuschia's, Buddleia, Hebe, Mahonia, Hellebore and loads of Columbine.

'It was, and hopefully is, still full of bee friendly plants.'

Tammy made careful notes of the grid references for the plants on the list and between them they decided that, all being well, on Monday morning, providing it wasn't pouring down, they would begin to tackle the garden.

'Have you anything planned for the weekend?' Liz asked Tammy when they had finished.

'Monica is taking me swimming tomorrow,' replied Tammy, 'and then we are going shopping. Monica said that we could decorate my bedroom, maybe even buy a sofa bed so I can have friends to stay over.'

'Wow, that's fantastic. So you will be busy over the next few weeks. How are you two getting on now?' Liz asked cautiously. She had not heard the back door slamming lately.

'She's alright,' replied Tammy grudgingly. 'She is trying to learn to cook. She made shepherd's pie yesterday and it was edible, except that the mash was a bit lumpy, and this weekend she is going to attempt spaghetti Bolognese.

Would you like to come to dinner?' she added hopefully.

'I'd love to,' said Liz, 'but I think you should check with Monica first. She might have other plans.'

*****

Adam was in the middle of a staff appraisal when his secretary buzzed that his wife was on the phone. He took the call knowing that their holiday was in jeopardy and hoping she had managed to sort something out.

'It's not good news, Adam,' she began. 'I've managed to get Leo sorted. He can stay with his friend Alex from school. Alex's parents have a holiday home in Devon and they are happy to take Leo with them for the Easter break. I have tried to get someone to look after Sasha but most of her friends are going abroad. So unless your mother can come and look after her we will have to cancel and I was so looking forward to it.' She sounded upset.

'Don't worry, darling,' Adam soothed. 'I will finish work a bit earlier and pop in to see Mum today. I am sure that it was just a misunderstanding and she will be able to come and stay. We don't go until Tuesday evening so there's still time,' and with that he put down the receiver.'

*****

When Monica arrived home from work she was shattered. She was really looking forward to the Easter weekend to re-charge her batteries. Work was so demanding. She could have done with taking some home but she tried not to work when Tammy was around, often finishing reports early in the mornings or when Tammy had gone to bed. She had stopped at the supermarket on the way home to buy everything she needed and dropped the shopping off at the flat before going next door.

Tammy opened the door to her and Liz shouted the offer of tea or coffee from the kitchen. Monica usually declined. She was always so tired after work she couldn't wait to get home and take off her high heels and put on some comfy clothes and flip flops but today she accepted. She hardly had time to sit down before Tammy asked if Liz could come to dinner on Sunday.

'That would be lovely,' said Monica, and warned Liz about her cooking. 'It's still early days. I am attempting spaghetti Bolognese but you might have to bring a sandwich just in case.'

'Don't forget the pie,' said Tammy. 'You said I could make a pie.'

'I haven't forgotten the pie,' replied Monica smiling smugly. 'I bought all the ingredients on the way home from work but I haven't got a pie dish. We'll have to get one tomorrow.'

'Don't worry about a dish,' interrupted Liz. 'I've got several. You can take one home with you. Keep it, I don't cook as often as I used to.' She got one out of the cupboard. 'Will this be big enough?'

'Perfect,' said Tammy.

They all sat in the kitchen chatting. Tammy showed Monica the list of plants and the grid. Monica looked out of the window at the lawn, or rather what used to be a lawn, the grass being completely squeezed out by taller, beige coloured stems of something or other that none of them knew the name of.

'I'm thinking of redesigning the garden,' Liz said eventually. 'I might replace the lawn with something else, maybe a pond with shingle or paving. I'll keep the flower beds but I'm not good with grass. I hear you're thinking of decorating,' she said quickly, not wishing to dwell on the grass for too long.

'Yes,' said Monica. 'All the rooms could do with a lick of paint, especially Tammy's. It's not at all girly at the moment is it?' Tammy nodded agreement. 'And there is nowhere for friends to stay over. So we thought we would decorate it. Although it's only a two bedroom flat the bedrooms are a decent size so there is room for a bed and a sofabed or bed settee. We also need some new wardrobes and a dressing table. The wardrobes are fitted in my room and they'll do for now but Tammy has nowhere to put anything in her room. I thought we'd brave Ikea for some inspiration.'

'Any thoughts on colours yet?' Liz asked Tammy.

'Not sure. I'm going to look around before I decide,' she replied.

'And who's doing the painting?' Liz added.

'Well, I don't get much time,' said Monica, 'so I'm not

doing it myself. I'd still be painting at Christmas. There is money in the budget to pay someone to do the walls and the ceiling. I'll find someone when we have decided on colours, maybe even paint the kitchen and living room too, brighten the place up.'

'It always feels good when a room has been decorated,' agreed Liz. 'I might think about decorating when I've finished the garden.'

Monica and Tammy were just getting ready to leave when the doorbell rang.

'I wonder who that can be?' said Liz. 'I'm not expecting anyone.' She opened the street door. 'Oh, it's Adam,' she said out loud, a hint of pride in her voice as she said it.

'Hi, Mum,' he said, smiling as she let him in. He was surprised to see she had visitors.

'Oh, Adam, this is Monica and Tammy, my neighbours. They live next door in Eve's old house.'

'Nice to meet you.' He smiled as he shook Monica's hand and said hello to Tammy.

'Well, we'll be off,' said Monica. 'See you on Sunday.'

'Don't forget the pie dish,' Liz called to Tammy, who ran back and collected it before running off after Monica.

'Well, Adam, it's lovely to see you. How are you?'

'I'm fine Mum. You?'

'Really well. Can I get you anything?' she added, before walking back into the kitchen.

'Tea would be good.' He followed her in and sat down at the table. He watched her as she filled the kettle.

'Something's different,' he said presently.

'I've had a haircut,' said Liz, subconsciously touching her hair.

'It looks great,' he added.

'Thank you, love. It was long overdue.' She made the tea and put a few biscuits on a plate on the table before sitting down.

'I'm sorry to come unannounced,' he said.

'It's always lovely to see you, Adam, you don't need an appointment.'

Liz knew he was about to ask her to look after the children. He had not popped in unannounced since he moved to Bury, even though he worked in Canary Wharf.

'I have just posted Easter eggs for the children,' said Liz. 'If I'd known you were coming you could have taken them with you.'

'Thanks mum,' he said, 'but I needed to see you because Georgina and I are in a bit of a bind. We planned a holiday over Easter and we were counting on Georgina's parents to look after the children, but they are now going on a cruise for their anniversary. We go on Tuesday. Leo is staying with friends but we have no one to look after Sasha.

Maybe I misunderstood but when I asked if you could stay you said you had plans. I wondered if it's something you could change.'

'There was no misunderstanding, dear.' Liz looked at him and tried not to look too pleased about it. 'I do have plans. I am not able to stay in Bury over the Easter holiday.'

'Well, what are you doing that is so important you can't cancel for your granddaughter?' He asked impatiently.

'Not that it's any of your business, Adam,' Liz kept her voice calm, 'but I have promised that I would look after Tammy over the holiday.'

'Who's Tammy?' said Adam incredulously.

'The little girl next door, the one you've just met,' she reminded him.

'I haven't heard you mention them before.'

'No,' said Liz. 'I've only known them since January when they moved in. We have become very good friends and Tammy and I are going to do some gardening.'

'Gardening?' said Adam. 'You hate the garden. You haven't touched it in years.'

'Exactly,' said Liz, 'it's long overdue.'

'You would choose to look after a stranger rather than your own grandchild?' he said, exasperated.

'I love Sasha, Adam, but I don't know her and she doesn't really know me. I've seen more of Tammy in the last two months than I have of you or my grandchildren in nearly seven years and although I would hate you to miss your holiday,' she said unconvincingly, 'I can't come to Bury.'

'Can't or won't?' said Adam bitterly.

'both,' said Liz defiantly.

She wanted to vent. She wanted to tell Adam what a selfish, thoughtless disappointment he was but she felt sorry for him.

'What can I do?' he said, pushing his fingers through

his thinning hair. 'What will I tell Georgina? She will be devastated.'

Liz thought of Georgina being devastated and what a ridiculous use of the word. Losing someone you love is devastating, missing a holiday is unfortunate.

Liz thought for a second. 'You can tell her that I would be happy to look after Sasha.'

'You will?' asked Adam hopefully.

'Yes,' said Liz, 'but not at your house. She can come to stay here with me while you're away. She can help me and Tammy sort out the garden.'

'I'm not sure Georgina will be happy with that. Sasha will miss her friends and her horse. I don't know what to say.'

'Thank you would be a start,' said Liz. 'You can drop her here on Tuesday on your way to the airport. It will be fun.'

Adam was not convinced. Georgina disliked Enfield, probably because it was too close to Edmonton where she had spent her teenage years before her parents moved out to Bury St Edmunds. She now considered most of Enfield as too rough for their delicate offspring who were used to private schools with well-spoken children who owned horses and played tennis. Not on neglected, litter strewn, public courts in run down parks but in local clubs and more often on courts in the grounds of houses owned by their friends. He resigned himself to the fact that he would probably have to cancel the holiday.

Chapter 7

When he finally got home around nine thirty Georgina was in the conservatory reading a book and drinking a glass of Amarone.

'Hi, Darling,' she said, getting up and putting the book down on the seat.

She poured him a glass of the deep purple wine and walked over to the door as he put his briefcase and jacket on a chair. He took the glass and sniffed it, breathing in the alcohol before taking a sip.

'Mmmmm, just what I needed,' he said.

'Would you like something to eat?' she walked towards the kitchen.

'Not now,' he called after her, 'this will do fine,' and he sat down on the sofa.

'Well, how did it go? Are we going on holiday?' asked Georgina, as she sat next to him.

'Good news and bad news, I'm afraid,' said Adam. 'Mum has agreed to look after Sasha.'

'Great,' said Georgina. 'What's the bad news?'

'Sasha will have to stay at her house. She will not stay here.'

'But what about her friends and her clubs, and Ebony? Who will ride Ebony?' Georgina whined.

'The horse is not really a problem is it.' Adam was irritated. 'You know that the stable can get one of the stable girls to ride her. She will be fine'

'Why didn't she want to come here?' she asked eventually. 'What are the 'plans' she spoke of.'

'She is looking after the girl next door,' Adam continued. 'She and Tammy, that's the girl's name, are going to sort out the garden.

'That's ridiculous,' said Georgina, 'you know how she feels about the garden.'

'How she felt about the garden,' repeated Adam. 'She seems different. She's had her hair done. She looked really well.'

'What do you really think is going on Adam? Do you think she has met someone?'

'Mum? Don't be ridiculous, sweetheart. She is nearly sixty and besides she doesn't go anywhere. Where would she meet someone?'

'Well, it just seems strange. We don't know anything about this child next door or even if she really exists.'

'She definitely exists,' replied Adam. 'I met her and her aunt at Mum's today.'

'What is she like?' asked Georgina, wondering if she would be a suitable companion for Sasha.

'I don't know,' Adam laughed. 'About Sasha's age, brown eyes, curly hair. I didn't really take that much notice. I only had time to say hello after all. They were leaving as I arrived. You'll meet her yourself soon. Look, hun, if you want to go on holiday, you're going to have to trust Mum. I'm sure she will take very good care of Sasha but if you really feel that she may be in mortal danger we had better cancel.'

'I don't know, Adam,' said Georgina. 'Sasha is very sensitive and easily influenced. I don't think staying there is a good idea.'

'I'm not sure we are talking about the same child, Georgie. I love our daughter with all my heart but I am under no illusion. She is bossy, manipulative and very, very spoilt,' Adam replied, 'and on reflection I think it would do her the world of good to spend some time with Mum doing manual labour.'

He took another sip of his wine and laid his head against the back of the sofa. 'Anyway, if we don't go we will lose all the money which is eleven thousand pounds in case you have forgotten. The insurance only covers cancellation by the travel agent, injury or death of the insured or close relative and perhaps volcanic ash. Us not having someone to look after Sasha doesn't qualify for a refund. Anyway, I'm tired. I'm going to bed. Let me know what you decide and I'll give mum a call in the morning.'

Georgina was well versed in the art of getting her own way with Adam but she had no influence on Liz. She knew that it was pointless piling on the pressure. Besides, she had been looking forward to the holiday. She had spent a small fortune on resort wear and underwear to be seen in.

'It's only for ten days,' she reasoned. 'Sasha has a mobile, I could ring up every day and check on her. It will be fine.' She drained her glass and followed Adam up to bed.

*****

Monica woke up early on Saturday morning with the sun streaming in through the curtains. She needed blinds. It was impossible to go back to sleep with the room so bright. She stretched out as far as her limbs would stretch and then relaxed back onto the pillow. She thought about the Easter holiday and her promise to Joanna. She must make some time to take Tammy out. She leant over the side of the bed and pulled out a shoebox. She had to adjust her position and kneel on the mattress so that she could pull the box onto the bed without falling over.

Once in place she sat cross legged with her back against the pillow and the box in front of her. She lifted the lid and looked at the photographs. There were a couple of albums and several loose photographs scattered on the top. She picked up the loose photographs and spread them over the duvet. Just as she did so she heard Tammy call out.

'Come in,' she shouted. A very sleepy looking Tammy walked zombie like through the door.

'What are you doing?' she asked.

'I'm just reliving some memories,' said Monica. 'Do you want to look with me?'

Tammy walked over to the bed and saw the photographs. She just stood there for a second before climbing onto the bed next to Monica, upsetting a lot of the photographs and turning them back to front. Monica had picked one up.

'Wow, you were such a beautiful baby,' she said to Tammy, 'and so good, unless I held you of course, then you would scream the house down.'

Tammy laughed and picked up another photograph. It was a picture of the three of them, Joanna, Monica and Tammy who was about four or five at the time. They were at the zoo and Tammy was playing tug-o-war with a goat who wanted her crisps.

'Do you remember that?'

'Mum was beautiful wasn't she?' Tammy was running her finger over her mother's face.

'Yes, she was,' said Monica, 'and you are so like her. She would be so proud of you.'

Tears welled up in Tammy's eyes which made Monica cry too. Monica handed her a tissue and took one out of the box for herself. She put her arm around Tammy who let Monica hug her while they both cried.

'Well, look at us, what a fine pair we make,' Monica said eventually. 'Shall I put these away?'

'No,' said Tammy, 'I want to see them. Sometimes I try to picture her in my mind when she was well but all I see is her in hospital.'

'Oh, honey,' said Monica. 'If it helps we can pick out some photographs and put them in a frame to remind us of the happy times.'

They both pawed through the loose photographs and the albums. There was a gorgeous smiling picture of Joanna in a coral coloured dress with a matching hat at Tammy's christening. Monica was holding Tammy who appeared to be crying hysterically.

'You see, this is the baby I remember,' said Monica holding up the photograph.

'I love it,' said Tammy. 'Let's keep that one.' For the next hour and a half they laughed and cried as they sorted through the rest of the photographs, remembering conversations, occasions and places where the pictures had been taken. Tammy couldn't help but notice that Monica had been a lot slimmer when she was younger. It didn't go unnoticed by Monica either. The proof was right in front of her.

'Oh, I didn't realise I'd got so fat,' said Monica.

'Well, it can't have been on home cooking,' said Tammy laughing.

'Cheeky,' said Monica. 'I'm getting better.'

'That's because you couldn't get worse,' joked Tammy.

'OK young lady, out,' said Monica. 'That's it. Let's get up now and have some breakfast. We have swimming and some serious shopping to do and I hate that bloody Ikea at the weekends. It's always too crowded.' Tammy ran off back to her own room to get dressed as Monica put the chosen photographs to one side and put the box back under the bed.

*****

Liz had been up for a few hours. She was never one for lying in bed. As soon as she was awake she was up.

Jim, on the other hand, loved a lie in. He had a weekend ritual whereby the papers would be delivered early and she would take them upstairs to him with a cup of tea. He would read them in bed and then drop off to sleep for another hour before coming down to breakfast.

This suited her as she loved the quiet stillness of early morning. Whenever she had work to prepare or mark for her students this was the time of day when her brain seemed to be at its sharpest and she could work without interruption.

She poured herself another cup of tea before moving into the office. She had planned to go shopping and then start researching what to do first. Everything in the garden needed attention and there would probably be a bit of clearing and chopping down before she could get started. She'd have to get into the shed to get the tools and that would require clearing a path in the overgrown grass and cutting back the ivy so she could open the door properly.

She also thought about giving Eve a call. It had been a while since they had spoken and she wondered how she was doing. She envied the fact that Eve had three daughters. She would have loved a daughter. There was an old saying that Eve often quoted. 'A son is a son till he takes a wife, but a daughter's a daughter all her life.' Adam was certainly proof of those words. Most of her friends with daughters saw them often and even if not were still very involved in their lives. Adam couldn't be more distant.

The phone ringing interrupted her thoughts. It was only

eight thirty so she guessed it would be Adam. He knew she was an early riser.

'Hello, Mum,' he said, as she picked up the receiver.

'Hi, Adam, have you talked to Georgina?' she asked, getting straight to the point.

'Mum, Georgina and I,' (he lied) 'would be very grateful if you would look after Sasha over the Easter holiday. We will drop her off on Tuesday morning around eleven o'clock. We don't need to be at the airport until three so we could have a cup of tea with you, if that's OK.'

'Great,' said Liz. 'I'll see you then.'

She put on her coat and went to the garage to get the car before heading to the supermarket. With Tammy and Sasha to feed she would have to stock up. She wondered what sort of girl Sasha was and how she would get on with Tammy.

She hoped she would be kind and thought about telling Adam about Tammy's mum so he could talk to Sasha before she arrived, or whether she should have agreed to look after Sasha at all.

It was too late now anyway. She would tell Tammy on Sunday that Sasha would also be staying and hope that they clicked. Despite the fact that they came from entirely different worlds they were a similar age and probably interested in lots of the same things. She doubted that Sasha had ever had to worry about anything in her life, which made her admire Tammy even more just for getting through the day and keeping her amazing sense of humour.

*****

Monica and Tammy wandered around Ikea looking at the bedroom furniture. They soon found something they both liked. Although Monica had told Tammy that she could have whatever she wanted, and she meant it, she hoped that it would be something practical. Luckily the flooring in the flat had been done before they moved in so she didn't have to worry about carpets.

Monica hated flat pack furniture. It was a hang up from her student days. She remembered how long it had taken to assemble a chest of drawers. She was really happy to discover that for an extra fee the store delivered and assembled the furniture in situ. That settled, Tammy picked her furniture, plus a sofa bed and blind to match. Unlike most girls of her age she hated pink. Her only concession to girly at all was a pastel coloured laundry bin and storage boxes to match.

Monica was really happy that they found everything so quickly, especially as her feet were killing her and she was puffed out from walking along the arrowed lanes directing you to the tills and the exit. She would have loved to have found a shortcut. Instead she felt as though she had walked around the entire store. She needed a rest.

Tammy was worried about Monica's lack of energy.

'You're not sick are you?' she asked with concern in her voice.

'No, I'm not sick at all,' said Monica. 'I'm just too fat. I promise that I will do something about it. I need to go on a proper diet and I need to get some exercise. Perhaps we could start going for walks in the evenings, what do you think?'

'Definitely. I'll be your personal trainer,' said Tammy.

'Okay. Happy now?' said Monica. Tammy nodded that she was and they left the store hand in hand and headed home. Tammy picked up a catalogue as they went through the exit, keen to show her new bedroom furniture to Liz on Sunday.

*****

Georgina tried to speak to Sasha about staying with Liz but Sasha was far from pleased at the prospect of not seeing her friends or riding her horse.

'Why can't I stay here?' she whined.

'Because nana and grandpa are going on holiday too so there is no one to look after you.'

'Then I'll come with you,' she sulked.

'Not an option, poppet,' soothed Georgina. 'Daddy and I have already got the tickets and we can't change them now.'

'Then stay here, don't leave meeee!' She stamped her feet.

'You will have a lovely time with Grandma Liz whether you like it or not and that's the end of it,' said Georgina firmly.

She had no intention of continuing to argue with a ten year old drama queen, especially when she had been such an expert herself from an early age. She knew all the moves. Besides, she had a lot of packing to do. Not only did she need to pack for herself and Adam but now Sasha would need several changes of clothes to stay with Liz. There was still the manicure and pedicure to organise and the bikini wax to take care of. It was hard work looking fabulous.

*****

Adam had a grudging respect for his mother for standing her ground. She had, in the past, always appeared weak and submissive and he hated himself for saying it but she got on his nerves.

It wasn't nearly so bad when Dad was alive because he was fun and they laughed together. Not that he saw his parents much then either but at least they had each other so he had no need to feel guilty.

Dad dying had completely ruined that and he now felt so guilty that it was hard to talk to his mother at all. It didn't seem to occur to him that by actually doing something for her and making an effort now and again he could have eased his guilt no end.

*****

Monica and Tammy picked up a DVD on the way home. Monica would usually have ordered a pizza and a two litre bottle of Coke but instead she made a healthy tuna salad and a low calorie drink. While eating it she pictured the local takeaway owners wearing black and wringing their hands as they mourned the demise of their businesses. Tammy was content with a salad too. She wanted to encourage Monica, although she did eat half a packet of biscuits with her hot chocolate before she went to bed.

*****

Meanwhile Liz was studying the internet, looking for hints and tips on what to do first. Instinctively she felt that the wilderness that was the grass should be cut down so they could see what they were doing. She would have to do this job herself as she didn't want either of the girls handling sharp tools. They could rake the cuttings and keep the compost heap well stocked. It wasn't a huge lawn so it shouldn't take that long.

She wondered what she might find under there. It was so wild now. She could see nettles and dandelions and docks had staked a claim. Those were the ones she knew the names of anyway. She doubted that there would be any grass left to save. In a way she didn't mind. She was thinking about replacing the grass, maybe adding paths next to the borders and putting decorative stones or shingle in the middle. She had often thought about putting in a pond before Jim died.

Sunday morning was not as bright as Saturday had been. Grey clouds hung menacingly in the sky threatening heavy rain, maybe even thunder and lightning. Liz was glad that she would be going out. She hated being in by herself in a thunderstorm.

She decided to head up to the garden centre to get Monica some flowers and more tools so that Sasha would have some of her own too.

The garden centre had only just opened when she arrived, which was fantastic as there were no queues and she could breeze in and out, but once inside she decided to look at the gardening books to see if there was anything that could help with the task ahead. She flicked through a couple of books on the shelves for inspiration. As she walked past the coffee shop she heard a familiar voice.

'Hello again, Liz.' She turned to see Nick sitting at the same table he had sat at before, a folded newspaper in his lap.

'Morning,' she said smiling. 'You're up early. You must be a very keen gardener,' she added.

'No, not at all,' was the reply. 'I'm a very keen coffee drinker. I moved into a flat up the road last year and this is the nearest place to get coffee in the mornings. It's usually nice and quiet at this time. How about you? You're here early too.'

'I'm not one for lying in bed,' she said self-consciously.

'Will you join me for coffee?' he asked.

'Why not,' said Liz. 'I'm not in a hurry.'

She ordered a cappuccino and sat down at the table. Nick was easy to talk to. She found out that he had two ex-wives. The first marriage had been to his college sweetheart Susan. They had married at eighteen and had two children, Heather and David. 'We were married for twenty years. It would have been a lot less but for the kids.'

'Are you still in touch?' asked Liz.

'I see them all often. We have a standing arrangement to meet for dinner at least once a month. Susan plays host to me, our children and grandchildren.'

'That's great,' said Liz. 'Did she remarry?'

'Ah, yes,' said Nick. 'Susan is very happily married to

my brother.' Liz was surprised and it must have shown on her face. 'It's not a bad thing,' said Nick. 'Patrick has most of my good traits and none of the bad so she very wisely divorced me and married him,' he was smiling broadly.

'You don't sound too bitter about it,' Liz ventured.

'I'm not,' said Nick. 'Oh, I was at first but when I got over my wounded pride I realised that they are much more suited than we ever were. Patrick is brother, step-dad, granddad and uncle and I couldn't be happier. We all get on fantastically well.'

'How very modern,' said Liz, fascinated, 'and the second?'

'The second was an even bigger disaster. I guess it was me trying to cling on to my youth.'

'Ah, that reminds me of the old joke,' said Liz. Nick look puzzled. 'How does a man hold on to his youth?'

'Tell me,' said Nick.

'expensive jewellery,' Liz replied. They both laughed.

'I guess it was something like that,' he said smiling. 'I was in my early forties and she was in her late twenties.'

'Mid-life crisis?' asked Liz.

'Panic,' said Nick. 'I was never good at being on my own.'

'What happened?' Liz was curious.

'I don't think I made enough money at the time to support her in the lifestyle which she wanted to become accustomed. She moved on to bigger fish.'

'Oh, I'm sorry,' said Liz.

'Don't be,' said Nick. 'It was a big mistake. Besides, I am very happy doing what I do now. Enough about me. How about you, are you married?'

'I was married for a very long time. I have a son, Adam, who is married to Georgina and they have two children, Leo and Sasha.'

'Was married,' repeated Nick. 'Are you divorced too?

'No, no,' said Liz. 'Jim died five years ago.'

'Oh, I'm sorry,' said Nick. 'He must have been a good man.'

'He was. We laughed a lot.'

'You miss him.'

'I do,' said Liz, 'but it's getting easier all the time. I had to pull myself together eventually. I was scaring the neighbours.'

'Are you fond of gardening?' asked Nick.

'I wouldn't say I was fond of it,' Liz replied, 'but I have a project to finish. I have neglected the garden over the last few years and have recently decided to get to grips with it, restore some of it and change the rest. I hope I'm not being too ambitious. Anyway, it was either the garden or get a couple of cats and that's a slippery slope.'

Nick laughed. 'You wouldn't consider going back to teaching?'

'I don't know,' said Liz. 'I'll think about it when I've finished the garden.'

Chapter 8

Liz got home around eleven thirty having bought a mottled pink orchid in a white glazed pot for Monica. Liz loved having flowers in the house but hated cut flowers. She thought they were a terrible waste, especially as they only lasted for a few days. Whenever Adam had sent her flowers she had kept them far too long, throwing the dead flowers away and rearranging what was left until the bouquet resembled something Morticia Adams would have in her boudoir.

She thought about Nick. She had an idea that he was a bit younger than she was. The teaching staff always collected money for birthdays and she had a vague idea that there had been a collection for Nick's fortieth birthday. They had all gone to the pub after work. It stood out in her memory because it was rare that she ever went anywhere without Jim but he was working away at the time.

She remembered the general opinion of Nick formed by the other female members of the teaching staff at school. He had a nice smile and was fairly fit, in the good looking sense of the word, but he had a pony tail back then which was a real turn off. He took himself much too seriously.

*****

Monica was panicking next door. Although her cooking

was definitely improving the timings were still a bit off, which is why spaghetti Bolognese was a great choice. She could make the Bolognese sauce in advance and cook the spaghetti when Liz arrived. Tammy was busy making a pie and covering most of the kitchen in flour, which was the other thing Monica was worried about. She wanted the house to be tidy.

She had forgotten to take the minced beef out of the freezer on Saturday night and had only remembered when she got up this morning, hence the meat was still frozen solid in the centre. She would have to microwave it to thaw it enough so she could cook it. Damn.

She put it on a plate and selected defrost on the microwave. 'Thank god for microwaves,' she thought to herself. She would have hardly eaten anything hot in the last fifteen years if she hadn't been able to zap it. It was hard breaking the habit.

She turned the dial to ten minutes and while she waited for the meat to thaw she opened the red wine and chopped the vegetables before taking the smoked bacon bits out of the fridge.

She was relieved when the microwave pinged. She had loads of time. She examined the meat. It was still slightly frozen on the inside so she separated the unfrozen bits and took them out of the microwave before selecting another five minutes to tackle the stubborn centre. Disaster averted she put the meat into a frying pan and poured herself a glass of wine.

Tammy, meanwhile, had successfully made the pie and was now busy decorating the crust. The pie was so good she had to sign it in pastry letters across the centre. Neither of them had any idea how long to cook it for so decided to check on it every few minutes until the crust started to brown, or until the sweet smell permeated the room, whichever came first.

Monica sipped the wine as she added the chopped onion, green pepper and carrot to the olive oil in another pan, adding garlic, herbs and bacon bits as they softened. It was all going so well. 'I've got this cooking cracked,' she thought smugly. 'I can do this.' A burning smell interrupted her reverie as the minced beef had stuck to the bottom of the frying pan.

She hastily rescued the bits that could be salvaged, which luckily was most of the meat. She put this in another pan and set the gas to low while she scraped the charred remains from the base of the frying pan and shoved it in the sink to soak. She then turned her attention back to the vegetables which had softened and were on the cusp of burning. She managed to rescue them in time so added the contents of her wine glass and a tin of tomatoes, finally combining these with the meat and set it to simmer. So far so good. It actually looked very professional.

'Just spaghetti to conquer now and I will be queen of the kitchen.' She looked around the rest of the room. She had used almost every pan and Tammy had used any she had missed. Luckily she still had a clean saucepan left to cook the spaghetti in but between Tammy's pie and the Bolognese sauce the kitchen resembled the horror show that used to be the kitchenette in her student digs. She imagined Gordon Ramsey saying, 'I don't fucking believe it!' She poured herself another glass of wine before starting the clean-up.

There was no separate dining room in Monica's ground floor flat. When Eve had sold the house it was bought by a builder who did the conversion. He extended the ground floor at the back making it big enough for a kitchen diner and small bathroom, which left two decent bedrooms and a spacious living room. She also had the larger of the gardens but it was all crazy paving and the garage took up a lot of the space.

The entire kitchen would be on show while they sat at the table.

She turned off the Bolognese sauce. It was done. It looked exactly like the picture in the recipe book. She was so impressed she called Tammy to come and admire the similarity.

'Wow,' said Tammy. 'It looks like a real cook made it.' That was as close to a compliment as Tammy could manage. 'Are we having garlic bread?' The garlic bread was also on display in the picture, set out on an oblong dish in a neat row with each perfectly round slice resting on the one behind like dominoes.

'I've got French bread,' said Monica smiling. 'That'll do. Don't push it.'

The pie crust had turned golden brown indicating that it was cooked and not burnt, which Tammy was immensely proud of as Monica took it out of the oven.

'We did it!' said Tammy.

'We did indeed,' Monica replied, as she put the pie down on the counter and gave Tammy a hug. Liz arrived an hour later with the plant under her arm. Monica was feeling a lot more relaxed after blitzing the kitchen with Tammy in tow, wiping as Monica washed. Liz gave Monica the plant as she walked into the flat.

'Oh it's lovely,' said Monica, as she looked around the flat for somewhere to put it before deciding on the windowsill in the kitchen.

Tammy had set the table and the boiling water was ready to accept the spaghetti, which Monica had broken in half rather than risk burning the ends as she waited for it to melt into the water. It was all good.

Tammy and Monica were both amused by Liz's method for testing the spaghetti was cooked. She used a fork to tease a strand out of the water and then threw it at the tiles behind the hob. It stuck, which apparently meant that it was ready to eat.

Monica drained and rinsed the spaghetti, zapped the Bolognese sauce so it was nice and hot and grated some parmesan cheese.

They all sat at the table and there was complete silence as they concentrated hard on trying to twist the spaghetti onto a fork, using a spoon as a brace. Before long they were all laughing at their failed attempts at eating quietly with Tammy giving up completely and sucking the spaghetti until her cheeks hollowed and the spaghetti disappeared into her mouth in a flash.

'Oh no,' said Monica, as they finished their meal. 'I forgot the French bread.'

'I couldn't have eaten bread as well. It was so filling. I've just about got room for Tammy's pie.' Tammy was beaming with pride as she sashayed over to retrieve her masterpiece.

'Every artist should sign their work,' said Liz, observing the word Tammy in pastry on the pie crust.

Monica sliced the pie and gave a large piece to Liz and Tammy and a very small piece to herself.

'I'm on a diet,' she said to Liz. 'And I mean a real diet this time, not the pizza and chips diet I used to be on. I'll eat some more tomorrow.'

'She is too tubby,' chimed in Tammy, rather than use the 'F' word.

'I know,' said Monica. 'I don't think I'd have a weight problem if I were taller. I'm just too short.'

'Oh, I almost forget,' said Liz, as she pulled out three parcels from her bag. 'This is for you.' She gave one to Monica. 'And these are for you,' she said to Tammy. 'Happy Easter.' Monica was shocked.

'Liz, this is too generous, you already do so much for us.'

'Don't be silly,' Liz replied. 'It's lovely having you here and you have done more for me than you know.'

Monica opened her present and looked at the labels on

each of the bottles.

'I thought they might help you relax a bit,' said Liz.

'I'm learning. Thank you so much,' Monica replied. Then it was Tammy's turn. She opened the first box. Inside was a very large chocolate rabbit.

'Don't eat it all at once,' said Liz. 'You'll get stomach ache.'

'Thank you,' said Tammy. 'I won't, and I won't let you have any,' she addressed Monica who feigned a hurt expression. 'I'm helping you,' said Tammy by way of explanation for being mean. Then she opened the second box containing the gardening tools and gloves. Her face lit up.

'I've got my own tools,' she said to Monica, 'and gloves.'

'Yes, you'll definitely need the gloves in my garden,' said Liz. 'We start clearing tomorrow. Oh, and I've got some good news, at least I hope it's good news,' Liz added. 'My granddaughter, Sasha, is also coming to stay this week. She is around your age. I am sure you'll get on well and we can all work in the garden together.'

'Great,' said Tammy. 'I can't wait.'

'I hope you don't mind,' she said to Monica, 'but Adam and Georgina are going on holiday and they were stuck for a sitter so I volunteered.'

'Don't be daft,' said Monica. 'She is your granddaughter. It will be lovely for you and for Tammy.'

They sat at the table chatting for a while, sipping wine and laughing. Tammy grabbed the catalogue to show Liz her new furniture and she then insisted on showing Liz her room now so that she would see the before and after, when the furniture arrived and the room was decorated. It was a big, bright room and Liz could see the potential.

'I need to look for a decorator this week,' said Monica. I would like to get it done before the furniture arrives in a couple of weeks' time.'

Just then the phone rang and Tammy picked up the receiver. It was Molly on the phone, asking her if she could come to her house to play. Monica had met Molly's mother quite a few times at school and was happy for Tammy to play there. She left Liz for a few minutes while she walked her round the corner to her friend's house.

'What time shall I collect her?' she asked Ann, Molly's mum.

'No need to collect her. I'm dropping Lauren off at six thirty and I can drop Tammy off too.' Monica thanked her and walked back round to the flat.

By the time she got there Liz had washed up the dinner plates and cutlery and had just started on the serving bowls.

'Liz, you're a guest,' exclaimed Monica. 'Come and sit down, have a glass of wine.'

'All done,' said Liz. They took their wine and moved to the living room. They both sunk down in the well-worn sofa and breathed out a contented sigh.

'That was a fantastic meal. You've come a long way.'

'I'm getting better,' said Monica. 'I'm trying to be more organised and make a serious effort to lose some weight. Tammy is worried that I'll keel over if I don't. The trouble is I sit at a desk all day. The busier I am, the more I sit. Tammy and I have just agreed to go walking in the evenings after dinner. Why don't you come along? Not that you need to lose weight,' Monica added.

'I'd like that very much,' said Liz. 'I used to love walking. I have sort of got out of the habit.'

'Tammy is a fantastic motivator', added Monica. 'When I say motivator, I mean nagger,' she laughed, 'but I don't want her to worry about anything so I am fully focused on getting thinner and healthier.'

'Don't you ever get lonely, Monica?' Liz said, changing the mood.

'Not really. At the moment I need to concentrate on getting Tammy back to a good place where she feels safe and happy. Believe me I have kissed a lot of frogs and there are no princes out there so I don't think I'm missing anything in particular. Besides, I need to get back to my fighting weight before I will have the confidence to even think about dating again, and all of that will have to wait until I am sure that Tammy is settled. I won't do anything to cause her worry.'

'She is lucky to have you,' said Liz.

'Actually, I think I'm lucky. She is a great kid. How about you, Liz?' Monica's face was serious. 'Don't you ever get lonely? You've been living by yourself in that house for a long time now. Wouldn't you like to meet someone?'

'Me, meet someone, at my age? I think that ship has definitely sailed.'

'Don't be daft,' said Monica. 'You look amazing and you've got loads of energy. You could have another twenty five years or more left. Don't spend it on your own. If Joanna's death has taught me anything it's that you have to take every chance offered to you. You never know when it will be your last.'

'I think that's easier said than done,' said Liz smiling. 'Even if I wanted to meet someone, and I'm not saying that I do, I think my disco days are over. I would have no idea how to go about it. Besides, I doubt that Adam would approve.'

'I'm sure he would like to see you happy,' said Monica. 'It might take some adjustment on his part but he's a grown up, he'd get used to it.'

'Actually you're right,' said Liz. 'I just don't think I'd have the confidence to meet anyone. Adam is just an excuse. I am even feeling a bit apprehensive about looking after Sasha, after all she hardly knows me,' Liz confided. 'I rarely see the children since they moved. Oh, I get a fleeting visit at Christmas and flowers on my birthday and Mother's Day, from his secretary, I might add. But I doubt I've seen Sasha for more than half an hour at a time for the last few years. I think I probably made it worse after Jim died. I was so lost, I don't think Adam could cope with my grief. It was easier for him not to see me at all.'

'I think that's a terrible excuse and I'm not sure that you really believe it any more than I do,' said Monica. 'He sounds selfish and thoughtless in the extreme. Families help each other, which means being there when you're needed.'

'Was it just you and Joanna?' asked Liz. 'Or do you have any other brothers or sisters?' she added, trying to deflect attention away from Adam.

'No, just us,' said Monica. 'Our Mum died a couple of years ago. She was seventy when she died but she had been ill for a long time. She had early onset Alzheimer's and was in a home for the last five years. She didn't really know us in the end.'

'I'm sorry,' said Liz.

'Oh, don't be. That's life,' Monica continued. 'She was a great mum. She bought us up on her own. She divorced dad twenty five years ago. He was a gambler and womaniser. He eventually married again and moved to Barbados.'

'Do you ever see him?' asked Liz.

'Don't really want to,' said Monica. 'Anyway, I've lost contact over the years. He could be dead for all I know. He knew where we were if he wanted to stay in our lives. Mum had two younger sisters and a brother and we still see them, so I have lots of cousins which is great for us.'

'I have a brother,' said Liz, 'but we are not close. He emigrated to Australia thirty years ago now. He came over for Jim's funeral, which was nice of him, but I felt as though I was talking to a stranger.'

'Have you ever been there?'

'Where?' said Liz.

'Australia. Have you thought about visiting him?'

'No. I must admit, I haven't thought about it. It's so far

away and I'm not keen on flying.'

'Me neither,' said Monica, 'but I will have to arrange a holiday abroad soon. It was on Joanna's list.'

'Joanna's list?' repeated Liz.

'Yes,' said Monica. 'Joanna gave me a list of the things she had planned to do with Tammy and they had never been abroad on holiday together. I promised to take her as many places as I could. I also promised her a party for her birthday in August. Not a small party, a big family party with uncles and aunts and all of her classmates from school.'

'Where will you put them all?' said Liz.

'I have no idea,' said Monica. 'I expect I'll have to hire a hall.'

'How about my garden? It's certainly big enough and if we can sort it out it should be presentable by August.'

'Oh no,' said Monica. 'I can't expect you to do that.'

Liz put her hand on Monica's shoulder. 'I would love to have a party in the garden again,' said Liz, 'and it would be a wonderful thank you to Tammy for all her help. Please, it's no trouble, and apart from anything else it's great to have a goal to work to.'

'Are you sure, Liz?' asked Monica. 'We would make all the food and help as much as we can.'

'I'm sure,' said Liz.

Chapter 9

Monday morning saw Georgina packing a suitcase for Leo for his trip to Devon with Alex. Leo was delighted that he would be escaping his grandparents and his bossy sister to spend Easter with his best friend. He was small for his age and despite being younger was continually outmanoeuvred by Sasha. He didn't know how to play the youngest card. If Sasha was losing an argument or caught out in some misdemeanour she would lie, and if that didn't work feign tears. Grandpa Joe was particularly gullible so often told Leo off, despite the fact that he was usually the innocent party.

This morning it was his turn to be smug. He was going on holiday to Devon with his best friend and Sasha was staying with Grandma Liz in boring old Enfield, and worse would be gardening. Leo was really enjoying the fact that Sasha was stomping around the house, crying and throwing herself on the soft furnishings.

'I'll miss my horse, I'll miss my friends,' she wailed, overacting as if her life depended on it. Leo loved the fact that his mother didn't seem to be paying any attention to her at all.

Georgina usually gave in to Sasha's tantrums but not today. Her own holiday depended on the children going their respective ways and although she felt a slight tinge of guilt, especially as she regarded Grandma Liz as being slightly unstable, it wasn't enough to prevent her from sunning herself on the beach. She put the case in the car, Leo sat in the front passenger seat and a screaming Sasha was eventually frogmarched out to sit in the back seat for the short drive.

Once Leo was delivered to his friend's house it was home again to pack for Sasha and Adam. Georgina always did Adam's packing. He couldn't put matching socks on without her help, or so she thought. She was just as meticulous with Adam's clothes as she was her own, not because Adam was incapable of packing but she wanted to make sure they didn't clash when they were out together. She viewed him pretty much as an accessory and therefore his clothes had to compliment hers.

*****

Tammy was up earlier than usual. On school days Monica had to virtually prise her out of bed but in the holidays she woke at dawn and was full of beans. She got up and made herself breakfast. Monica was still half asleep as it was just gone six o'clock and as the alarm clock did not go off until six thirty she was trying to force herself back to sleep. Tammy had dressed in tee shirt and jeans tucked into her wellington boots. She had a cardigan and coat on standby in the hall along with her gardening tools and gloves. She was really keen.

Monica moaned. It was no good. No matter how hard

she tried she couldn't nod off. She'd have to get up. She threw on her dressing gown and stumbled sleepily into the kitchen to find Tammy already sitting at the table eating toast.

'This is a first,' she said, as she headed for the toaster. Tammy sprang up and told Monica to sit down, she would make the toast and Monica was very happy to oblige. Tammy put two slices of brown bread in the toaster and got the honey out of the cupboard. As soon as the toast popped up Tammy had it on a plate and on the table.

'No butter?' asked Monica.

'No,' said Tammy. 'Diet. Remember?' Monica wanted to forget but Tammy wouldn't let her.

'I need coffee,' said Monica, desperate to wake up. Tammy poured hot water over the granules in a cup and put the black coffee in front of Monica.

'Have we run out of milk?'

'No,' said Tammy.

'Oh, I get it,' said Monica, 'Starvation diet. Tammy, I am willing to give up butter, cheese, cream, pizza and every other fattening food item that I love but if you don't pass the milk I'll have to kill you. I can't drink black coffee.'

'Okay,' said Tammy, getting the milk from the fridge, 'but I'll be watching the scales.'

'We'll have to buy some first,' said Monica, smiling.

'Can I go next door to Liz now?' said Tammy.

'No, not yet,' Monica replied. 'It's not even six thirty. Liz might not be up. You can go at seven thirty when I leave for work. I'm sure that will be early enough.'

Tammy watched the clock and reminded Monica of the time every few minutes as seven thirty approached. 'I'm coming, I'm coming,' said Monica, as Tammy was being helpful by finding Monica's shoes and briefcase before Monica was actually looking for them.

It was a bright spring morning with a slight chill in the air. 'You'll need your coat,' said Monica, as they walked up the path. 'Have you got a waterproof?'

'No,' said Tammy. 'I forgot to put one in the bag. I don't think it matters, I'm sure we won't be outside if it rains.'

*****

Liz had been mentally preparing herself to tackle the garden but she was pleased that she wouldn't be attempting it on her own. She was waiting at the door as Monica and Tammy came towards her.

'Morning girls,' she said, smiling broadly as they approached.

'Morning Liz,' replied Monica. 'Are you sure it's OK to come so early?'

'Of course, I've been up since six o'clock.'

'You see,' said Tammy triumphantly. 'I could have come at six thirty.'

'Have you got time for a cuppa before work?'

'Best not,' 'I'd like to get into work early. I need to find a decorator who can start next week if possible. I thought I'd get the local paper on the way in and look at the ads. I want to make some calls to get prices before my boss arrives.'

'Okay,' said Liz. 'Maybe tomorrow?'

'Thanks again for this,' said Monica as she was leaving. I really appreciate it'

Tammy came in and put her bag and coat on a chair in the kitchen.

'You're well prepared,' said Liz, eyeing her colourful wellies.

'I've bought my tools too,' said Tammy, holding them up.

'So I see,' Liz replied. 'Sasha isn't coming until tomorrow so I thought that today you and I could clear a path to the shed so we can get out the shears and maybe the strimmer so we can tackle the lawn.' Liz put her secateurs in her jacket pocket.

She asked Tammy if she wanted anything to eat or drink before they got started. 'No thanks,' said Tammy, who was very keen to use her gardening gloves.

Liz put on her jacket and gloves and they went outside. Together they trampled a path to the shed, pushing down the weeds and grasses with their boots as they went. Some of the plants sprang back up as soon as their feet had moved on but others stayed horizontal, resembling the wake behind a speedboat.

The plants were wet and dark patches had formed on their jeans by the time they reached the shed. Liz was relieved. She didn't say anything but she couldn't help thinking about Jim lying dead on the grass. She pushed the memory from her thoughts as she took out the secateurs. The ivy was so thick in places that it had almost entirely obscured the windows. Now she was up close she could see that in other places it had found a way inside the shed itself. The door no longer fitted properly and was lopsided and the resulting gap had meant that the ivy had easy access to the inside.

She cut the stems blocking the door first. Tammy pulled the long strands as Liz cut through them and before long there was a pile of ivy mounting up next to the shed. A few more snips and there was enough room to manoeuvre the door open and let the light in. Tammy was in like a shot. Apart from the ivy it was just as Jim had left it. Liz let Tammy explore while she cut the ivy away from the windows so there would be a little more light inside. Once this was done she wedged open the door with a plant pot and walked inside.

She caught her breath. The workbench was neat and tidy apart from a clock which Jim had been repairing when he died, the box of tiny screwdrivers left open on the shelf and the insides of the clock scattered around the casing on the bench. It reminded Liz of an autopsy or an operation. She shuddered. There was nothing else out of place. The cabinets and drawers were neatly closed and the drills and sanders hung on hooks above the bench as they always had.

At the far end of the shed the lawn mower was still against the wooden slatted wall alongside the strimmer. Jim also had a hedge trimmer and various rakes and shovels hanging along the same wall. He was meticulous about his tools and always put them back in the same place. Liz looked around for an extension lead. She thought that the hedge trimmer might be useful in tackling the lawn.

As she reached to open the cupboard she spotted a small wasp nest no bigger than a tennis ball which looked as though it had been there for a few years. Parts of it had flaked onto the linoleum floor but most of the delicate structure was still in place.

She pointed it out to Tammy who was keen to have it to take into school. Once they were absolutely sure that it was no longer inhabited. Liz carefully removed it without breaking much more of it and put it into a flower pot for Tammy to take home.

Liz looked around the shed.

'What do you think?' she said to Tammy.

'It's Okay as a work shop,' said Tammy, 'but I think it would make a great summer house. You could paint it pale blue or yellow, like the ones by the seaside,' she added. 'I don't like grey.'

'Me neither,' said Liz, before proceeding to cut away all the ivy that had made its way inside the shed. Together they took all the tools they needed outside and lay them on the patio, the extension lead, the strimmer, the hedge cutter, and a couple of pairs of shears.

Tammy was getting hot already and took off her coat. Liz did the same before going back into the house to get some garden sacks to put the waste in. Before long they had one sack full of ivy. It was a satisfying feeling, being busy and making progress no matter how small. Liz plugged the extension lead into the socket in the shed before trying out the hedge trimmer. It worked at the higher level but she couldn't angle it low enough to get as near to the bottom as she would have liked. The strimmer looked more promising.

However, she was nervous of using it in case she managed to catch any wildlife that was lurking in the undergrowth with the plastic blade. Tammy had no such scruples and was happy to whizz through.

'Hang on young lady,' said Liz. 'You're a bit nearer to the ground than I am. You will have to wear goggles in case something shoots up and hits you in the eye.' She went back into the shed and returned with a pair of plastic goggles that resembled a snorkelling mask. 'These will keep you safe,' she said, as she slipped them over Tammy's head.

It took a few goes but they soon worked out the best method of hacking back the weeds. Tammy strimmed and Liz followed behind with the garden shears and secateurs to cut down any fatter stems that resisted the strimmer.

Every so often they would both stop what they were doing and pick up the cuttings and put them into sacks. Before long they had two more sacks full and the lawn was starting to look flatter. Still nothing like a lawn, more brown and straw coloured than green, but definitely flatter.

Tammy really enjoyed using the strimmer and was eager to find new areas to attack. Liz had to keep a sharp eye on her and once or twice had to restrain her from going too near the flower beds in case she decapitated something Liz wanted to keep.

It was hard work and at about ten thirty they decided

to stop for a break. Liz went off to make a cup of tea while Tammy searched the garden for signs of life. She was very keen to find a frog. Liz came out with a tray and set it down on the garden table. She hadn't bothered covering the furniture again. Instead she had set the chairs at an angle with the tops resting on the table to make sure any water would run off.

She pulled two of them back so they could sit down. Tammy sipped a Coke and nibbled on a biscuit while Liz drank her tea and they both admired their handiwork.

'Monica will be amazed,' said Tammy eventually. 'Perhaps you should take a photograph,' she said to Liz, 'before and after.'

'That's a great idea,' said Liz and she went inside to get the camera.

When she came outside again Tammy was walking around the perimeter of the grass area and looking at the plants. She leant over to smell a few before stopping in front of a bush. She made a fist around one of the branches and, pulling her hand up towards the tip, brushed the leaves against her palm as she did so before cupping her hand over her nose and mouth and breathing in.

'Rosemary,' she said eventually. 'Mum had this in a pot in our garden.'

'Would you like to take some home with you?' said Liz. 'There are several clumps in the garden. We can find one of the smaller ones and dig it up.'

'Maybe,' said Tammy.

'Well, you don't have to decide now,' said Liz. 'We have loads of time. Right let's take this photograph.'

'Hang on,' said Tammy. 'I need to get ready,' and she rushed over and put her gloves and goggles back on although these now nestled on the front of her forehead so as not to obscure her face. Finally she held the strimmer in one hand and a pair of shears in the other. She looked like a garden warrior.

'Ready,' she shouted, as Liz clicked the camera.

'That's a good one,' she said to Tammy, looking at the photograph. 'Here, come and see.' Tammy threw down the strimmer and shears and rushed over to Liz. It was a great picture. Tammy was very photogenic and was smiling broadly.

'It looks as though you're doing all the work,' said Liz.

'The camera never lies,' said Tammy. Liz laughed. 'I'm sorry,' said Tammy.

'Sorry for what?' asked Liz.

'For throwing rubbish in your garden and calling you a witch,' she said.

'Don't worry,' said Liz, 'I probably looked like a witch at the time but thank you anyway. Now, back to work.'

They continued cutting and strimming the lawn throughout the day, only stopping for lunch and ice cream later in the afternoon. By the time they finished they had seven sacks of garden waste and a very uneven, prickly looking mass which was beginning to resemble a lawn.

'I think I'll run the mower over it a few times,' said Liz,

'try to get it as low as possible.

When Tammy took off the goggles she had the imprint of the outside of them in a line around her head as though she had been wearing a mask. Liz grabbed the camera for another photograph.

'When can we get started on the plants?' Tammy asked.

'I should think in a few days' time. I have a plan of sorts. The first priority is to sort out the lawn, at least when it's back to ground level we can see what's here. Then we will need to weed the flower beds. There will be lots of unwanted bits 'n' bobs amongst the plants we want to keep. I'll have to get some advice from the garden centre. Hopefully we can then take out the dead plants and replace them with new bee friendly plants, and finally paint the shed and the fences.'

'In bright colours,' added Tammy.

'Definitely not grey,' said Liz. 'I thought that we could also have a few days out. Perhaps you and Sasha would like to go to the pictures or skating at the weekend. Do you think Monica would like that?'

'Monica would love that,' said Tammy.

'Don't forget your project either,' reminded Liz. 'You need to get cracking.'

'I will,' Monica said. 'I could go out with my friends, too. I am almost eleven you know.'

'How could I forget,' said Liz.

When Monica came home at six o'clock she was amazed at the progress made in the garden. With the middle now cleared the flower beds were revealed. The edges still required a lot of work and the beds were full of weeds but it already looked much better.

'You have worked hard,' she said. 'Perhaps I can come and help at the weekend too. We'll soon have it back in shape.'

'That would be great,' said Liz. They all stood on the patio and looked out towards the shed.

'Tammy suggested that I turn the shed into a summerhouse. What do you think?'

'I think it would be fantastic, if you can bear to do it. Are you ready for that?'

'I am,' said Liz, surprising herself. 'Did you manage to find a decorator yet?'

'No. A man called Wojtek gave me a verbal quote for painting the walls, ceiling and woodwork, but it was seven hundred and fifty pounds and he specified cash. I thought that was a bit steep. It's just a bedroom, not the ruddy Sistine Chapel. I'll have to make a few more calls or wait a bit longer until I can afford it.'

When Monica and Tammy had left Liz went outside and sat in the garden. With the lawn cleared it was possible to see the precise spot where Jim had died. She began to recall details.

It was a very bright day. They had cleaned the windows and Jim had noticed that one of the clocks on the windowsill had stopped working. Jim had collected clocks at one time and although he had sold most of them he liked this particular clock so he kept it. He had bought it at auction. Apparently it had a very good movement. He knew a lot about clocks.

He tapped the glass a couple of times before inserting the key to wind it. It flatly refused to tick so Jim opened the door at the back to inspect it.

'Probably the spring,' he said with authority. 'I'll take it down to the shed.' He had been in the shed for an hour or so when she called him for some lunch.

'Coming, luv,' he shouted back. He had been walking down the path towards the house when he suddenly stopped in his tracks, his face wracked with pain and fear as he gripped his chest. It was almost in slow motion as he fell to the ground.

She couldn't get to him in time, it was too late, but it would have always been too late. The autopsy revealed he had a massive coronary and there was nothing she or anyone could have done. He'd often said that when his time came he preferred a heart attack to a long drawn out illness but it was much too soon.

What was she doing? Renovating the garden was not going to be enough. It would be like putting a plaster on a gaping wound. It really required something major. Something completely different. A garden to make new memories in.

'I am responsible for my happiness,' she said to herself. She was exhausted. She knew that she would sleep well despite Adam and Georgina's impending visit.

Chapter 10

Tammy was already up, dressed and at Liz's door by seven o'clock. Liz woke early but her back ached terribly and she'd had a hot bath and a painkiller before Tammy arrived.

'Breakfast?' she asked, as Tammy walked through the door.

'Toast please,' said Tammy.

'Yes, madam,' said Liz with a curtsey. 'Come and sit down.'

'I have thought of a plan,' said Tammy. 'What if we make lots of small pots of bee friendly plants and give them to all the neighbours to plant in their gardens or window boxes. That would be helping the bees.'

'Great in theory,' said Liz, 'but you would need an awful lot of plants.'

'I have thought about that too,' said Tammy. 'I wondered if we could look in Jim's book to see if there is something we could take cuttings from now.'

'You could cross reference with your bee friendly plant list,' said Liz. 'Let's have some breakfast and then we'll take a look.'

After breakfast Tammy brought the book into the

kitchen and put it on the table. She followed the list down with her fingers, mumbling the plant names until eventually, 'Lavender,' she said. 'Take cuttings in spring before it comes into flower. This is it,' she said. 'There is loads of Lavender in the garden.'

'Was,' said Liz pointedly. 'We'll have to see what's still out there. I'm not sure how much of it has survived.'

'Can we look today?' said Tammy.

'Sure,' said Liz. 'You have the list of grid references so you know where it should be so you can go on the hunt. You will also need some potting compost and lots of small pots. I don't think I have any.'

'I'll buy some with my pocket money,' said Tammy. 'I've been saving up. Can we go to the garden centre?'

'We'll go at the weekend,' Liz replied. 'My granddaughter, Sasha, is coming today and I'm sure she'd like to help you. Let's get on a bit more with the garden and I'll take you both out somewhere tomorrow. How does that sound?'

'Great.' said Tammy, and she settled down to eat her toast. 'Can we go bowling? I'd like to get some practice in before Molly's party.'

'Bowling it is,' said Liz. While Tammy was eating Liz put on a little make up.

'You look nice,' said Tammy as Liz came downstairs.

'Thanks, I want to look my best when Adam and Sasha arrive. Before they get here I would like your advice,' said Liz. 'I'm thinking of changing the garden.'

'You're not going to get rid of all the plants are you?' said

Tammy.

'Definitely not,' said Liz. 'In fact, I'm thinking of adding more, perhaps something exotic. Palms maybe? Come outside with me and I'll explain.' Liz opened the back door and they both went outside and stood on the patio. 'I'm thinking of getting rid of the lawn, or at least some of it, and maybe adding a pond or water feature and maybe a larger summer house there. She pointed to the shed. 'I could get someone in to do the landscaping work. What do you think?'

'Brilliant,' said Tammy. 'It would be like a park.'

'A very small park,' added Liz.

Tammy spent some time looking around the garden for Lavender. She found it in several places, big bushes of lavender surrounded by weeds. The plants had grown thin and straggly in their efforts to get to the light.

'Found loads,' she shouted through the back door. Liz was busy cleaning the house.

'Better look up how to take cuttings,' she called to Tammy. 'If it doesn't tell you in Jim's book we'll look it up on the computer.'

Tammy was busy with the book when the doorbell rang. Liz looked through the curtains at the front to see Adam, Georgina and Sasha on the doorstep. Adam was holding Sasha's suitcase. It was huge. As well as the suitcase Sasha had a backpack. Tammy appeared behind Liz to get a good look at her would be companion before Liz opened the door.

'Hiya,' Liz said to Adam and Georgina as she opened the door. Georgina came forward first to plant an air kiss either side of Liz's face. Liz wasn't quite sure how to react. This was as close to affection as she was ever likely to get from Georgina. Adam gave her a hug and Sasha just said, 'Hello grandma,' in a very sulky voice. Liz gave her a kiss on the cheek.

'Hi sweetie. Come in, come in, it's lovely to see you. This is Tammy,' she said to Georgina and Sasha as Adam had already met her.

'Hello,' said Georgina, and offered her hand. Tammy shook it vigorously and said 'Hi' to Sasha.

'Hello,' said Sasha quietly. Adam looked at his daughter. This was so unlike her he suspected she was up to something.

'What can I get you all?' said Liz, leading the way into the kitchen.

'Tea would be great,' said Adam.

'Tea is good for me too,' added Georgina.

'Can I have a glass of water? asked Sasha meekly.

'Tammy, would you like to take Sasha up to the spare room and show her where she will be sleeping? Adam can take the case up later.'

'Come on,' said Tammy, leading the way. Sasha rolled her eyes to her mother which Georgina recognised as, 'Do I have to?' Georgina's eyes narrowed in response, meaning, 'Yes'. Sasha stomped up the stairs behind Tammy.

'How are you, Liz?' said Georgina presently.

'I'm good,' said Liz.

'Adam tells me you're sorting out the garden,' she continued.

'I was intending just to sort it,' said Liz, 'but now I've decided to redesign it instead. I'd like a summer house and maybe a pond.'

'Oh,' said Georgina, 'that will be nice.'

Adam looked surprised. 'You can't change the garden. Dad loved it the way it is.'

'I know,' said Liz, 'but dad's not here and I am so I have decided to give it a makeover.' She softened her voice. 'Tammy is helping me, and now Sasha's, here I'll have two helpers, it will be fine. Don't worry, just have a great holiday. We won't be gardening all the time, I promise. I do intend to take them out. We're going bowling tomorrow and the girls can go to the park with Tammy's friends on some days.'

'I'm not sure I'm comfortable with Sasha being in the local park.' Liz knew exactly what Georgina meant by that. She didn't want her privately educated daughter mixing with the local poor people.

'Tammy is a lovely girl,' Liz reassured them. 'She will look after Sasha. They will be fine. How's work?' she said to Adam, changing the subject.

'Oh, really busy as usual.'

'Thank you for the flowers,' Liz added, 'they were lovely.'

'Oh,' Adam looked blank.

'For Mothers' Day.'

'Oh, that, yes, glad you liked them.' Conversation was

strained. Liz asked after Georgina's parents. Georgina seemed to take great pleasure in informing Liz that they had just moved into a gorgeous little apartment just up the road from their house which was so much easier for them since her dad had stopped driving. Adam looked embarrassed.

Liz thought again about explaining to Adam and Georgina about Tammy's mum but she was worried that Tammy would hear and so she said nothing. She would leave it to Tammy to tell Sasha if and when she wanted to.

Adam let Georgina do all the talking about the holiday and the house and the children.

'You look really well, Liz,' said Georgina eventually. 'You look happier.'

'I am,' said Liz. 'Monica and Tammy are wonderful friends and neighbours and I'm really looking forward to getting to know Sasha.'

'Thanks again, mum, for stepping in at the last minute,' said Adam, with real sincerity in his voice. 'I'd really like Sasha to get to know you too.'

'You're welcome, darling.' Georgina looked a little put out as Adam gave his mum another hug.

*****

Meanwhile Tammy was upstairs with Sasha who was unpacking her backpack. She took out her iPhone followed by an iPad and put them on the bed. Tammy sat down on the bed next to the iPad.

'Don't touch that,' said Sasha harshly.

'I wasn't going to,' said Tammy. 'I was only looking.'

'Don't you have one?'

'Not yet,' said Tammy. 'Might get one for my birthday but that's not until August. Did you get yours for your birthday?'

'Don't be silly,' said Sasha. 'I'm planning on Disneyland for my birthday. This is for school and recreation. Don't you use them at school?'

'No,' replied Tammy, 'We have computers but not iPads or laptops yet. We have a PC at home.'

'How about a phone, a mobile?' said Sasha, as if she was talking to someone of inferior intelligence.

'I have an old phone, a basic one,' said Tammy.

'What about Facebook?' said Sasha.

'What about it?' said Tammy. 'I'm not allowed on Facebook yet.'

'Well, how do you stay in contact with your friends?'

'I talk to them,' said Tammy, 'face to face. You should try it sometimes,' and she laughed.

'Who do you think you're laughing at?' said Sasha

'Well, you're the only one in the room,' replied Tammy.

Sasha put her hands on her hips. 'Let's get one thing straight. This is my grandma's house and she will believe anything I say, so you had better not cross me.'

Tammy just laughed again. 'You've been watching too many movies,' as she turned to go out of the room.

'I warned you,' said Sasha.

Tammy turned back to see Sasha breathing heavily, her face distorting and getting redder and redder before bursting into tears which quickly turned to full blown hysterics. She hopped up and down on the spot before running down the stairs shouting that Tammy had hit her. Liz was bewildered.

Adam seriously doubted it and although Georgina wasn't sure of Sasha her natural suspicion of anyone she considered inferior convinced her that Sasha was telling the truth and the motive was probably jealousy. She tried to comfort Sasha.

'Liar,' shouted Tammy.

'I knew this was a mistake,' Georgina hissed at Adam.

'I want to go home,' Sasha sobbed.

Liz was about to say something when Adam, his face contorted with anger shouted, 'Oh, for God's sake Georgina. We are going on holiday and mum is going to look after Sasha and that is the end of it.'

Georgina and Sasha were both shocked into silence. Georgina looked like she'd been slapped in the face and Sasha stopped crying immediately. Tammy came and stood behind Liz, who put her arm around her shoulder for reassurance. Adam smiled at his mum while Georgina glared at Tammy, then at Adam, but she said nothing.

Tammy moved to sit beside Liz. She hadn't encountered anyone like Sasha before. 'I think you two should start again,' said, Liz looking at Sasha. Tammy stood up with her hand outstretched. Sasha remained steadfastly at Georgina's side. 'This is going to be fun,' thought Liz. Adam and Georgina said their good-byes. Georgina was holding on to Sasha as if her life depended on it and promising to call her every day.

Once they had left Liz took out the gardening gloves and tools that she had bought for Sasha. She asked her if she would like to come out and help in the garden. Sasha declined and went upstairs to get her iPad.

Liz had called a couple of landscape gardening companies and had made appointments for them both to come to the house to give her an estimate. Now she had made up her mind to change the garden she couldn't wait to get some ideas.

She imagined herself sitting on the porch of her summer house, reading a book from the comfort of a soft armchair as she caught the last rays of the afternoon sun.

Jim had often talked about installing a pond but it was a 'someday' topic. Like someday we'll go on a cruise, or someday we'll learn a language or move to France. She was sorry that they had waited but imagined Jim looking down on the garden, not sure if he would approve.

Tammy had inspected the borders for Lavender and was pointing out all the places where it had been planted. It was easy to walk on the lawn now. It didn't look much like a lawn but Liz was happy in the knowledge that it would soon be gone anyway.

'I don't think Sasha likes me,' said Tammy.

'What's not to like?' said Liz smiling. 'She will.'

'I didn't hit her' Tammy continued.

'I know, said Liz, I think she is just used to getting her own way so it might take a while for her to come round.

When she gets bored with her own company she'll come outside, you'll see.'

Liz asked Tammy to put her gloves on and get her tools as they were about to tackle the weeds in the flower beds. Both of them knelt beside the soil and Liz pointed out the plants that could be removed.

After sulking for an hour or so Sasha came outside. 'I'm going to watch', she announced, as she flounced onto one of the chairs on the patio.

'Fine,' said Liz. Tammy got a bit carried away and started on the Forget-me-nots. 'Hold up,' said Liz, 'those aren't weeds.'

'They are Forget-me-nots,' said Sasha, who had been watching everything and couldn't resist giving them the benefit of her knowledge.

'How do you know?' asked Tammy.

'We have a gardener,' said Sasha, with her nose in the air, and the emphasis on gardener as if everyone had one. 'He tells me the names of all the plants,' she continued.

'Then we could definitely use your help,' said Liz, winking at Tammy.

Sasha stood up slowly. 'Oh, all right. I'll advise you,' she said as she came over to kneel next to Tammy as if she was doing them both a big favour. 'This is a weed,' she said, pointing to the plantain, 'and this,' pointing at Lamb's Ear.

'I don't get it,' said Tammy. 'They are all just plants. What makes them weeds?'

'I don't know,' said Sasha. 'Some of them are nice. Our

gardener pulls up the Forget-me-nots. He says they crowd the Lilies but I like them.'

'I like them too,' said Liz, 'so we'll leave them in.'

'These definitely have to come out,' Sasha continued with authority, pointing to the stinging nettles gathering at the back. Tammy leant forward and pulled at a clump as she was wearing her gloves but as she did so she managed to brush the leaves against Sasha's hands and knees.

'Ouch, that hurt. You did that on purpose,' said Sasha, about to cry again as the bumps started to appear and throb.

'I did not,' said Tammy, 'but if I had I wouldn't lie about it. It was an accident and I am sorry but you don't need to make such a fuss.'

'You need a Dock leaf,' said Liz.

'I know where they are,' said Tammy, jumping up and rushing to the spot where she'd seen them. She quickly picked off some leaves and tore them into smaller strips before rubbing them between her hands to squeeze out the juice.

She came over to Sasha. 'You need to rub this on the sting.' She offered the leaves.

'That looks disgusting,' said Sasha.

'Suit yourself,' said Tammy, 'but it definitely helps.' Tammy put the leaves down next to Sasha who grudgingly picked them up and rubbed them onto the stings. After a few minutes the stinging subsided. Sasha thought about saying thank you but that went against all her natural instincts so instead she asked how Tammy knew what to do.

'Mum told me,' was the reply.

Sasha seemed to settle quickly after that. It must have been obvious to her that Tammy would not be indulging her tantrums the way her mother and grandparents did and therefore they were redundant. It was a great help having Tammy around. Liz wasn't sure how she would have coped with Sasha on her own. Tammy was easy going and completely able to handle Sasha who warmed to her eventually. With no one she could manipulate Sasha gave up trying and just enjoyed being a ten year old girl having fun in the garden.

It was a warm day and Liz kept the girls well stocked with lemonade, ice lollies and toasted cheese and tomato sandwiches. It would all work out.

Bob from Living Landscapes, one of the garden design companies that Liz had rung earlier, turned up at three o'clock to look around. He had a young boy with him that Liz assumed was his son. The boy, who could only have been about twelve, held the end of the tape measure as his dad took measurements and wrote them down in a book. After the measurements had been taken Bob accepted Liz's offer of tea and sat with her at the table to discuss her ideas.

The boy sat next to his dad, self-consciously sipping his Coke and avoiding eye contact with either of the girls, who had decided between them that he resembled Harry from One Direction. They stared and giggled making him feel really uncomfortable and self-conscious which was, of course, their intention.

Liz explained what she wanted to keep and what was going. The shed was going. She would put all the useful power tools in the garage and keep the other garden tools in the new summer house. It was time to let go of the past. Liz explained that she might like a pond or at least the sound of water in the garden.

She would also like some exotic plants, palms or bamboo. Bob asked her what she wanted to do with the grass and Liz was quite specific on this point. It had to go. She felt that she was betraying Jim by replacing the grass but if she was to move on it had to go. Besides, it was Jim who loved the grass. She thought that some kind of statue or other garden feature could occupy a bit of the space. She wanted the garden to look completely different.

Finally, she wanted lights, lighting up the pergola and the trees. She wanted to be able to turn on a switch from inside the house that would illuminate the garden and banish the unhappy memories. The next time she went to the cemetery she would explain it all to Jim.

Bob from Living Landscapes informed her that he would come up with a design and get back to her, adding that she may be looking at around ten thousand pounds for the work, but Liz had been frugal for the last five years and she could certainly afford it. She wasn't hard up for money. Jim had a fantastic insurance policy and pension and it was about time that she spent some of the money. She was looking forward to getting started. They would have Wednesday off to go bowling and on Thursday Finn from Fantasy Gardens would be coming round to give her a quote.

By the time Monica arrived at six o'clock Tammy and Sasha were well on their way to being friends. Sasha assumed that Monica was Tammy's mum and Tammy said nothing to make her think otherwise. She came in and had a cup of tea with Liz while Sasha and Tammy watched TV in the living room.

'How's the diet going?'

'I think I've lost a few pounds,' said Monica, 'but I haven't got any scales so I can't be sure.'

'I have got some in the bathroom upstairs,' said Liz. 'You could make this your weekly weigh in station.'

'I'm definitely feeling fitter,' said Monica. 'I don't think I could have made the stairs a few months ago.' She came down a few minutes later, smiling.

'Well?' said Liz, curious to know how she'd got on.

'I used to weigh almost eighty kilos.'

'What's that in old money,' said Liz.

'Twelve and a half stone,' said Monica

'And now?' said Liz, excitedly.

'Seventy three kilos.'

'Well done. Have you told Tammy?'

'Not yet,' Monica replied.

'What are you aiming for?' said Liz.

'I'm trying not to be too ambitious. At my height I should be around fifty eight to sixty kilos, which is a size ten to twelve, so I still have a way to go. At the moment I'm a

144

size sixteen going on eighteen. Tammy is very keen on me losing weight. We are going for a walk this evening. She is trying to get me to go running but until I lose some weight I don't think there's a sports bra strong enough to prevent me knocking myself out with my boobs.' Liz laughed. 'Why don't you come with Sasha?' Monica added.

'I could do,' said Liz. 'The girls have already eaten.'

'I am now the queen of organisation,' said Monica. 'Poached salmon and three bean salad await me in the fridge next door. I'll nip back and eat it, get changed and come back. You can tell me all about the garden.'

*****

Adam and Georgina had arrived at their hotel, which was stunning. Georgina had booked a suite which was big enough to accommodate a family of ten although furnished for only two. She was never, ever frugal with Adam's money. Besides, the views were amazing. They approached the room via a huge marble hallway. The double doors opened to reveal a sitting room, fully furnished in various shades of cream and ivory.

A bowl of fruit sat on the ultra-modern chrome and glass coffee table. A low white cupboard on one wall housed the fridge, which was well stocked with drinks, and a flat screen TV reflected the room on the wall above it.

A door from the living area led to the equally luxurious bedroom. A king sized bed dominated the room which was sparsely decorated apart from the bedside tables and a smaller sofa. Doors led from the bedroom to the bathroom and dressing room. Cool beige and white flecked tiles covered the floors, which were occasionally obscured by coffee coloured shag-pile rugs dotted like islands in a white speckled sea.

Folding glass doors in the living room opened to a wide terrace where a table, chairs and sun loungers were neatly arranged. Folds of voile curtains gathered each side of the glass doors which could be drawn to cover the pale beige blinds waiting, coiled and ready to block out the morning sun. The terrace was completely private, not overlooked by anything other than the sea birds. Opaque glass partitions gave complete privacy from the suites either side.

Georgina stood on the terrace and imagined herself sipping champagne in her evening gown with the cool sea breeze wafting over her tanned body. She had sulked for most of the journey but now she was here she decided that it was time to forgive Adam. Despite the fact that he had been willing to leave their darling daughter in the care of his demented mother in the cheaper end of Enfield with only a rough comprehensive school pupil as a companion. After all, she had survived it.

'Thank you darling, it's wonderful,' she said sincerely.

'You found it,' said Adam

'But you work so hard to pay for it,' Georgina pouted. 'What would I do without you?'

Adam had left the cases by the door and taken his shoes off to lie on the white sofa. Georgina decided to demonstrate her gratitude in a much more physical way so while Adam closed his eyes and rested Georgina jumped into the shower and came out of the bathroom wearing nothing but a smile.

'Aren't you going to ring Sasha?' he said sarcastically, as she undid his shirt buttons.

'I'll ring her tomorrow,' she replied.

Chapter 11

Monica was buoyed by the fact that she had started to lose weight, and not the one or two pounds that usually marked her previous half-hearted attempts. She had lost over half a stone. Tammy was thrilled with the news and encouraged Monica to walk faster to knock off a few more pounds. Liz didn't need to lose any weight but the exercise was welcome as she rarely walked anywhere nowadays.

'How's the hunt for a decorator going?' she asked as they strolled along.

'Not that great,' said Monica. 'I've rung a few numbers but I hate it when there is just a mobile and no landline or address. I have to leave them in the house by themselves so a business address is vital.'

'I know what you mean,' Liz sympathised. 'I'm having some people round to give quotes for the garden. I have finally decided to change it. Sasha and Tammy can help with the planting but the landscaping needs a professional.'

'Sounds expensive,' said Monica.

'I suspect it will be,' agreed Liz, 'but it needs doing. I have my heart set on a water feature. I've already had Living Landscapes in,' Liz continued, 'and I've got Fantasy Gardens coming to take a look on Thursday. Let's hope the prices are realistic.'

Sasha interrupted to ask Liz and Monica if Tammy could sleepover. Monica was more than happy not to be woken up at six o'clock in the morning. A lie-in would be fantastic. When they got back from walking Tammy grabbed a toothbrush, pyjamas and clean clothes so she could stay with Liz.

Monica went home to catch up on some work and the girls sat to watch a DVD.

Liz had the urge to paint. She had hardly picked up a pencil since Jim had died. The drawing with Tammy had made her laugh and made her think. She missed it, so while the girls watched TV Liz went to the garage to sort out her paints.

The next morning Liz woke early but the girls were still fast asleep.

'I bet they were chatting all night,' she thought, as she put the kettle on. She wasn't wrong. Tammy told Sasha about her mother and Sasha was really sad to hear it. Sasha searched her memory for a similar story of loss. She did have a hamster once. Her mother had told her that it had escaped but Leo had found it in the bin.

'Not that you can compare a hamster to your mother,' said Sasha trying to empathise.

'Don't worry about it,' said Tammy. 'Mum was the best but Monica is great too.'

The girls got up around nine o'clock and while Liz was upstairs making the beds the girls sat in the kitchen eating breakfast. Sasha's mobile rang.

'Hi darling, it's mummy,' Georgina cooed. Sasha's face changed immediately.

'Hi mum,' she said sadly.

'Are you having a lovely time?' Georgina continued hopefully.

'It's fine,' said Sasha in a monotone voice.

'Are you all right sweetie?' Georgina was concerned.

'I'm fine,' said Sasha, trying to convince her mother otherwise. 'Don't worry about me. You just have a nice holiday and I'll see you when you get back.'

'OK,' said Georgina, really worried now. 'I'll call you tomorrow.'

'What was that all about?' said Tammy, when Sasha had put the phone down.

'It's all to do with guilt,' said Sasha wisely. 'The guiltier they feel the bigger the holiday present will be when they get back.'

'What is it that you want?' said Tammy, to the girl who appeared to have everything.

'I'm working on a weekend in Disneyland for my birthday,' said Sasha, before becoming more animated again.

'You're scary,' said Tammy, laughing.

Liz was heartened to hear the girls laughing. She knew she could relax.

'No gardening today,' she said, as she walked into the kitchen. 'We are going bowling instead.' They both jumped up excitedly and ran to get dressed. Liz phoned Monica to ask if she would like to come for dinner to save her cooking for herself as Liz was cooking anyway. She promised to make diet food for Monica, who was happy to be fed.

They had a great day out and when Monica came over in the evening Tammy was really pleased to see her and gave her a hug as she came through the door.

'What was that for?' she asked.

'Nothing,' said Tammy smiling, before rushing off to watch TV with Sasha. They went for a walk in the park after dinner, the girls running on ahead.

'Liz, I want to ask your advice,' said Monica seriously. 'I bumped into an old friend at the coffee bar near work.'

'When you say old friend, do you mean old boyfriend?' asked Liz.

'That would have been great,' said Monica, 'but I do mean old friend. We started work the same week for a magazine group. We were inducted together.'

'Sounds painful,' said Liz.

'It was,' said Monica. 'It could have been the most boring week of my life but Kevin made it fun. He has a great sense of humour. He only stayed for a year. We were just friends. Besides he had a girlfriend.'

'Sounds like you were sorry,' said Liz.

'I was,' said Monica, 'but I doubt I'd be in with a chance anyway.'

'Why ever not?' said Liz.

'Well, for a start he is a six foot tall, slim, white guy and I am a short, fat black woman. We're hardly a match made in heaven. Don't you think we'd look odd together?'

'Now who's being daft?' said Liz. 'He must like you or he wouldn't have asked you out. Besides, you're beautiful and getting slimmer all the time. What does he do?'

'Not sure what he does now but he used to work for the IT department, so something techy I suppose. I think he said that he's a web designer.'

'What did you say?' asked Liz. 'Are you going to go?'

'I wasn't sure so I told him that I only had time for coffee. I haven't been on a date in such a long time I've forgotten the dating etiquette. Do I offer to pay half or let him pay? I wouldn't feel so bad about coffee but lunch would be different. Plus, I don't want Tammy to worry.'

'It's only coffee at the moment,' said Liz. 'Aren't you jumping ahead a long way? Why don't you meet for coffee and think about the rest when you have to.'

*****

The doorbell rang at nine o'clock on Thursday morning. Liz looked through the curtains before opening the door, a habit she acquired after Jim had died. Up until then she would always open the door without checking first. Mormons, Jehovah's witnesses, political candidates and door to door salesman could rely on the fact that if they were in they would answer the door.

Liz could see two men on the front step. There was a very thin man with dyed blonde hair, shaved at the sides, with the remaining hair standing up two inches from his head like the stripe down a badger's back. He wore purple skin-tight jeans and a pale blue denim jacket. He had studs in both ears and a hoop piercing his left eyebrow. A multi coloured stripy scarf was wrapped around his neck and there was a large black portfolio case tucked under his arm.

The other man was demure in comparison. He was equally thin but with short brown hair and brown eyes. He had a smooth face with even, handsome features. He wore chino trousers that were slightly creased and brown leather boots and his tweed jacket would not have been out of place on a country estate with its leather patches on the elbows. The sports holdall he carried looked incongruous compared to the rest of him. 'It could only be Fantasy Gardens,' thought Liz, as she went to open the front door.

The blonde man introduced himself as Finn, the brown haired man was Devlin, and they were here to talk to Liz about her Fantasy Garden.

Liz offered them tea or coffee which they both declined. Tammy and Sasha were fascinated with Finn who was as camp as Christmas but gushingly warm and friendly. Devlin on the other hand was much quieter. However, it was apparent that they were partners both in and out of work as they bickered like an old married couple while discussing ideas for the garden.

Finn in particular was very theatrical. Liz took them out to the garden. Finn stood on the patio and held his arms out wide with his chin slightly raised while he got a 'feel' for the space. The girls thought this was highly amusing. Devlin, on the other hand, sat at the table with a sketch pad making a plan of the garden and asking Liz what she would like to keep.

Finn walked up and down the garden, taking photographs with a digital camera and saying things like, 'That'll have to go,' and, 'That'll never do.' Every now and then he threw in a, 'Will you look at that!'

Out of sight the girls were imitating him. After half an hour Liz joined them both at the table. Finn sat directly in front of Liz and then, adopting the style of a supportive friend, leant forward before asking earnestly what she wanted from the garden. She told them what she had told Bob regarding the late afternoon sun and the sound of water, and definitely no grass.

Finn was excited. 'We could put a bold water feature there.' He pointed to the centre of the garden. 'Not too tall, we don't want it to obscure the view of the summer house. I'm thinking different textures, rattan, sea grass, raffia. Soft lights and soft lines. Swirling patterns. Bamboo, pampas and palms.'

'Maybe,' said Devlin cautiously trying to reign in Finn. 'Let's draw up some designs and see what Liz thinks.'

Finn opened his portfolio on the garden table. Inside there were tracing paper plans of designs they had already done and pictures of the finished gardens. They were fantastic. Some were completely over the top with statues of fairies and butterflies and arches everywhere. There were huge gardens and small discrete hideaways, all beautifully balanced and coordinated.

Liz could imagine herself in all of them. She thought that her fantasy might be too modest in comparison to some of their other designs but Devlin had listened intently and told Liz that he was sure they could come up with something that she would love. Liz liked both of them very much and was equally sure that they would do exactly that. She couldn't wait to see it.

The house was a lot quieter when Fantasy Gardens had vacated the premises.

'You haven't forgotten the bees?' asked Tammy when they left.

'Definitely not,' said Liz. 'We will make sure we plant a lot of bee friendly plants everywhere in the garden and you will make sure that our neighbours all have Lavender in theirs. In fact, why don't you and Sasha design a flyer to go with the Lavender? You'll need instructions on how to care for it and when to re-pot it. You could also add some advice about other bee-friendly plants.' Liz went outside to carry on weeding while the girls made the flyer.

Tammy was surprised that Sasha thought it was a good idea. She suspected that Sasha would only think ideas were good if she'd come up with them herself. Of course, Sasha knew all about the fate of bees. There was not much that Sasha didn't know something about. Back home, one of her friend's parents had several hives in the grounds of their estate. Tammy noticed that Sasha's friends had grounds and estates, not gardens.

Tammy looked up how to take cuttings and between

them they designed an information sheet that they would eventually attach to each pot. They would then distribute them to any house or flat with a garden or window box in the immediate vicinity.

'I have an idea. Why don't we make it a pyramid scheme,' suggested Sasha. Tammy had never heard of a pyramid scheme. Sasha explained. 'The instruction sheet can include information on how to take cuttings and we could suggest that when the plant gets to a reasonable size each person takes at least two cuttings from it to give away. Not everyone will do it but even if only a few do it the plants will be spreading.'

'That's a fantastic idea,' said Tammy.

'I know,' said Sasha, smiling smugly. It wasn't entirely her idea. She had heard Georgina trying to explain the principle to her friends as she tried to sell them Aloe Vera products. They were a lot less impressed than Tammy had been.

'What about pots?' asked Tammy eventually.

'They could use yoghurt pots,' said Sasha. 'Everyone eats yoghurt.'

Monica popped in after dinner as usual for the walk around the park. 'Any news of Kevin?' said Liz hopefully.

'He emailed me,' replied Monica. 'He suggested meeting next Friday at one o'clock.'

'Great,' said Liz smiling.

'Let's not get ahead of ourselves,' said Monica. 'It's just coffee. Don't go rushing out to buy a hat.'

*****

It had taken a few days but Adam was finally relaxing into his holiday. Georgina always found people to hang with.

She was great at networking. Most of the time she managed to find a couple that were like clones of themselves, in that they consisted of professional men with stick thin wives. Either that or rich, old, bald men with their second or third trophy wife draped in designer goods and looking every inch like the advertisements in the duty free shops at the airport.

In many ways Adam and Georgina had bucked the trend. They were, after all, still on their first marriage. Adam loved Georgina and Georgina loved Adam in her own way. He was successful so she was happy. It did cross Adam's mind in the early days that Georgina would be off in a flash if he didn't have money but he had already amassed a small fortune so that wasn't really a problem. And they did get on. Georgina understood him. After all, isn't that the reason that most men stray? Their wives don't understand them?

*****

Saturday morning was gloriously sunny. Liz woke up to find several letters on the mat. She picked them up and found a business like envelope which she guessed was a utility bill, a plain brown envelope which was handwritten and an A4 window envelope with Fantasy Gardens emblazoned on the left hand side and covered in glitter dust. She couldn't wait to open it. She poured herself a cup of coffee and sat at the kitchen table.

She opened the other two envelopes first. She hoped

that Fantasy Gardens would be the antidote to whatever bad news was in the other two. She was right to suspect as the first one was a utility bill. Three hundred and thirty six pounds for gas in the last quarter. 'Scandalous,' she thought as she pinned it to the notice board so she'd remember to pay it.

The brown hand-written envelope was very disappointing. It was the estimate from Living Landscapes and it was set out like a list.

Remove grass and topsoil from an area of (approximately 30 sq feet) £300.00.

Excavate an area of approximately 4 metres £240.00

Supply and install 15 square metres of Bredon Gravel etc

Take down and remove existing shed £400

Supply and fit 4 metre x 2 metres log cabin - £2,500

Paint log cabin etc….

She couldn't be bothered with the rest.

She scanned down the list for the total. The job came to just over eleven thousand eight hundred pounds. 'Where's the pictures,' thought Liz, 'the vision. How can I make a decision based on a list?'

She turned her attention to Fantasy Gardens. She opened the envelope carefully to reveal several pieces of paper and a folded plan. She could hardly bear the excitement as she unfolded the plan to reveal her new garden. It was spectacular. The summer house was set to the left hand side at the back of the garden with folding glass doors to the entire front and a porch where a very modern rattan sofa looked out towards the back of the house with a view of the garden.

There were exotic looking plants and raised areas, pathways and focal points and not a blade of grass in site, bar the ornamental grasses in the new beds. They had not included a pond but instead a large water feature consisting of a lump of smooth stone with water cascading over it and falling into a pebbled tray that was set to one side and lit by small round lights set into the stones.

The plan showed views of the garden from different angles, all very hi-tech. 'This is it,' she thought to herself. She looked at the other pieces of paper. One was a contract which she was to sign and return if she agreed to the design. The other was the price. She took a deep breath before turning the page, fourteen and a half thousand pounds. Wow! This was more than she had intended to spend but she loved it so she found a pen and signed on the dotted line.

Liz couldn't wait for everyone to see it. As soon as the girls came down for breakfast she showed them the design.

'Oh, my God. It's amazing grandma,' said Sasha.

'It is,' said Tammy. 'Are you keeping the Lavender?'

'I am and I'm thinking of planting lots more. We'll talk to Finn and Devlin about the details of the design when they start work. We need to look at all the plants on your list, Tammy, and move anything we want to keep to the beds that are staying.'

Monica was equally impressed. 'It's definitely different.

Are you sure this is what you want?'

'It is,' said Liz. 'It's time for a change.'

They were all dressed and at the garden centre by ten thirty and decided to stop for a coffee at the café before they started shopping. As they approached Liz could see Nick getting up from his usual spot. He was about to leave.

'Hi Nick.' She was smiling as she introduced Sasha and then Monica and Tammy as 'my lovely next door neighbour and her niece.'

'How's work?' she enquired.

'Still quiet,' he replied. Liz explained to Monica that she and Nick used to teach at the same school but that now he was a self-employed painter.

'Oh, that's great,' said Monica, who was still looking for someone to decorate Tammy's room. 'Do you live locally?'

'I do,' said Nick, 'just up the road from here.'

Monica was optimistic so continued, 'Do you have a land line and a mobile?'

'I do,' said Nick, bemused. 'Even a website if you'd like to take a look.'

'Fantastic,' said Monica. 'You wouldn't be interested in a job would you? I need someone to paint Tammy's bedroom.' Tammy smiled hopefully at Nick.

Nick hesitated. He was considering making an excuse but both Liz and Monica were looking at him expectantly.

. 'Why not? He said eventually, I have some time on my hands.'

Monica searched her handbag for something to write her

address on. 'Would you be able to start on Monday?' she asked. Nick had no plans so Monday was agreed. 'If you can't get there for eight o'clock don't worry. I'll leave the key with Liz.'

'Number seventy three,' added Liz.

'Great,' said Nick, smiling warmly at Liz as he took the address from Monica before saying his goodbyes.

Monica, Tammy and Sasha had all noticed that Liz seemed to be in a Doris Day haze as her eyes followed Nick to the exit. It was fairly obvious that he liked her too.

'He seems nice,' said Monica to Liz, 'and he seems to like you.'

'Oh, really?' said Liz. 'I hadn't noticed.' Tammy raised her eyebrows.

Chapter 12

Tammy and Sasha went off to find potting compost and small plastic flower pots. Liz and Monica had sat down with coffee and were talking about decorating Tammy's room.

'Any idea on colours?' asked Liz.

'I'll leave it to Tammy. She seems to know what she wants.'

'Oh, that reminds me,' said Liz. 'I need to pick up some more plants. The ones in the garden are looking a bit ragged. Have you heard from Kevin?'

'He emails me a lot,' said Monica, 'mostly jokes and funny things that he has seen and thought I might like.'

'That's good,' said Liz. 'He sounds like he has a sense of humour.'

'He'll need one,' added Monica. 'I know I'm leaping ahead but so much has happened since we last met. I now have a ten year old to look after.'

'It's way too early to tell,' said Liz, 'but if he cares about you enough he'll make the effort to get on with Tammy. I know it's none of my business but what was Tammy's dad like? Is he around?'

'Max? No, he was off like a rocket when Joanna told him

162

she was pregnant. Not that she minded. He was a great boyfriend, fun and unpredictable, but not father material, at least not then.'

'Are you in touch?'

'No, not for a very long time. I think he did try a couple of times when Tammy was four or five but Joanna would have none of it by then and I've not heard anything since.'

'Did he come to the funeral?'

'I don't think he knew she had died. Besides it would have been awkward.'

'Does Tammy ever ask about him?'

'It's strange,' said Monica. 'I thought she might have when Joanna died. I thought it might be important to her to find her dad, not to feel so alone, but she hasn't asked yet. I've got pictures of Joanna with Max and I have gathered some things together just in case. Tammy has his smile and his sense of fun. I would help her find him if she wanted to but I'll wait until she asks. I'm not going to do anything to seek him out unless Tammy wants me to.'

Monica had tears in her eyes. Liz had never seen her cry. She had often been overwhelmed, frustrated, angry even but never tearful.

'What are you thinking?' asked Liz.

'I miss her,' said Monica. 'I miss Joanna. I didn't think we were close when she was alive. We led very different lives and we only caught up now and again but I miss not being able to give her a call when I have some news. I would have been on the phone to her soon after bumping into Kevin to ask her what she thought.'

'I know what you mean,' said Liz. 'I still have Jim's mobile number on mine. I can't bring myself to delete it even though he sometimes drove me mad. I'd be at work or out somewhere and he'd call me to ask me to make a note of something because he didn't have a pen. He called me when he was bored or stuck in traffic. Other times he'd ring to tell me about things that happened during the day. After he died I used to ring it, just to hear his voice, which is funny when I look back because all it said was, 'Jim here. Sorry I can't get to the phone right now,' and she started to laugh, 'but if you leave me a message,' she laughed more and Monica started laughing too, it was infectious. Liz laughed so much that she could barely get out the last bit, 'I'll get back to you when I can'. The pair of them were now laughing hysterically as other people at the café looked on completely bemused by the sudden outburst.

'Thank you,' said Monica when she finally recovered, tears of laughter rolling down her face. 'I needed that.'

The girls came back from exploring the garden centre. Tammy told Monica about the pots and compost that she wanted to buy and Sasha had found a display of water features. Liz bought the girls lemonade and crisps before going to collect a trolley. When they finished at the café Liz pulled the trolley over to the aisle where pallets were piled high with bags of compost and picked up a small one. They could always come back for more if it wasn't enough.

Tammy ran off and came back with five packs of small

brown plastic pots, ideal for her Lavender cuttings, and Liz picked up more Lavender plants. She had decided to border one of the beds with Lavender. She also picked up a few bedding plants although she had no idea where she would put them. They parked the trolley and went to inspect the water features. Sasha knew something about ponds as one of her friends had a huge pond in the garden containing Koi Carp.

The garden centre had several troughs with fish at various stages of development. Despite the sign that asked visitors not to touch the girls couldn't resist putting their fingers into the water and then squealing with delight as the fish approached, assuming they were food. The water features were next to the troughs. Some of the ponds were very ornate with fountains in the centre and water cascading out of the mouths of dolphins or the tops of jugs or urns. The girls were highly amused by one fountain where a nude cherub appeared to be peeing into the water.

Next to these were the modern fountains. Liz found one that had water cascading over the top of an oblong granite block.

'I think I'd like something like this,' she said to Monica.

'I like it,' said Tammy, 'although I would like to have some fish too.'

'No fish,' said Liz. 'I want to know that I can go away for a few days without worrying about feeding the pets.'

'Are you planning a trip.' said Monica.

'Not exactly,' said Liz. 'I have no idea where or when but

I definitely intend to go away somewhere this year.'

When they had finished at the garden centre Tammy and Monica went off to buy paint for Tammy's room. Liz asked Sasha what she wanted to do next and Sasha decided on the cinema. Liz hadn't been to a cinema in years. The last time was a Star Wars film when Adam was a small boy but she remembered the rubbish everywhere and the way people spoke throughout the film. It was an experience she wasn't keen to repeat. She much preferred to wait for the DVD to be released.

Her fears turned out to be unfounded. The cinema in the town had since been developed into a multiplex. It was now a large glass fronted building with ten screens showing new releases for the Easter holiday. Sasha made her choice and Liz bought the tickets. They stocked up with a selection of sweets from the wall of containers in the foyer before going in to find that it was fairly quiet.

Liz was relieved to find that Sasha seemed to be enjoying herself as she had been worried that she would be bored. After all it was a world away from her life of privilege. At home she had a games room and an indoor swimming pool, she played tennis and rode her pony. Liz was pleasantly surprised at how easy she was to amuse.

Sasha was just as chatty as Tammy and had opinions on everything and everyone. Liz found out more about the lives of Adam and Georgina in an afternoon with Sasha than she had from talking to Adam in the last ten years.

Grandpa Jo had lost his driving licence. He had apparently

driven the wrong way down a duel carriageway. His eyesight is now so poor he would be dangerous behind the wheel of a car and Grandma Betty is very forgetful and tends to repeat things all the time. Georgina gets irritated with both of them and says their days are numbered. She's started to collect brochures for residential homes in the area.

Sasha told Liz all about Georgina's ideas for going back to work. She once opened a tea shop but apparently she couldn't stand the customers, or the staff for that matter, so it didn't last very long. She joined some sort of pyramid scheme but stopped when her friends started to avoid her.

She tried selling costume jewellery and resort wear on the internet but became very disillusioned when she had to start returning goods and fending off dissatisfied customers. Her latest venture was party planning. It was Adam's idea. He said she was made for it so she hired someone to build her a website. Sasha was hoping her birthday trip would be her mum's first project.

Adam played golf badly, probably because he hated it. He only played for work. Leo also played golf and was really good at it and had won lots of tournaments. Adam was hardly ever home nowadays and even when he was there he was working. Leo was at boarding school during term time and only came home for the holidays so she was very lonely sometimes, even with Grandma Betty there as she just liked to knit and watch TV.

Sasha loved her pony. She called it Ebony and she couldn't wait for Liz to meet her. She had won quite a few rosettes already. She really wanted a dog for her birthday but Adam and Georgina had categorically refused to get one because live in pets were too much of a tie. Besides, daddy had been offered a job in New York. 'Ooops.'

'Ooops,' repeated Liz.

'That was a secret. I wasn't supposed to talk about it.'

'Don't worry,' said Liz. 'My lips are sealed.'

'It's a five year contract,' continued Sasha, 'and we would only come back for holidays once a year. Mum and dad can't decide whether it's best to sell or let the house. I don't want to leave,' said Sasha miserably.

Liz thought about Adam. He would be mortified to hear his daughter telling his secrets, especially as he was very unlikely to tell her about it himself.

She wondered how Georgina would feel about leaving her parents behind. They were at least ten years older than Liz. She couldn't imagine them upping sticks and moving to America, unless they would be able to move in with Adam and Georgina, of course, or they could find an appropriate retirement home which seemed more likely, especially in the light of Sasha's revelations.

She was tempted to ask Sasha but decided against it. It hurt her to think that Adam had known about this for a while and had not bothered to tell her. She doubted that he had given a moment's thought to the fact that she was on her own. She felt sad for Sasha too, the girl who appeared to have everything, especially now she knew her better. She would really miss her.

'It will be fantastic,' said Liz, trying to sound cheerful to mask her own disappointment and not wanting to upset Sasha. 'I'll come to see you in the holidays. I've never been to America.' Sasha smiled.

*****

Monica had taken Tammy to the local DIY store to look at paint colour charts and she picked out a couple of colours. Monica wasn't convinced that the colours would gel on the walls but she had promised Tammy that it was her room and therefore her choice so she bought two tins of each and white paint for the woodwork and ceiling. It had been a long day and she couldn't wait to get home, although she was starting to feel she had more energy. She picked up fish and chips on the way home.

'Don't worry,' she said to Tammy, 'I'm only eating the fish.'

*****

On Sunday Monica had planned to visit one of her aunts. She wanted Tammy to get to know them all a bit better but she had to change her plans. Nick was now coming to paint on Monday morning so they would have to clear everything out of Tammy's room.

'You'll have to sleep in my bed for a few days,' she said to Tammy as they took the bedding off. 'Unless you can stay next door with Sasha.' Tammy was quite happy about either arrangement.

After breakfast they emptied all the cupboards and drawers. Monica had been saving boxes, which was very unlike her.

She was definitely getting more organised. Between them they moved clothes, shoes and anything Tammy still played with into boxes that Monica labelled as they went along before stacking the boxes in her room and in the corner of the living room. She also managed to free some hanging space in her own wardrobe so she could squeeze some of Tammy's school clothes in for the time being.

Tammy had a couple of boxes containing things that had belonged to her mother. They were still taped up. Monica assumed that Tammy hadn't looked at them since they collected them from the flat after Joanna's funeral. She had encouraged Tammy to pick up anything she wanted, anything at all no matter how big or small. So while Monica searched for photographs and papers that she might need Tammy was incredibly brave and boxed up the hairdressing equipment, brushes and curling tongs that had made such a difference to the friends and clients that came to the house and held so many happy memories.

Monica's old place was a tiny one bedroom flat so there was definitely no room for all of Joanna's clothes and furniture. Joanna had the knack of making something out of nothing. She was always finding abandoned bits and pieces. She couldn't go past a skip without looking in. Monica would cross the road to avoid it, too embarrassed to be next to Joanna as she rummaged. Joanna didn't care at all.

'One man's trash is another man's treasure,' she would say,

as she transformed old cupboards and chairs into shabby chic works of art. Her home was an eclectic mix of unique items cobbled together from her imagination. She was such a hard act to follow.

Initially, after Joanna died Monica tried to live in Joanna's flat with Tammy to avoid disrupting her, but it was a bad idea and Tammy rejected everything that Monica tried to do.

Joanna's essence was in every nook and cranny and Tammy didn't miss an opportunity to let her know that she was a poor substitute for her mother. She spent a lot of the time angry and confused, and being in Joanna's flat with the furniture she had made and her paintings on the walls was a constant reminder of what they had both lost.

After a few months Monica decided that things might improve if they moved away so she put what she could of Joanna's in storage and let Tammy bring whatever she wanted to her tiny flat until she had saved a bit more money and could look for something a bit bigger. Tammy was very unhappy to leave familiar surroundings and her behaviour worsened.

Monica had done everything she could to ensure Tammy could be with her and had been granted kinship care of Tammy. Social Services were really helpful but Monica knew that Tammy had only agreed to it because she felt it was the lesser of two evils, foster care or Monica. She lost count of how many times she had heard Tammy scream the mantra, 'You are not my mother.' That was the better behaviour. Worse was when she would sink deeper and deeper into silent rage where she would not speak for days on end.

When Monica had moved next door to Liz she was at the end of her tether. She had decided to give it three more months before seeking help from Social Services or giving up Tammy altogether. She didn't think she would ever get to the point where Tammy would accept her.

Now Tammy's old bed and the tatty wardrobe were all that remained of her old furniture. It didn't look the same in the new flat anyway. It was time to let it go.

'What shall we do with it?' said Monica. 'We could just pile it up outside and ask the council to come and collect it, or,' she paused for effect, 'we could break it apart and ask Liz to help us take it to the dump.'

'I think breaking it apart would be more fun', said Tammy.

'I think you're right,' Monica agreed. 'It's falling apart anyway.'

Tammy ran next door to ask Liz and Sasha if they would like to take part in the ceremonial trashing of the old furniture. Sasha was very keen. She never did anything like this at home. Her parents would definitely disapprove which made it a lot more fun and she couldn't wait to tell them.

Liz went down to the shed and brought back screwdrivers and one of the drills. She had seen Jim using it to put up shelves, to push screws in and remove them when necessary too. She had never used it herself but how hard could it be?

'Flat head or Phillips?' she asked Monica, who didn't have a clue what she was talking about. Liz explained the difference between screw heads.

'Phillips,' Monica replied, once she'd inspected them. She was impressed as Liz set the drill to reverse and used it to loosen the screws which the girls then took out completely with the screwdrivers.

They enjoyed breaking up the wood and carrying it outside, each taking an end and trying to steer each other into obstacles as they went out the door. They ferried drawers and bits of broken panels to the front of the house. When Monica and Liz came out to see where they were putting it they were amazed to find that they had fashioned a seesaw from the broken furniture. They had piled wood in the centre as the cantilever and each sat on one end of the plank from the long side of Tammy's bed to go up and down.

'Can I have a go?' said Monica.

'I wouldn't risk it,' said Tammy seriously.

Liz took the larger pieces to the dump in her car as it was bigger than Monica's and the back seats folded down. Sasha had to sit at the back as the sides of the bed went almost up to the windscreen and Liz had to fold the front seat back to accommodate them. They loaded the smaller broken bits into Monica's car. Tammy wanted to keep the slats that held the mattress in place. She thought that they would make great shelves.

Monica suspected that it would be one of those things

that you never get round to doing but she had room in the garage so agreed.

'You are definitely your mother's daughter,' she said to Tammy.

Chapter 13

It was raining hard on Monday morning. Monica held on until eight fifteen before leaving for work but she couldn't chance leaving any later. She had escaped a formal warning earlier in the year and she didn't want to give them any reason to doubt her commitment now. She was worried that Nick wasn't going to turn up at all but she left her keys with Liz, just in case.

Tammy had already made a dash for Liz's house in between showers. She was sitting at the kitchen table eating toast and drinking tea when the doorbell rang. Nick was standing on the doorstep, soaking wet.

'Sorry I'm late,' he said to Liz, as she invited him in. 'I didn't like to assume I could park on the drive so I found a space around the corner.'

'When the rain stops you can park on Monica's drive,' replied Liz. 'She's not usually home until six at the earliest. Would you like a cup of coffee before you start?' Liz offered.

'I would love one,' Nick replied, as he sat at the table where Tammy was finishing her toast.

'Hello again,' he said, smiling.

'Hi,' said Tammy. Sasha had heard the doorbell and came downstairs in her pyjamas. She said hello to Nick before pouring herself a bowl of cereal and retreating into the living room with Tammy to watch TV.

'How's the garden coming along?' he asked Liz.

'I've changed my mind,' said Liz smiling. 'I have decided against doing the work myself. I am now going to completely revamp it and I have just signed a contract with a company called Fantasy Gardens to redesign the whole thing.'

'Sounds expensive,' said Nick, looking out of the window.

'It is,' said Liz, 'but I think it's worth it.'

'Is that your son?' he asked, pointing to a picture on the windowsill.

'Yes, it is,' Liz picked up the framed photograph of Adam taken at Christmas the year before.

'You don't look old enough to be his mother,' said Nick.

'Thanks,' said Liz, a little unsure. She wasn't used to compliments.

Tammy and Sasha appeared at the door. 'What are we doing today?' they asked.

'We'll settle Nick in so he can get started,' Liz replied, 'and then we'll pot up the Lavender plants for Tammy's project.'

'Great,' said the girls, as they ran upstairs so Sasha could get dressed. Nick finished his coffee and stood up.

'Right, let's get this show on the road. By the way, you wouldn't happen to have a ladder would you?' Liz was surprised that Nick didn't have one but she didn't say anything. She knew, without the need to check that Jim would have at least one and probably two in the garage somewhere, that Nick was welcome to use.

*****

Upstairs in Sasha's room Tammy was lying on the bed with her chin supported in her hands.

'I think Nick really likes your grandma.'

'I think grandma likes Nick too. He seems nice and she looked really happy to see him at the garden centre.'

'Wouldn't it be cool if he asked her out,' said Tammy smiling.

'I'm not sure,' said Sasha. 'I think grandma is too old for a boyfriend.'

'Rubbish,' said Tammy. 'She's too young to be on her own. Would you prefer her to be lonely?'

'Not when you put it like that,' said Sasha. 'It would be nice for her to have a friend but you're forgetting that he may already have a girlfriend, or a wife.' She added dramatically.

'You're right,' said Tammy. 'We need to find out.'

The girls accompanied Liz to let Nick in, Tammy was particularly keen to show him her room.

'I chose the colours,' she said proudly as she picked up the pale green and cream tins of paint.

'Lovely,' said Nick, not convinced. 'The room will be really bright.'

'I want cream on this wall and this one,' said Tammy, pointing to the window and the wall opposite, 'and the

177

green paint on the other two. The ceiling and the paintwork will be white.'

'What colour would you like the alcove?' said Nick, pointing out the fact that it was on a wall that was to be green. 'I think it would look better if we painted the inside cream.' Tammy agreed.

'Well, we'll leave you to get on with it,' said Liz. 'I'll pop in at lunch time with a sandwich, unless you have brought something with you.'

'No, I haven't,' said Nick. 'Anything would be good. It's kind of you.'

'You haven't tasted it yet,' said Liz laughing. 'Thank me when you've eaten.'

Liz and the girls went back to her house. They had serious re-potting to attend to. 'I think we'll need a production line,' said Sasha, her natural bossiness surfacing. 'If grandma takes the cuttings, you and I can fill the pots with soil and plant the Lavender.'

Liz put on her gardening gloves and went outside. She decided to take cuttings from the old plants as they were really straggly now and probably on their last legs anyway. She would think about replacing them when the garden was finished and made a mental note to discuss where to put the new plants with Finn and Devlin for best effect. They would be starting on Monday of the following week and she couldn't wait. She was only sorry that Sasha would be going home and was unlikely to see the finished garden, at least not for a while.

Her mind wandered back to Nick and she blushed at the thought of the compliment. The years had been kind to him too. He was still slim and his hazel eyes twinkled when he smiled. 'He is too young for you,' she said to herself.

'Don't be ridiculous, you're much too old for this nonsense.' She had lost count of the number of snips she had made with the secateurs but she had a little pile of cuttings in a heap on the floor in front of her so she took them back into the house.

The pots full of compost were now lined up on trays on the kitchen table, draining board and side-board. The remaining compost appeared to be scattered all over the floor.

'Great,' said Liz, as she came back in, 'but I think you two will have to sweep up before we continue. I'm not having soil walked all over the house.

'You get the broom,' said Sasha, 'and I'll get the dustpan

'Oh no,' said Tammy. 'You get the broom and I'll get the dustpan.

'Toss for it,' said Liz reaching for a coin. Tammy called and won, Sasha did the sweeping. 'Another new experience,' thought Liz, as Sasha seemed to spread the soil around even more.

'I'm no good at this,' Sasha whined.

'Then you need more practice,' said Tammy laughing.

It seemed to take ages but Liz resisted the urge to help Sasha sweep. It would do her no harm to learn how to do it properly. Besides she was sure that Sasha was making a meal of it so she didn't get asked to do it again. Big mistake. Liz was wise to that and every other trick. What she hadn't learnt from Adam growing up she had picked up teaching the children in school over the years.

Sasha had just finished sweeping while Tammy held the dustpan in place when her mobile rang. 'Saved by the bell,' she said smugly, as she took it out of her pocket.

It was Georgina. 'Hi Darling, how are you?'

'Fine,' said Sasha, in the sad voice she reserved for her mother.

'Are you having a nice time, darling?' Georgina added hopefully.

'It's okay,' said Sasha.

'What have you been up to?' asked Georgina.

'Well,' replied Sasha, in the saddest voice she could muster. 'During the day we work in the garden. After dinner we usually go for a walk around the park and yesterday we smashed up some furniture and took all the wood to the dump. Oh, and today I have to clean the kitchen and then plant a hundred pots of Lavender.'

Georgina was horrified. Sasha sounded so miserable and now she was being forced to do the housework and gardening. She couldn't wait to get home and rescue her.

Liz looked on baffled. It's not that Sasha was lying, because she wasn't. It was just that the way she conveyed the information made it sound as though she had been sold to a sweatshop and forced to do hard labour.

'What was that all about?' asked Liz, when Sasha had

turned off her phone.

'Guilt,' interrupted Tammy. Sasha shot her a look.

'Why the sad voice?' Liz continued in a sterner voice. Sasha stayed silent. She was slightly ashamed that she had answered the phone in front of Liz. She was really enjoying staying with her grandma but that information wouldn't pay for Disneyland.

Liz was not very happy. 'If your mother thinks that you are miserable here I doubt that she will ever let you stay again, not to mention the fact that you are making her worry unnecessarily.' Sasha hadn't thought it through. 'I think the next time she calls you had better make sure you put a happier spin on it.'

'Yes grandma,' said Sasha sulkily.

'OK, let's get on with the planting.'

Once the floor had been swept Liz set about trimming the leaves off an inch of the stem at the bottom of each cutting so they would not be buried in the soil. Sasha and Tammy used a pencil to force a shaft in the centre of each pot where they placed the cuttings before pushing the soil back in around the stems. After the first dozen or so plants had gone in they became quite expert and the production time rapidly sped up.

'You'll have to take them outside to water them and then you will need to cover the pots in something waterproof or your instructions will get too wet and the ink will run. No one will be able to read them.'

'We could use sandwich bags,' said Tammy. 'We have got

loads of them next door.'

'Good idea,' said Liz. 'I think I've got some of the small ones here somewhere too. I don't use them anymore.'

Liz opened various cupboards in the kitchen until she found what she was looking for and the girls went off to the office to print off the instruction sheets. They had made them look very professional. The heading stated 'Help the Bees'.

There were a couple of paragraphs about why we need bees and how they are under threat followed by the instructions on how to care for the plants and when to re-pot them. Finally there was the request to take cuttings and pass them on when the plant got big enough.

'Stage one complete,' said Tammy. 'Now we have to deliver them.'

By the time they had finished it was lunch time, the girls went into the living room to watch television, while Liz made cheese and ham toasties. She made an extra one and took it next door for Nick. When he came to the door his hair looked almost white and his eyelashes and eyebrows had a layer of white dust on them. 'Rubbing down,' he said, by way of explanation. Liz knew what he meant as she was the one that did all the decorating at home. Jim loved the garden but he hated painting and he certainly never got involved in rubbing down if he could help it.

'I've brought you a sandwich,' said Liz, holding out a foil wrapper. 'Better eat it while it's warm.'

'Thank you,' said Nick. 'I appreciate it. I will make sure I bring food with me tomorrow.'

'No need,' said Liz. 'I'll be making something for the girls anyway. How's it going?'

'I should be ready to start painting soon,' he said.

'I can't wait to see it finished. Tammy is really excited,' said Liz. 'Anyway, I'd better get back to the girls. I'll see you later.'

'Thanks again for the sandwich.'

'We're making cakes this afternoon. I'll bring you some later if they are edible,' she laughed.

Liz had bought some cupcake cases and cake mix as a contingency plan. She thought that if the weather was fine they could do a bit more outside and if not they would make cakes. It was still raining so it was plan B. She had never met a child who didn't like to bake. Adam loved making cakes when he was little and she was really happy to have the opportunity to cook with Sasha. Liz asked her if she ever made cakes with her mum at home.

'No,' said Sasha, sadly, 'but I've made loads with Grandma Betty.'

'Mum and I were always baking,' said Tammy. 'It's one of the things I miss. I can't make cakes with Monica. She's on a diet.'

'She won't always be on a diet,' said Liz, 'and anyway, I'm not, so get your pinny on.'

Liz gave aprons to Sasha and Tammy. She knew that if the planting was anything to go by she would need to take precautions to minimise the mess. She got out the food mixer and the weighing scales. The girls grabbed the eggs, butter, sugar and flour. Liz gave them the recipe and let them get on with it. The initial stages of cake mixing went fairly well. The creaming of the butter and sugar in the mixer was relatively calm. The eggs proved to be a bit more difficult with one or two casualties on the floor and the worktop before successfully targeting the mixing bowl.

It was the flour that caused the biggest upset. 'Add the sifted flour gradually,' were the instructions in the recipe. Of course, the girls tried to add it gradually and it would have worked had they turned the mixer off before adding it, but instead they tipped the bowl of flour into the mixture when the mixer was going full pelt. This resulted in everything in the immediate vicinity being smothered in white dust, which included Liz who was attempting to turn the knob on the mixer to slow it down. Just as she did so the doorbell rang.

Liz opened the door to find Nick standing on the doorstep.

'Is this a bad time?' he asked apologetically, looking at Liz who was blinking flour from around her eyes. He laughed at the sight.

'No, no, come in. We were just decorating the kitchen with flour, weren't we girls.' They both stopped giggling for long enough to nod. Nick was still covered in dust but now several specs of white paint, like extra-large freckles, dotted his cheeks and his forehead.

'I wondered if you had a dust sheet, or failing that any

184

old newspapers that I can put down on the floor while I paint the ceiling?' he asked.

'We used to have some,' said Liz. 'They may still be in the garage. I haven't seen them in a while but you're welcome to them if I can find them.'

He followed her out to the garage and stood in the doorway as she looked on the shelves. 'Who's the artist?' he asked, looking at the half finished canvas on the bench.

'Artist is pushing it a bit,' said Liz. 'I dabble, or rather I used to.'

'It's good,' said Nick sincerely. 'You should finish it.'

'I will eventually,' said Liz. 'Ah, here they are.' She pulled at a black bin liner.

'Let me get that,' said Nick, and he stood on a toolbox and lifted the bin liner off the shelf.

'I'll bring them back in a day or so.' He added, 'I'll wash them when I've finished.'

'Great,' said Liz. 'No problem.' Nick went back to decorating and Liz went back to the kitchen.

'You've got flour all over your face,' said Tammy.

'It's probably an improvement,' said Liz smiling. 'It certainly improves you two. You're not allowed to leave this kitchen until you have brushed all that flour off your clothes. I don't want it walked through the house.'

'You too,' said Sasha laughing. Liz looked down. Her navy blue shirt was almost grey.

Monica was outside Liz's house by five but popped in to see Nick before picking up Tammy.

185

'How's it going?' she asked, as she walked through the door, the smell of paint assaulting her nostrils. She opened the kitchen window.

'Good,' said Nick. 'I've done the ceiling and undercoated all the woodwork. I'll give it another coat tomorrow and then start on the walls.'

'How long do you think it will take?' she asked.

'Three days tops,' said Nick.

'That's fantastic,' said Monica. 'I hope you don't mind but I forgot to ask how much you charge. I might not be able to afford you.'

'A hundred and twenty a day,' said Nick, 'as you're a friend of Liz.' He winked.

'Thanks,' said Monica, relieved. When Nick left Monica popped next door.

'How's the decorating going?' asked Liz.

'Great,' replied Monica. 'He'll be finished by Wednesday. I think I'll organise the furniture to be delivered on Thursday. You wouldn't mind letting them in would you, Liz? Nick might be finished. They didn't confirm whether it would be a morning or afternoon slot but apparently if you ring them on the day they'll give you an exact time.'

'It's no trouble,' said Liz. 'Just give me the details and I'll make sure I'm here.'

Chapter 14

The next day Nick arrived at Monica's flat early enough to miss the commuters that parked there to avoid paying to park at the station. He got a spot right outside her house. Monica let him in still wearing her pyjamas and after a cursory hello and the offer of coffee she went off to get dressed. Tammy was as chatty as usual and told him all about her project to help bees before giving him a pot of Lavender to take home.

'I don't even have a window box,' he said, as he tried to think of reasons not to take it with him. He didn't want to be responsible for anything living. He tried to live a life devoid of pets or plants including live yoghurt and watercress. He hated responsibility. It was one of the reasons that both his previous wives had left him.

'You can put it on your window sill. You must have space in your house somewhere.' Tammy argued. Eventually realising that resistance was futile he accepted the plant and the instructions, feigning gratitude as Tammy sat and watched him pull overalls over his trousers.

She studied him for a while longer before asking him how old he was.

'Old enough to look after a Lavender plant,' he said laughing.

'Are you over sixty?' she said, refusing to leave the subject until she got an answer.

'Cheeky. I'm fifty seven,' he said eventually. 'I'll be fifty eight in August.'

'My birthday is in August too, on the fourteenth. When's yours?'

'Twenty eighth,' replied Nick, wondering where this was leading.

'Are you married?' she continued. Nick laughed out loud.

'No, definitely not. No one would have me.'

'Have you ever been married?' She looked serious.

'I've been married twice and divorced twice. Why all the questions?'

'Oh, just curious,' said Tammy unconvincingly. 'Do you have any children?'

'Yes,' said Nick. 'I have a son, a daughter and two grandchildren.'

She suddenly remembered that not married didn't mean not involved so she tagged on an extra question. 'Do you have a girlfriend?'

'No,' said Nick emphatically.

'Good,' said Tammy. Interview over she left him to get on with painting.

Monica made coffee and handed Nick the cup as he stood in the doorway surveying Tammy's bedroom.

'It needs something else,' he said. 'The colours are fine

but it will be a bit bland. I would like to paint something on one of the walls if you don't mind. Don't worry, there will be no extra charge.'

'That's kind of you,' said Monica. 'What are going to paint?'

'I'll think about it,' he said, smiling as he drank his coffee.

It was a gorgeous sunny day as Liz accompanied the girls to deliver the Lavender cuttings to residents in their road and the surrounding neighbourhood. The instruction sheets were neatly folded and attached by a staple to one corner of the sandwich bag. It all looked very professional. Liz had emptied a couple of shoeboxes so the girls could have one each to keep the plants upright as they went on their rounds. Sasha and Tammy walked up and down Liz's road leaving plants on doorsteps before knocking and retreating down the path.

If someone did manage to open the door before they got to the front gate the girls would smile sweetly and explain that the plants were for a school project to help bees. Sasha exaggerated the problem and included the fact that the world would starve if we didn't do something now to protect them. She could be very melodramatic. Most people were very sympathetic and took the plants in, assuring the girls that they would take good care of them. Occasionally someone would reject it out of hand saying they didn't have time, suspicious that somewhere along the line the project would involve parting with money.

As they walked Tammy told Sasha that Nick was not

married and did not have a girlfriend.

'Well, that's something,' said Sasha, 'and how old is he?'

'Nearly fifty eight,' Tammy replied, really pleased with herself.

'He could be fibbing,' said Sasha. 'Lots of people lie about their age. Mum has been thirty five for a few years now.'

'We could look him up on the internet,' said Sasha. 'See what we can find out about him. We can't let Grandma go out with him until we've checked him out.'

'I don't think he has asked Liz out yet,' said Tammy, reeling Sasha back down to earth. 'Besides we need his full name and I didn't ask that bit.'

'I think Liz might know,' said Sasha. 'I heard her tell Monica that she used to work with him so we'll have to ask her later. Anyway, that can wait. At the moment we need ideas for how we can get people to plant Lavender.'

'We could try to get some publicity,' said Tammy hopefully.

'That's it!' said Sasha, excited. 'We need to let people know.' Her eyes opened even wider as she visualised the two of them on breakfast television or Talk Radio, not to mention the effect on her profile on Facebook if the project went viral. Her popularity rating would be through the roof. She suddenly stopped in her tracks. 'We need to contact the press. We'll look into it when we get back.'

Tammy couldn't help but admire Sasha's determination. 'Monica might be able to help you,' suggested Liz. 'She works for a magazine doesn't she? She may know how to put together a press release. Why don't you ask her tonight? I'm sure she'd like to help.'

*****

Nick was getting on well with the painting. He was grateful for the fact that there was no wallpapering involved. He didn't mind painting but wallpapering was not his forte. Liz left Sasha and Tammy writing notes for the press release and popped next door to give Nick a couple of scones she had made the day before.

'It's really coming on now,' she commented, from the doorway. 'When will you be finished?'

'Should be done by Thursday,' he assured her.

'Did you remember to bring food or would you like a sandwich later?' asked Liz.

'I remembered today,' said Nick, pointing to a Tupperware container on the windowsill.

'What have you made? It doesn't look like a sandwich.'

'It's not. You may be surprised to learn that I am a very good cook. I made a curry last night and this is the leftovers.'

'I'm impressed,' said Liz. 'I'm surprised that either of your wives could bear to let you go with your painting and culinary skills,' she laughed.

'The cooking was a necessity. I soon got sick of beans on toast and takeaways. The painting… You've seen nothing yet.'

'Modest too,' added Liz, as she left.

Liz went back to get the girls a snack before the three

of them went out into the garden to carry on weeding. Liz told them that Devlin and Finn were going to start on the following Monday and Sasha was really disappointed that she wouldn't be there to see them. She hadn't spoken to them at all but she already had a little crush on Devlin and she loved the way Finn's personality filled every space despite the fact that he was only a slip of a thing. You couldn't miss him, he was imposing.

'Mum and dad are back on Friday,' said Liz. 'Remember,' she said, looking at Sasha seriously, 'a positive spin if you'd like to stay again.'

'Will do, grandma, I love it here.'

*****

Monica popped in for a coffee after work as usual and Tammy and Sasha collared her as soon as she walked through the door. Sasha wanted to know exactly what she did and how she could help the cause. Monica was not really sure that she could do anything other than possibly advise on the wording for the press release and ring up the local rag to find out who the features editor was.

Sasha was already going global. She thought that they could contact garden centres and ask them to give away plants or provide information on bee friendly gardens. It was hard to believe that Sasha's motives were entirely altruistic but you couldn't fault her commitment. She was already planning on how she could set up the Bury St Edmunds branch of the 'Be kind to Bees Campaign'. All campaigns need a slogan she informed Tammy.

The girls were busy in the office writing the press release. Meanwhile Liz and Monica sat at the table. 'Are you still on for coffee with Kevin on Friday?' Liz spoke quietly.

'I am,' said Monica. 'Ooh, while I think about it can I go up and weigh myself please? I feel certain that I've lost another few pounds.'

'Any time,' said Liz. 'In fact, why don't you take the scales home with you? I haven't used them for years.'

'Thanks, Liz, but I think I'll leave them here. I don't need Tammy starting a daily weigh in. She is obsessive enough about my weight as it is. When I told her the other day that I thought something I was wearing had shrunk in the wash she suggested I take myself to the launderette.' Liz laughed. 'It's like living with Jimminy Cricket.'

Monica came down the stairs grinning. 'I've lost another one and a half kilos. The weight is positively falling off me now.'

'That's fantastic.' Liz was really pleased.

'I think I'm going to have to go and buy new clothes soon. I've gone down a size or more already so I'm running out of things to wear.' Tammy was highly delighted when she heard the news.

They were all in the kitchen now. Sasha was half sitting on Liz's lap.

'It's my last day tomorrow, gran.' She made a sad face. 'Mum and dad are back on Friday.'

'I know poppet,' she gave her a hug. 'How about we all go out tomorrow night? My treat. We could eat somewhere first and then go bowling or skating. 'Bowling,' the girls said together.

'I need more practice. It's Molly's party on Saturday and I'd like to win.'

Monica and Tammy said their goodbyes and popped in to see Nick who was just cleaning the brushes before leaving for the night.

'Don't touch anything in there,' he warned Tammy as she approached the door. 'The paint is still wet. One more day and you'll be able to sleep in your own room again.'

'Thanks, I can't wait,' said Tammy.

'I'll finish up tomorrow.'

'Don't forget your plant.' Tammy noticed that Nick had left it on the windowsill along with his Tupperware box.

'Oh, no,' said Nick. 'Must not forget that.'

*****

Liz had made chilli and instead of eating at the table as they usually did she put the plates onto trays and took them into the living room where Sasha was watching TV. She placed the tray on the side table and moved it in front of Sasha.

'Thanks,' said Sasha, happy to have her grandma all to herself.

'Are you looking forward to going home?' Liz asked.

'Yes and no,' said Sasha. 'I am looking forward to seeing my friends and riding my horse but I have loved being here.'

'I've loved having you here,' said Liz. Neither of them mentioned New York.

Thursday was another bright and sunny day and Nick, who seemed to get earlier every day, was at the door of Monica's house before seven o'clock. Monica was relieved it was the last day although by necessity she set the alarm for six thirty during the week anyway. This week she had been forced to make the effort to actually get up. She had to keep her hand away from the snooze button. She usually hit it once or twice before getting out of bed and trudging around in her pyjamas for half an hour before getting dressed. This morning she had sprung out of bed at the first beep, just in case Nick was early. She caught the alarm before it woke Tammy.

She made Nick a cup of coffee and they both stood cupping their mugs at the doorway to Tammy's bedroom. It looked so different. The ceiling and paintwork were gleaming white and the walls green and cream. Monica had to agree it did look a little bland, but she thought it would look a lot different when the furniture was in.

'Where are you going to add the wall art?' she asked Nick.

'I'm thinking I'd paint a tree on that wall,' he pointed to the wall to the right of the door, 'with a brightly coloured bird of paradise sitting on one of the branches.' There was no window on the wall to break up the space. It was like a huge blank canvass. 'You can hang pictures where the branches are,' he added.

'That's a great idea,' said Monica. 'Tammy has recently picked out some pictures of her mother to be framed.'

'It will be finished by the time you get back from work,' Nick added, 'and if it is not entirely to Tammy's satisfaction I will paint over it at my expense.'

'Confidence,' said Monica. 'I like that. I hope it's justified.' She left Nick painting the alcove as she went off to work and Tammy went next door to Liz.

Liz stayed at home for the morning, just in case Nick finished before the furniture arrived. She got a text message at nine thirty telling her the furniture would be delivered at eleven so she left the girls playing in the garden while she popped next door to see if Nick would be able to let them in.

She was pleased to find him still there. She hadn't said goodbye the day before. He had just finished painting the contrasting colour in the alcove and was about to start the tree.

'Are you here for the day?' she asked.

'Not sure yet. I was hoping to be finished around two thirty,' he replied.

'Did you bring lunch? I've got some leftover chilli if you'd like it.'

'That would be great, thank you,' he said, putting down the paintbrush. 'I forgot to bring food today.'

'The furniture will be here at eleven,' said Liz. 'Are you sure it's not going to be in your way?'

'No,' said Nick. 'I'm only working on this wall now. The rest of the room is all theirs.'

'That's great. Tammy will be so pleased.'

'She's a great kid,' said Nick. 'She gave me a Lavender plant yesterday and made me promise to put it on my windowsill.'

'Yes, it's her project at the moment to help bees. She is very dedicated.'

'Bossy,' said Nick smiling.

'Yes, probably. I think Sasha is rubbing off on her. Anyway, I'd better get back to the girls. I'll pop back around twelve thirty with the chilli, unless you're starving now.'

'No, I don't think I could face chilli for breakfast. I look forward to seeing you later.'

When she got back in she was just in time to take a call from Adam. 'Hiya,' she said with a smile in her voice. 'Are you enjoying yourselves?'

'It's a fantastic place and we have had a great time,' said Adam

'I'm glad,' said Liz. 'Sasha and I have had great fun too.'

'Mum, we get home around ten o'clock tomorrow so should be with you by lunch time.'

'Great,' said Liz. 'I'll get you something ready to eat before you drive home.'

'Thanks, mum, that would be lovely,' he added warmly, before putting the phone down.

When Liz popped back with the chilli at lunch time she was with Tammy and Sasha. On hearing their voices Nick closed the bedroom door. He didn't want Tammy to see the room until it was completely finished.

'Can I look?' she asked, as soon as she came in.

'Not until tonight,' said Nick. 'Let me finish it first. I might not be here when you get back but you can ring me and let me know what you think. Monica has my number. And Liz, I'll pop the ladder and dust sheet back this afternoon if that's okay.'

'No hurry,' said Liz. 'See you later.'

*****

Monica was back from work early so she went to the flat first. She was keen to see Nick's masterpiece before she saw Tammy. Nick was in the kitchen cleaning his brushes and the door to Tammy's room was shut.

'All finished?' she said airily as she breezed in.

'I am,' said Nick. 'Come and take a look.' He put the brushes down and went ahead, opening the door with a theatrical sweeping gesture. 'Ta da!'

'Wow!' She stood at the threshold to take it all in.

The furniture was now in place in the room and although the bed wasn't made up it looked gorgeous. Nick had even put the blind up at the window. The sofa fitted neatly into the alcove and the bed was now framed by a huge stylised tree. Nestling in one of the branches near to the trunk Nick had painted a beautiful bird with long flowing tail feathers in different colours. It looked spectacular. The trunk of the tree grew out from the skirting board on the wall at the bottom end of the bed with the branches leaning up and over towards the headboard.

Monica had tears in her eyes. 'Tammy will love it, I can't thank you enough. I think I'll make up her bed and put down the rug before she sees it. You've done a fantastic job. How much do I owe you?'

'Just pay me for three days,' said Nick. 'The tree is on me.'

'How come you're not busy?' said Monica, tilting her head to one side to get a view of the tree from a different angle. 'You've done such a great job.'

'I'm not a decorator, Monica, I'm a painter.'

'I know,' said Monica, confused as to what the difference was.

'Painter as in artist,' Nick clarified.

'Aaahhh,' said Monica. 'Hence the fantastic tree. I think Liz thinks you're a decorator.'

'I thought that was the case,' said Nick, 'but I don't have much work on at the moment and anyway, I would like to be a friend.'

'My friend or Liz's friend?' asked Monica pointedly. Nick appeared to blush.

'Both,' said Nick, 'but particularly Liz.'

'That's fantastic,' said Monica, really pleased.

'I'm having an exhibition of my work next weekend. I thought I might ask Liz if she'd like to come along to the press preview on Thursday evening so she can see what I really do. You're welcome to come too. Bring Tammy if you can.'

'Unfortunately I've got quite a bit of work on at the moment with a new venture the magazine are planning, so you may get Liz all to yourself,' said Monica smiling. She had no intention of being a gooseberry. Nick left Monica

199

making up the bed and went next door to drop off the ladder and dust sheets.

'Thanks for your help, and the food,' he said, when Liz opened the door.

'No problem. Have you time for a cuppa?'

'No, not today,' he replied apologetically. 'I have to get something sorted out.'

'Oh, well perhaps we'll meet in the garden centre.' She was a little disappointed. She enjoyed talking to Nick.

'I'd like that,' he replied. He paused before adding, 'Liz, I wondered, since you're interested in painting, if you'd like to come to the preview of an art exhibition next week. It's nothing too pretentious, just a few people exhibiting their work. I'll be one of them. It's on Thursday evening.'

'You kept that under your hat,' said Liz. 'I'd like that. Where is it?'

'I have all the information here.' Nick fumbled in his pockets for a flyer, which he was unable to find despite patting down all the pockets in his jacket and jeans. 'Sorry, I must have left it in the car.' He smiled as he asked for paper and pen so that he could write down the address.

'What time?' asked Liz, scanning the paper and not finding the information.

'It opens at seven thirty,' he replied, 'but I'll be there from seven so come as soon as you can.'

'OK,' said Liz. 'Thank you. I will probably see you next week.'

When Monica popped in to collect Tammy Liz told her

about Nick's invitation and the fact that she had more or less accepted but was now having second thoughts.

'Don't panic,' said Monica. 'It doesn't sound like you'll be alone. He's just being friendly. He did mention it to me too but I've got loads of work on. Why not go? You might actually enjoy yourself.'

'He is younger than I am,' said Liz.

'How much younger?' asked Monica.

'I'm trying to work it out, but maybe two or three years.'

'Scandalous,' said Monica teasing. 'That's nothing. Besides you look great together. I don't think anyone will look at the two of you and assume he is your toy boy.' She laughed. 'Anyway, why worry. Life's too short.'

'I'll think about it,' said Liz.

Chapter 15

Tammy was too excited to wait to see her room. As soon as Monica appeared at the door Tammy had grabbed Sasha physically by the hand and ran next door to check it out.

She was stunned. It all looked so beautiful. Monica followed on with Liz who, with Sasha's help, had potted up one of the lavender plants into a coral coloured glazed pot to put on the window sill.

'Nearly done. I can't wait to get my bed back.' Monica smiled at Tammy. 'No more balancing on the edge of the bed while you make like a starfish.' She grabbed the back of Tammy's neck making her squeal. She was very ticklish.

'I love it,' said Tammy. 'Can we move my things back in tonight?'

'Not tonight,' said Monica. 'We are all out tonight. Perhaps Liz and Sasha can help you tomorrow while I'm at work.'

'We could start early. I've got Adam and Georgina coming at midday tomorrow to collect Sasha and hopefully they'll be staying for lunch,' said Liz. Sasha made a sad face and Tammy gave her a hug.

'Don't worry, we'll stay friends. Perhaps you can stay in

the summer holidays.'

'I hope so,' said Sasha, 'or maybe you can come and stay with me. I'll have to work on mum and dad.'

'If anyone can do it, you can,' said Tammy confidently.

Liz went back home, leaving Sasha with Tammy while Monica got ready. When the three of them knocked at the door Monica was grinning.

'Look at this,' she said, holding the waistband of her skirt three inches from her body. 'I'm not even breathing in. I've lost almost two dress sizes.'

'You'll have to be more careful where you put them in future,' said Liz laughing. 'Congratulations. It's really starting to show.'

'Oh, I feel so much better and it's all down to my personal trainer here.' She put her hands on Tammy's shoulders. Tammy did a curtsey.

'Well, where shall we eat? We could go to the pizza place down the road, or would you like Chinese or Indian? What do you fancy?'

'I think it's easier to have a salad or something lighter in a pizza place than an Indian or Chinese.'

'How about Thai?' said Liz. 'The pub up the road does Thai food and children are allowed in until eight. We could go there. You could have a green curry and plain boiled rice. That shouldn't be too bad.'

'Hang on,' said Monica, getting her smartphone out of her bag. 'I've got an app.' She keyed in Thai green chicken curry and rice. 'Three hundred and sixty eight calories. Not bad. I can eat that.'

They all piled into Liz's car. The restaurant was at the back of the pub. Sasha was very accustomed to eating in restaurants but for Tammy it was a rare treat. Apart from family occasions the nearest Tammy got to a restaurant was McDonalds and then only drive through. Sasha and Tammy linked arms like an old married couple, chatting away as if they'd been friends all their lives.

After dinner Liz drove them to the local bowling alley. They decided that they would play in teams rather than as individuals, Tammy and Sasha against Liz and Monica. Sasha was a dab hand but Tammy still needed the bumpers for the first round until she got the hang of it. Liz was the worst player. The others could barely contain themselves as she bowled for the first round and forgot to let go of the ball.

Not surprisingly the girls won, with Monica declaring that Liz was a liability and not sure if Sasha and Tammy hadn't bribed or blackmailed her to be as awful as she actually was. Liz of course denied it. Bruised and aching all over she was keen to opt out of the second game, leaving the girls to play on by themselves.

'You two seem to be getting on really well now,' said Liz, as the girls played another game.

'We are,' said Monica. 'I guess I've got over my fears. It's taken me a while.'

'What were you afraid of?' asked Liz.

'Oh, lots of things. That I wouldn't be good enough, that

I could never be a patch on Joanna, but the worst fear, the one that kept me awake at night, was that I wouldn't be able to love her. I wasn't sure I had it in me.'

'And now?' asked Liz.

'Now I can't imagine my life without her. I love her as much as I would if she were my own.'

'How about your date tomorrow?'

'It's hardly a date,' said Monica, playing it down. 'It's just coffee.'

'Oh, I see. What are you wearing for just coffee?' asked Liz.

'Well, I spent an hour or so last night trolling through my wardrobe to try to find an outfit that made me look less like a barrage balloon.'

'Just for coffee,' Liz laughed. 'Thank God it wasn't dinner. You'd have been there all night.'

Monica ignored the jibe and carried on. 'Eventually I came across a bag with some of my old size fourteen clothes in. Some were still a bit tight but I did find a couple of outfits that fitted me. I settled on a pair of black trousers and a brightly coloured kaftan style top.'

'And you hair?' asked Liz.

'What about my hair?' said Monica.

'How are you wearing your hair? The bun makes you look too serious. Why not wear your hair loose for a change.'

'Have you seen my hair loose?' asked Monica.

'Yes, and it looks great,' replied Liz.

'No it doesn't,' said Monica. 'I look like I've been

electrocuted. Joanna was the only one who could tame my hair.'

'You should let Tammy loose on it. She seems to know a lot about hair,' said Liz.

'Maybe if I get to a second date I'll seek help,' said Monica. 'I'm just going to have coffee and try to relax. How about you? What are you wearing for your date on Saturday?'

'I'm not sure yet but mine is definitely not a date,' said Liz emphatically. 'Nick and I are just friends. Besides, I am a bit too old for dating.'

'You're wrong,' said Monica. 'Life is short. You should eat dessert first. Skip the formalities of dating and move him straight in.'

'You old romantic you,' Liz laughed. 'Besides, I'm sure he just thinks of me as a friend.'

'I hope not,' said Monica. 'You've got too much to offer to be wasting away on your own.'

'Thanks,' said Liz. 'I'm getting there. I don't need to go to the exhibition for any set time so I could wait until you're back if you would like to come,' Liz was hoping.

'No, don't wait. Just go and enjoy yourself. We'll catch up later and compare notes.'

They were home by ten o'clock and Liz and Sasha went straight to bed. Tammy stood at the door of her room having a final look before turning in. The blinds were open leaving just enough moonlight coming through the window to make out the furniture and the tree painted over the bed. 'Can we get some frames for the photographs tomorrow?'

making a mental note of where she would hang each one.

'We'll go on Saturday.' Monica joined her in the doorway. Tammy stood for a second or two more before suddenly turning to Monica and putting her arms around her waist.

'Thank you so much.' She was really happy. Monica was taken by surprise. She closed her arms around Tammy's shoulders and hugged her, fighting back tears. Happy tears.

'You're welcome, it was a pleasure.' She hugged Tammy a little tighter. 'Come on, let's get to bed. I've got to be up early.'

The alarm went off at six but instead of fumbling around for the snooze button as she usually did she snapped the reset button with lightning speed so she didn't wake Tammy before inching her way off the mattress as quietly as she could and heading to the bathroom. She looked in the mirror and took a deep breath before saying to herself. 'You're sexy, sassy and fabulous.' She didn't believe it but she repeated the mantra three more times in the hope that saying it would make it so before jumping in the shower.

She washed her hair and slapped on conditioner. She shaved her legs although she had no idea why. After all, it was just coffee. She didn't usually wear much make up but today she carefully applied eyeliner, mascara, a bit of blusher and lip gloss. She put the makeup in a bag to take to work. It was only six thirty and coffee was at one so she'd need to touch it up during the morning. She slipped on her dressing gown and tiptoed to the bedroom to retrieve her clothes.

While her hair was wet it stayed relatively straight but as it dried it started to spring out at the sides and the top. 'Uuurgg, bloody hair.' She said this out loud. She was tempted to cut it off. Luckily she couldn't think where the scissors were, which was just as well as she would have regretted it. Instead she reached for the Kirby grips and moulded her wayward locks into a bun, teasing a couple of strands of hair out at the sides and back to soften the look. 'That will have to do,' she said to herself.

Unusually for Tammy she didn't wake up until seven thirty and then it was a mad rush as Monica had to leave for work by eight.

Liz and Sasha had been up since seven. Liz had washed most of Sasha's clothes the day before and was busy ironing them in the kitchen before packing them back into her case. Sasha was sitting at the kitchen table playing on her iPad when Tammy arrived.

Tammy had brought her camera with her. She wanted to take some photographs of Sasha so she could put them on her wall. The sun was streaming in through the window. 'Let's go outside and take them in the garden. You can sit by the Lavender.'

'It could be your campaign photo,' piped up Liz.

'Good idea,' said Sasha, before rushing into the bathroom to check on her hair.

Liz took several photographs as the pair of them pulled all sorts of silly faces. The girls then flicked through the images together and decided which ones they liked the best.

Tammy intended to take the memory stick to the shop on Saturday and get the pictures printed.

They exchanged mobile and land line numbers. Sasha had an email address which she gave to Tammy who asked Liz to keep it safe. Liz promised to sort out an email address for Tammy so they could exchange pictures and keep in touch.

Sasha was still hoping for Disneyland at the end of May. She promised to invite Tammy although she hadn't been able to work on her parents long enough to guarantee that it would be Paris. She didn't want to lose touch although she knew it was a real possibility with New York looming large on the horizon. She hadn't mentioned it to Tammy. She really didn't want to go.

The morning seemed to fly by and before long Adam and Georgina were standing in the hallway looking bronzed and relaxed. Sasha rushed out to give them both a hug. Adam swooped her up in his arms and kissed her on both cheeks. Sasha pretended to be embarrassed and, shrieking with laughter, wiped her hands over her face to rub off the kisses. Tammy looked on, a little jealous of the fuss that Adam made of his daughter.

Georgina bent over to give Sasha a kiss. Anything more animated would have left her creased. Adam gave his mum a big hug too. He was really pleased to be back. Georgina said hello to Liz and then came towards Tammy to greet her. She was about to put her hands on Tammy's arms so that she could plant her customary air kisses on either side of Tammy's face. Tammy was having none of it. She grabbed one of Georgina's hands and shook it vigorously. 'Hiya,' she said as she did so. Georgina looked a bit ruffled.

She then turned her attention to Liz who had also decided against the air kissing fiasco and instead just said hello without moving from the spot. There was an embarrassing pause before Liz urged them to sit down and ushered them into the living room. Adam and Georgina sat together on the large sofa with Tammy and Sasha linking arms on the chair opposite while Liz made tea.

'Come and sit here sweetie,' said Georgina, patting the cushion next to her.

'I'm fine here mummy,' said Sasha, refusing to budge.

Georgina couldn't wait to get Sasha outside where she could interrogate her thoroughly about her terrible ordeal.

'Mummy, I'd like Tammy to come and stay with us.'

'Of course,' said Adam enthusiastically, 'that would be great.' Georgina said nothing. She had worked hard to make sure her children mixed with the right people and she didn't include Tammy in her definition of the right people, or Liz for that matter.

Adam had bought a couple of presents on the plane coming home to give to Liz and the girls. He'd bought perfume for Liz. He had no idea which perfume she liked but he bought the most expensive one they had for sale. He had bought Sasha and Tammy a necklace and bracelet each. Tammy was delighted but Sasha knew better. This was just the token gift. The real one was in the suitcase.

Liz had prepared lunch for all of them but Georgina didn't want to stay. She said she had a headache and couldn't wait to get home. Adam looked uncomfortable, especially as Liz had gone to the trouble of making Lasagne and salad, but Georgina was adamant that the headache was escalating to a migraine and would only get worse. Adam was not happy but he didn't want the embarrassment of an argument with her in front of his mum and the girls so he acquiesced and got up to leave.

Georgina was already standing at the front door as Adam said goodbye to Tammy and gave his mum another hug. Sasha promised to ring her new friend as soon as she got home.

'Thank you, grandma,' she said to Liz. 'I've had a wonderful time.'

'Me too sweetie,' said Liz, squeezing her a little tighter. Georgina choked out a thank you to Liz, trying to make it sound as if she genuinely meant it, before reaching to take Sasha's hand.

Sasha turned away and ran back to her grandma to give her an extra-long hug. She knew that she might not see her again for a very long time. Adam promised to pop in one evening after work. Liz and Tammy stood at the front door and waved them off with Sasha turning round and waving and blowing kisses until they were out of sight.

'Come on,' said Liz to Tammy. 'We've got a lot of lunch to eat.'

Chapter 16

When Monica arrived at work she felt self-conscious. Out of her protective uniform of smart suit and court shoes she felt vulnerable.

Nadia was new to the company. She had only worked on the main reception desk in the building for a month or so and seemed to know everyone already. She was particularly nosey. 'Eeewwww, where are you going?' she remarked, as Monica waited for the lift.

'Nowhere,' said Monica defensively. Nadia was around the same age as Monica but much taller and slimmer. She was always immaculately turned out with bright red lipstick and long talons to match. Monica wondered how she managed to do any typing, not that she'd ever seen her typing for that matter. 'Just feeling a bit yuk,' she replied.

'I know what you mean,' said Nadia. 'A bit of lippy gives you a lift. You should do it more often, it suits you.'

'Thanks,' said Monica smiling. She felt better.

At twelve thirty she was in the toilets trying to touch up her makeup with the aid of a small handbag mirror perched on the side of the basin nearest the window. The mirror in the ladies was distorted somehow in that you had to move your head up and down to get the whole picture, plus the light was terrible. She wasn't used to wearing much makeup either and her eyesight was not great. At the first attempt she only managed to apply the mascara to the lens of her reading glasses. By twelve forty five she'd given up and instead applied a little blusher and more lip gloss.

She was grateful for the fact that there was no full length mirror in the ladies toilets. She made a point of not looking at herself in full length mirrors at all, preferring to see herself in small sections. She liked the mirrors in shoe shops that only showed you how you looked from the knees down. The bathroom mirror at home was just above the basin so you could only see from the waist up. She could go days without seeing her bottom half reflected anywhere at all.

She began to wish that she had worn her work clothes. After all, when she had met Kevin she was wearing work clothes. It was almost as if the smart jackets and skirts were like armour and she could play the part of professional business woman.

She regretted choosing something casual. She didn't suit casual. Besides, she didn't want Kevin to think she had made an effort, although obviously she had.

She got to the coffee shop just gone one o'clock and went inside. Kevin was nowhere to be seen. She looked at her watch. He had definitely said one. It was only a couple of minutes past so no need to panic yet. She walked up to the counter as confidently as she could, ordered a skinny latte and sat on the armchair backing onto the wall near the window so she was facing the door.

At ten past one there was still no sign of him. An elderly man came into the coffee shop and ordered a cup of tea and a slice of carrot cake. He sat on the empty chair on the other side of Monica and though she was tempted to say it was taken, she didn't because she was conscious of the fact that Kevin may not turn up at all and then she'd be embarrassed.

She got out her mobile phone and began scanning her emails as if sitting by herself in coffee shops was something she was used to doing. She tried to look relaxed although she felt anything but. She was convinced that everyone in the coffee shop knew she had been stood up and were feeling sorry for her. She had almost finished her coffee and was about to leave when a very embarrassed and breathless Kevin was suddenly standing in front of her.

'I'm so sorry,' he began. 'I ran all the way. I was worried that you would have left by the time I got here. I had to finish a rush job and hadn't realised how long it would take me to get here from work. I would have called but I don't have your number. I was praying you would still be here.'

'Don't worry,' said Monica, relieved that she hadn't been stood up and giving a 'See, I'm not a desperately sad case' smug look to the other patrons in the coffee shop.

'Can I get you another one?' he said hopefully.

'Sure,' said Monica. 'I'm in a very boring meeting this afternoon. It will help keep me awake.' She didn't want to sound too keen.

He laughed and joined the queue. Monica had spotted a

couple who were just leaving and indicated to Kevin that she was going to nab the table. She picked up her coat and handbag and moved nearer to the back of the coffee shop. She watched him as he waited for the coffee at the counter.

His hair was longer than it had been when they first met but he still had the same easy manner and friendly face. He looked a little bit like a younger version of Jamie Oliver but with slightly darker hair.

She wished she'd started dieting earlier or that she had worn one of her suits. She felt more confident in a suit. She tried not to look too keen as he came over to the table carrying the coffees. He smiled as he sat down.

She hoped that he hadn't noticed the makeup, she didn't want him to think that she had made the effort just for him.

'You look different,' he said, as he pushed the coffee glass towards her.

'I am trying to lose weight,' she said smiling.

'I've never met a woman who was happy with her weight,' he said, 'but you look great.'

Monica blushed. She felt uncomfortable with compliments. 'Thank you, but I can't lend you any money until pay day.' She forced a smile.

'No, it's your hair,' he said after a while. 'I'm sure when I worked at Gibson's you had auburn hair.' Monica blushed again but this time it was the memory of the auburn wig. She promised herself she would throw it away when she got home.

'Oh, that was a long time ago,' she glossed over. She

laughed out loud.

'What's funny?' he asked.

'I was just remembering when we met,' she said.

'Ah yes. Induction.' They laughed as they remembered how they had found themselves sitting next to each other in the meeting room where all the new staff had been gathered to learn about the internal procedures and practices of Gibson Media. After the initial get to know your neighbour exercises they knew they were sharing a table with Ann, Purchase Ledger, Bob, Facilities and Estates and Anita, Readers Letters and Horoscopes.

They got on particularly well as Kevin had a wicked sense of humour and made the rest of them laugh their way through the most boring bits by initiating a game which involved them all writing down the title of a film, TV programme or song on a piece of paper and then passing it to the person on their right. The winner was the first person to work their title into the discussion or question and answer session at the end of each talk.

Monica had marvelled at the fact that Kevin seemed to win most of the time with phrases like, 'Surely no one would make such a Titanic mistake,' or 'things like that are a Basic Instinct.' He had come completely unstuck during the talk by the Finance Department on purchase orders when he tried to get Ghostbusters into the discussion. The Head of Finance thought he was an idiot but Ann from Purchase Ledger nearly wet herself laughing and had to leave the room.

She had initially thought he was gay. No heterosexual man she had ever met was so well turned out. There was never a hair out of place, and his hands always looked so neat with perfectly manicured nails, which is probably why they got on so well. There was no pressure. It was only after a month or so that he mentioned his girlfriend, Alice, who was apparently moving in.

This piece of information had consigned her to the friend zone. Pushier women with romantic inclinations would have gone for it anyway but to Monica, Alice made Kevin off limits. As far as she was concerned he now had a barbed wire fence surrounding him with machine gunners on the turrets.

'How is Alice?' Monica asked, vocalising her thoughts. She hated Alice. She had never met her but she hated her for being the object of Kevin's affection.

'You've got a good memory,' he said, nearly choking on his coffee before stuttering through an explanation of how they were no longer together. Monica thought she noticed him blushing.

'Alice and I parted company a long time ago.'

'I'm sorry,' said Monica, but inside her head mini Monicas were punching the air shouting, 'yes, yes, yes'.

'I often thought of you,' said Kevin. 'I imagined that you would be married with kids yourself by now.'

She laughed a nervous laugh. She would not mention Tammy at all until he was completely under her spell.

He glanced at his watch. 'One forty. Oh, I'm sorry, I've

made you late for your meeting.' He stood up. Monica was about to say 'What meeting?' when she remembered her earlier excuse, just in case she didn't like him as much as she used to. The problem was that she did like him as much as she used to and now she would have to rush off.

'Do you think we could meet for dinner next time?' he added hopefully.

'That would be great.' said Monica, the mini Monicas running round in circles in her head swapping high fives. They exchanged mobile numbers and Kevin promised to email her later. He pecked her on the cheek before parting.

She felt lighter walking back to work, buzzing from the lack of food and the caffeine overload. How would she be able to concentrate on work? She sat at her desk, staring into space, and deeply regretted making an excuse to curtail lunch.

When Joanna was alive they had often discussed their ideal man. They had both agreed that it would be the sexiest thing in the world to have a boyfriend who could play an instrument or sing. Preferably play and sing. That was partly the reason for Joanna's attraction to Max. He played guitar in a band. It was also the reason he didn't stick around. He was certain he was destined for greatness. Eleven years on she still hadn't seen his name anywhere to indicate that he was any nearer to his ambition.

*****

Liz had promised Monica she would help Tammy move all her things back to her bedroom now the room was finished.

They brought the boxes in from the living room and Liz put clothes on hangers and hung them in the wardrobe while Tammy folded up her tops and bottoms, separating school clothes from other clothes as she put them away in the drawers. She then filled the shelves with her DVDs, books and CDs and placed her jewellery box on top of the desk.

After they had finished Tammy pulled out the box of family photographs to show Liz. 'Your mother was very beautiful.' Liz was holding a picture of Joanna and Monica at Tammy's christening. 'You look just like her. I nearly didn't recognise Monica with her hair down.'

'Mum did it. She was brilliant with hair and make-up.' Tammy's face was animated. 'Mum just liked people. I miss her so much. I wish I could talk to her to tell her about my project and you and Sasha.' Liz gave her a hug.

'When my Jim passed away I used to talk to him constantly. I gave a running commentary on everything I did. I think I spent so much time on my own I just needed to hear my voice out loud. I was scared that I would lose the ability to speak.'

'I used to have nightmares' said Tammy. I would dream that I was on my way to school and would catch a glimpse of mum just up ahead in the crowd. I would run after her as fast as I could, shouting for her to stop, but she was always just out of reach, too far ahead or disappearing around a corner. It was so real.'

'Do you still have dreams like that?'

'No, not for a while now, in fact I think I would like to go to the cemetery to plant something on mum's grave. I didn't take anything for Mothers' Day. Will you take me?'

'Of course,' said Liz, 'but I think we should give Monica a call to see if she would like to come too.' Liz dialled the number. Monica was actually quite pleased that Tammy wanted to go to the cemetery and didn't mind Liz taking her at all.

'Do you think she'd like Lavender?' asked Liz. 'I've still got some in pots, or would you prefer to go to the garden centre on the way.'

'No, she would love Lavender. I'll get my tools.' They finished putting everything away. Tammy picked up her backpack before they popped next door so Liz could grab the plant and her car keys.

The sun was still shining when they arrived at the cemetery. Liz parked her car at the entrance and took the Lavender out of the boot. Tammy had only been to the cemetery twice, once for the funeral itself and then once with Monica just before Christmas to bring a holly wreath.

The cemetery looked so different in sunlight. Tammy led Liz to where half a dozen plaques were set on a sunny bank. They all had flowers planted around them apart from one. Tammy walked towards a plaque where a faded Christmas wreath lay next to a fresh sheath of flowers which she guessed were from Monica. She hesitated before approaching.

'We brought that, me and Monica,' Tammy pointed to

the wreath. 'We wanted to make it look nice for Christmas. I didn't really want to come,' she continued, 'but I felt I had to.' Liz put her arm around Tammy's shoulders.

'You don't have to come here to prove you love your mum,' said Liz. 'She knows. I'm sure she's always in your heart.'

'I didn't think I'd ever be able to come here,' said Tammy. 'How do you talk to Jim?' she asked.

'In my head,' said Liz. 'I say all the things I want to say in my head, especially if there are people around. You get some very funny looks talking to yourself but you can say them any way you want to. Write them down if you like. There is no right or wrong way.'

Tammy knelt on the ground in front of the plaque. She got the tools out of her back pack and Liz placed the plants on the ground. She then carefully dug a hole on one side of the plaque and then, holding the Lavender at the base of the stem, turned the pot upside down and shook the plant free. She placed the ball of earth into the hole and pushed the soil in around it.

'Very professional,' said Liz. 'I'll go and get some water.' Liz went off to fill the bottle. Tammy ran her hand over the small marble plaque and as she did so she spoke softly to her mother.

'I don't know if you can see me,' she began, 'but we have moved into a new flat. I have got a big bedroom there and Monica has just had it decorated for me. Nick, he's the painter, painted a big tree over my bed and we are going to hang photographs from the branches. You would love it, Mum. It's just like something you would have made.

'I'm sorry I haven't been here much but I didn't know what to say to you. I came today with my new friend Liz. She is the lady who lives next door. You might know her husband, Jim, Jim Bailey, he's been here five years. He likes gardening. I am helping Liz in her garden.'

'You probably know this already but I am doing really well at school. We get our end of term report in July and I'll bring mine here to read it out to you so you can see for yourself how I'm getting on.

'Lastly, I don't know if you can help but I'd like Monica to meet someone. She needs a husband. I don't want her to be lonely like Liz.'

Liz was just coming back with the water. It was quiet in the cemetery apart from the occasional bird or car horn in the distance and although Tammy spoke quietly Liz heard Tammy say that she was lonely. She sat on the bench with the water until Tammy had finished speaking. She didn't want to interrupt.

She felt odd, not quite sad but something she couldn't define. It was strange to see yourself through someone else's eyes. Lonely, she didn't feel nearly as lonely as she used to feel but she obviously still gave the impression she was lonely to other people. Why couldn't Adam see that? She vowed to make more effort with friends and family. 'I will go to the art show,' she said out loud, 'and damn Adam.' She was suddenly conscious of the fact that Jim

222

might be listening so added, 'Nick's just a friend.' Tammy gave her a sideways glance, the way you would if someone was a bit odd.

Chapter 17

Monica couldn't wait to tell Liz all about her encounter with Kevin. Luckily Tammy was busy on the computer emailing Sasha when Monica arrived so she was able to sit in the kitchen and talk to Liz without interruption.

'He was late,' said Monica quietly, not wanting Tammy to hear. 'I thought he was going to stand me up. I felt really self-conscious in the coffee shop, cupping my latte and pretending to read my non-existent messages. Just as I was going to give up and leave he was there, standing in front of me apologising.'

'Is he single?' said Liz, cutting to the chase.

'He is,' said Monica, hardly able to contain herself. 'He split up with his girlfriend ages ago and he wants to take me out to dinner.'

'Wow,' said Liz. 'This is progress. And are you going to go?'

'Yes,' said Monica. 'I am going to seize the day. It's not often you get a second chance.'

'That's my girl,' said Liz, really happy for her. 'You don't need to worry about Tammy. She can always stay with me.'

'Oh, Tammy,' Monica's face changed. The beaming smile disappeared. 'What about Tammy? Do I tell her? Do I wait?'

'I don't think you need to worry about Tammy,' said Liz, as she relayed the chat at the cemetery. 'She is keen for you to find someone to love. She doesn't want you to be lonely.'

'That settles it,' said Monica. 'I will meet up with Kevin for dinner and see how it goes. Anyway, back to you. Have you decided to go on Thursday or are you still dithering?'

'I am going,' said Liz, 'although I would feel better if you were going too. I get on well with Nick but I haven't been out with anyone other than Jim. Besides, I am sure I'm too old for him. I think his last wife was several years his junior and I must seem positively ancient, although I really don't feel old.'

'You don't look old,' added Monica.

'Thanks. You will be pleased to know that I have promised myself to make an effort and get out and about more. I might even go back to the gym.'

'What will you do at the gym?' said Monica, assuming yoga or Pilates.

'Fight gravity,' said Liz.

'Great idea,' Monica agreed. 'I might come with you.'

Meanwhile Tammy had told Sasha that Nick had asked Liz to go to the art exhibition. Sasha was really excited. She liked the prospect of Liz being with Nick. She hardly knew Grandpa Jim anyway so she didn't really miss him.

'Grandma smiles more when Nick's around. Have you noticed?' Tammy didn't miss much and had observed Nick paying close attention to Liz whenever she spoke. He also laughed a lot when they were together which is why she thought that they would be perfect together.

*****

Saturday morning was bright and sunny but with a slight nip in the air. Monica and Tammy were up and out early as Tammy wanted to buy a present for Molly and Monica promised Tammy a new outfit to wear for bowling.

Liz was also thinking about shopping for clothes. She hadn't actually bought anything new since before Jim had died. This would not have been so bad were it not for the fact that she had lost over a stone in the first few weeks after his death which she had never managed to regain. She couldn't have cared less and was happy to disappear inside dark coloured clothes that hung loosely on her small frame. But now there was nothing for it, she had to go shopping.

She had always hated shopping for clothes and had avoided it unless absolutely necessary. On the rare occasions that she had to buy an outfit it usually took several attempts, with the first forays resulting in shoes or a handbag, sometimes both. She decided to take the tube up to the West End and look in the big department stores.

It had been ages since she'd been on a train, not since working at the school. She was grateful for the fact that she could get a seat. There were only three other people in the carriage at the start of the journey. By the time she arrived at Oxford Circus it was ten o'clock and the train was bulging fit to burst, she was worried that she would be stuck in her seat and forced to go on to the next stop. Luckily loads of people were getting off and forged ahead towards the exit, blazing a trail so Liz was forced out with the throng.

She had forgotten how much she hated shopping uptown. It was crowded and dirty and she worried about her handbag. She wished that she had brought one with a longer strap so that she could wear it like a sash across her shoulder rather than tucked up under her arm as she had it. She pushed her way along the pavement to the first big store she came across and walked in. This was an oasis of calm compared to the melee outside; although still fairly busy considering that it was still only ten fifteen.

She must have looked a bit bewildered when she walked into the ladies wear department as she was immediately approached by a smartly dressed shop assistant. The navy blue suit reminded Liz of an air hostess. 'Can I help you, madam?' she said with a smile.

'I don't know,' said Liz, feeling completely out of her depth. 'I'm not really sure where to start.' Liz explained her dilemma to the shop assistant whose name was Kirsty according to the badge on her lapel.

'I have the perfect solution,' she said to Liz reassuringly as she went off to enlist the help of a colleague. Five minutes later Kirsty was back with Ali, whose name was underlined with the words Personal Shopper. Ali was tall and slim and incredibly glamorous with a perfectly made up face and, although wearing the same blue uniform as Kirsty, the jewellery and scarf strategically placed made Ali's uniform smarter still. She looked stunning. Liz was about to protest but decided against it. This might just be the answer.

Ali was indeed a very personal shopper. She asked Liz about the occasion, the colours she liked and disliked and her budget. Liz hadn't thought about budget. She had no intention of buying anything from the more expensive designer brands in the shop but what the hell. She hadn't bought anything at all for the last four years, bar underwear. She was owed a bit of a spree.

Ali walked around the store with Liz, picking out things that Liz would never have considered in a million years and all the time talking about lines and this season's colours and statement jewellery. Liz settled on half a dozen items and headed for the changing room, convinced that none of it was suitable, while Ali paced up and down outside the changing room like an expectant father.

Liz tried on the first dress. It was sleeveless with slightly cut away shoulders. She would never have considered a dress without sleeves but Ali was convinced that this dress would accentuate her long neck. Liz had never thought much about her neck before but she had to agree when she looked in the mirror. The fitted dress was really flattering and the cut away shoulders did indeed make her arms and her neck look longer. Teamed with the matching bolero cardigan she looked okay. Actually she looked better than okay

The second outfit of navy fitted trousers and patterned silk shirt looked fantastic with the olive green coat that Ali popped around the changing room door. Liz looked at herself in the mirror. 'Not bad at all,' she thought, as she surveyed this new version of herself. Ali continued to fawn a bit and Liz wondered if the personal shoppers worked on commission. Not that it mattered. Ali was very good at her job and without exception Liz really liked the outfits she came up with.

Two hours and seven hundred and forty pounds later Liz left the shop with four large shopping bags. Luckily she didn't need shoes or handbags as she still had loads of those at home. Although she hadn't worn anything higher than a two inch heel since her teaching days she still had a cupboard full of shoes just waiting to be pressed into service.

*****

Monica also had a very successful morning. Tammy had bought Molly some nail varnish and a One Direction CD, plus a birthday card and wrapping paper. 'Are you sure Molly wears nail varnish?' said Monica. Tammy's look said it all. She didn't need to speak. It was one of those 'Have you been on another planet' looks. Obviously Monica didn't understand eleven year olds. 'You're all in too much of a hurry to grow up,' she said to Tammy, thinking to herself that she sounded just like her mum.

Tammy tried on skinny jeans, denim shorts and cute tops with sparkly bits, the bright colours looking fantastic against her cappuccino coloured skin. Monica felt a flush of pride as she watched her posing in front of the mirror. They picked out a couple of outfits before moving on to the underwear department.

Tammy couldn't wait to wear a bra although she really didn't need one. Apparently all the girls in her class were wearing them. Monica resisted the balconettes and padded bras that Tammy insisted on picking up and instead chose a couple of very sedate starter bra and brief sets in pastel colours.

'You're almost eleven, not sixteen,' she pointed out, as Tammy pouted her disapproval of Monica's choice.

Finally they bought some picture frames and headed home. Monica was surprised at how good she felt even after three or four hours shopping, which was just as well with bowling scheduled for the afternoon.

*****

Liz had taken a taxi home. She was feeling extravagant but, more so, she couldn't face walking up the hill from the station with her bags in tow. She had forgotten how much hard work shopping for clothes could be.

Monica and Tammy were in a rush but popped in briefly so Liz could see Tammy all dressed up for the party.

'Wow, you look so grown up.'

Tammy did a twirl and looked very pleased with herself.

'Wait, I have to take a picture.' Liz ran into the kitchen and snatched up the camera. Tammy stood still and smiled as Liz clicked. 'Now both of you,' said Liz as Monica and Tammy arranged themselves in the doorway, Tammy almost as tall as Monica and jostling for position as Liz snapped.

Once Monica and Tammy were on their way Liz put

the kettle on and thought about contacting her friends. It was three years or more since she had cut herself off completely. They had tried to stay in touch but she didn't bother taking calls or replying to emails, she just wanted to cocoon herself in her memories and not let the outside world in. They gradually stopped trying. Liz was nervous. She wasn't sure if she would be welcome and she had some apologising to do. She poured the tea and sat down at the computer.

*****

Tammy had a wonderful time bowling. Monica marvelled at how grown up her classmates were with some of the girls looking like teenagers already. She thought about Tammy's impending birthday party and how she was going to keep the whole class entertained and briefly considering employing their class teacher who had complete control of them.

The background music at the bowling alley decided her. She would hire a disco. She talked about the idea of a disco to Tammy who was really keen and straight on the phone to Sasha, followed by Molly and Lauren. No decision could be finalised without first conferring with the other inbetweenies. Monica made a note to talk to Liz about it in the week.

*****

Sunday dragged lazily. Liz considered working in the garden but there really was no point as Finn and Devlin would be starting work on Monday. She needed to talk to them before planting anything.

Instead she got the easel out of its box and searched out the watercolour paper and paints before setting the easel up in the garden.

She walked around the garden, settling on a spot to sketch before attempting to paint. Looking up for a second from her pad she briefly had a flashback of Jim in the garden but he wasn't clutching his chest as she usually pictured him. Instead he was leaning on his shovel surveying the lawn. She didn't look away. She just smiled to herself and looked beyond the image in her mind's eye to the Lavender where bees were busying themselves on and off the flowers. She started to draw.

Chapter 18

Devlin and Finn arrived at seventy three Elm Close at eight thirty on Monday morning. When Liz opened the door she was greeted by the sight of Finn resplendent in lime green skinny jeans tucked into floral wellington boots. Unusually for him he was sporting a very ordinary looking, outsized grey sweatshirt on top of a white tee shirt.

'I'm ready to work,' he exclaimed, as Liz invited him in. Finn stood to one side in the hall as Devlin followed him in, wearing his trusty crumpled chinos and today, brown no nonsense work boots.

'God, it's cold today,' Finn remarked, as Liz was about to shut the door. 'Wait,' shouted Finn. 'There's more.'

Coming up the path was another man around six feet tall with a sturdy frame and rugged face. He looked to be around the same age as Finn and Devlin but there the similarities ended. He was not nearly as neatly dressed or self-contained. In fact he looked like he had slept in his clothes.

The man nodded to Liz as he came through the door and pushed out his hand for Liz to shake. 'Rory,' he said, in a soft Irish accent, shaking her hand vigorously.

'This is our assistant. He'll be helping us dig up and lay the paths,' said Finn by way of explanation.

'Yes, that's me. Navvy to the queens,' said Rory with a wink.

'He means us,' said Finn laughing.

'You know who you are,' said Rory, laughing louder. 'Lizzy and Mary over there.' He winked again at Liz.

Devlin raised his eyes and shook his head slightly in disapproval before going through to the kitchen. Finn trotted gaily behind.

Liz scanned the area outside her house to see if any of her neighbours had noticed them arrive. There was no one around but even if they had managed to slip in unnoticed no one could miss the van parked outside Liz's house, painted grass green and emblazoned with Fantasy Gardens in pink on every panel.

'Tea?' asked Liz, as she closed the front door.

'I'm dying for a cuppa,' said Finn theatrically.

'Yes please, no sugar,' added Devlin.

'Me neither,' said Rory. 'I'm sweet enough.'

Liz smiled. She could see it was going to be fun having the three of them around. They all went out to the garden and Finn was soon engaged in deep and meaningful conversations with Devlin as Rory started to plot out where they needed to dig.

'Can we use the side entrance?' he shouted to Liz as she came outside with a tray.

'Yes, of course,' said Liz. 'I'll get the key.' She was grateful that they wouldn't be trudging their muddy boots through the house.

'Great,' said Rory, before shouting out to Finn, 'Have you got the digger coming?'

'I have, sweetie,' Finn replied, teasing Rory. 'Don't worry, you won't have to ruin your nails with the pick and shovel.'

Liz glanced at Rory's nails. He looked as though he'd been digging for potatoes with his bare hands already.

Liz placed the tray on the garden table. 'Help yourself,' she called, before turning to go inside. Rory and Devlin were marking out the garden with chalk and bits of string.

'Liz,' said Finn, 'can I borrow you for a few minutes?'

'Of course,' said Liz, turning around.

'I need you to walk around the garden with me and decide what's staying put, what's being moved and what will be going to that great compost heap in the sky.' He linked arms and led her around the garden.

Finn had a system. He used different coloured ribbons and stickers. Red was staying, orange was moving and yellow was going. Rory would be pulling up all the plants with yellow ribbons or stickers on and adding them to the compost heap with what remained of the lawn. He then pointed out the spots where they would be building tiered planting areas. He didn't like boring flat gardens. His vision included creating different levels of interest. 'Little hills of heaven,' he explained. 'Trust me, darling,' he added when they had finished their tour.

The forecast promised dry weather for the next few

235

weeks which meant that there would be no down time.

Liz talked to Finn and Devlin about the planting scheme, stressing her wish for a Lavender border somewhere in the garden and giving them the list of bee friendly plants they were to keep, as Tammy had instructed. Happily, Finn was a fan of the industrious little insects, which would please Tammy.

Rory proved to be a great all-rounder. Not only could he work the digger with crack-shot accuracy he would eventually be running the electric cables up the garden for the lighting and dismantling the shed. But not before he had helped Liz box up all the tools and move them to the garage which now contained everything except the car. Tammy was home from school by three thirty and couldn't believe the change in the garden, which now resembled a bomb site.

Ribbons abounded on most of the plants and deep trenches had been dug in the ground to accommodate gravel paths and block paving. Without a shred of shyness she rushed out to say hello to Finn, who made a big fuss of her.

'Can I help?' she asked. 'I've got my own tools.' She pulled out her floral fork and trowel.

'Definitely,' said Finn. 'You can start here.' He took her over to a section of the garden where some of the smaller plants had orange ribbons on them. 'We are moving these, sweetie, so they need to be dug up and put in here.' He pointed to a wooden crate next to the flower bed. 'You need to keep a good root ball,' he explained, before getting down on his knees to demonstrate and then watching while Tammy did the first one. 'Remember, only the orange ones,' he said as he moved to help Rory.

Liz kept them all supplied with refreshments, sandwiches and doughnuts. She learned that Devlin was very into health and fitness and therefore resisted doughnuts and coffee, instead preferring fresh orange juice and salads for lunch. Finn would occasionally waft the hot bacon rolls or doughnuts under his nose to tease him. Devlin smiled indulgently at Finn before tucking into his couscous and vegetable medley.

'It's alright for you,' he would moan. 'I have to watch my weight. You can eat like a horse and still look like a stick insect.'

'You're only jealous of my fast metabolism and sylph like figure,' Finn would counter. 'Anyway, you eat like a stick insect and look like a horse.'

Whenever they bickered too much Rory would intervene, like a marriage guidance counsellor or referee, and tell them both to shut up. This always had the desired effect as they would then both start on Rory who knew exactly what he was doing. In the end they would all be laughing and the good humoured teasing would continue for the rest of the day.

Liz loved having them there. It was a breath of fresh air. The garden was taking shape and looking better every day and the fun they had spilled over to Liz and Tammy, who would spend most of the time laughing at their banter. Tammy couldn't wait to get home from school to get out in the garden to help Finn. Devlin didn't usually stay for the whole day, preferring to direct operations and then leave to prepare plans for other jobs.

By Thursday all the digging was done and the concrete base for the summer house had been laid. A huge skip was delivered and took up most of the space outside Liz's house, filled to the brim with wheelbarrow loads of earth and turf and wood from the old grey shed. Large lorries deposited huge bags of gravel and sand followed by low loaders with grabbers which dropped pallets of bricks and slabs onto the drive.

The new summer house arrived mid-morning. It looked nothing like a summer house but Liz was assured that when Rory had worked his magic she would be dazzled at the spectacular sight of it. Finn never used one word when ten would do. It still had a way to go but Liz could see that Devlin's design was taking shape and she was promised she would really be able to see a difference the following week when the summer house was erected and the new plants started to go in.

When Tammy got home from school Liz was in a tizzy. She had been trying on outfits for the art exhibition. She didn't want to look as though she had tried too hard. There was nothing effortless about effortless glamour. Liz decided it was either something you had or didn't have, and she didn't have it.

'Let's face it,' she said to herself, 'I've reached the age where it takes three times as long to look half as good.'

'You look great for your age,' said Tammy helpfully. Liz smiled but didn't really believe it.

'I know,' said Tammy. 'You wash your hair and let me style it for you. I used to help mum all the time.' Liz wasn't entirely convinced but didn't want to hurt Tammy's feelings so she made her some cheese on toast and left her eating it while she went upstairs to have a shower and wash her hair.

Tammy went outside to say hello to Finn who already had a job lined up for her. She was to dig up some of the Lavender and move it to another flower bed.

'Can't help tonight,' said Tammy earnestly. 'Liz is going on a date and I'm doing her hair.'

'How exciting,' said Finn, genuinely interested. 'Where is she going?'

'To an art exhibition with Nick,' said Tammy. 'He's a bit younger than she is.'

'Toyboy, eh?' said Finn smiling. 'Good for her. I can help,' said Finn. 'I used to be in fashion before I started gardening. If she wants any advice with what to wear, I'm her man.'

'Huh,' said Rory, 'you could be done under the Trade Descriptions Act for saying things like that.'

'I'll have you know that I have worked in some of the best fashion houses in London.' Finn was indignant.

'Not that,' said Rory laughing, 'you being a man.'

Liz came down half an hour later with damp hair and

wearing a baggy tracksuit. Tammy ran next door and brought back her hair hairdryer and straighteners. Liz then sat at the kitchen table while Tammy deftly blow dried her hair.

'This will give it some lift and bounce,' she informed Liz, as she pulled up strands of hair and rolled them around the large hairbrush before blasting them with the dryer. Liz was not a fan of blow drying but she had to admit that Tammy was pretty good. Once the blow drying was finished Tammy plugged in the straighteners to tame the ends.

'Now you can look in the mirror.' Liz shook her head like the girls in the adverts for hair products on TV before going to look in the hall mirror. She hardly recognised herself.

'Wow!' Tammy had done a great job. 'It doesn't look like me at all,' said Liz.

'You should always have your hair like this,' said Tammy. 'It really suits you.'

'I can see that I'll have to employ you to do my hair in future.'

Tammy looked really pleased with herself. 'Let's look at outfits now.' Liz brought down the four outfits that she had recently bought.

'Hang on a minute,' said Tammy, and she ran out into the garden to call Finn. Liz went to protest but Tammy was out in a flash and back with Finn, who was pleased to be press ganged into service. He took off his muddy boots at the backdoor and sashayed into the living room where Liz had laid each outfit over the back of the sofa.

'No. No. No,' said Finn, pointing at three of the outfits in turn. 'Too simple, too plain, too dressy. Now this could be great.' He picked up the navy pants and brightly coloured silk shirt. 'Shoes,' he snapped.

Liz wasn't sure. She pointed him in the direction of the cupboard under the stairs where most of her shoes were kept. She felt a bit like Cinderella with Finn as her fairy godmother.

He was mumbling to himself, 'Too red, not black, aahhh Tan.' He emerged with a pair of dark tan court shoes. 'This is it,' he announced. 'What do you think?' he said to Tammy, who had now cast herself in the role of fairy godmother's assistant. 'Do you have a bag to match?' he asked.

'I do,' said Liz, and she went to rummage in the cupboard before emerging triumphantly with a small shoulder bag in the same colour.

'My work here is done,' said Finn. 'I want to hear all about it tomorrow,' he said, as he flounced out the back door.

'Just make-up now,' said Liz. 'Have you any tips?' she asked Tammy.

'Less is more at your age,' she said seriously. 'You don't want to look like you're trying too hard.' Liz laughed. It was all a bit too serious. She hoped that if she could look the part she might actually feel more confident, that somehow the hair and make-up would endow her with confidence by osmosis. She went upstairs to apply make-up sparingly before getting dressed.

Tammy went out into the garden to talk to Finn as she

waited for Liz to come down all made up. Liz had carefully applied a little eyeliner and mascara, blusher and a hint of lip gloss. She put on the trousers and the silk patterned shirt. She looked slim and elegant. 'So far so good,' she said to herself, as she tried on the shoes and the coat to get the finished effect. Silver earrings and necklace completed the look. 'Not bad at all,' she said to herself. She was pleased that she felt comfortable, smart but casual.

She came downstairs so Tammy and Finn could give her the final thumbs up.

'Wow, you look amazing.' Tammy had only ever seen her in casual trousers and jumpers. Finn put his hands up as she walked into the room as if someone had pointed a gun at him.

'You look fantastic,' he said.

'You look nice Mrs B,' shouted Rory, who could see her through the open kitchen window. 'Where are you off to?'

'She has a date,' shouted Finn.

Liz was embarrassed. 'It's not a date,' she protested. 'Nick is just a friend.'

She took off her coat as she wouldn't be leaving for another forty five minutes or so. Rory shouted his goodbye's followed soon after by Finn.

'Relax and have a great time,' said Finn, giving her a peck on the cheek as he left.

'Thank you for all your help,' said Liz, blushing slightly.

As they were coming out through the side gate Monica was coming up the garden path to collect Tammy.

As much as she valued Tammy and Finn's opinion Liz was keen to hear if Monica approved. Tammy opened the door. She was really excited.

'I helped Liz get ready. I did her hair,' she blurted, as Monica came in. Liz poked her head around from the kitchen door before walking catwalk style down the hall and then doing a turn at the front door.

'I love it,' said Monica. 'You look great.'

'Thank you. I should make more effort. I used to but I sort of got out of the habit.'

'Remember, I want all the details tomorrow,' shouted Finn, as he boarded the Fantasy Gardens van. Liz felt herself blush again and looked to see if any of the neighbours were watching before closing the front door.

'I will have to employ Tammy to do my hair, too,' said Monica. Tammy was beaming.

'Have you got time for a cuppa? I'm not going for a while yet.'

'Not tonight,' said Monica. 'I've still got a bit of catching up to do but if you're free tomorrow night perhaps we can all have dinner?'

'That would be great.'

'I love the outfit, very chic.'

'I would never have picked this out for myself,' said Liz, studying her reflection in the hall mirror. 'I feel a bit guilty for spending so much money.'

Monica stayed chatting for another ten minutes before going home and then Liz looked up the address on the computer. The venue was an industrial looking warehouse in Crouch End which looked very trendy, and she started to worry that she wouldn't fit in. The confidence she had felt fifteen minutes ago was starting to drain away. She wrote down the postcode so she could put it into the satnav and began to transfer some of the contents of her every day handbag to the small tan bag she would be taking with her.

As she was doing so the doorbell rang again. She assumed that Monica had forgotten something and was shocked to see Adam standing on the doorstep. 'Hi, mum,' he said, surprised to see her all dressed up. 'You look nice.'

'Thank you darling,' she said warmly. 'Come in, come in. I'm afraid I'm in a bit of a hurry. I have to leave soon but I can make you a cup of tea and you're quite welcome to stay and make yourself something to eat if you want to.'

'No, don't worry, I'm fine. I just thought I would pop in on my way home. Where are you off to all dressed up?'

'I'm going to an art exhibition in Crouch End.'

'Good for you,' said Adam. 'Are you going with the lady next door, Monica isn't it?'

'Not Monica.' Liz didn't really want to tell him but she didn't want to lie either. 'I'm going with an ex colleague, an old friend.'

'Oh, what's her name, anyone I know?

'I don't think so, dear,' said Liz, and then biting the bullet added, 'His name is Nick. Nick Roberts. She emphasised the word his. 'He is exhibiting his paintings and tonight is the press preview.'

'So this is a date?' he said sounding concerned.

'No, no,' said Liz, laughing, 'he's just a friend.'

'How long have you known this Nick?' said Adam, probing.

'We worked together for a couple of terms a few years ago now but we recently bumped into each other in the garden centre. He lives nearby. Plus he's been decorating Tammy's bedroom next door so I've seen him a lot.'

'Don't you think you're a bit too old for a date?'

Liz prickled. 'Adam, it is not a date, he is just a friend.' She sounded a little put out.

'You have made a lot of effort for a friend,' he said sarcastically.

'I'm glad you think so, Adam, but that's all it is and now you come to mention it,' she was getting angry, 'no, I do not think I am too old for a date. Of course, I realise that in your eyes I should be perfectly happy to stay at home and wait for you to visit once in a blue moon but I have decided that it's about time that I started getting back into the world. So if you're staying don't wait up,' and with that she grabbed her coat and bag and left.

Adam was sitting in the kitchen with his mouth open. He couldn't get his head around the fact that his mum was going anywhere, let alone with a man. He viewed his mother as completely asexual.

He took his mobile out of his pocket to call Georgina but hesitated before dialling. He was looking out onto the garden and couldn't believe his eyes. The garden looked like a building site. There was no grass. In its place were the skeletons of various pathways and his dad's shed had been demolished. He didn't know what to do.

He rang Georgina. 'I think mum is having a midlife crisis,' he said seriously.

'Liz Is too old for a midlife crisis,' she replied.

'Well, she's all dressed up to go to an art exhibition with someone called Nick,' he said hysterically, 'and she has completely destroyed dad's garden. What would you call it?'

'Oh dear,' said Georgina. 'You don't think that she is being conned do you? You hear stories in the news about vulnerable lonely women being bamboozled by heartless lotharios who are only after their money.'

'Don't be melodramatic,' said Adam. 'It couldn't be, could it? She said that he is just a friend.'

'That's how it starts,' said Georgina, before hanging up.

*****

Liz was immediately sorry that she had vented. She had often wanted to tell Adam that she thought he was selfish but had held it in, not wanting to rock the boat. Well now the boat was rocking and she didn't care.

'He has a damn cheek.' She said this out loud. 'How dare he mind that I am going out? He should be pleased.'

Chapter 19

Adam was distracted all the way home. He was determined to find out more about Nick and make sure that his mother was not parting with her life savings. He would ask Sasha what she knew about him.

*****

Liz was so mad with Adam on the drive to Crouch End that she forgot to be nervous, although the anger had subsided by the time she arrived and she felt a little ashamed of herself for losing her temper. Perhaps she over-reacted. She would call him tomorrow.

Her face was still flushed as she parked the car. None of the buildings had either names or numbers but luckily she was able to stop a passer-by who lived in the area and he directed her to a building which looked like an abandoned warehouse. As she got closer she could see a large poster advertising the exhibition next to the entrance.

The entrance itself was very deceiving. It looked quite narrow from the outside but once inside it opened out into a huge industrial looking space. She looked around for Nick.

She was pleased she had worn trousers and not opted for

one of the dresses. She felt a bit more at ease in trousers. She could see a couple of men in suits but most were wearing casual jackets and jeans. She tried to imagine what Nick would be wearing. She doubted he owned a suit. She felt that for once in her life she had got it just right. A waiter walked past with a tray of glasses containing something fizzy and she took a glass and sipped it before moving further into the room.

She hated standing on her own and the longer she stood by herself the more she felt her confidence ebbing. She didn't know anyone here except for Nick and he was nowhere to be seen, she started to feel very self-conscious. She considered backtracking and slipping out of the room again. It was a mistake to come here. Adam was right, what was she thinking?

She took a deep breath. 'Don't panic,' she said to herself, 'just look around. It's an art exhibition. People go to art exhibitions by themselves all the time. Breathe.' She took another sip from the flute in her hand and scanned the room. Where to start? She wondered which paintings were Nick's. There was so much to look at, sculptures in stone, marble and metal, portrait and landscape paintings, abstracts and still life. She walked over to the nearest display as confidently as she could manage.

Paintings were hanging from the ceiling as well as from screens and walls separating the different artists work. This particular artist painted nudes and there were pictures of men and women in various stages of undress. The artist was good. They had managed to capture muscle tone, skin and hair in great detail. Liz noticed a woman talking enthusiastically to a group of people about the paintings and guessed that this was the artist.

She took another sip from her glass and moved around the screen where she was confronted by a huge oil painting of a man reclining on a bed, every aspect of his naked body painted in minute detail. She was eye level to his genitals. Had she been with someone she would have stopped to admire the skill of the painter but on her own she blushed and tried not to stare, turning her head to look at something else. Luckily she spotted Nick out of the corner of her eye.

He didn't see her immediately. He was having an animated conversation with a serious looking couple who were very smartly dressed in suits, which looked a little out of place in the warehouse. Liz watched for a while, wondering if she should go over or stay put until he'd finished. In the end she didn't have to make a decision as Nick looked in her direction and smiled. She waved, as if she was asking permission to leave the class, and self-consciously walked towards him. As she did so he excused himself from his companions and came to greet her.

'I wasn't sure you'd come,' he said smiling.

'I wasn't sure I'd come either,' said Liz.

'You look great,' he added, standing back in admiration.

'Thank you,' she said gracefully. 'I wish I could take the credit but it's hair by Tammy and outfit by Ali and Finn.'

'Designers?' asked Nick.

'No,' Liz replied. 'Ali, personal shopper, and Finn of Fantasy Gardens. Nick laughed. 'No seriously,' said Liz smiling. 'I needed help. It's been a while since I've been shopping and I had nothing to wear.'

'I suspect that you'd look good in a sack,' said Nick.

'I'll remember you said that next time,' said Liz.

'So there will be a next time.' There was a twinkle in his eye.

Liz laughed. 'I must say you scrub up very well too.'

Nick was wearing jeans with a white shirt, tan shoes and a well cut navy jacket. 'We sort of match,' said Liz.

'We do,' said Nick. 'It's a sign. Now, come on over. I'd like your opinion on my work.' He led her to a stand on the far side. She started to relax. Nick's paintings were an eclectic mix of contemporary and modern styles. He had several portraits on display. 'Always a hard sell,' he informed her, 'unless it's someone famous or it has been commissioned. I roll them out to show what I can do.'

'Who's this?' said Liz, pointing to a portrait of a lady who looked to be around thirty five.

'This is my daughter, Heather,' he said, brimming with pride.

'She's beautiful,' said Liz.

'She is,' said Nick. 'Obviously takes after her dad.'

Liz laughed. 'And this one?' Liz was standing in front of a picture of an old man.

'Aah, now this is a man I used to see regularly in the park. He has an interesting face don't you think?'

'He looks sad,' said Liz, staring into the watery grey eyes. 'These are really good. I wonder you had time to paint Tammy's room.'

'Well, I was in between jobs. It's not a steady business but it's getting better.'

They moved on to another stand. This one had four abstract paintings on it. Liz stood back to get the full effect. 'I'm not feeling these,' she said to Nick.

'Not my best work,' he agreed, 'but they help to pay the bills.'

'Do you sell a lot of these?' she asked.

'I have just been discussing a commission to paint thirty like this one.' He pointed to a huge canvas with splashes of colour scattered randomly in primary colours. 'It's for a chain of wine bars opening in July.'

'Ah,' Liz smiled. 'Were the couple I saw you talking to earlier the owners?'

'No. Not sure what that's about yet. They are from one of the regional TV channels, they said they have a project they want to discuss. I have made an appointment to see them in a couple of weeks' time. They just popped in to the look at my work.'

'Sounds intriguing,' said Liz.

'Something always comes up.' Nick was smiling. 'And if it doesn't I could advertise my services as a decorator.'

Liz laughed. 'You'd have to buy a ladder.'

'Let's hope it doesn't come to that. Shall we take a walk around the room and scope out the competition?'

'Let's,' said Liz. Nick grabbed another couple of glasses of sparkling wine and led Liz towards the sculptures.

They were both amused by the titles of the works, especially as you would need a very vivid imagination indeed to be able to work out what it was without them. Liz was particularly amused by two blobs of marble on a plinth entitled 'Mother and child'.

'Looks like a deformed potato,' she said to Nick, who had to agree.

The evening whizzed by, Nick was great company and they spent the whole time chatting and laughing. She liked being with Nick, there were no awkward silences and she didn't feel the need to censor her conversation. Not that censorship would have been possible with two glasses of wine. She was completely relaxed.

Nick introduced her to some of his friends from the art club and he told them all about Liz's painting. She argued that it was a very unworthy effort. Nick disagreed and they urged her to join. She said she would think about it.

By ten she was feeling tired and decided to head home. She could still feel the effects of the sparkling wine and it made her a little light headed, so there was no way she would be able to drive. She asked Nick to call her a cab.

'I can take you home if you don't mind waiting half an hour or so. I don't think the sponsors would be very impressed if I left early.'

'No, I wouldn't hear of it,' said Liz. 'This is important to you. I'll be fine.' She didn't trust herself to be alone with him under the influence of sparkling wine. She liked him a lot more than she cared to admit, even to herself.

'How about if I pick you up in the morning and drive you back here to collect your car?'

'That is really kind of you but I don't want to put you out.'

'It's no trouble, Liz. I'm coming back here tomorrow anyway. Is nine o'clock okay?'

'Perfect,' said Liz. 'Thank you.'

The minicab was outside in ten minutes and Nick walked her to the car. She was praying that he wouldn't kiss her but equally thrilled at the thought that he might. She hadn't kissed anyone except Jim, apart from Tony Rolfe when she was seven, and she was nervous but excited at the same time.

Nick must have been a little unsure of himself too. When they got to the taxi he took both her hands in his and thanked her for coming. Just the touch of his hands around hers made her tingle, warm and soft like his voice.

'I've had a really good time,' he said. 'Perhaps next time you'll let me take you somewhere less crowded.'

'That would be lovely.'

On her way home she thought about her argument with Adam. Was he right? Was she too old to start again?

As she pulled up outside her house she half expected his car to be there but it was gone. She was relieved. She thought he might be waiting up for her like her father did when she was a teenager. She felt really happy and didn't want anything to intrude on the feeling. She'd had a wonderful evening. It felt so good to have someone to laugh with and who was actually interested in her opinion.

*****

When Adam finally got home Georgina was waiting with the red wine. He looked stressed. Sasha had gone to bed so Adam was unable to interrogate her. Had it been entirely up to him he would have woken her up and sat her in front of a spotlight. He was that worried.

'Let's not panic until we know more,' Georgina soothed.

'She is spending so much money. You ought to see the garden.' Adam's voice was sounding more and more agitated.

'Well, she can't be giving loads of money away can she,' said Georgina, 'if she's spending it.'

'No, that's true,' said Adam.

'But she could be making changes to the house to sell it. Or worse, move him in,' said Georgina.

'That's not helping,' he said, putting his head in his hands.

Adam tossed and turned all night. He looked dreadful in the morning and didn't get up until almost seven o'clock. He would be late for work but luckily he was the boss. Sasha was sitting at the breakfast table eating toast when he came down.

'Morning Daddy,' she said, in between bites.

'Morning poppet. What do you know about Nick?' said Adam, getting straight to the point.

'Who's Nick?' said Sasha, still sleepy.

'Nick. Nick the artist,' said Adam, 'the one who painted Tammy's room.'

'Oh, that Nick,' said Sasha.

'That Nick,' repeated Adam. 'What do you know about him?'

'Not much,' said Sasha. 'He painted Tammy's room and it was really good.'

'Is he married?' asked Adam.

'Not now,' said Sasha. 'I think he's been married twice but he's divorced. He used to be a teacher with grandma at the same school years ago. We've met him a few times at the garden centre. He lives just up the road.'

'How old is he?' asked Adam, convinced that he must be a lot younger than his mother.

'I can't remember exactly,' said Sasha. 'Younger than grandma I think.'

'I knew it,' said Adam to himself.

Georgina was now absolutely convinced that Liz was being taken in and would lose the house and all her money.

Adam was concerned that artist was a euphemism for layabout sponger. He shouldn't have to worry about his mother like this. What was she thinking? He would have to talk some sense into her. He would call when he got to work.

*****

Liz didn't wake up until seven thirty, which was an hour later than usual. She had slept like a log. 'Must be the wine,' she concluded. She was grateful for the fact that she didn't have a headache. She had to get up and dressed quickly as Rory and Finn would be arriving soon and she made a point of giving them tea and a bite to eat as soon as they got there.

She looked in the mirror. Her hair had pretty well kept its shape and still looked really good. She had a quick shower and put on tee shirt, jeans and sandals before going downstairs in time to greet Rory and Finn. 'No Devlin today?' she enquired through the open kitchen window.

'No,' said Finn, 'we've another job in a few weeks' time so he's working on his vision,' and he made a great show of moving one hand above his head in a sweeping gesture worthy of a musical to indicate the scope of Devlin's vision.

Liz had hardly put the kettle on when Finn was at the kitchen door. 'Well, how did it go?'

'It was lovely,' said Liz. She really liked Finn, he was so easy to talk to. 'I was a bit nervous so I had a couple of glasses of sparkling wine.'

'Nothing like bubbles to relax you,' said Finn smiling.

'That's true,' she said, 'but I felt a little tipsy. I had to leave my car there and get a taxi home. Nick is picking me up this morning to drive me back to collect it. He'll be here soon.'

'Sounds promising,' said Finn, with a little squeal of delight.

'Hold your horses,' said Liz, 'we are just friends.'

'Me thinks thou dost protest too much.' He was now grinning like a Cheshire cat. 'What was the art like?'

Liz was animated in her praise of Nick's painting. 'Just

friends, eh?' said Finn, as he went back outside.

*****

As soon as Adam had gone off to work Sasha was on her mobile. 'Dad's got his knickers completely in a twist about grandma and Nick,' she told Tammy. 'He thinks that Nick is trying to con Gran out of her money.'

Tammy laughed. 'Why would he think that?'

'I don't know,' said Sasha. 'It's probably because gran hardly ever went out before so he always knew where she was.'

'We'll have to see what we can do,' said Tammy. 'I'll give you a call tonight.'

*****

Liz busied herself washing up the breakfast things and tidying the kitchen before popping out to the garden to give Rory and Finn another cup of tea before she went to collect her car. Nick rang the doorbell while she was chatting to them both and getting no reply at the front door decided to go through the side entrance to the back.

'Hi Nick,' said Liz, smiling, as soon as she saw him.

'Wow, the garden will be spectacular,' he said, amazed at how fast the project was moving forward. Not much of the old garden remained.

Finn almost ran over to shake his hand. 'Thank you so much,' said Finn. 'It's completely gone to plan.'

'This is Nick,' said Finn (winking at Rory). Liz introduced Finn to Nick and then Nick to Rory, or at least she indicated the spot where Rory was bending over a flower bed, his low

257

slung trousers revealing the crack of his arse. Not a pretty sight.

'Hi,' he said, without standing up and instead moving his head to one side of his bottom to make eye contact.

'I hear you're an artist,' said Finn.

'I'm trying,' said Nick.

'What do you paint?'

'Anything and everything,' said Nick, 'portraits, landscapes, anything really.'

'Gardens?' asked Finn.

'Sometimes,' said Nick.

'Now and again we have clients who ask if we know anyone who could paint a picture of their garden,' said Finn. 'Perhaps we could pass on your details?'

'Thanks,' said Nick, shaking his hand, 'that's really kind of you but wouldn't you like to see what I do first before you recommend me? You might not like it.'

'Liz has told me all about it,' said Finn. 'I'm sure it's great.'

Liz left Nick in the garden talking to Finn as she went inside to get her bag and coat before going to pick up her car. She was just about to leave when the phone rang. It was Adam. She was pleased. She had calmed down a lot. After all, it wasn't unreasonable for Adam to be concerned.

'Adam, about last night,' she began.

'No, it's OK mum, you don't have to apologise.'

'Adam, this isn't an apology. I just wanted to tell you that you don't have to worry.'

'I'm glad you've come to your senses,' he said.

Liz sighed loudly. He wasn't listening. She knew this conversation was going nowhere. 'Adam, Nick is a friend. I had a really nice time last night and I will be going out with him again.'

'Mum, you could be making a complete fool of yourself.'

'Thank you for your support, Adam,' her voice was completely calm, 'but that's up to me. I am a grown up. Anyway, I have to go. Nick is taking me to collect my car. I will give you a call later.'

Adam was left holding the receiver again when his secretary announced that his wife was on the other line. 'Georgie, it's worse that I thought, I think Nick stayed the night.'

Georgina laughed. 'Don't be so ridiculous.'

'I'm serious,' said Adam. 'I think this may have been going on for a while.'

'Are you sure?' said Georgina.

'Of course,' said Adam, 'it all makes sense.'

Liz's face was a little flushed when she came out to the car. Nick had stayed by the passenger door so he could open it for her as she approached.

'Thank you,' she said, as he nimbly ran around the front of his battered old Jeep to sit in the driver's seat.

'You don't look happy,' he said, as he turned the ignition to start the car.

'Oh, it's nothing, just family,' not wishing to elaborate but despite herself blurting out that her son was trying to control her life.

259

She tried not to sound bitter as she told him that Adam hardly came near or by, not even after Jim died, but that now she was starting to get back into the world, changing the garden and going out more, he seemed to be upset. 'I think he was happier when I was sad and lonely. I don't want to argue with him but that's all we seem to do now. I wish he had more faith in my judgement.'

'It's understandable for him to be concerned, Liz,' said Nick. 'He doesn't know me.'

'Thank you, Nick'

'For what?'

'For last night. I haven't laughed so much in a very long time and I must admit to feeling nervous about going, but everyone was so lovely. I have decided to join the art group, if you would still like me to.'

'That's fantastic,' said Nick. 'We can go together. I had a very successful evening. I picked up a couple of commissions as well as the wine bar work and the mystery meeting with the TV execs. So I thought that you might help me celebrate.'

'That would be lovely.' She didn't want to get her hopes up. She liked Nick a lot but didn't trust herself to read the signs. He may just see her as a friend and if that was the case it was better than nothing. She would wait and see. She was scared of making a fool of herself but despite her reservations she hoped.

Chapter 20

Monica was in work early. It was one of those rare mornings when the planets aligned and all the lights turned green as she approached them. There were no hold ups at all and better still there were parking spaces left in the car park.

This was so different to the usual routine of driving into the car park, finding no spaces and having to walk back half a mile or so from the parking space she eventually found a few streets away. She considered buying a lottery ticket it was that rare.

She was up to date with work, the accounts had been finalised and Tammy was doing well in school and at home. She felt complete contentment. She grabbed a coffee from the café downstairs before heading up to her office.

Nadia was there to greet her as she exited the lift, looking immaculate as usual. 'Morning,' she almost sang the word. She was always so cheerful.

'Morning,' Monica called back. It was going to be a good day.

She sat at her desk trying to decide what to do first. She had auditors coming in a few weeks so had plenty to do but her workload was manageable for the moment so no pressure. She decided to give Liz a call as she was curious to know how her evening had been. She dialled the home number but only got the answer phone. She made a note on her blotter to give her a call at lunch time before turning on her computer.

Kevin had sent several emails, most of which were jokes, but one was asking when they could meet up next. Monica decided not to rush into anything. After all there was Tammy to consider now. She accepted his invitation for dinner the following week and decided that she would tell him all about Tammy. If there was to be any relationship between them Tammy would be a big part of it. He would have to like Tammy and, more importantly, Tammy would have to like him.

*****

On the journey back to the gallery Liz told Nick about how she came to meet Monica and Tammy and what a lifeline they had turned out to be. She really admired the way Monica coped despite having no experience with children. Tammy could be a handful. She laughed as she recalled the day that Tammy had called her a witch.

'I can't imagine anyone thinking that you looked like a witch.'

'You didn't see me,' said Liz. 'I was seriously scary.'

'I can see that Tammy can be quite forceful.' He was recalling the Lavender plant Tammy had given him. Apparently it was holding on by a thread.

'You had better not let Tammy know,' said Liz. 'She is

very serious about her project.'

'I wouldn't dream of it,' said Nick. 'If I do manage to kill it I will replace it.'

'On pain of death,' added Liz.

'Scouts honour,' said Nick, who went on to confide that he had never been good at looking after things. He was terrified of responsibility, which is why he had been such a lousy husband.

'It took me a long time to grow up,' he said seriously. 'It has taken me a few years to get the hang of being a father. In fact, if I'm honest I didn't get it until my wife finally kicked me out.'

'How is your relationship with your children now?' asked Liz.

'It's great. We see each other all the time and the kids come and stay. I would even say that they are proud of me and my grandchildren think that being an artist is cool, which is amazing.'

Liz relayed the circumstances of Jim's death and the reasons behind changing the garden. She also spoke of how sad she was that her relationship with Adam had deteriorated after he married Georgina.

'It made me angry at first. I admit to blaming Georgina but then I realised that it could only have happened if Adam had let it, and he did. It got even worse after Jim died. I am fairly certain they think of me as a neurotic nuisance.' She hadn't actually said this out loud to anyone before. It was something that she had kept to herself. She felt almost ashamed.

She relayed to him the conversation she had with Sasha about Adam's job prospect in America.

'I didn't notice it when Jim was alive, maybe it was always there but just not so obvious because I was busy,' she said. 'I am pleased to say that I have decided to stop wallowing in self-pity and start living a bit. I'm only sorry that I will not be able to have a relationship with my grandchildren. I loved having Sasha to stay. She is a wonderful girl and if they move abroad it would be painful, but it's not something I have any control over.'

'I'm no expert,' said Nick, 'heaven knows I've mucked things up more times that I care to admit, but I would say keep in contact as much as you can. The kids are getting older. They will be able to make up their own minds in a few years' time.'

'That sounds much too sensible to have come out of your mouth,' said Liz, trying to lighten the mood.

'Well, I act my age occasionally,' said Nick. 'I have even managed to be organised enough to get my granddaughter's birthday present. She will be sixteen on Wednesday.'

'That gives me an idea,' said Liz. 'It's Sasha's birthday in June. I wonder if you would undertake a commission for me and paint a picture of her as a surprise?'

'I'll need a recent photograph if it's going to be a surprise,' said Nick.

'That's easy,' said Liz. 'She loves having her picture taken. Georgina sent me a picture of her riding her horse a few months ago and I took one of her in the garden with Tammy. I'll give them to you the next time I see you.'

They made arrangements to meet up the following week. Liz promised to take Monica and Tammy to the gallery at the weekend and to have dinner with Nick the following Saturday. She drove back home feeling calmer. She would keep her cool the next time she spoke to Adam. There was nothing to be gained by arguing. What will be, will be.

*****

Finn and Rory were on schedule for the garden transformation. They had managed to lay most of the paths and the base for the summer house and the fountain. Finn had brought a portfolio with him showing fountains they had installed in other gardens so Liz could get a feel of how she would like it to look. She pretty much had her mind made up about the stone until she saw a picture of three steel columns at different heights with water cascading down each of them. It was only slightly more expensive than the stone boulder but it looked so much more sophisticated. It would make a spectacular centrepiece.

She made them a cup of tea and sat at the garden table with them, enjoying the morning sunshine.

'Well, come on woman,' said Finn eventually, 'tell us all about it.'

'It was nice,' said Liz, a little guarded. 'Nick is a nice man, easy to talk to and fun to be with, but he is just a friend.'

'Saying it doesn't make it so,' said Finn. 'I think he likes you, you look good together.'

'Do you think so?' said Liz, feeling a little embarrassed. She marvelled at her own garrulousness. Six months ago she hardly spoke to anyone about anything and now every aspect of her life was open for discussion and she didn't care.

She told Finn that she was going to join the art group.

'I didn't know you painted Mrs B,' said Rory.

'I haven't for a long time,' Liz replied, 'but I'm thinking of starting again.'

'Let's have a look,' said Finn. Liz went into the garage and dug out a few of her old canvasses. She had painted the garden as it was before Jim died.

'This is really good,' said Finn. 'I think we should recommend you to our clients.'

'Thank you,' said Liz, 'but I am a little out of practice.'

*****

Adam was pacing up and down in his office. He had called Georgina and asked her to do a bit of internet research on Nick. He couldn't quite remember the surname although he was sure it began with R, maybe Robson or Rogers. He did remember that the exhibition was in Crouch End so Georgina didn't take long to find a list of art exhibitions in London and then narrow it down to Crouch End. There was only one entry, which made the job easy. She found the website for the exhibition but was frustrated to find that although there was a list of the artists, which included a Nicholas Roberts, there were no photographs.

She tapped the name Nicholas Roberts, artist, into the

search engine and found that he had exhibited in several places in England and there was a web-site. Georgina opened the tab with the tag line 'About the artist' and there in the top right hand corner was a picture of Nick standing next to an easel but it was an old photograph taken several years ago and Nick had never got round to updating it.

'Adam was right,' thought Georgina. 'He is much younger than Liz.' She called Adam.

Adam had to put it to the back of his mind to concentrate on work. The deadline for America was looming large and he had to think about what to do with the house. He also needed to speak to the children at some point although he was sure that they would love living in America and Georgina couldn't wait.

The only fly in the ointment was his mother. He hadn't given her a second thought when he was first approached by the Head of the New York branch but now he wasn't so sure he was doing the right thing.

Adam was a man who could compartmentalise his life. His wife and children fitted neatly into their slots, his work was under control and he found success easy. His mother and father were happily doing their own thing and did not give him any cause for concern until his father died suddenly and his mother became completely unhinged. Even then he had managed to keep things on an even keel. He wasn't sure why he felt so put out now.

*****

During the week that Finn and Rory had been working in

Liz's garden they had worked out a little routine. Liz would make tea and bacon rolls in the morning when they arrived. Tea and biscuits would be dispensed around eleven o'clock. Between twelve thirty and one thirty she would offer them a sandwich and at three thirty when Tammy got home from school they would get more tea and toast or buns, with Tammy and Liz joining them in the garden. Tammy would then help to dig up plants or fetch and carry in the garden until Finn and Rory left just before six.

Today was no exception. Finn was looking forward to seeing Tammy at three thirty as usual. He had a surprise for her. He had prepared a wage packet as a thank you for all her help. She came breezing in through the side gate. She didn't bother knocking at the front door now she could go straight through to the back. She went over to the table, poured herself some juice and then slumped into one the chairs before letting out a huge sigh.

'What's up with you?' said Liz.

'I think we need to start planning my birthday party,' she said seriously. 'There's so much to do.' She looked at Finn. 'Are you quite sure that the garden will be ready in time?'

'My word is my bond,' said Finn.

'I need to get the invitations out before the end of school.'

'We've still got six to eight weeks yet I think,' said Liz. 'Don't worry. You're starting to sound a lot like Sasha.' Tammy pulled a face to reflect her disapproval of Liz's statement.

'Will you be able to come to my party with Devlin, and you Rory?' said Tammy. She was fond of them all but especially Finn as he made a fuss of her.

'We wouldn't miss it for the world, sweetheart,' said Finn. 'Who else is coming to this party?'

'I'm inviting my whole class. If they all come that will be thirty children, plus Sasha,' she looked at Liz.

'Of course,' said Liz.

'And Nick. Do you think he would come?'

'I'm sure he will if he can,' said Liz, realising that this was Tammy doing her best to match-make.

'Plus some of my mum's family, not sure how many yet.'

'Now, young lady,' Finn addressed Tammy. 'The landscaping will be finished by the end of next week. If Rory manages to finish the lights and the wires in the pump for the fountain,' he nodded in Rory's direction. 'We will also be putting up the summer house. The following week will be the soft planting and then it's Mother Nature's turn, and when Mother Nature has a day off I expect you to help water the plants so they will be perfect in time for your party.'

'I will,' said Tammy.

'Good. Now let's get on with it, we still have some bricks to move.'

Finn and Rory worked hard for another hour or so with Tammy in tow. At a quarter to six they packed up their tools and Finn called Tammy to give her the wage packet. She held the envelope in her hand for a few minutes before opening it.

'Come on,' said Rory, 'what are you waiting for?' Tammy felt suddenly embarrassed.

She opened it slowly and was delighted to see the money inside but she didn't take it out. Instead she closed the envelope immediately and gave it back to Finn. 'I can't take it,' she said. 'I don't deserve it.'

'Will you let me be the judge of that?' said Finn, pushing it back into her hands. 'It's not much for all your help and you definitely deserve it. I won't take it back.' He turned his head to one side.

'Thank you,' said Tammy, before giving Finn a big hug.

'You're welcome, sweetie.' Finn had tears in his eyes. He was such a softy. 'Come on Rory, time to hit the road.' He said goodbye to Liz. 'See you on Monday,' they shouted as they got into the van. 'Be good,' shouted Finn to Tammy. 'Don't spend it all at once.'

Monica was just pulling up as the van sped off. Tammy was really excited when Monica arrived and so pleased with herself. 'Time for tea?' asked Liz.

'I have,' said Monica, feeling relaxed. She was getting so organised. Dinner had been prepared the night before and only needed heating up.

'Great, I'll put the kettle on.'

Liz bought the tray out to the garden as it was still quite warm outside.

Tammy told Monica about the pay packet. 'Can I keep it?' she asked.

'I guess so,' said Monica. 'I think Finn would be offended if you gave it back.' Tammy gave a happy little squeal as she opened the envelope and took out the money to count it.

'Twenty five pounds!' she exclaimed.

'Wow,' said Monica, 'you are a lucky girl. That is so generous. What are you going to do with the money?'

'Not sure yet.' said Tammy. 'I think I'll just save it for now.' Liz poured the tea.

'Well?' asked Monica.

'Well what?' said Liz, knowing exactly what Monica was referring to.

'How did it go? Are you friends?' She made the speech-mark sign with her hands as she said the word friends.

'We are.' Liz smiled. 'I had a wonderful time. Nick is great company and we laughed a lot.'

'It's a good sign,' said Monica. 'You need to be able to laugh with someone. What was the art like?'

'There was a real mixture of styles, some of it was terrible. I hate it when you have to read an essay to understand what you're looking at.'

'I know what you mean,' agreed Monica.

'Other pieces were fantastic.' She relayed the story of the full frontal assault on her eyeballs as she was confronted by the reclining man. Monica and Tammy both laughed.

'Did you like Nick's paintings?' asked Tammy.

'He's very versatile,' said Liz. 'His portraits were really good. I wasn't so keen on the abstract stuff but it seems to sell.'

'Are you seeing him again, friend or otherwise?' asked Monica.

'I am,' said Liz. 'He's taking me out to dinner soon.'

'Progress indeed,' said Monica.

'Can we talk about my party now?' interrupted Tammy. 'It's going to be sick.'

'Sick?' repeated Monica.

'Great,' Tammy translated. Tammy ran inside to get a pad.

'She's very organised isn't she?' said Liz.

'You have no idea,' Monica smiled.

'I want to invite everyone in my class,' she announced as she came outside again.

'How many is that?' asked Monica.

'Thirty, if they all come, but I think that some of them may be on holiday. I also want to invite Sasha and Leo, Finn, Devlin and Rory. Oh, and Nick of course and anyone else you can think of.'

Liz didn't want to mention her row with Adam in front of Tammy. She felt fairly certain that Adam would not be speaking to her for a while. In any case, knowing Georgina she doubted that Sasha would have been allowed to come to the party anyway. She felt really sad at the prospect of not seeing her granddaughter again.

'I think we may be looking at around forty five people,' said Monica. 'What do you think?'

'Wonderful,' said Liz, 'the more the merrier. I am really looking forward to it. What will we feed them?'

'I thought about a barbeque at first,' said Monica, 'but that entails someone cooking all the time and I'm hopeless so I thought maybe a buffet instead.

'Cupcakes,' Tammy announced. 'I'd like cupcakes instead of a birthday cake.'

'Well that's easy,' said Liz.

'I thought we'd have a disco too,' said Monica. 'Perhaps we can rig up the summer house as the chill-out area. That's what it's called isn't it Tammy?' asked Liz.

'That would be great said Tammy, as she sat on Monica's lap. It's going to be wicked.'

Chapter 21

Liz woke early on Saturday morning as usual. She hadn't given the house a good going over for a couple of weeks now. The cleaning caddie had remained in the cupboard under the sink for two successive Saturdays. She was out of her routine. Not that the house was really dirty, most of the time she had cleaned it for something to do, but now she had real things to do and cleaning the house had to fit in.

She had made plans to go shopping with Monica and Tammy. Monica had weighed in on Friday night and was getting closer to her goal weight and therefore in desperate need of a wardrobe overhaul as her clothes were starting to hang on her. They were all going to take a trip to the West End, Liz having recommended the personal shopper, popping into the gallery beforehand so Monica and Tammy could appraise Nick's artwork for themselves.

As soon as Tammy got up she was on the phone to Sasha to let her know that the garden was on track and that she had been paid twenty five pounds in wages for helping Finn. Sasha was back in her routine and after breakfast would be off with her friends to go riding. She had asked her mother if Tammy could come to stay in the summer holidays but got the customary, 'We'll see, darling,' which Sasha knew meant no. Georgina would never actually say no. She liked to hedge her bets in case she changed her mind. Sasha had to be really persistent to wear her down.

Tammy told Sasha about the disco and the chill out area and the fact that her whole class would be invited, including the boys. This really excited Sasha who attended an all-girls school and, apart from her brother and his friends, knew very few boys. She really had to work on her parents now, not only that but she had to plan what she was going to wear. She would ask for clothes for her birthday and forget Disneyland for now.

'I'll do my best to get there,' she promised.

Tammy wondered whether Liz might have any influence. 'I doubt it,' said Sasha. 'Daddy didn't tell her he was going to America either.'

'Perhaps it will be different now,' said Tammy, 'now that you have already been to stay and survived the ordeal. I hope you told them what a nice time you had.'

'I did,' said Sasha earnestly. 'I had a great time but now dad has a bee in his bonnet about Nick. He can be such a child.'

'I know what you mean,' said Tammy. 'I'll call you later.'

'I have to go too,' said Sasha. 'Mum's dropping me off at the stables in half an hour.'

Liz had also telephoned to talk to Sasha. Now that she was in her life Liz had no intention of letting go again without a fight. She called the house and Georgina answered the telephone. She was surprised to hear Liz's voice but keener than usual to talk and therefore very pleased to be able to tell her that Adam had gone off to play golf.

'That's great,' said Liz. 'How are you and the children?'

'Oh, we're all fine,' said Georgina brusquely, keen to get onto the subject of Nick.

'I wondered if Sasha was around?' asked Liz. Georgina was delighted to tell Liz that Sasha had gone riding and was then going to her friend's house for tea.

'Not to worry,' said Liz as lightly as she could manage. 'I'll call her another time.'

'How are you, Liz?' said Georgina warmly. Georgina couldn't usually wait to get off the phone, and more so didn't give a damn about how she was, but now she wanted to find out anything she could so launched her charm offensive. Liz was determined not to part with any information but as much as she disliked Georgina she was Adam's wife and Sasha and Leo's mother.

'Really well,' said Liz. 'I'm feeling fantastic.' She knew what Georgina was up to and had no intention of obliging, in fact she decided to tease her a little instead.

'Nice talking to you,' said Liz, 'but I have to go. I have a date.'

Georgina leapt on the word. 'Date?' she exclaimed.

'Yes,' said Liz after a slight pause, 'with a personal shopper then the hairdresser.'

'Oh,' said Georgina, clearly disappointed.

'Speak to you soon.' Liz hung up before Georgina had a

chance to ask any more questions.

Liz then called Sasha's mobile. 'Grandma,' said Sasha excitedly.

'How have you been, poppet?'

'Great,' she lied. 'I'm just at the stables about to go on a hack.'

'Sounds exciting,' said Liz. 'Be careful.'

'I will grandma. How's Nick?'

'Nick's fine. We had a great time at his preview.'

'Fantastic,' said Sasha. 'Does this mean that he is your boyfriend?'

'No,' said Liz. 'We are still just friends but he is taking me out to dinner soon so you never know.'

'That's great grandma but dad doesn't seem too pleased.'

'I know, but there is no need for him to worry. Is there any news about the move?'

'No. Dad hasn't mentioned anything about it at all.'

'Perhaps he has changed his mind,' said Liz hopefully.

'I doubt it grandma, it's just that my opinion doesn't count.'

'I'm sure that's not true. I expect it's because nothing is certain and he doesn't want to worry you until he is sure.'

'Nice try, grandma,' said Sasha, 'but I heard them. It has already been decided. Dad is just waiting for the date.'

'It will all work out in the end, you'll see.' Liz tried to be optimistic. 'I'll call you tomorrow. Have fun.'

Monica and Tammy arrived at Liz's house just after nine o'clock. It was a really warm sunny day so Liz made tea and they all sat in the garden before heading off to the shops. 'It's going to look spectacular,' said Monica, trying to visualise the garden finished. Tammy was the expert, having spent every evening after school listening to Finn extol the virtues of the planting scheme and the natural materials so she was able to fill Monica in on the minute details of what would be where.

'It will look even more spectacular at night,' she said with authority, before going off to water the plants, leaving Liz and Monica chatting at the table.

'Any news from Kevin?' asked Liz.

'As a matter of fact there is,' said Monica, looking pleased with herself. 'We are going out to lunch on Tuesday week and then dinner on Friday. I was going to ask if you could look after Tammy.'

'It would be my pleasure,' said Liz.

After tea they all piled into Liz's car for the trip to Crouch End. Parking was even harder on a Saturday morning and Liz had to park several streets away. Luckily it was a beautiful day and walking was a pleasure. When they got to the gallery Nick was deep in conversation with two women and a teenage boy. She recognised one of the women from the painting she had seen at the preview. She felt a little awkward. The older lady looked like an older version of the younger one and Liz guessed that they were mother and daughter. The boy looked to be around fourteen.

Nick waved them over as soon as he clapped eyes on them. Liz was pleased that she was with Monica and

278

Tammy otherwise her courage would have failed her. Nick introduced the two women as Susan, his wife. 'Ex-wife,' corrected Susan. 'Ex-wife,' Nick laughed, and Heather, his daughter. Both women said hello to Tammy and shook hands warmly with Liz and Monica. Nick then introduced his grandson, Bradley, who barely mumbled hello without taking his eyes away from his phone screen. 'My granddaughter, Milly, is here somewhere,' said Nick, 'but I can't see her at the moment.'

Within seconds they were joined by another man who looked very much like Nick, only a little older and fuller in the face. 'This is my brother Patrick,' said Nick. Patrick shook hands with Liz and Monica.

'You look so alike,' Liz was quite taken aback.

'Yes,' said Patrick smiling, 'but as you can see I got all the looks and charm.'

Nick grinned. 'But I got all the talent.'

'That you did,' said Patrick indulgently.

'We can't stay long I'm afraid,' said Patrick, putting his arm around Susan's waist. 'We are going to stay with some friends in Bath for a few days.' Susan said her goodbyes to Heather and Bradley before giving Nick a peck on the cheek and making him promise to bring Liz over to the house for dinner at the earliest opportunity.

As soon as the introductions were over Bradley sidled off to a bench where he could view YouTube in comfort. Tammy thought about tagging along but suddenly felt shy so she stayed with Monica.

'I'm just going to see where my granddaughter Milly went,' said Nick. 'She was here a moment ago.'

'Don't worry, dad,' said Heather, 'she's here somewhere. You show Monica and Tammy around and I'll take Liz to find Milly. I'd like to introduce her.'

'I've heard good things about your work from Liz,' said Monica. 'I am really looking forward to seeing it. You did such a great job in Tammy's room.'

She caught a glimpse of the huge picture of the naked man to her right and was keen to go off in the opposite direction, wishing to spare her own and Tammy's blushes.

They were both really impressed by Nick's painting. He explained about the commission for the wine bars. Monica had heard of them. Apparently they were up and coming on the singles scene, playing host to regular speed dating events. Nadia at work was a big fan.

'Your daughter is very attractive,' said Monica.

'Yes, she is,' said Nick. 'She looks a lot like her mother, and just like her mother she really looks after me.'

'It's great that you all get on so well.'

'I think that life's too short to be bitter, especially if you have children together. Besides, we get on much better now we are divorced.'

'I bet lots of couples could say that,' said Monica.

'You're probably right. She thinks I'm a lost soul.'

'Are you lost?' said Monica.

'No, not now. I did go missing for a while but I was never lost.' He laughed.

Heather, meanwhile, was asking Liz how she knew her dad. Liz explained that she had first met him years ago when they were teaching at the same school, although they didn't speak very much at the time.

'Ah, yes,' said Heather, 'his academic phase.'

'Has he had a lot of phases?' asked Liz.

'Quite a few,' said Heather, 'in fact the only constant in his working life has been his art. He always goes back to it.'

'He is very talented,' said Liz enthusiastically. 'He deserves to be successful.'

'He is,' agreed Heather, 'but it's hard to make a living at it. It's just great to see him happy. I haven't seen him enthusiastic about anything for a while.'

'Oh, I doubt that's down to me,' Liz was smiling. 'We've only recently met but I do enjoy his company, he makes me laugh.'

'Well that's a good omen,' said Heather, 'because that's exactly what he says about you.' Liz blushed.

'I'm pleased he has met someone nice. Dad pretends he's OK and he comes over to our house whenever he likes, but we worry that he is lonely.'

'I know what that feels like,' said Liz.

'Yes, of course,' said Heather, 'dad told me that your husband died. It must have been awful.'

'It was,' said Liz, 'but it's getting easier all the time.'

Nick had now joined them with Monica, Tammy and Milly in tow. 'Ah, there you are,' said Heather. 'This is Liz.'

'Hi, Liz,' said Milly smiling.

'I'm going to have to go too now dad. John's picking me up. We're going shopping for a new sofa.'

'We'll stay with granddad,' said Milly. 'He promised us breakfast.'

'Is that okay dad?' Heather looked at Nick.

'It's fine.'

'They would rather poke their eyes out with a sharp stick than come shopping,' said Heather, 'unless it's something they want, of course.'

'I know that feeling,' said Monica, recalling her trip to Ikea.

'Honestly, it's no trouble,' said Nick. 'I'll drop them off later.'

Heather said her goodbyes and headed for the exit.

'I hope she said nice things about me,' said Nick grinning.

'How much did you pay her?' asked Liz.

'No money exchanged hands I can assure you.' Nick held up one hand as if swearing on the Bible. 'She is just one of my many, many fans.'

'She's lovely,' agreed Liz, 'and she cares about you a lot.'

'She does. I'm very lucky. Have you got time for breakfast?' he added. 'I promised Brad and Milly a fry up. There is a fantastic little place across the road. What do you think?'

Liz looked at Monica hopefully. 'Fantastic,' said Monica. 'We've got all day to shop.'

'Great,' said Nick, 'wait here while I try to find my grandson.'

Nick came back a few minutes later with Bradley. Despite his earlier reluctance to mix, once the phone had been prised out of his hands Bradley was an enthusiastic chatterbox. Tammy was even more impressed with Milly who was about to go to a festival with her friends for her sixteenth birthday.

'No parents?' Tammy repeated incredulously. It was clear she thought that Milly was the coolest. Monica could see she was taking it all in to store up as ammunition for future requests. There will be trouble ahead.

Milly was equally keen to know how Liz had met her granddad and was at pains to point out his good points. Liz was enjoying herself but at the same time it all felt a bit overwhelming. She also couldn't help feeling a pang of jealousy when comparing Nick's family relationships with her own, and as they chatted and laughed together she wondered where she'd gone wrong.

Breakfast seemed to fly by. It felt as if they were in and out in a flash, despite sitting at the table for an hour and half. It was getting on for lunch time and Liz and Monica had some serious shopping to do so they had to break up the gathering. Nick said goodbye to Monica and Tammy before pressing Liz's hands in his and promising to call in the week. Milly gave them all a hug before they parted on the pavement outside.

'I think I'll invite Milly to my party,' said Tammy, hoping to impress her friends by way of association with someone so grown up.

They had a really successful afternoon's shopping. Monica was initially reluctant to employ the services of a personal shopper when she saw how stick thin she was, convinced that she would be unable to pick out clothes for someone bigger than a size ten. Instead she opted to go it alone and rely on Liz and Tammy for advice.

Despite dropping two and a bit dress sizes Monica still had a more curvaceous figure. Although for the most part she could now get into anything she wanted to wear the problem was she didn't know what she wanted.

She gathered up a few bits to try on which included some dresses for going out (she had Kevin in mind) and pictured herself sitting opposite him in a romantic candlelit restaurant, looking glamorous and sexy. Trying on the dresses soon burst that bubble. They were not very flattering. They were the wrong shape for her shape so she swallowed her pride and called in the professional.

Two dresses and one handbag later they were on their way home. Tammy and Liz were exhausted. Monica could have shopped for England. She had acquired a new zest for shopping since losing weight. Liz declined the offer of dinner and opted to go home to a hot bath and the sofa instead. She just wanted to relax at home by herself for a while and think things through.

Chapter 22

As she lay in the bath she thought about calling some of their old friends, maybe even Jim's sister. She had met Jim when she was very young and they had almost grown up together. Most of their friends were their friends as a couple. She had a few acquaintances, girls she had met at work and went out with occasionally, but no real close female friends. Until Eve that is. Eve was so kind when Jim died and Liz regretted not making more effort to be a better friend to Eve while Jim was alive.

When Jim was alive they had socialised a lot with other couples, most of who were still together. As nice as they were on the telephone it was apparent that she would not be welcome as a single entity, she would unbalance the group. They didn't say so but there was a reluctance to commit, she could hear it in their voices when she suggested meeting up. She made a conscious decision to abandon any guilty feelings she harboured for not staying in touch. Life was too short. Her withdrawal from the old social collective was inevitable.

She reflected on how easy it was to lose your identity. She had almost disappeared, lost in grief and pulled back from the brink. She hadn't thought much about friends when Jim was alive. She didn't feel the need to make an effort, after all Jim had been her best friend. But what would she have done without Eve and now Monica, Tammy and Nick. She felt lucky to have a second chance and promised herself that she would never make the same mistake again.

The date for the party had been fixed for Sunday the nineteenth of August. Tammy's birthday actually fell on the Wednesday before but weekends were easier for most people. Tammy had decided to design the invitations herself and was busy scouring the internet for suitable templates and pictures.

Liz spent almost an hour talking to Eve, telling her all about Monica and Tammy. She went through the changes to the garden, which she couldn't do without mentioning the lovely boys from Fantasy Gardens who she now considered friends.

She didn't mention Nick. She would hold him in reserve. She wasn't entirely sure where it was going and she didn't want to jinx it. Nick was so different to Jim and just thinking about him set her pulse racing in a way that she didn't think possible at her age.

Eve was pleased to know that nice people were living in her house and that Liz had made some new friends. She had made great progress health wise and living in a bungalow meant that getting around was a lot easier. She wasn't sure if she could make the party on the nineteenth as her daughters were planning a holiday in Devon in August and the whole family would be going.

'Lucky you,' said Liz, knowing full well that a family holiday was unlikely to be something she would ever experience. They said their goodbyes and promised to meet up soon.

*****

On Monday morning she thought about ringing Adam. She hated arguing with him and wanted to reassure him that she wasn't about to give away her pension and that Nick was a really nice man who earned his own money. Adam would probably like him a lot if he gave him a chance. She decided to think about it a bit more before making the call.

Finn and Rory's arrival interrupted her reverie. They were earlier than usual as they were expecting a delivery.

'Morning.' Finn's musical voice wafted in through the window as Liz made a pot of tea and popped some crumpets into the toaster.

'Morning boys,' she replied.

'How are you Mrs B?' shouted Rory.

'I'm great,' said Liz, as she opened the back door and came out with the tray.

'You're too good to us,' said Rory, picking up a crumpet and devouring half of it with one bite.

'Philistine,' hissed Finn, as he delicately pecked around the edges of his. Liz joined them on the patio and sat drinking tea and laughing as they batted good humoured insults back and forth.

*****

Monica had made arrangements to meet Kevin for lunch on Tuesday and was already planning what to wear and where to go. That was until she received a text from him an hour later apologising. He said that something urgent had come up at work and he would have to cancel lunch. He asked if she was free for dinner on Friday instead. She did a little dance on the spot before calling Liz to ask if she could look after Tammy. It was no problem. Excited, she sent him a text confirming that Friday would be fine.

*****

The garden was coming on spectacularly well. All the pathways and raised beds were now in place. The summer house had been erected at the back of the garden, no glass in the windows yet but you could see the effect. Rory had run the electrics for the fountain and the lights and Finn was busy planting. Liz surveyed the garden and felt happy and a little lighter, as if a huge weight had been lifted. She smiled to herself. 'What do you think Jim?" she said in a whisper, looking up to the sky. 'I think it will be wonderful.'

*****

Friday came round fast. Monica decided not to mention Tammy to Kevin, nor Kevin to Tammy. It was much too soon. After all this was their first proper date and she didn't want to complicate things. She let herself in the side gate to find Tammy and Liz in the garden planting Lavender to edge the border where the summer house sat overlooking the garden. Liz had tea and biscuits waiting on the table.

Monica told Tammy that she was going out with some

friends from work. Tammy was disappointed it wasn't a date. She was keen for Monica to find someone.

'Mind if I weigh in before I sit down?' said Monica in a rush.

'Go ahead,' shouted Liz, 'I'll pour the tea.'

Monica came back out into the garden grinning. Liz and Tammy looked at her expectantly. 'Well?' they said together.

'I'm down to a size twelve.' She was really pleased with herself. 'I'm back to my old weight.'

'That's amazing,' said Liz. 'Well done. Would you like a biscuit to celebrate?'

'Yes please,' said Monica smugly, 'but only one.'

'What are you wearing?' asked Liz.

'I can wear almost anything I want to now,' said Monica, 'but I think I'll wear the red dress.'

'I'll do your hair,' Tammy volunteered.

'That would be lovely,' said Monica hugging her, before going off to get dressed.

Liz had made quiche and salad for dinner and set the table in the garden. Tammy loved eating outdoors. They had just finished putting the dishes in the sink as Monica rang the bell. Liz opened the door to find Monica posing with her hands on her hips. She was wearing a deep red dress and high heels and the dress complimented her dark brown skin and flattered her curves.

'You look amazing,' said Tammy, taken aback a little. She looked more like her mother than ever, except for the hair.

Monica had done the usual; that is she fiddled about with

it for ten minutes or so before losing patience and scraping it up into a bun.

'It ruins the look,' said Tammy with authority. She set about straightening Monica's frizzy mane, finally taming it into a sleek style which totally transformed her face, making it appear longer and thinner. When Monica looked in the mirror she couldn't believe it.

'Wow. I hardly recognise myself. Thank you so much.' She squeezed her arms around Tammy's shoulders. 'I love it.'

'Told you,' said Tammy. 'You should trust me more.'

'Have a fantastic time and enjoy yourself,' said Liz.

'I'll be back around eleven o'clock,' shouted Monica, as she got into her car.

'Don't worry. Tammy can stay over, it's no trouble.'

Tammy liked having Liz all to herself. They washed up together and then looked through Liz's small collection of DVD's. Tammy found Pride and Prejudice which they had both watched a few months back. Liz had seen it four or five times but she loved it so they snuggled down on the sofa with a bowl of popcorn to be mesmerized by Mr Darcy.

*****

Monica was late. She managed to catch every red light on her way to the restaurant. Kevin had suggested picking her up but she didn't want to risk Tammy seeing him so arranged to meet him there. She turned into the street but there was nowhere to park. Damn. She was getting agitated.

'It's a bad omen,' she started to worry.

Luckily, as she turned the corner a car was just pulling out and her little Nissan could slip in without the need to parallel park. She was relieved. She'd never been good at parking. A good omen. She locked the car and walked towards the restaurant as it started to rain. 'Two to one to the bad omens,' she thought to herself.

The restaurant was dimly lit and intimate. She felt self-conscious as she pushed open the door she hoped and prayed that Kevin would be there. She needn't have worried. He was sitting on a sofa next to the small bar having a drink. He stood up as soon as he saw her and came towards her, smiling.

'You look great,' he said, reaching for her hand.

'Thank you,' said Monica, feeling a bit like a princess.

'Would you like a drink or shall we sit down at the table?'

'Can we go to the table?' said Monica, allowing herself to be led. This was her reward for starving herself for the past few months.

'I hope you like Italian.' He pulled out her seat for her to sit down.

'I do,' Monica gushed.

He scrubbed up really well. He was wearing a suit. She caught the scent of his aftershave as he kissed her on the cheek and it made her feel slightly lightheaded. She still fancied him like mad. 'Steady girl,' she thought to herself. It had been so long since she had been on a date and she had to fight the urge to climb across the table and ravage him.

She looked at the menu and was grateful that the Italian dishes had English subtitles underneath which made ordering so much easier.

'Have you been here before?' she enquired.

'A couple of times.' He peered at her over the top of the menu.

'What would you recommend?'

'I'm a bit boring I'm afraid,' he said. 'I always have the same thing, Chicken al Forno.'

She briefly considered spaghetti bolognaise but recalled the trouble she had eating it when she had made it for Liz. She pictured herself with spaghetti worms sticking out of her mouth as she struggled to keep them in check. Not a good look for a first date. She decided on penne arrabiata instead, neat, fork sized bits of pasta she could manipulate easily.

Kevin had already ordered a mixed starter of olives and roasted vegetables and a bottle of Chianti. The decision to drive also meant that she would be unable to drink too much wine. She needed to have a completely clear head. She didn't want to risk making a fool of herself or letting her guard down. First date rules included not getting too drunk so you're not tempted to sleep with him. She fancied him too much to risk it.

The waiter brought the food and Monica was very grateful that it was easy to eat. However the chef overdid the chillies in the arrabiata sauce. She could feel the steam coming out of her ears, it was so hot.

She tried to skim the sauce off the pasta before taking each bite without making it too obvious. Kevin didn't notice, he was too busy eating his chicken and talking about his project. In the end she gave up and merely pushed the pasta around the plate rather than risk the need to fan her mouth which felt like it was on fire.

Despite the diet she ordered ice cream for dessert. She was still hungry after leaving half of the pasta and, besides, she needed to cool down.

After dinner they sat at the table chatting. Kevin expanded on his idea for a new web-based app and was really keen to find a buyer. He talked so much about his work he barely asked her any questions for which Monica was grateful. She wasn't ready to talk about Joanna or Tammy and she was happy not to be thinking of sad things that would bring down her mood.

There was only one other couple left in the restaurant at the end of the evening and the waiters had begun stacking the chairs ready to lock up.

'Would you like to come back to my flat for coffee? It's just around the corner?' Had she drunk a couple of glasses of wine the sensible Monica would be consigned to a deep dungeon while the reckless Monica would enjoy an evening of carnal pleasure. But the stone cold sober Monica panicked a little. She imagined Joanna sitting on her shoulder and whispering words of wisdom in her ear, 'If he's getting free milk he has no need to buy the cow'.

'I can't,' she spluttered. 'I've got something important on

in the morning and I need to be alert.'

He made a sad face. 'Just for a little while,' he pouted.

She nearly gave in. 'No, not tonight.' Her mind was made up. She surprised herself, 'I have to go.'

He signalled the waiter for the bill. Monica moved to open her handbag. 'Don't you dare. I've got this covered. Come on, I'll walk you to your car.'

They both stood up and the waiter helped Monica on with her coat. It was almost midnight and outside the street was eerily quiet. Monica felt nervous, not the scary nervous but the butterflies in your stomach feeling of anticipation. She felt the mood had changed and dreaded the awkward moment when they said goodbye.

When they reached the car she turned to thank him.

'Thank you for coming,' he said and took her hands in his as he said goodnight. He didn't even attempt to kiss her. This was not how the evening was supposed to end. He would kiss her passionately and she would swoon. She expected him to repeat his invitation to go back to his flat but instead he just said, 'Night, night gorgeous.' Then he held open the car door as she climbed in, waited while she started up the engine and watched her drive off down the road.

Wow, he was the perfect gentleman. It felt a bit like a scene from a romantic movie except for the lack of the lingering kiss, the one where everyone in the audience goes 'aahhh.' Kevin was almost too good to be true. It was much too late to collect Tammy which meant that she could lie in bed and try to analyse the evening.

She definitely fancied him but she wanted a relationship and not just a quick roll in the hay. She was puzzled. Did he fancy her? She couldn't decide if he felt the same way she did. Maybe he didn't fancy her at all and was just being polite, after all he didn't even attempt to kiss her when they parted, but he did ask her up to his flat. She was confused.

Perhaps he was a player and this was all part of a strategy to disarm his victims. Did he do this on a regular basis? Her head was spinning.

*****

Finn and Rory had come to work on Saturday, which was a first. They only had a little bit left to do and a new job to start on Monday uptown so time was of the essence. The garden was looking spectacular. Liz's next door neighbour had been in to have a look and had taken the telephone number for Fantasy Gardens. The garden was now the envy of all those who set eyes on it.

Liz had decided to give Adam a call, she had nothing to lose. Sasha answered the telephone.

'Hello darling,' said Liz on hearing Sasha's voice, 'how are you?'

'Great grandma,' said Sasha enthusiastically. 'How's Monica and Tammy, have you seen them?'

'Tammy is here with me,' said Liz, mouthing the word Sasha to Tammy. 'I'll put you on to her when I've had a chat with Daddy. The garden is looking fantastic. I can't wait for you to see it.'

'Me neither. I'll ask Daddy if I can come to stay in the summer holidays.'

'That would be wonderful,' said Liz. She really missed her granddaughter.

'Hang on Grandma, I'll fetch Dad.'

Liz waited on the telephone and listened as Sasha trotted off into the distance and shouted, 'Grandma is on the phone.' She listened intently for his footsteps, which seemed to take forever. She was considering hanging up when she finally heard his sulky voice.

'Hi Mum.'

'Hi Adam, how are you?' She didn't wait for an answer but instead continued. 'Adam, I wondered if you would pop in to see me one day during the week so that we can have a chat. I think we need to clear the air.'

'No need, mum,' said Adam, who obviously felt there was a need. 'You don't owe me an explanation. You can do what you like.'

'Thank you, Adam, but I would like you to understand. I am not a silly old woman being taken in by a conman. Nick makes a living as an artist. He is a really nice man with a lovely family and I am sure you would like him if you gave him a chance. That's all. No one can ever replace your father.'

'I know mum,' said Adam, who had calmed down considerably, 'but isn't he a bit young for you?

'What makes you say that? There's only a couple of years between us.'

'I don't want to see you make a fool of yourself.'

'I won't, Adam, please trust me, but don't take my word for it. Come and meet him. I am going to have a garden party on the nineteenth of August for Tammy's eleventh birthday. I would love it if you, Georgina and the children could come. You could all stay over. Tammy would love for Sasha to be here. They really are good friends.'

'I'm not sure, I might be away. I'll let you know nearer the time.'

'Of course, I understand. I know you're busy.' She was disappointed. 'If you are, you are. Perhaps if you are away the children could come and stay with me for a few days. I would love to have them.'

'We'll see. Anyway, I have to go, I'm off to play golf,' and with that he put down the receiver.

Liz was distracted. 'Ooops! Sorry dear,' she said to Tammy, 'I forgot to ask to speak to Sasha again.'

'Don't worry,' said Tammy, 'I'll give her a call on my mobile.' Tammy went outside into the garden to make the call. Sasha answered the phone.

'Hiya,' said Tammy, really happy to be speaking to her friend. 'Liz told your dad about the party. I hope he lets you come.'

Sasha had missed Tammy. Her friends were mostly the over-indulged spoilt brats that she had been herself before a little dose of reality had made a difference to her outlook.

'I don't know,' said Sasha honestly. 'I think he is upset with grandma. He doesn't seem keen to meet Nick.'

'Doesn't he realise that she is lonely?' said Tammy.

'I don't think so,' said Sasha, 'he is much too selfish for that but I will try to talk to him.'

'It's not that long to go now. I'll email you an invitation and I'll put one in the post for the whole family, including Leo. I'd like to meet him.'

'I'd love that,' said Sasha honestly. 'How's the project going, you know, helping the bees?

'Have you given away any plants where you live?

'I haven't had time,' said Sasha. 'I've been much too busy with my horse. I'm competing in a gymkhana next weekend. What about you?'

Tammy had little or no expectation that Sasha would do anything at all to help the bees on her own. She told Sasha that she might use some of the money Finn gave her to buy more pots. She had kept a list of addresses for those people who accepted the plants last time and thought about leaving plants on the doorsteps of the flats around the corner. They could certainly do with brightening up.

'I don't really have the patience for that sort of thing,' admitted Sasha. 'I need you to motivate me. Anyway, I'm more of an organiser. I need to be in a supervisory role.'

'So what have your organised?' asked Tammy.

'I have sent a press release to the Enfield Gazette, or at least I am going to.'

'Did you mention my name?' said Tammy, wondering if Sasha had taken credit for the whole project.

Of course,' said Sasha earnestly, 'it was your idea. I just

helped.'

'Thanks Sash, I miss you.'

'I miss you too. Don't worry, I'll work on Dad. See you soon.'

Tammy had just put the phone down on Sasha when the doorbell rang. Monica had come early. Tammy looked through the window before rushing to open the front door.

'Did you have a nice time?' she asked'

'Great,' said Monica, trying not to give anything away.

'Did you meet anyone?'

'Loads of people,' said Monica, teasing. She knew full well what the question implied. 'But no one special.'

'Awww. Maybe next time,' said Tammy.

'You never know,' said Monica, as she followed Tammy into the hall, 'especially if you keep doing my hair.' She hated lying to her but she didn't want to give her any false hope either.

'Hiya.' Liz poked her head round the door of the kitchen. 'Come in, come in. Come and look at the garden. It's finished.'

Monica walked straight through to the back door and stood with Liz and Tammy on the patio. 'Wow!' The summerhouse looked stately, set up three or four feet higher than the path with stairs leading up to it, its large windows and double glass doors making it bright and airy. It had a veranda to the front which would lend itself beautifully to a couple of easy chairs and a table.

'That is an ideal spot for a glass of wine on a balmy

summer night.'

'I can see it all now,' said Liz. I think I'll use it as my studio.'

'Very posh,' said Monica, admiring the view.

Liz led the way around the garden, following the pathways as Monica admired the shady nooks and the exotic planting schemes that weaved in and out of the tiered flower beds. All the pathways lead to and from the central fountain. Exotic grasses in various shades of green edged the higher beds while smaller, dark, almost beetroot coloured grass bordered the lower levels and contrasted with the Lavender.

'It is absolutely stunning,' said Monica. 'The boys have done an amazing job. It actually makes the garden look bigger.'

'Can we see the fountain running?' asked Tammy. Liz went over to the kitchen and flicked the switch just inside the door. Soon water began to gurgle and splutter until it bubbled through the top of the steel columns and cascaded down the sides.

'Well, what do you think?' said Liz, beaming with pride. 'Don't you think this would be a great place for a party? It's fabulous and there is still enough room to put a couple of small tables and chairs around the fountain. I can't wait to see it in the evening with all the lights on. Finn assured me that it will look magical when it's lit. Now we can really start to plan,' said Liz. 'How are you getting on with the invitations?'

'I'll show you,' said Tammy, and she went off to find the

picture that she had decided on as the background to the invites.

'Well,' said Liz as soon as Tammy was out of earshot.

'Don't know,' said Monica. 'I felt a bit like a princess at first but I'm not sure that he is the prince I imagined him to be. When I think about it he talked an awful lot about himself although he did pay for dinner and walked me to my car, both of which are a bit of a novelty I might add.'

'Well that's something,' said Liz. 'Are you seeing him again?'

'Not sure,' said Monica. 'I don't want to rush anything. I haven't mentioned Tammy yet. It may be a deal breaker.'

Chapter 23

Monica was in a funny mood as she walked into work on Monday morning. She wasn't sure that Kevin would bother contacting her at all having failed to get her back to his lair on Saturday night. She was convinced that the dating desert she had been wandering around aimlessly in for the last few years was likely to stay on the horizon for the foreseeable future.

She wondered if she would ever meet a decent man and thought that perhaps it was time to consider dating websites or perhaps lowering her standards.

Nadia was busy painting her nails as Monica arrived at work.

'Hiya.' Nadia paused between her thumb and index finger on her right hand to chat. Monica felt miserable. On Friday she had a prospective boyfriend. Today she wasn't so sure. She was convincing herself that she was already on the dating scrapheap. She was sure Kevin would move on to more amenable pastures.

'You look a bit fed up,' Nadia observed as Monica reached the reception desk. Nadia was nothing if not perceptive. Monica was certain that she could detect a mood at fifty paces.

'Oh, just a bit,' said Monica, not wishing to elaborate and hoping Nadia wouldn't ask.

'Don't tell me,' said Nadia, who obviously did want Monica to tell her. 'Man trouble. They're all selfish shits.' She said this without taking a breath. Monica didn't reply but merely nodded agreement.

'Why don't you come out with me and the girls from advertising this week? There's a speed dating event at the new wine bar on Thursday night. You never know, you might meet the man of your dreams.'

'I might,' said Monica, who had never been out with the girls from advertising before. Monica considered it briefly and thought that would probably mean rejection at a faster than average rate.

'At least you don't have to waste too much time talking to them if you don't want to,' said Nadia. Monica had certainly kissed a lot of frogs but had serious doubts that she would find her prince in five minutes of polite conversation.

'Come on, it will be a laugh,' said Nadia. Monica could imagine Nadia picking off the poor unsuspecting hopefuls, chewing them up and spitting them out. She doubted that Nadia was fussy anyway, at least not as fussy as she was. 'What do you think?' Nadia looked hopeful.

'I may have to work,' said Monica honestly, 'but I will if I can.'

'That's more like it,' said Nadia, 'don't let the bastards get you down.'

Monica moved off to go to her office and Nadia continued with her manicure. As soon as she got to her desk she turned on her computer and went straight to email. Nothing from Kevin. She refreshed the page as if doing so would cause the flurry of emails from Kevin to rush through. Still nothing. She checked her mobile. Maybe he'd sent a text and she hadn't heard it. No, no text either.

'Well, that's it. He is only interested in one thing. I've had a lucky escape.' She didn't feel lucky. 'How wrong can you be about someone?' She was talking to herself.

Ten minutes later when she had decided to stop mooning over Kevin her mobile pinged. It was a message from Kevin. She opened it quickly. 'Thank you for a lovely evening, wondered if you fancied meeting up next week. I'll cook. Smiley face, and four X's.' I'll cook was the new come up and see my etchings. It was too soon. It's breaking the five date rule. Joanna had a five date rule, bar any deal breakers on dates leading up to date five. Deal breakers included bad breath or BO, excessive body hair, scruffy clothes, bodily noises or talking about their ex, being too touchy feely, clingy or whiny. Baby talk, couldn't bear a man who resorted to talking like a child to get their own way. Being rude to waiters or bar staff, too controlling or jealous. The list was endless. Deal makers, on the other hand, was a much shorter list. Clean and smart, great smile, good listening skills, sense of humour, kind, patient and employed. Not too much to ask for.

She thought about Joanna and Max. Max had at least

been funny and loosely employed as a guitarist for a reggae group, which was odd for a middle class white boy. He was in the happy position of being supported by his very well off parents.

She hadn't known Max for very long at all. Maybe if she had obeyed her own rules she wouldn't have been pregnant by date five.

What to do, she couldn't decide. Should she make an excuse and maybe suggest something else, or go into the lion's den and remain sober, although she wasn't sure she could trust herself.

Maybe she should take him to dinner and mention Tammy before it went any further. If he was frightened off then there was no point at all in continuing to see him. If not she would consider testing his culinary skills. She texted back. 'How about letting me take you out?'

'I'm a modern man,' came the reply, 'I could live with that. Where will we go?'

'I'll think about it.'

She was pleased with this exchange. She expected some resistance but he seemed happy enough with the suggestion. Maybe she had misjudged him. After all, he did tick many of the other boxes. He was clean and well dressed, with a great sense of humour, and he was employed. What's not to like?

*****

When Tammy got home from school she had only one thing on her mind, her party. It was obviously the highlight of her social calendar and was coming up fast so she wanted to make sure that she got the invitations out before the end of term. She also decided to make sure that she had contact details for all of her class mates so she could do a ring round during the week before the party. Invites could be lost between the end of the school term and her birthday, which was three weeks later. She was nothing if not practical. She didn't want to leave anything to chance.

She had found a picture to use as the background for her invitation and Liz helped her with the wording which she was able to overlay on the picture. She left a line of dots at the top of the words so that Tammy could write the name of the invitee, then followed it with the words, 'You are invited to a garden party/disco to celebrate my 11th birthday. Please come to (they filled in Liz's address) 2.00 – 6.00 on Sunday 19th August. Refreshments will be provided. RSVP: Tammy,' and she added her mobile number and her new email address.

'What do you think?' said Liz, holding up a copy she had just printed out.

'They look OK,' Tammy had her index finger resting on her chin, 'but I think they would look better on different coloured paper.'

'Hang on a mo,' said Liz, rummaging around in the desk drawers. 'How about this?' She was holding up several sheets of bright yellow paper which was slightly thicker than the usual copy paper.

'Perfect,' said Tammy. Liz fed one sheet through

the printer as a test copy. The invitations looked very professional.

Liz printed out fifty copies. 'OK young lady, now it's your turn to fill in the names and get the addresses.' Tammy got out the list of classmates and wrote twenty nine invites to give out at school. She asked Liz for the address for Finn, Devlin and Rory. Fantasy Gardens must be represented. She didn't actually mind if Devlin wasn't there but Finn and Rory were a must. She wrote one out for Nick and for his grandchildren, Bradley and Milly, and then Sasha and family. The family were not really a necessity but Tammy doubted that Sasha would be allowed to come without them. Monica could write out the invites for the aunts and uncles.

Nick had called up earlier to remind Liz that the art group would be meeting on Wednesday evening and he would pick her up at seven o'clock. She had forgotten all about it but was pleased to be going out to meet new people. 'This is what life is meant to be like,' she thought to herself.

She thought of Jim. It was strange but she hadn't thought about him for a few days. She felt a little guilty for being happy.

Monica popped in after work and the three of them sat in the garden soaking up the late afternoon sun. As soon as Monica had settled with a cup of tea Tammy ran inside to retrieve the party invites.

'What do you think?' she said, looking really pleased with herself.

'Fantastic,' said Monica, holding one up. 'Very professional. We will have to find a DJ now.'

'I think you can hire a jukebox,' said Liz trying to be helpful. 'It might be cheaper than a DJ, although Saturday afternoon is probably a good time. It should be more reasonable than an evening slot. What are you wearing Tammy?' asked Liz.

'I don't know yet.' She looked at Monica. 'I need something new.'

'I could buy your outfit for your birthday,' said Liz.

'That's too generous,' said Monica.

'No, no,' said Liz, 'I insist. It will save me having to think of something.'

'No high heels or crop tops,' said Monica.

Tammy gave her the 'are you serious face'. 'I wouldn't wear a crop top,' she insisted.

'Good,' said Monica.

'We will only look at clothes up to your neck and down to your knees,' said Liz seriously. Tammy laughed and raised her eyebrows.

'What would you like me to get you?' asked Monica, thinking that she probably already knew the answer.

'How about a new phone,' said Tammy, 'mine's a bit ancient. I'd like a smartphone so I can FaceTime and send emails n'stuff.'

'I'll think about it.'

'Everyone else has one,' said Tammy in a whiney voice.

'If everyone jumped off a cliff would you jump?'

countered Monica, sounding just like her mother. She laughed at herself. She had already decided to buy Tammy a new phone but wanted it to be a surprise. 'Right, party food suggestions.'

'I like burgers,' said Tammy.

'I'm sure you do,' said Monica, 'but we're not having a barbeque and we have around forty five people to cater for.'

'How about pizza and salad with a few snack foods and cakes thrown in,' said Liz.

'I think my friends would prefer burgers and don't forget the cupcakes.' Tammy was making a list.

*****

On Tuesday when Monica went into work she had decided against speed dating given that Kevin seemed keen on her taking him out. She would put off meeting more frogs for a while longer. She had sent him a text suggesting an early dinner followed by a comedy club in Crouch End. 'Great,' came the almost immediate response, which put her back in the happy place she was in prior to her last date. Liz was able to look after Tammy so Monica booked the tickets.

*****

When Nick came to collect Liz on Wednesday night he looked different. She had been in the living room and watched as his car pulled up outside the house. She studied him as he walked up the path and thought to herself that he didn't seem at all like a man approaching sixty. He had a real spring in his step. He still had a full head of hair and the greying temples gave him a distinguished look. He was lightly tanned and wearing a chunky jumper over faded jeans and boots. The casual style really suited him. Not that there are many rules relating to clothes for men. They could wear more or less anything.

He was so different to Jim. Jim always wore a shirt and tie, summer or winter, never without a shirt and tie. Even working in the garden he wore a tie.

She wasn't sure that Nick even owned a tie but she liked the way he dressed, the way he walked, the way he made her feel. He was addictive. She felt a little frightened by the strength of her own feelings. What if Adam really objected, what would she do? She wasn't sure whether she was ready to rock the boat but Nick made her happy and she didn't want to go back to being lonely either. She would content herself with being friends for a bit longer.

'Hiya.' He smiled as he reached the door. 'All ready?'

'I am,' said Liz, indicating the bag containing all the art materials she thought she would need.

'I've got you a present,' he said, holding up a parcel. She opened the bag. Inside was a book, 'How to Draw Everything.' It was a huge tome explaining techniques and different styles.

'I hope you don't mind,' he said, 'I know you're not a beginner but you said you were a little rusty. I thought this might help.'

'Thanks,' said Liz a bit lost for words, 'it's lovely of you. Well, shall we go?' Liz put the book on the table in the hall, locked the front door and followed Nick to his car. 'We can always take turns driving,' said Liz, 'I don't want to put you out.'

'It's no trouble. I'm only up the road.'

The car was another big difference. Jim always had a sensible saloon car which he washed religiously every Saturday morning, rain or shine. He also bought a new car every three years. Nick had a battered old Jeep which suited his more rugged appearance.

He was growing on her more every time they met. She really liked his family too, so different to her own. She thought about Adam.

The art group was a mixture of old and young, Liz guessed at ages anything from thirty to eighty. As they walked in the room it had a buzz about it. The teacher looked like she had been dressed from a fabric warehouse and wore a long multi-coloured skirt and a turban on her head. Her batik top had bell shaped sleeves which she constantly folded back up her arms so she could demonstrate without painting herself. Her large dark eyes were underlined with kohl, making them look even larger and her bright pink lipstick bled into the wrinkles around her mouth. She was definitely what people would refer to as a character.

Nick introduced Liz to Angela. Liz was slightly disappointed. She expected her to have an unusual, exotic name like Diandra or Jacquetta. Angela belied her bohemian appearance. She welcomed Liz enthusiastically to her 'little group' as she called them before directing her to a desk near the front and proceeding to demonstrate the technique of the week.

Nick smiled at Liz as Angela fussed over her new pupil, guiding and correcting her mistakes. Every now and then she looked over at Nick, who didn't need lessons. He seemed to be doing his own thing. He would smile broadly and give her work the thumbs-up. After an hour and a half they stopped for a break.

'Come on,' said Nick, 'I'll take you to the coffee bar and introduce you to some of the others.'

The coffee bar was set up in what looked to be an old office. It had a wooden counter with a proper coffee machine and not the old tea urn that Liz had expected. There was also a glass fronted cabinet containing chocolate bars, biscuits and cakes. A vending machine dispensed fizzy drinks and crisps. Painting and drawings were on every wall and Liz thought she recognised some of the styles she had seen at the exhibition the week before.

Nick bought two coffees and pointed to a table where a couple of seats were still empty, the other two seats occupied by a couple having an animated discussion.

'I'll help you,' said Liz, not feeling quite confident enough to go and introduce herself although she thought that she recognised the woman from the exhibition the week before. When she had her coffee in her hand she followed Nick over to the table.

'Hi folks,' said Nick as they sat down, 'this is Liz, a new recruit. Liz this is Marie and Carlo.'

Liz guessed that Marie was probably in her early fifties

and Carlo maybe mid-thirties. They shook hands with Liz enthusiastically.

'I recognise you from the exhibition last week,' said Liz. 'You painted the fabulous nudes.'

'Thank you,' said Marie. 'I sold quite a few paintings that week. Carlo was there too, weren't you darling.' She patted his thigh.

Liz looked at Carlo. 'I'm sorry, I met so many people. I didn't recognise you,' said Liz a little embarrassed.

'Carlo was the subject of the paintings,' said Marie, waiting for a reaction and hoping to shock.

'Well that explains it,' said Liz, nearly choking on her coffee. 'I didn't recognise you with your clothes on.' Marie and Carlo laughed out loud causing Nick and Liz to erupt into a fit of giggles. Liz hoped that her initiation was over and she could relax. She doubted she would have been so brave without Nick's support.

She learnt that Marie and Carlo were a couple and had met six years ago when Carlo was in his late twenties. Marie had advertised for a life model and Carlo had answered the call. He had a fairly ordinary looking face but Marie was not interested in his face and they really hit it off, so much so that after the first week's work Marie had moved him in.

'How fabulous,' said Liz, genuinely interested. 'It takes all sorts,' she thought to herself. They drank their coffee quickly and went back to the class.

Lessons finished at nine o'clock and usually moved from the classroom to the pub on the corner.

'Coming Nick?' shouted Frank, a man of at least eighty if he was a day.

'It's up to you,' said Nick, addressing Liz. 'Would you like to go to the pub?'

'I'd love to.' She was really starting to feel comfortable. They were an interesting group of people and Liz was fascinated. She couldn't wait to talk to them.

The pub was only a couple of minutes' walk away.

'How did you find this group?' asked Liz, as they walked along the pavement. 'You certainly don't need art lessons.'

'I didn't find it, my daughter found it for me. After my second wife left I did a lot of soul searching and began to try to rebuild my relationship with my children and grandchildren. I was spending a lot of time on my own. Heather noticed the ad in the local paper and they were looking for new members, so I came along. It was just something to do initially. I was fairly reluctant in the beginning but I found I really liked it. They are a bit weird and wonderful but they support each other. Angela and the group encouraged me to give up my old job and helped me put on my first exhibition and I've never really looked back. The group arrange social events and exhibitions. I feel lucky to be a part of it.'

'It does have a nice feel to it,' said Liz. 'I should have tried something like this myself ages ago.'

'Well, you're here now,' said Nick smiling.

'Yes, I am,' said Liz, smiling back and feeling utterly content.

'Now you just need to practice. I could always give you a hand if you're interested.'

'That's kind of you,' said Liz. 'I'm thinking of making my summer house into a studio.'

'I'd love to help,' said Nick. 'What about this weekend?'

'Great,' said Liz, without giving herself time to mull it over first.

'It's a date,' he added.

She watched him as he went up to the bar. He was warm and friendly with everyone. She really enjoyed his company but still had a nagging thought in the back of her head that he was just being nice and she shouldn't read too much into it. She wasn't sure how to react. Besides, girlfriend sounds very odd when you're over fifty.

She had even started to think about sex. It was strange because as much as she loved Jim they had drifted into an entirely sexless marriage. They slept in the same bed but boredom had set in years ago and the physical side of their marriage had deteriorated in their late forties.

They still did lots of things together, and he would occasionally hold her hand or give her a hug, but it never lead to anything physical. She told herself that it didn't matter and it didn't with Jim. But with Nick she felt butterflies in her stomach whenever she was close to him and it was a little scary.

Chapter 24

'Found one,' said Monica, when she popped in after work on Thursday.'Found what?' said Liz.

'A disco,' said Monica. 'Hundred quid. That's not too bad, and he'll do from three to five. What do you think?'

'I think it's a nice little earner for a couple of hours work. How did you find him?'

'Nadia at work is a mine of information,' said Monica. 'She did ask me to go out tonight to a speed dating event in a wine bar but I'm not quite sure it's me. Besides, I couldn't have gone. The auditors turned up yesterday so I'm rushed off my feet.'

Liz told Tammy and Monica about the art group and the fact that Nick would be coming over on Sunday to help with the summer house.

'There's not really much to do, we're just adding some cupboards for the art materials and moving all the stuff out of the garage.'

'Sounds cosy,' said Monica grinning.

'Heh, why don't the two of come for lunch? It's going to be hot at the weekend, we could barbeque?'

'Please,' said Tammy, looking longingly at Monica.

'We would love to Liz.' She made a face at Tammy. 'I need to go to the garden centre at some point,' added Monica. 'We need some extra chairs and tables for the party.'

'Don't spend too much money,' warned Liz, 'the supermarkets are selling patio furniture and bistro sets at the moment and probably cheaper. Plus we can use our kitchen tables and chairs too.'

'Do you fancy shopping on Saturday?'

'That would be great,' said Liz.

'Has anyone replied to your invitation yet?' asked Liz, addressing Tammy.

'I only gave them out yesterday at school,' she replied, 'and most of my class mates are coming. Except Holly who will be on holiday, which is a shame, but Lauren's coming.

I've emailed Sasha and I need to send one in the post to Finn and Rory. Will you give this to Nick?' Tammy was holding an invitation addressed to Nick, Milly and Bradley. 'Monica is sending out the family invites.'

*****

Sasha was doing her homework in the den when Adam came in from work.

'Dad,' she called, as she heard her mother saying hello.

'Hang on poppet,' Adam replied, as he gave Georgina a peck on the cheek. Five or ten minutes passed before he put his head around the door.

'Need help with your homework?'

'No dad,' said Sasha earnestly. 'Tammy has sent me an invitation to her party at grandma's. It's not long now and I want to go. I could stay with grandma.'

'We'll see,' said Adam.

'No, I don't want to see,' said Sasha. 'We'll see usually means no. I really want to go. Why doesn't mum like Tammy?'

'Mum doesn't dislike Tammy. It's just that she doesn't want you mixing in that area.'

'You mean she doesn't want me having mixed race friends unless they are rich and go to a school like mine.'

'No, it's not that,' said Adam.

'Then why can't I go?

'It's complicated,' said Adam.

'No, it's not,' said Sasha. 'It's not just Tammy. You're not very nice to grandma. You should be pleased she has met Nick. He is really nice and she likes him. Tammy will be going to secondary school in September and grandma will be home on her own again. Would you prefer her to be lonely?'

'No, of course not,' said Adam, clearly flustered. 'It's not what you think. We might not be here. I have been offered a job in America so we may be moving at the end of the summer. Won't that be great?'

'No it won't.' Sasha had tears in her eyes. 'I don't want to leave, I like it here. I won't go,' and with that she ran out of the room crying.

Adam pulled himself up from the sofa and lumbered into the kitchen. 'Sasha is upset,' he said to Georgina.

'She'll get over it.' Said Georgina, without looking up

from the magazine she was reading.

'I think maybe we should go to Tammy's party at mum's on the nineteenth,' said Adam.

'No,' said Georgina firmly. 'I don't want to encourage her friendship with that girl and New York beckons. It wouldn't be fair.'

'We could always put the date back and go a couple of weeks later,' said Adam. 'Besides, I'm not so sure it's the right thing. I don't want the kids to be miserable.'

'What about me being miserable?' Georgina looked up from her magazine. 'I've got my heart set on New York. They'll thank us when they're older.'

'Georgie, we hardly see mum now. We'll see her even less if we move and she must be lonely or she wouldn't be so keen on this guy Nick.'

'Well, we can do the same as we're doing for mum and dad and find her a nice home nearby.'

'You really are a cold hearted bitch, aren't you,' said Adam seriously.

'And you have always been the perfect son,' said Georgina with a tight lipped smile. Adam winced. Georgina had definitely hit a nerve.

*****

Monica was happy as she walked into work on Friday. The party was coming together nicely and she had a potential boyfriend again. Life was good.

'Hiya,' said Nadia, clearly very pleased with herself. 'You missed a great night.' She was beaming.

'Were there lots of potential mates?' asked Monica, curious to know if she'd really missed anything.

'There was the usual desperate bunch, the ones still drinking in the last chance saloon. They try too hard but if you drink enough they start to look better. I did meet one nice guy early in the evening.'

'Fantastic,' said Monica. 'What was he like?'

'Gorgeous! His name is Kevin and he's something in IT.' Alarm bells started ringing in Monica's head. There must be loads of guys working in IT and Kevin is a common name she reasoned.

'He was really charming. Apparently he split up with his girlfriend recently and is only just getting out and about again. Her loss is my gain. We got on really well, so well in fact that he has invited me to dinner at his flat on Sunday.'

'Wow, that's fast,' said Monica.

'What the hell. Life is short and I do love a man who can cook.'

'Yes it's great,' Monica agreed, trying not to sound too interested. 'What did he look like?'

'He's tall with dark hair and a great smile. He reminded me of someone, someone from the telly. I can't think of the name right now but it'll come to me.' Monica had to force a smile as she moved away from the desk.

She was sure that if she'd stood there for much longer she wouldn't have been able to stop herself asking for his contact details so she could check. Could it be the same man? Thank god Tammy hadn't met him.

'You haven't got an aspirin have you?' asked Nadia, 'my head is really thumping.' Monica searched around in her handbag until she found the Paracetamol that she kept for emergencies.

'You're a lifesaver,' said Nadia, as she threw two of them in her mouth at the same time and took a swig of water from the bottle on her desk.

As Monica got out of the lift she thought about what she should do. Nothing yet, just in case, although every instinct told her that this was probably the same Kevin who said he had divorced years ago. She wondered if he was actually divorced at all. Still, it could just be a coincidence. There are loads of men on the telly. It could be someone completely different.

It was hopeless, another bloody frog.

In any case it would have to wait until Nadia's memory came back. Luckily Nadia was keen to talk about the previous night's triumph and asked Monica if she fancied meeting up for a chat in the canteen at lunchtime. Monica couldn't refuse.

However, if it was the same Kevin it threw up an additional dilemma. Should she tell Nadia? She'd cross that bridge when she came to it.

When she got to her desk and switched on her computer there was an email from Kevin. 'Morning Gorgeous. Looking forward to Saturday, lots to talk about. What time shall I pick you up?' Prior to the conversation with Nadia she would have been over the moon. But now there was a spanner in the works and she wasn't sure what to do. She started to look at Kevin with a much more critical eye. Was he a bit too intense? After all, they'd only had coffee and dinner.

Unfortunately she was unable to find out if it was her Kevin. Nadia had started to feel unwell around ten o'clock due in most part to the copious amounts of vodka and tonic she had consumed the night before. She was finally sent home at eleven o'clock after being sick in the waste paper bin on reception. There was nothing for it. She had to cancel her date with Kevin.

She replied to his email. Had she not spoken to Nadia and suspected Kevin of being a liar she might have worried about the wording and been a bit more sensitive. What plausible excuse could she give to make sure she got another date? She had no such scruples now 'Sorry Kevin, but I'm going to have to cancel dinner on Saturday as something urgent has come up. Monica (no kisses).' Short and to the point. Now she just had to hope that he was the same guy that invited Nadia to dinner at his flat or she had just blown any chance she had of a potential mate.

*****

Saturday was hot, almost Mediterranean. It was fantastic to wake up to brilliant sunshine. Liz had made an appointment for the hairdressers at eight thirty to get her highlights done and her roots touched up. Tammy had taken over the task of blow drying Liz's hair, for which Liz now paid her ten pounds per week, money that Tammy was using to make sure every house in the neighbourhood grew Lavender to help bees.

Liz was up at six thirty and by six forty five she was washed, dressed and sitting on the patio drinking tea, just like old times. 'Well Jim, what do you think?' She spoke to the sky. 'I hope you like it,' she added sheepishly.

Tammy was going to Laura's house for the day so Liz and Monica were able to go shopping on their own. They decided to go to the superstore on the edge of town as it saved all that trudging around from one shop to another and they were almost certain to find what they were looking for. When Monica rang the bell at eleven o'clock Liz had just finishing mopping the floor.

'I've cancelled my date for tonight,' she told Liz as soon as she was in the door.

'Oh, what's happened? I thought you liked him.' Monica relayed Nadia's encounter at the speed dating event.

'It could just be a coincidence,' said Liz, trying to reassure her.

'I'm not lucky enough for that,' said Monica. 'It's more likely that he's still married and probably has a couple of kids. I bet it's not even his flat. It's amazing how fast you can go off someone.'

Liz smiled. 'Come on, let's get out and have a coffee before we start shopping.'

As soon as they got to the shopping centre they headed off to the nearest café.

'How are things going with Nick?'

'It's great,' said Liz, 'his friends at the art club are brilliant. I met the artist and model responsible for the nude paintings. You know, the huge canvas I almost bumped into.'

'Oooh, can I meet him too?' asked Monica teasing.

'His name is Carlo and he is the partner of the artist. They are a really nice couple.'

'Shame,' said Monica, turning the corners of her mouth down to make a sad face. 'Let's get back to Nick,' said Monica, refusing to be waylaid. 'Have you had your first kiss?'

'No, we have not,' said Liz, with mock indignation. She had definitely thought about it. 'I know young people nowadays don't wait for anything but I spent nearly forty years with the same man. I am very,' she hesitated, 'very out of practice. Apart from the fact that Nick's last wife was twenty years his junior. I can't compete. What on earth does he see in me? No. I'm happy just being friends.'

'Liz, I've seen the way he looks at you. It's obvious he likes you. If you like him as much as I think he likes you, you should just go for it. I'm not convinced that you two can just be friends. Let's face it, no one knows how much time they have on this earth. Don't waste time. You're good together.'

'We'll see,' said Liz, 'anyway he'll be here tomorrow when you come for the barbeque so you can observe closely and tell me what you think.'

'Are you still OK to look after Tammy in the summer holidays?'

'I am,' said Liz. 'I'm looking forward to seeing more of her, she's such a lovely girl. I'm going to invite Sasha to stay too. I really miss her but I don't hold out much hope that Georgina will agree. She's such a snob, and worse, I can't even talk to Adam at the moment. We just end up arguing. He's got a bee in his bonnet about Nick.'

'Do you think they will come to Tammy's party?'

'I don't hold out much hope of that either I'm afraid. Sasha told me that Adam has accepted a job in America. He hasn't even mentioned it to me.'

'Oh, that's a shame.'

'I must admit that I am really disappointed. I barely see them now, if they move to America I don't suppose I'll see them at all. Still, I guess Adam has to make the most of these chances. After all, he has a very important job and a family to provide for.'

'Of course,' Monica agreed. She didn't want to upset Liz by saying what she really thought of him.

They finished their coffee and went off to look for garden furniture and to buy food for the barbeque. Every big store had patio sets for sale so competition was fierce. It wasn't long before Monica had found a table, six chairs and a parasol at a very reasonable price which she planned to use in her own garden until the party. Liz couldn't resist a bargain either so ended up with a couple of rattan recliners and a coffee table. She could picture herself sitting on one of them on the veranda of the new summer house with the sound of the fountain in the background and a glass of wine in her hand.

'That makes fourteen chairs,' said Monica. 'Will it be enough? I doubt the kids will sit down for long but they will have to sit down to eat.'

'We could put some picnic blankets out with cushions on top,' suggested Liz, mindful of the fact that without grass the ground was quite hard. 'I'm sure we could beg or borrow some chairs from somewhere,' Liz assured her, 'worse way, we'll ask the adult guests to bring their own.' Sadly the bargain furniture wasn't such a bargain when it wouldn't fit in the car and they had to pay a twenty five pound delivery charge.

Monica's mobile pinged on the way home. When she looked it was Kevin. 'Hope everything is OK, please give me a call if you need me. Kevin xx.'

'Awww, that's nice,' said Liz when Monica read it out. 'Maybe you're wrong about him. It might not be the same man.'

'I know,' said Monica confused, 'but I'd like to wait and see before I commit to any more dates. Besides, it's difficult with Tammy. We come as a package now. I have to be sure.'

Chapter 25

Liz had slept badly and she woke up feeling tired. She had finally got off to sleep around three in the morning. When she thought about it she realised that it was Nick coming to the house that was on her mind. She wasn't worried about being alone with Nick, she loved his company, but it was Jim's house. She felt almost as though she was committing adultery, betraying him in some way, which was ridiculous. Nick made her happy and that made her feel guilty, but what for? She had been a good wife.

She wasn't sure that Nick coming over was such a good idea. Maybe she should ring him and make an excuse to put him off. It was nearly nine o'clock now and he was due to arrive by eleven. She tried his mobile and when he didn't answer she resigned herself to the fact that he was coming and she was being silly. She got washed and dressed quickly and carefully applied a little make-up which she now did on a regular basis. She made a cup of tea and went outside to sit in the garden.

Nick turned up at eleven on the dot and getting no reply after ringing the bell went to the side gate and knocked loudly.

'Coming,' shouted Liz, who had been busy watering the plants. She spent as much time as she possibly could in the garden now, she couldn't get enough of it. It would only get better as the plants matured and the paving weathered.

'Hiya,' said Nick, smiling as he walked down the path behind her. 'I thought you'd be out here.'

'We don't get enough summer to waste any being indoors,' said Liz, leading the way. 'Would you like a cup of tea?'

'I'd love one.' He sat down at the table and opened a newspaper he had brought with him. Liz looked out the window while she waited for the kettle to boil. It felt so familiar. Jim would sit and read the papers in the same spot while she made tea and breakfast and watched him from the window. Except that she didn't look at Nick in the same way.

'Monica and Tammy are coming by later. I thought we could barbeque if you don't mind.'

'Great,' said Nick, 'I'm a dab hand on the barbeque.'

'Well that's good to know,' Liz shouted through the window. 'Monica and I are both useless. I hope you've looked after the Lavender. Tammy is bound to ask you how it's doing.'

'I have,' said Nick, who surprised himself. 'It's positively thriving.'

'Great. Tammy may demand evidence. She is busy supplying the rest of the neighbourhood with plants at the moment.' She brought out tea and biscuits on a tray.

'Oh, in case I forget,' Liz ran inside and brought out

an invitation to Tammy's party. 'She has invited Milly and Bradley too. I hope you can all come? She would be so disappointed if you weren't here.'

'I'm not sure about Bradley,' said Nick, 'you know what teenage boys are like but Milly is much more considerate. I'm sure she'd be happy to come, especially as it doesn't interfere with her going out later. Bradley on the other hand does his best to stay in bed all day at the weekend. I know he has Heather pulling her hair out. I hope you weren't too fazed by Marie on Wednesday. She likes to shock.'

'On the contrary, I thought she was trying to make me feel at home. After all she did feed me the line so I didn't want to disappoint her.'

Nick laughed. 'You didn't. You seem different,' he said, when he'd stopped laughing.

'I do? How?'

'A little distracted, what's wrong?

'Oh nothing,' said Liz, lying through her teeth and feeling a bit unnerved that he was so perceptive. 'I didn't sleep very well, that's all.'

'I hope you weren't worrying about me coming over.'

'No, I'm pleased you're here. I've been really happy lately and that's the problem.'

'Being happy is a problem?' asked Nick confused.

'No, no, I didn't mean that. I mean that I feel guilty for being happy.'

'I'm sure Jim wouldn't want you to be miserable.'

'No, I don't think he would. I'm not so sure about Adam

though. I don't think he likes the idea of me having a male friend.'

'Liz, I'd be happy to be your friend if that is all you want me to be but I hope you have realised by now that I'd like us to be more than friends.'

Liz smiled as Nick reached over and took her hand. 'I'd like that too.' She cupped her hand around his.

'Well, that's great. Come on let's get on with kitting out your studio.' He pulled her out of the chair and they walked up to the summer house hand in hand.

By the time Tammy and Monica arrived at two o'clock Nick had put up several shelves and moved a lot of the boxes from the garage. Liz decided to leave the tools where they were for now, at least until after the party. While Nick drilled and banged in nails Liz marinated chicken and chopped up salads and vegetables for the barbeque.

'My, you have been busy,' said Monica when she came in and saw the table already laid. 'Here,' she gave Liz a Tupperware container full of fresh fruit salad, 'and these.' She handed over a couple of bottles of white wine. 'They are nice and cold,' she added. 'They've been in the fridge since last night.'

'It's so nice of you,' said Liz, 'but you shouldn't have.'

'I helped,' said Tammy, making sure she got her share of the credit.

'Well it looks fantastic,' said Liz, and she gave Tammy a big hug.

'Hi Nick,' shouted Tammy as soon as she saw him coming

down the steps. 'How's the Lavender?'

'I told you,' said Liz, as he reached the patio.

'I have had to re-pot it,' he said proudly. 'It's grown a couple of inches. So have you I think. Are you sure you're only eleven on your next birthday?' Tammy laughed. 'Monica you're looking great.' He pecked her on the cheek. 'Well, are you getting hungry? The barbecue's ready, shall I start cooking?'

'Yes please,' said Tammy. 'Would you like to hear about my party?'

'I'd love to,' said Nick. He was a captive audience after all. Tammy proceeded to tell him who was coming and what they would be doing and the outfit she planned to wear as Nick slapped chicken breasts onto the grill, leaving Monica and Liz to sit at the table with a glass of wine.

'This is a lovely domestic scene,' said Monica, smiling mischievously as she sipped her wine.

Liz smiled. 'The weird thing is it feels perfectly natural and yet every now and then I get this nagging feeling in the back of my mind that makes me feel as if I'm doing something wrong.'

'Like what?' said Monica.

'Oh, I don't know. I guess I just feel guilty for being alive and happy and probably for having Nick here in this house, Jim's house.'

Monica reached over and put her hand on Liz's. 'Jim's been dead for how long? Five years? I think you've been miserable long enough.'

'I'm not so sure,' said Liz. 'He always joked when he was alive that he'd come back and haunt me when he died. I prayed that he would, I was so desperate to see him.'

'I think this house needs some happy memories,' said Monica, 'but if you really feel too guilty to be happy with Nick here perhaps you should think about moving.'

'Oh, I don't think I could ever do that, could I?'

'Why not? You are a free agent, so to speak.'

Nick came and joined them at the table and Liz poured him a glass of wine.

'I hope you don't mind but Tammy and I have been discussing her party and I have volunteered to man the barbecue.'

'That was cheeky of you,' Monica said to Tammy.

'I didn't ask,' said Tammy defensively, 'Nick volunteered.'

'Yes,' said Nick, 'it was completely of my own volition.' He made a big gesture of winking to Tammy. 'Besides, I hate pizza.'

'Told you,' said Tammy, 'people prefer burgers.'

'Are you sure?' asked Monica.

'Of course,' said Nick, 'it will be my pleasure.'

'Well that's settled then, burgers it is.'

The afternoon was warm and breezy, just enough to ruffle the edges of the tablecloth every now and then. The sound of the fountain was drowned out by the chatter and frequent bursts of laughter. Tammy's party was going to be the highlight of the summer. Liz soaked it all up. It was fantastic to be using the garden again.

'How about a holiday, are you going anywhere?' asked Nick.

'Haven't thought about it,' said Liz and Monica together. 'How about you?'

'I have a small house in France that I go to sometimes. It's been a project for a few years. I still haven't managed to finish it.'

'How lovely,' said Monica. 'Where is it exactly?'

'It's in a little village outside Toulouse in the south of France, near to the border with Spain.'

'Wouldn't you like to live there?' asked Tammy.

'Not on my own,' said Nick looking at Liz, who blushed. 'Can we see it?'

'Tammy!' Monica moved her head from side to side to indicate to Tammy that asking was rude.

'I'd love you to see it,' said Nick. 'I was thinking of going there later in the year. Perhaps you could come for a holiday?'

'Can we?' said Tammy, her big brown eyes pleading with Monica to say yes.

'We'll see.'

'We could go by aeroplane,' added Tammy.

'We'll see,' said Monica a little more forcefully. Tammy realised that going on would not aid her cause so she changed the subject to art.

'I'll show you my drawing of Liz.' She ran into the kitchen to retrieve Liz's picture from the fridge. 'What do you think?'

'It looks just like her,' said Nick laughing.

They stayed in the garden until the sun started to go down.

'Come on Tammy, time to go home I think.'

'Oh, do we have to?'

'Yes, we do,' said Monica. 'You and I have both got homework and it's getting late. Thank you both for a lovely afternoon, we've really enjoyed it..

'Me too, 'said Liz. 'Thanks for coming. See you both tomorrow.'

Liz and Nick took all the plates and cutlery into the kitchen and put them in the sink. Nick started to run the water.

'No,' said Liz, 'you are my guest. I'll do that later. I'd like to sit on my veranda and watch the sun go down.'

She flicked the switch in the kitchen which turned on the garden lights. It was only just starting to get dark enough and the chrome columns of the fountain glistened in the mixed rays of spotlights and fading sunlight. Nick poured a couple of glasses of wine and held them both as he led the way to the summer house. He set them down on the table next to the chairs and turned to take Liz's hand as she walked up the three small steps. She stumbled on the top step and fell forwards. Nick managed to catch her in his arms and pull her up. Her face was now just inches away from his and she was aware of his breathing and his strong arms holding her. There was no hesitation and it seemed to be one fluid motion of gathering her up in his arms and kissing her full on the lips.

She didn't resist. The wine had softened the edges. She closed her eyes and felt butterflies in the pit of her stomach. She could easily have just let herself go with it, be carried away in the moment, but after the kiss she pulled back, scared by the force of her own feelings.

'I can't do this here,' she said softly. 'Not in this house, not yet. This is a little fast for me.' She was now aware of her own breathing. 'I'd like to take it slowly if you don't mind. It's been a long time since I have even kissed anyone,' she said eventually, 'let alone…' She didn't finish the sentence.

'There's no hurry. I just haven't met anyone in a long time that I have felt so at ease with.' He held her hands in his. 'I'm not going anywhere Liz.'

She smiled. She was relieved. She felt as though she could relax now the first kiss was over. She couldn't deny the chemistry between them and knew the first kiss would not be the last.

They sat on the veranda, drinking wine and talking way past midnight, Liz snuggled up to Nick on the chair next to his.

*****

Back in Bury St Edmunds Adam was tossing and turning. Georgina would be so angry if they didn't move to New York. Would she leave him? On the other hand, Sasha definitely did not want to go. He hadn't even discussed it with Leo and deep in his heart he knew he was putting it off because Leo loved his school and his friends. He probably felt the same as Sasha. He would have to speak to the children in the morning.

Then there's mum. Georgina was right, he had been a lousy son, aided and abetted by his scheming wife who only ever did anything that suited her. She certainly didn't go out of her way to let Liz into their lives but she was his mum and he should have behaved better. She might never have even met this Nick if he had looked after her more. He looked over at Georgina who was sleeping serenely. He did love her but he was under no illusions about her.

What if he didn't take the job? Would it damage his career? Would there be other offers? He had planned to retire at fifty five at the latest, buy a yacht and maybe sail around the Med. The kids would be at university and he would buy them a flat each.

And then there's mum. What to do about mum.

*****

Nick and Liz had fallen asleep in the garden and Nick woke around two o'clock. Liz was fast asleep with her head on his shoulder. He kissed her gently on the forehead, which woke her up.

'I'd better be off,' he said. 'Come on, I need a cab.'

Liz woke up wondering where she was for a second or two. 'What time is it?'

'It's after two, we both fell asleep.'

'Sorry,' said Liz, 'it must be the wine.'

She shivered with the cold and Nick put his arm around her. They walked back to the house with Nick's arm still around her shoulders to keep her warm. The garden looked magical with the spotlights illuminating the plants and the fountain and the fairy lights twinkling on the pergola.

The mini cab promised to be there in ten minutes.

'Thanks Nick,' said Liz.

'For what?' asked Nick.

'For being patient with me. I love being with you too.'

'I told you Liz, there's no hurry.'

The cab company rang Nick's mobile to indicate that they were outside in the street.

'I'll call you tomorrow.'

She watched him walk up the path. She was grateful that he hadn't kissed her again, although part of her wanted him to.

Chapter 26

Monica had Kevin on her mind on Monday morning as she drove to work. She couldn't wait to catch up with Nadia to see if she remembered who the speed dating guy reminded her of but when she got to work Nadia was not on reception. Instead there was another girl who Monica had never seen before. She wondered if she was still ill from the Friday before. Maybe it wasn't a hangover, or maybe she had stayed over for dessert when she had gone to Kevin's flat for dinner.

There was also an email waiting for her from Kevin when she switched on her computer. 'Hi Monica.' A bit formal, what happened to Hi Gorgeous? She could sense that something had changed. 'Hope everything was OK at the weekend. XX.' It sounded more like an email to a friend than a girlfriend. She wasn't sure how to respond. She would think about it before writing back.

*****

Finn was now working for one of Liz's neighbours a few doors up and had popped in for a chinwag after work. As soon as Tammy saw him she almost leapt on him, she was so pleased to see him.

'How's Rory and Devlin?' she asked. Although she liked Rory and Devlin she had a little crush on Finn. She knew that Devlin and Finn were partners but that didn't matter. She was still planning her wedding to Finn when she grew up.

Finn told them that Rory had left to start his own business. He was now working at the local industrial workshops where he had hired one of the units and was now busy making arty farty furniture.

'We'll have to go and see him in the holidays,' said Liz and Tammy together.

'I'll take you,' said Finn, 'let me know when you want to go. I do miss him. The jobs aren't half as much fun without him. We've now got a Polish guy called Thomasz, Thomas to you and me, working for us. He's built like a small tank and works like a navvy but he has no sense of humour whatsoever.'

'That will never do,' said Liz, remembering how much fun it was listening to Rory and Finn's good humoured bickering.

'I know,' said Finn. 'We'll have to work on that aspect of his character.'

Finn was keen to hear all about Nick. Liz relayed the fact that they now went to the art group together and saw each other quite often. She told him about Nick's house in France and how he had asked her to go with him later in the summer. Tammy added that she would also be going to Nick's house for a holiday at half term. She had practically invited herself.

Finn asked about the arrangements for the party. Tammy was in her element as she told him about the disco and chill out area, adding that Nick would now be manning the barbecue and burgers were on the menu.

'It will be fantastic,' said Finn, 'I can't wait.'

Liz showed Finn her studio inside the summer house. 'Love it, love it, love it,' he said enthusiastically. He then walked around the garden inspecting the plants which had grown quite a bit over the past few weeks. ''I hope you've been watering these well,' he said to Tammy. The garden was, he assured her, one of their best designs ever. 'I've done bigger,' he said to Liz, 'but I don't think I've done better.'

'I adore it,' added Liz, 'it has changed my outlook in so many ways.'

Monica popped in to collect Tammy after work and sat in the garden chatting to Finn until he left just after seven o'clock. Tammy was enjoying herself watering the plants with the hosepipe. Liz had an adjustable spray nozzle and Tammy was trying hard to spray next door's cat as it walked along the top of the fence. Luckily the cat was far too fast.

'Any news?' Liz waited until Tammy was out of earshot.

'No, Nadia wasn't in work.'

'Well, maybe she's ill,' assured Liz.

'Maybe,' said Monica, not convinced.

'Have you spoken to Kevin?'

'He emailed me, a business-like email.'

'Well what do you expect?' said Liz. 'You've hardly seemed keen. What if it's not the same Kevin? He must be confused.'

'I am too,' said Monica, 'and maybe it's too late but I can't go forward until I know for sure.'

Nadia was not in work the next day either which was beginning to affect Monica's mood. Not knowing was gnawing at her insides. She felt grumpy and short tempered which was so unlike her. 'It was only dinner,' she reasoned. One date, she didn't own him. What if he did ask Nadia out? She hadn't seemed that keen so maybe he thought she didn't like him. Maybe he decided that it wasn't going anywhere so he may as well put himself back on the market.

By Thursday Monica had decided that if Nadia was not in work she would find out where she lived from Personnel and pay her a visit. Luckily that wasn't necessary. As Monica walked through the door Nadia was sitting at her desk looking all pleased with herself.

'Hi,' said Monica, relieved to see her, not least because it would put her out of her misery. 'How are you?'

'I'm great,' said Nadia.

'Have you been ill?' asked Monica.

'No,' said Nadia, speaking very quietly. 'That's just what I told the agency. I'm in love.' She was grinning from ear to ear.

'Wow, that was fast.' Monica couldn't hide the shock and disbelief from her face. Nadia didn't notice, she was too loved up. 'Kevin has asked me to move in with him.'

'He has?' said Monica, incredulous.

'I went to his flat for dinner on Sunday and ended up staying for three days. We talked and talked and the sex was incredible. He's such a great kisser. When I was leaving on Wednesday he asked me to move in and I thought why not? I know it's impulsive but I have a good feeling about him. He is the one.'

Monica was shell shocked. This could have been her, if only she'd accepted his invitation to go back to his flat. He was obviously looking to settle down. She would have been the one having incredible sex and moving in. She was so shocked she forgot to ask Nadia who he reminded her of, instead she went up to her office to mourn the loss of the life she would have had if she had just taken a chance. She didn't bother replying to his email.

The rest of the day she was in a daze. When she finally got home from work Liz and Tammy were painting in the garden.

'Tea is in the pot,' shouted Liz, as Tammy opened the front door.

Monica didn't seem her usual happy self. She poured herself a cup of tea and came outside, slumped into a chair on the patio, took off her shoes and rubbed her feet.

'Hard day?' asked Liz.

'Sort of,' she said miserably.

'What's up?' said Liz, when Tammy had gone to the far end of the garden and knew she could not hear them.

'Nadia is moving in with Kevin.'

'Oh,' said Liz, 'and are you sure that this is your Kevin?'

'Not a hundred percent,' said Monica. 'I haven't got proof it's the same one but I have a very strong feeling that it is.'

'I'm sorry,' said Liz, 'I know you liked him.'

Monica laughed. 'I only met him a couple of times, not really enough to plan the wedding.'

'There are plenty of fish in the sea,' said Liz, at a loss to think of any wiser words.

'What's worse,' Monica continued, 'I had an email from him today.'

'What did it say?' Liz was almost frightened to ask.

'Well, it started by saying that he was sorry that we couldn't meet up before and then asking if I had thought any more about his ideas for the website. He hoped that I liked them enough to help him set up a meeting with the advertising department.'

'I see,' said Liz.

'I don't think he was actually interested in me at all, he just wanted an introduction.'

'Oh, I'm sorry,' said Liz. 'He was just sounding you out?'

'It just goes to show how desperate I am,' said Monica. 'It's my own fault, I only saw what I wanted to see.'

*****

The next few weeks went by really quickly. Liz had been out with Nick several times to dinner and to the art group. She had met Heather and her husband John and would be meeting Nick's son and his new wife in a few weeks' time. She loved being with Nick and his family. She loved the fact that he made an effort with people. She couldn't quite believe that he was interested in her. Nick didn't push things either, apart from the occasional lingering kiss. He was prepared to wait until Liz felt happy about moving forward.

Of course she didn't need Adam's permission to go forward but she couldn't be happy without it and it was part of the reason she was holding back. If Adam really disapproved it would never feel right and there was a very real possibility that he wouldn't approve. He hadn't called for a couple of weeks despite the fact that she had left messages at home, at his office and on his mobile. She knew she would have to do something to break the deadlock. Adam was far too stubborn.

Evelyn answered the phone at the office. Liz didn't need to explain who she was. 'Mrs Bailey,' said Evelyn warmly, 'how nice to talk to you. Adam is on a conference call right now I'm afraid. Is it something urgent or can I ask him to call you back later?' She thought about leaving a message but decided that much more drastic action was needed. She was never sure if Adam was as busy as he always seemed to be when she called or whether he had briefed his secretary that part of her gate-keeping role included fending off calls from his mother.

In any case she had nothing to lose so she continued, 'Evelyn, are you the lady I need to thank for the wonderful flowers I received on Mothers' Day? They were absolutely stunning. I knew it couldn't be Adam, men are never very good at that sort of thing.' Ever loyal Evelyn didn't like to own to the fact that Adam merely paid for them. Instead she tactfully said that Adam was always very thoughtful. Liz knew she was lying. Adam had never been thoughtful; at least he had never given her much thought.

However, pressing on she asked if Adam would be free for lunch any time soon as she would like to surprise him. Evelyn opened up the Outlook Calendar on her computer.

It was almost wall to wall meetings until the end of August. 'He might be able to squeeze something in on Friday week.'

'It can't wait that long.' She was almost ready to panic. The party was just over three weeks away and she needed to speak to him now.

'Hang on Mrs Bailey, I think I've found a slot. The Management Committee Meeting has moved to Friday which means that he has a couple of hours late Thursday morning when he is not in a meeting. If you could make it an early lunch, say eleven thirty to twelve thirty, I can fit you in.'

'Perfect. I'll see you on Thursday. Thank you so much for all your help.' Liz knew that Tammy would be breaking up from school on Friday so time was of the essence.

She was nervous on Thursday morning and took extra care getting dressed. She wanted to look her best. She had never, ever gone into town to meet Adam for lunch and now, as she boarded the train, she wondered why it had never occurred to her to do it before. She should have made the effort. He might have been pleased to see her. She wondered if she would get a phone call at the last minute cancelling the appointment but when none came by ten thirty she wasn't sure whether she was pleased or not.

She exited the tube at Aldgate and found that she quite liked the buzz of the City. It was different to the West End which seemed much more crowded but much less focused. Here people walked with intent, no aimless meandering along the pavement. Here people strived determinedly forward. You could almost feel the ambition.

She got to the bank at eleven twenty five and asked the receptionist to let Adam know that she was there. She was surprised to hear the voice on the other end of the phone instruct the receptionist to ask her to come up to the tenth floor.

'Oh dear,' thought Liz, 'he's waiting with an excuse.'

When the lift doors opened Adam was nowhere to be seen and instead Evelyn lunged forward to shake her hand. 'Hi Mrs Bailey, we've spoken on the telephone.'

'Yes,' said Liz, 'nice to finally meet you and thank you so much for your help.'

Evelyn smiled broadly. 'Come this way, Mr Bailey is waiting for you.' She led her along the corridor to a meeting room.

Liz wasn't sure what to make of it. The fact that they were meeting in a meeting room made it so much more formal. She felt as though she was about to be interviewed for a job, or worse was being fired. 'Can you fire your own mother?' she wondered as she walked in.

Adam was already in the room, waiting and looking tense. 'Hi mum,' he said nervously. Evelyn came back with coffee and biscuits, discretely leaving them on a side table before slipping out as quietly as she came in.

'This is a first,' said Adam, forcing a smile.

'I don't know why I didn't think of it before, it was such an easy journey.' Liz took off her coat. 'So this is it, the place where you spend so much time. It's impressive.'

'Come on, I'll show you round.' He opened an adjoining door. The office was spectacular. It had huge floor to ceiling windows which looked amazing but apparently made the room far too hot in the summer and freezing cold in winter. In the centre of the room was a very modern semi-circular oak desk with a big black leather chair facing towards the wall. An assortment of chairs and side tables were scattered about the room.

She pictured Adam in this huge office and it suddenly seemed like a very lonely place. He looked tired.

'I'm sorry I didn't get round to calling you back.'

'Don't worry,' said Liz kindly, 'I'm here now. I know how busy you are,' Liz reassured him, 'which is why I thought it would be easier if I popped in to see you. I wanted us to have a chat. Have you got time for lunch?'

'Hardly ever,' said Adam, 'unless it's to impress a client.'

'Pretend I'm a client,' said Liz. 'You look like you could do with a break.'

She gathered up her coat and the pair of them headed to the lift. Passing Evelyn on the way Adam instructed her to shift his one o clock appointment to one thirty as he was taking his mother to lunch.

For a few seconds Liz got a glimpse of the old Adam. He seemed a little more human than usual.

Outside it was a beautiful day. He led the way along the pavement to a small café where a couple of tables and chairs had been placed outside. It wasn't quite noon so there was no rush. They ordered the food and drinks and sat in the sunshine. There was a little bit of an awkward silence after they ordered and Liz decided to be the first one to speak.

'Adam, I'd like to apologise for not telling you about my plans for the garden. I realise that it must have been a shock and I'd like to explain.

'After your father died I think I had a bit of a breakdown. I retreated into the house and I can see how hard that must have been for you. I couldn't bear to look at the garden, it held such terrible memories for me and it would have stayed exactly as it was if Tammy hadn't been so curious and then so keen on helping me change it. It seemed to me to be the answer I was looking for.'

'You could have told me what you planned to do Mum. I wouldn't have tried to stop you.'

'You're right, Adam. I should have let you know how I felt but I hardly see you. We haven't exactly been close over the last few years. I didn't think you'd care. We barely talk nowadays.'

Adam must have thought he had the moral high ground so he tagged on, 'And what about Nick?'

'What about Nick?' said Liz indignantly. 'Where Nick is concerned I have nothing to apologise for. He is an old acquaintance and a really good friend. We met up again a few months ago and I really like him. I would love you to meet him to see for yourself.'

'Why would I want to meet Nick?' Adam sounded more like a petulant teenager. 'You don't need my permission.'

'No, I don't,' Liz agreed, 'but your good opinion is very important to me. I have been very lonely since your Dad died. I have only started getting back to my old self since meeting Tammy and Monica. I'm sure that you would not prefer me to be on my own? Especially with your planned move to America. Were you going to tell me or just surprise me with a change of address card?'

Adam looked embarrassed. He knew the moral high ground had slipped from his grasp. He didn't ask how she knew. He guessed it must have been Sasha.

'She didn't mean to tell me Adam, so please don't be cross with her, but we were chatting one day and it just came out. She was very unhappy about it.'

'I had my reasons for not discussing it with them,' said Adam defensively.

'I'm sure you did,' Liz sounded sympathetic. 'Have you discussed it with them now?'

'Yes, and Sasha does not want to go.'

'How about Leo?'

'He seems quite excited at the prospect of moving.'

'And Georgina, is she keen?'

'She can't wait. She's already scoping out apartments and planning her shopping sprees.'

'Will this be a permanent move Adam?'

Adam nodded before speaking. 'The contract is for five years initially. I'm not sure after that. I'll see how it goes.'

'Why didn't you tell me?'

Adam looked sheepish. He thought for a few minutes before saying, 'Because I felt lousy about it and wasn't sure I could cope with your reaction.'

'Well, I have known for a while now Adam and I haven't fallen apart.' Adam said nothing.

'When are you planning on leaving?' asked Liz

'If it all goes according to plan I should be flying out at the end of August with Georgina following me nearer to Christmas with the children. It's a great opportunity and Georgina has her heart set on it.'

'Do you have to go?' asked Liz.

'No, but if I don't go it may harm my career.'

'Well, only you know what's best. You do not need to worry about me; the children are your main concern.

Still, if you're not going until the end of August there is nothing to stop you coming to Tammy's party with Sasha and Leo, and if you are not free perhaps you would let Sasha and Leo come to stay for a few days. Sasha and Tammy are good friends and it would mean so much to Tammy and to me.'

The food arrived which stopped the flow of conversation momentarily. They both thanked the waiter as he put down the plates but as soon as he left Liz continued. 'Please try to come on the nineteenth Adam, I would love you all to be there. I don't see nearly enough of you.'

'Georgina is absolutely adamant that she does not want to encourage Sasha's friendship with Tammy.'

'Tammy is a lovely girl and they get on so well. I can't see what possible harm it could do. Promise me you'll come.'

'I can't promise, mum.'

'You could Adam, if you wanted to.'

'I'll try. Can we eat lunch now?' he smiled. 'I have to be back in the office in twenty minutes.' They ate the rest of the meal in silence. Liz wanted to talk about Nick but sensed that Adam did not want to hear any details. Instead she talked about Tammy's party and the disco that Monica had hired.

She told Adam all about Monica's amazing weight loss and about the garden and how spectacular it looked. Lunch over, Adam called for the bill as Liz picked up her coat. 'Come on, I'll walk you to the tube station.'

When they got to the station to say goodbye Liz hugged him briefly which made Adam feel awkward and self-conscious, the way a small boy does at the school gates when his mother gives him a kiss goodbye.

'I love you so much Adam, and I'm very, very proud of you. Whatever you decide please don't be afraid to talk to me. Let's be honest with each other.'

'I love you too Mum,' he said as she walked through the barrier, although not loud enough for her to hear him.

*****

Friday was the last day of school and Tammy wore a crisp white shirt which was part of the uniform. It would be the last time she wore this particular shirt as all of the pupils in class seven would be autographing them for posterity.

'You never know, one of us might be famous one day,' she told Monica as she got dressed in her uniform for the last time. 'I hope it's me.'

School finished at two o'clock. It was a gorgeous day and rather than wait at home Liz thought that she would walk up to the school gates. She arrived just in time to see all of the children in Tammy's class proudly sporting their shirts, now covered in graffiti. She waved as soon as she saw Tammy who looked really pleased to see her.

'Don't forget to remind your friends about the party,' Liz mouthed the words as Tammy was too far away to hear. Tammy looked puzzled so Liz did a little dance and a mime of someone pulling the string of a party popper. Tammy laughed. She knew exactly what Liz meant, because she ran around frantically reminding her friends to come to her party.

They walked home in the sunshine hand in hand. 'What shall we do for the next few weeks?' Liz asked. 'I thought we might go to the seaside one day. What do you think?'

'Yes, please,' said Tammy. 'Is Sasha coming?'

'Not sure,' said Liz honestly, although she hoped that her

meeting with Adam had made it a little more likely.

'Monica said I could go out with Molly and Lauren to the park in the holidays. I am nearly eleven you know.'

'How could I forget,' said Liz. She swung her hand forward and back.

*****

Monica had a lull in her workload as the forthcoming audit had been cancelled. She decided to take a couple of days off work before the party and a week or two at the end of the summer recess so she could spend some quality time with Tammy.

Nadia continued to be completely loved-up. It was depressing. Even worse, whenever she spoke about the object of her affection now it was always preceded by the word 'my', as in 'my Kevin is so handsome', 'my Kevin is so clever', 'my Kevin is such a good cook'.

Monica avoided conversations with Nadia about her Kevin whenever she could possibly help it in case Nadia discovered that she knew him too. It was bad enough having to listen to how great he was all the time without Nadia suspecting that Monica could confirm all of these things, having known him. Monica realised she didn't know him at all and was beginning to wish they had never met.

Liz and Tammy both spoke to Sasha all the time on the telephone or email. One evening during their usual internet exchange Sasha told Liz that the local Gazette had contacted her because they were looking for an article for a filler and had picked up her letter about the Lavender plants. She had given them Monica's number. She wasn't sure if they would actually ring but they might.

'How wonderful.' Liz was really impressed with her granddaughter who now seemed so grown up, not at all the spoilt brat she had first encountered at Easter. 'Has dad said anything more about New York?'

'He spoke to me and Leo a few weeks ago, gran,' said Sasha. 'I told him I don't want to go but Leo was really excited at the idea so it's one for and one against. Actually two for, mum is really keen. I think she has found a residential home for grandma and grandpa. I don't think they will be moving with us to America.'

'It might not be as bad as you think, darling,' Liz tried to reassure her. 'I promise that I will visit as often as I can.'

'Thanks gran,' said Sasha, 'perhaps you could bring Tammy too.'

'I'm sure she'd love it,' said Liz. 'Has mum or dad mentioned the party?' Liz had her fingers crossed.

'No, nothing. I have spoken to Dad about it. I'm not even going to try to work on mum.'

'Oh, I've got some great news about Nick. He has been commissioned to work on a television programme about iconic art. Apparently he did a portrait for some TV executive a year or so ago and when they were looking for someone to co-present the programme he thought of Nick. He's had an audition and according to Nick he's a natural. The first programme goes out in September and he will be off filming in Suffolk next week. Isn't that exciting?'

'Wow, gran, he'll be famous.'

'I'm not sure about that,' said Liz, 'but apparently there will be an article about the programme in one of the Sunday magazines soon so it will probably generate some commissions. He has had his photograph taken by a professional photographer. He really deserves to do well.'

'Does this mean the tree in Tammy's bedroom may be worth something one day?'

'You never know,' said Liz. 'It worked for Banksy.'

During the holidays Tammy and Liz visited Rory at his new studio although Finn was too busy with work to accompany them. They stood at the entrance to the workshop, looking around. Rory was hand turning a chair leg on a lathe. The radio was on in the background and he hadn't heard them come in. He was singing away to Bohemian Rhapsody, nodding his head from side to side in time with the music.

Tammy made a big effort to clear her throat, loud enough to drown out Freddy Mercury. Rory looked up, startled for a second, before registering them. He pulled the goggles up onto his forehead, his face turning a little pink as a big grin replaced the song on his lips.

'Sorry about that,' he said, apologising for his fairly bad karaoke performance. 'Come in, come in. How are you?'

He was really pleased to see them. Tammy had bought him a Lavender plant and Liz had made muffins. 'Mrs B, I've missed you,' said Rory, stuffing his face.

'You have to guard this plant with your life,' said Tammy,

placing it on the windowsill.

'I will, I will,' Rory promised.

Tammy got out her notebook. 'You are still coming to my party, aren't you?' the expression on her face daring him to say no.

'I am, said Rory. 'Look,' he pointed to the calendar on the wall where he had circled the date in red pen and written 'Tammy's birthday' underneath. 'You see, I'm all organised.' Tammy smiled.

*****

Nick was away the following week so Liz didn't go to the art group. She wasn't quite confident enough to go by herself yet despite the fact that she had been practising with Tammy in her studio and improving rapidly. Monica came in most nights after work and the three of them sat in the garden chatting.

The party was only a week away now and both Liz and Monica had started planning and prepping. Tammy did a ring round of her friends. Lauren's mother had offered some fold up garden chairs and Nick's daughter Heather had also promised the use of all her garden furniture. Nick would be collecting it a day or two before the party. So they were all set.

Chapter 27

Sasha already had her outfit planned as she prayed for a miracle that would make her mother change her mind. It was no good working on her dad. She knew from a very early age that her mother made the decisions in the house and mostly her dad liked it that way. But now, for the first time in her eleven years, there was tension at home. Her parents were not the lovey-dovey pair that made them different to her friend's parents. They were arguing a lot more than usual and she hated it.

She considered going on strike and not speaking to her mother at all but that only lasted until Georgina took her shopping and she saw something she wanted. Her mother was being extra nice and spoiling both of them more than usual in her attempt to win allies.

Sasha would normally have relished this state of affairs and made sure that she took full advantage but she was too unhappy to get any pleasure out of material things. Leo, on the other hand, was highly delighted each time he got the latest game as he was completely missing the bigger picture.

Adam had not spoken to his mum since they met for lunch. He didn't know what to do or say. He was still undecided about New York. He had tried discussing it with Georgina but she was convinced that it would be for the best. Adam knew that if he didn't take the job he may risk missing out on future promotions or even being frozen out completely.

Nick got back from Suffolk the Wednesday before the party, a bit too late for the art group so instead he took Liz out to dinner. He was keen to tell her all of his news. Apparently filming was due to start late autumn with the first programme scheduled to go out in December. The line-up looked really impressive with actors and politicians signed up to talk about their favourite pieces of art. 'We even do a bit of painting together.'

'It sounds wonderful,' said Liz. 'I am thrilled for you.'

'I must admit the timing is perfect. I was running out of work and this will definitely help to pay the mortgage for the time being. I expect I'll also get some more work off the back of it, especially when the article comes out. If it goes well I might consider moving.'

'Oh. Of course you'll be really busy now.' Liz looked disappointed and bowed her head slightly, a little embarrassed. Nick realised immediately what was going through her head and lifted her chin so he could look into her eyes.

'Liz, I wouldn't go far. I'd hate to be away from you. In fact, I was hoping that you would move with me, maybe even consider France. I wanted to ask if you would come with me next month for a holiday. I'd love to show you the house.'

Liz looked visibly relieved. The tension in her shoulders ebbed away and she held his hand. 'Yes, I will,' she said smiling, without a second's hesitation. 'I'd love to.'

'Great, that's fantastic.' He signalled the waiter for the bill.

The pair of them were now grinning inanely at each other and walked out of the restaurant arm in arm.

*****

The next few days were a flurry of activity. On Monday Tammy went out with Lauren and Molly shopping in the town and then to the park. Liz took the opportunity to go to the cemetery. She hadn't been for a few weeks. The truth was that she no longer needed to be there all the time and she was thinking about Jim less and less. She had stopped living in the past.

'I will always love you my darling Jim, but I can't mourn you forever. It's time to say goodbye. I will still come and see you from time to time but I intend to start a new life. I am in love with Nick.' She stopped and repeated the words. 'I am in love with Nick, am I? Yes I am.' She laughed. 'I hope you understand.' She watered the plants and placed a red rose on the plaque before leaving.

*****

Monica had some news about Kevin and couldn't wait to relay the information to Liz so she rang her from work.

It turned out that Kevin was still married to Alice. Nadia found out that the flat belonged to one of his friends.

Kevin was only looking after the flat while his friend was working away in Dubai. Unfortunately for Nadia the friend came back unexpectedly while Kevin was back in Chester.

Kevin's friend was not that happy to have a new flatmate and informed her that Kevin had a house in Chester which he shared with his wife Alice. He had let him use the flat whenever he was working in London. Needless to say the relationship came to an abrupt end when Nadia broke Kevin's nose with a frying pan on his return. She was now living in the flat with Brian who had decided not to go back to Dubai. It was love at first sight. Monica was pleased that she'd had a lucky escape.

It was Tammy's actual birthday on Wednesday. Monica presented her with a smartphone which she was highly delighted with, promising to guard it with her life and not use more minutes or texts than her allowance in any given month, on pain of death.

She had proudly texted and emailed all her friends and relatives to make sure they had her new number. Liz had already given her money for her party clothes plus she had other money from various aunts and uncles. Monica had bought her a birthday cake and the three of them ordered a takeaway as a treat.

They had just finished their fish and chips when Finn called round with some really pretty wind chimes for Tammy's bedroom. He also had an announcement. He and Devlin would be getting married next year. Tammy was bereft when she first heard the terrible news but consoled herself with the fact that Finn wanted her to be a bridesmaid.

Thursday was spent looking for the perfect outfit. Luckily Monica's stamina had improved and she could easily out-shop Tammy who was busy texting Sasha after every shop and sending photographs of proposed outfits. Sasha, in turn, was giving advice on Tammy's wardrobe choices. Neither of them wanted their outfits to clash, or worse, to turn up in the same outfit. Sasha was still hoping against hope that her mother would relent.

Friday was spent shopping for food and party paraphernalia. Monica had a very long list which included burgers, salad, tablecloths, paper plates, cutlery, balloons, banners, candles and party favours.

Apparently, each child had to have a party bag to take home. Tammy was overseeing the party bags.

They had to be just right. Not too babyish, after all she was eleven. The party favour had to be something cool. She decided on lip gloss for the girls and something funny for the boys. Liz suggested jokes in the form of fake bluebottles or chewing gum that dyed your tongue black. Tammy loved that idea so it was settled.

On Saturday Liz checked the weather forecast. It was going to be sunny all day, perfect for a garden party. While Nick, Monica and Tammy were outside setting up the furniture and getting the barbecue ready Liz sneaked inside unnoticed to ring Adam.

Georgina answered the phone. 'Hi Georgina,' said Liz,

trying to sound cheerful through gritted teeth. 'I'm just checking numbers for the party tomorrow. I wasn't sure if you were all coming?'

'Sorry,' said Georgina. She almost sounded sincere. 'No, no, I have much too much packing to do I'm afraid.'

'Oh, that's a shame,' said Liz, not that she was sorry not to be seeing Georgina but knowing that it meant Sasha would not be allowed to come either. Liz asked anyway. 'Will Adam be bringing the children?' She knew the answer, but forced Georgina to say it.

'No Liz,' Georgina sounded sharp, the question had obviously irritated her. 'We are all too busy,' with the emphasis on the word all.

'Oh dear, Tammy and Sasha will be so disappointed. They were really looking forward to seeing each other.'

'I think it's for the best,' said Georgina. 'There is no point in encouraging the friendship. Better to put a stop to it now.'

Liz had never, ever disliked anyone before but she felt a real loathing for Georgina and desperately sorry for Sasha and Adam, although she realised that Adam only had himself to blame for letting it happen and creating a monster. She hadn't really expected her to change her mind but she had hoped.

Tammy was so excited on Sunday morning. She woke up at five thirty, jumped up and knocked on Monica's door. A bleary eyed Monica made a noise which Tammy translated as come in.

'Time to get up,' she said excitedly.

362

'What time is it?' said Monica with her eyes closed tight.

'It's seven,' Tammy lied.

'It's Sunday,' replied Monica, 'I'll get up in half an hour.'

'OK,' said Tammy. 'I'll bring you a cup of tea,' and out she went.

At six o'clock she came back with tea and biscuits on a tray.

'Mmmm,' Monica opened one eye. Tammy had angled the bedside clock to face away from the bed and put the tray on the bedside table. Monica opened the other eye. 'Awww, this is so nice of you.' She put her hands on either side of her bottom and pulled herself up into a sitting position so she could drink her tea. 'What's this for, what have you done?'

'Nothing,' said Tammy, feigning indignation. 'It's just to say thank you.'

'Well, you're very welcome,' said Monica. 'I'll drink this and we'll get started.'

Tammy went off to get dressed, not in her party clothes yet but leggings and tee shirt as she intended being very hands on in the party preparations.

Monica sat in bed sipping tea and thinking about how much things had changed since they moved in. She had given up her takeaway addiction and had lost weight as a result. On the other hand she was still single and may well be for the rest of her life, but things could be worse. She felt happy, until she turned the clock around that is. 'Tammmeeeeee!!'

Tammy was chuckling away in the kitchen.

Monica couldn't be mad for long, it was a great cup of tea after all. She swung her legs over the side of the bed and sat there for a few seconds before heading to the shower.

*****

Unusually for Liz she was still in bed. The realisation that she did in fact love Nick was a revelation to her too. She knew how she felt when he touched her, that butterfly churn in the pit of her stomach and the tingling at the back of her neck. It was definitely love. She felt lucky to have another chance at happiness and snuggled down under the covers.

The phone rang at seven o'clock. It was Tammy asking when she could come over.

'Give me fifteen minutes,' said Liz.

Tammy was on Liz's doorstep at seven fifteen on the dot. She was carrying a large box containing party bags, banners and balloons. Monica was struggling down the path with three bulging carrier bags of shopping.

'I'll take those,' said Liz, as she walked up the path to meet her.

'There's more.' Monica put the three bags down on the step. Liz carried them inside as Monica made two more trips to bring the rest of the food and decorations.

'Right, where shall we start?'

'How about if we start with the food and then we'll sort out the balloons and banners for the garden?'

The three of them got to work and employed every

single Tupperware container they owned between them to fill with lettuce, tomatoes, cucumber and cheese slices. The baps were already prepared and placed in polythene bags.

'Oh no.' Monica had her hand up to her mouth. 'I haven't got anything vegetarian.'

'Don't worry,' Liz assured her, 'I have a couple of mushroom and cheese pizzas in the freezer and I made a huge vegetable lasagne, just in case. I knew Devlin wouldn't touch a burger with a barge pole and there are bound to be a few more who feel the same.'

'Not Rory,' said Tammy, 'he eats anything.'

'Better allocate him three burgers. I don't know where he puts it,' added Liz. 'Considering how much he eats he ought to be the size of a house. I wish I could eat like that.'

'What time is Nick coming?' Monica was grinning.

'Not until around one. He's bringing Milly and Bradley.'

'She's coming!' said Tammy, jumping up and down on the spot.

'Yes, she is, and Bradley is bringing some of his CDs to play after the DJ has finished. Apparently he is an aspiring DJ so you are a lucky girl.'

'You two seem fairly cosy now,' said Monica.

'We are.' Liz was icing the cupcakes as she spoke. 'I realise that I can't worry about everything. I have no control over Adam's life. He is likely to move to America anyway so I have to get on with my own life and really, when I think about it, I'd hate for him to worry about me. It's a shame Georgina is such a cow.'

'Liz! I've never heard you say a bad word about anyone.'

'No, I don't say it out loud but I think it sometimes. But she is Adam's wife and Sasha and Leo's mother so I try very hard to bite my tongue.'

By eleven thirty they had all the food prepared and the napkins, plates and cutlery ready on the sideboard to be transferred to the garden tables. It was a gloriously sunny day.

'We had better put the umbrellas up on the patio. It will still be fairly hot at two and some of the older people might like to sit in the shade.'

They finished up in the kitchen and went outside to decorate the garden. 'I think fifty balloons may have been a bit ambitious,' said Monica, after struggling to blow up ten. 'It's making me dizzy.' Tammy couldn't even manage one so instead she was responsible for tying the string to the ends and hanging them up on the pergola and the summer house.

'Where will the DJ go?' asked Monica.

'That's a point,' said Liz. 'I doubt he would be happy for too long in the hot sun. He'll probably need an umbrella too.'

'Unless he sets up on the veranda of the summer house,' said Tammy.

'Actually, that's a good idea,' said Liz. 'It doesn't get the sun until late afternoon and there are electric sockets already there. We won't need to trail cables anywhere.'

'Time for a break I think,' said Liz as she put the last of

the tumblers on the table. They looked around the garden. It was a perfect setting for a party. 'What do you think Tammy?'

'Spectacular!' was the smiling response.

Liz flicked the switch to the fountain and felt a rosy glow as she looked around. Her new memories of the garden were definitely pushing back the old ones. Monica and Tammy left to get changed into their party frocks and she had just put the kettle on when the doorbell rang.

She looked out of the window to see Nick walking down the path. Milly and Bradley had run on ahead.

She opened the door. 'Hiya.' Milly lurched forward and kissed her on the cheek. Nick caught up and kissed her on the other cheek.

'You might want to put a sign on the door asking people to use the side gate,' said Nick. 'You won't hear the doorbell if you're all out in the garden.'

'You're right, I'll make one.'

Nick went through to the garden. It was the first time Milly and Bradley had been to Liz's house and they were both keen to have a good look round.

'Tammy will be back soon,' Liz informed them. 'She will be the perfect guide. She's the expert on the garden transformation.'

Liz had just started preparing a sign when she heard a car horn blast. It sounded like it was right outside the door.

It was. The DJ had pulled his car almost up to the front door on the drive, his head poking out of the window. 'All right to park here?'

'You can unload there,' Liz responded, 'and then you can pull your car forward a bit.

'Thanks Mrs'. He made a thumbs up sign before getting out of the car and heading towards the back to start unloading.

Liz went out to the garden to tell Nick that the DJ had arrived and where he was to set up before going back to the office to write the sign. It was fast approaching two o'clock and there still seemed to be so much to do. She was starting to panic a bit.

Nick came into the office. 'How are you doing?'

'Oh, it's just a bit overwhelming. I haven't had so many people in the house for years.'

'Don't worry, we will all help.' Nick took her hand and kissed it gently. 'It's going to be great.'

She stood up from the desk and hugged him before holding his face and kissing him passionately on the lips. She moved her arms around his chest and held him for a minute or two.

'What was that for?' He was taken by surprise.

'You make me really happy.' She was smiling.

'The feeling's mutual,' he said, holding her briefly before relaxing his arms. 'Now, shall I put this notice on the door while you go and get changed before everyone arrives?'

'Thanks Nick, I haven't had a minute.'

As she was getting dressed she heard Monica and Tammy arrive and then other children chattering as the side gate opened and shut several times. She looked in the mirror. Her blonde highlights were a little lighter due to the sunshine and her lightly tanned skin glowed healthily. 'Definitely not a witch now,' she said to herself, as she put on her new dress and sandals. She tried to see herself through Nick's eyes and when she did that, she liked what she saw. Nick made her feel alive and it was such a great feeling.

She came downstairs to find Tammy absolutely beaming. Her smile could not get any wider. She looked gorgeous in her peach leggings and patterned tee shirt and she was loving being the centre of attention.

She looked so grown up. Monica looked equally confident. Her smooth skin didn't need much make-up and with her dark eyes and red lips she looked exotic in her brightly coloured summer dress.

The DJ was ready and the tunes started pumping out. Monica was busy chatting to aunts and uncles that had come from far and wide. There was a little bit of reflection and sadness about Joanna but Monica did not let anyone dwell on it for too long. This was Tammy's day and it was going to be a happy one.

Rory arrived looking completely different. Liz had only ever seen him in his baggy work trousers and tatty tee shirts. Today, with his dark hair cut short and his pale blue tee shirt clinging tightly to his toned biceps he looked handsome. Tammy noticed Monica giving him a second look and later in the afternoon caught Rory watching Monica as she chatted to Liz.

Devlin and Finn arrived around two thirty. It was the first time Liz had seen Devlin looking relaxed. He was usually so tightly wound. He was sitting under the umbrella eating lasagne and chatting to one of Monica's aunts.

Finn, as flamboyant as ever, had dyed his thick hair red and was wearing a pair of white dungarees. He was a tall, pale, skinny man who didn't suit white. Rory told him he looked like a Swan Vesta matchstick and Finn laughed so hard he choked on his burger. Devlin looked on in horror as Rory performed the Heimlich manoeuvre on a spluttering Finn, whose face was now the same colour as his hair.

Monica hadn't actually chatted to Rory other than hello and goodbye. She had seen him at a distance coming and going and Tammy talked about him all the time but she hadn't realised what a hunk he was until today.

Nick was looking incredibly hot and bothered as he cooked the burgers and sausages, taking care to watch out for the screaming children who were now running around like lunatics. Liz grabbed a cold beer and headed over to the barbeque.

'Here, you look like you could do with this.'

'Thanks, that's just what the doctor ordered. You look great by the way.' He kissed her on the cheek and put his arm around her waist and although she didn't mind she was grateful that Adam wasn't there to witness such a public display of affection. She was only just getting comfortable with being in a relationship herself. She doubted Adam would have approved, especially in his father's house.

'Have you heard from Adam?'

'No, nothing. I did talk to Georgina yesterday and she said they had packing to do. They won't be coming, which is a shame. I was hoping that you could meet them. I am really disappointed for Sasha, she tried her hardest to persuade them and Tammy would have loved her to be here.' As she finished speaking Tammy ran up to her.

'I don't think Sasha is coming, do you?'

'No hun. They are really busy,' she lied. Tammy looked sad. 'Don't worry, we'll stay in touch.'

The conversation was interrupted by Lauren who needed Tammy to bolster her courage. Lauren was the oldest in the class and was therefore almost twelve. She wanted to be introduced to Bradley.

Bradley had the kudos of firstly being fourteen and therefore in Lauren's eyes much older, secondly not being that interested in girls and therefore more of a challenge, and lastly fairly shy which to Lauren made him a bit mysterious. Tammy was glad to help and the pair of them went off giggling.

As soon as Tammy left Monica replaced her at Liz's side. 'It's going really well don't you think?'

'I do,' said Liz. 'It's a great party. How are you holding up?'

Monica was pleased to be away from her aunts. 'I haven't seen them in ages and yet the first words out of both their mouths were haven't you got a man yet?' She imitated their accent. 'What's wrong wit you, a good looking girl like you going to waste.' Liz and Nick laughed.

All of a sudden Liz heard Tammy let out an almighty shriek and she turned to see her running across the garden as Sasha, wearing an almost identical outfit, ran down the path from the back gate. They met by the fountain and Tammy lifted up her friend and squealed with delight.

'You came!' Tammy's school friends were now heading towards them, including the boys who were intrigued by this blonde slip of a thing with a very posh accent. Liz looked at the two of them for a while, really pleased for both of them.

She looked towards the gate and waited with baited breath until Adam emerged holding Leo's hand. Leo pulled himself loose as soon as he saw the garden full of children and ran towards Sasha and Tammy. Adam stood for a second on the patio as Georgina caught up with him. He looked a little tense at first until he spotted Liz and relaxed into the biggest smile she had seen on his face in a very long time.

Georgina looked as if she was off to Ascot, minus the hat.

'Adam!' Liz exclaimed, rushing towards them and kissing him on the cheek. She said a polite hello to Georgina as Nick and Monica caught up. 'Nick, this is my son Adam and his wife Georgina.'

'Nice to meet you,' said Adam, as they shook hands.

Georgina didn't waste any time. She said a cursory hello to Liz and Monica before turning her attention to Nick.

'I've been dying to meet you.' She beamed a dazzling smile that most sharks would be proud of.

Liz looked on in wonder.

'Can I get you both a drink?' asked Nick.

'Yes please,' said Georgina. 'You stay here Adam, I'll help Nick. I've got so many questions.' She slipped her arm through Nick's and headed off to the kitchen.

Liz looked puzzled. 'How come?' she asked, when Georgina had moved out of earshot. 'I didn't think you were coming. Georgina told me you were packing.'

'We were,' said Adam, 'but there's been a change of plan.'

'You mean you're not going to America after all?' Liz was surprised.

'No, I'm going,' said Adam, 'but only me. Georgie and the children are staying here apart from a couple of holidays. I have taken the contract for one year only.'

'How does Georgina feel about that?'

'She sulked for a while, but she'll get over it.'

'Well, that's fantastic,' said Liz, really pleased, 'but that still doesn't account for her being here today. I thought you would have had to drag her here kicking and screaming.'

'No,' said Adam, 'you actually have Nick to thank for that.'

'Nick?' She was confused. 'How so?'

'There was an article about Nick in one of the Sunday magazines today. I saw it early this morning and made sure Georgina saw it too. The fact that Nick will be on television meeting the great and the good was something Georgina couldn't ignore. I think she has even brought Sasha's portrait for him to sign.'

Liz laughed. 'Well, whatever works.'

Adam put his arm around her shoulders and hugged her. 'The garden looks amazing. It was a great idea mum, and Nick seems like a really nice guy.'

Tammy and Sasha were sitting in the corner whispering conspiratorially about something. They stopped when they saw Monica coming towards them.

'What are you two up to?'

'Nothing,' they said in unison, as they walked off hand in hand towards Rory.

They waited until he sat down on the bench under the palm tree and rushed over to sit either side of him before anyone else had a chance to sit down.

'How are you Rory?' asked Tammy.

'Great,' said Rory suspiciously. He knew they were up to something.

'This is my best friend Sasha.'

'Nice to meet you,' said Rory.

'Rory makes furniture,' continued Tammy.

'How wonderful,' said Sasha. 'Are you married?'

'No, I'm not,' said Rory, wondering what that had to do with making furniture.

'Good,' said Tammy, nodding to Sasha.

'Do you have a partner or children?' added Sasha.

'No, not yet,' said Rory.

'Great,' said Tammy. Thirty seconds silence ensued

before Tammy added, 'My aunt Monica is thinking about buying some new furniture.'

'Really?' said Rory.

'Definitely,' said Sasha. 'Have you met Monica?'

'Not formally,' said Rory. 'I've said hello.'

'Don't worry, we'll get her for you,' and the pair of them rushed off.

The party wound down and all the children had been collected by their parents. Monica and Rory were still deep in conversation and Georgina, who had completely monopolised Nick, even looked as though she was enjoying herself. Sasha seized the opportunity to ask if she could stay with her grandma for a few days over the summer and Georgina agreed without hesitation. She was doing her best to make a good impression on Nick.

'In fact, if Liz doesn't mind we could all stay tonight and drive back tomorrow,' she suggested.

Liz looked at Adam, who winked.

'That's a great idea,' said Liz, hugging Sasha. 'In fact, you can sleep in my bed, Leo can sleep in the spare room and Sasha could stay with Tammy tonight if that's okay.'

'Great mum. Perhaps we can take you and Nick out to lunch tomorrow.'

'That would be wonderful,' said Liz. Sasha and Tammy hugged each other and squealed.

'But we don't want to put you out. Where will you sleep?'

'Oh, I can stay at Nick's flat,' said Liz smiling.

'You can?' Nick looked surprised.

'I can,' said Liz. 'We'll see you in the morning.'

Printed in Great Britain
by Amazon